Jennings shouted, "We're almost there." We topped a rise and below us was a narrow lake, stretching right to left in front of us. It was as if a marsh similar to the ones to the north had flooded. Scattered on the lake's surface were towering buildings, *skyscrapers*, at least a dozen of them. One of them, to the left, was a giant circular wall. And in the middle of the lake stood a piece of freeway, up on concrete pilings above the water. A white house stood on this platform. Flying above this house I could make out a little American flag, snapping in the breeze. I looked at Tom, my mouth hanging open in amazement. Tom's eyes were big. I took in the sight again. Flanked by forested hills, lit by the low sun, the long lake and its fantastic collection of drowned and ruined giants was the most impressive remnant of the old time I had ever laid eyes on. They were so big! Once again I had that feeling—like a hand squeezing my heart—that I *knew* what it had been like. . . .

"Now *that's* the Mayor's house," Jennings said.

"By God, it's Mission Valley," Tom said.

D1210964

Ace Science Fiction Specials edited by Terry Carr

THE WILD SHORE by Kim Stanley Robinson
GREEN EYES by Lucius Shephard
NEUROMANCER by William Gibson
PALIMPSESTS by Carter Scholz and Glenn Harcourt
THEM BONES by Howard Waldrop
IN THE DRIFT by Michael Swanwick

THE WILD SHORE

SHORE

KIM STANLEY ROBINSON

ACE SCIENCE FICTION BOOKS
NEW YORK

PS
3568
.O2893
W5
1985

THE WILD SHORE

An Ace Science Fiction Book / published by arrangement with
the author

PRINTING HISTORY
Ace Original / March 1984
Third printing / November 1985

All rights reserved.
Copyright © 1984 by Kim Stanley Robinson.
Introduction copyright © 1984 by Terry Carr.
Cover art by Andrea Baruffi.
This book may not be reproduced in whole or in part,
by mimeograph or any other means, without permission.
For information address: The Berkley Publishing Group,
200 Madison Avenue, New York, New York 10016.

ISBN: 0-441-88874-7

Ace Science Fiction Books are published by The Berkley Publishing Group,
200 Madison Avenue, New York, New York 10016.
PRINTED IN THE UNITED STATES OF AMERICA

INTRODUCTION

by Terry Carr

If you're getting a little tired of reading science fiction novels that are just like the ones you read last month or last year, this book is for you. It's published under the label "An Ace Science Fiction Special" because it's just that, something fresh and different and, we believe, a novel superior to most of those you'll find today.

I'll tell you why I think so a little later; first, though, I should say a little about the Ace Science Fiction Specials series.

The SF Specials program is specifically designed to present new novels of high quality and imagination, books that are as exciting as any tale of adventures in the stars and as convincing as the most careful extrapolation of the day after tomorrow's science. Add to that a rigorous insistence on literary quality—lucid and evocative writing, fully rounded characterization, and strong underlying themes (but not Messages)—and you have a good description of the stories you'll see in this series.

The publishers of Ace Books believe that there are many readers today who are looking for such books, at a time when so many science fiction novels are simply skilled (or not so skilled) rehashings of plots and ideas that have been popular in the past. Science fiction by its very nature ought to tell stories that are new and unusual, but too many of the science fiction books published recently have been short on real imagination—they are, in fact, timid and literarily defensive. The Ace SF Specials are neither.

The SF Specials began more than fifteen years ago, when the science fiction field was in a period of creative doldrums similar to the present: science fiction novels then were mostly of the traditional sort, often hackneyed and familiar stories that relied on fast action and obvious ideas. Ace began the first series of SF Specials with the idea that science fiction readers would welcome something more than that, novels that would expand the boundaries of imagination, and that notion proved to be correct: the books published in that original series sold well, collected numerous awards, and many of them are now considered classics in the field.

Beginning in 1968 and continuing into 1971, the Ace SF Specials included such novels as *Past Master* by R. A. Lafferty, *Rite of Passage* by Alexei Panshin, *Synthajoy* by D. G. Compton, *The Left Hand of Darkness* by Ursula K. Le Guin, *Picnic on Paradise* and *And Chaos Died* by Joanna Russ, *Pavane* by Keith Roberts, *The Isle of the Dead* by Roger Zelazny, *The Warlord of the Air* by Michael Moorcock, *The Year of the Quiet Sun* by Wilson Tucker, *Mechasm* by John Sladek, *The Two-Timers* by Bob Shaw, and *The Phoenix and the Mirror* by Avram Davidson . . . among many others that could be mentioned, but the list is already long.

Most of those books were nominated for awards. *Rite of Passage* won the Nebula Award; *The Left Hand of Darkness* won both the Nebula and the Hugo; *The Year of the Quiet Sun* won the John W. Campbell Award. Other books in the series won more specialized awards. Most of the novels have remained in print over the years since they were first published.

That original series ended when I left Ace Books and moved to California in 1971, but its successes hadn't gone unnoticed. Both writers and publishers saw that a more "adult" sort of science fiction could attract a large readership, and during the seventies more venturesome sf novels were published than ever before.

A number of critics have credited the Ace Science Fiction

Specials with bringing about a revolution in sf publishing, and I like to think this is at least partly true. But nothing would have changed if there hadn't been editors and publishers who *wanted* to upgrade the product; and in particular, it required science fiction writers who could produce superior novels. Fortunately, such writers were there; some of them had contributed to the SF Specials series, some had been writing quality sf novels already (Samuel R. Delany, Philip K. Dick, and Robert Silverberg are examples), and many writers of talent entered the science fiction field during this period who didn't feel constrained by the thud-and-blunder traditions of earlier sf.

So in the early seventies science fiction was an exciting field: quality sf novels appeared from many publishers, they sold very well, and science fiction moved toward the front of literary achievement. It was reviewed in *The New York Times* and analyzed by academic critics; major universities offered courses studying science fiction. It seemed that science fiction had finally become respectable.

But other trends began to be felt, and although they brought many new readers to science fiction, for the most part they caused sf to look back instead of forward. The television series *Star Trek* attracted an enormous following, as did the *Star Wars* movies, *Alien, Close Encounters of the Third Kind, E.T.,* and others; these products of the visual media introduced millions of people to science fiction, but though many were enthusiastic enough to buy sf books too, what they wanted were stories as simple and familiar as the films they had enjoyed. When they found science fiction books that were like the television and movie productions, they bought them in great numbers; when the books were more complex or unusual, sales were much lower.

So in recent years sf publishers have catered to this vast new market. The result has been that most of the science fiction published today is no more advanced and imaginative than the sf stories of the fifties, or even the forties: basic ideas and plots are reworked time and again, and when a novel proves to be popular, a sequel or a series will come along soon.

There's nothing wrong with such books; when they're well written they can be very good. But when authors are constrained to writing nothing but variations on the plots and styles of the past, much of the excitement of science fiction disappears. Science fiction is a literature of change; more than any other kind of writing, sf needs to keep moving forward if it's to be exciting.

The novels in this new series of Ace SF Specials do look forward rather than back. They're grounded in the traditions of science fiction but they all have something new to add in ideas or literary development. And they are all written by authors who are comparatively new to science fiction, because it's usually the new writers who have the freshest ideas. (Most of those novels in the original series that came to be called classics were written by authors who were then at the beginnings of their careers.)

Ace Books asked me to edit this new SF Specials series because they believe the time is right for such adventurous books. The new readers who swelled the science fiction market in the last several years are by now familiar with the basic ideas and plots, and many of them will want something more. This new SF Specials series offers stories that explore more imaginative territory.

Kim Stanley Robinson's *The Wild Shore* is a good example. It's the first published novel of a new sf writer whose short stories and novelettes have been nominated for both the Hugo and Nebula awards. Its story of life in the United States as it might be after a nuclear strike that destroys our cities and reduces the nation to isolated enclaves of people living in the ruins and working their way back to civilization is familiar in its opening premises, but it adds a depth of characterization and background that has rarely been approached in science fiction before now.

The Wild Shore is a novel of adventure, the story of a boy growing up rapidly in dangerous circumstances, and you'll find yourself turning the pages to see what happens next; this is the criterion for any good novel. But there's much more in the book, and I'll let you discover the rest for yourself.

There will be more Ace Science Fiction Specials coming soon, and each will be as different from the usual science fiction fare as this one is. I hope you'll watch for them.

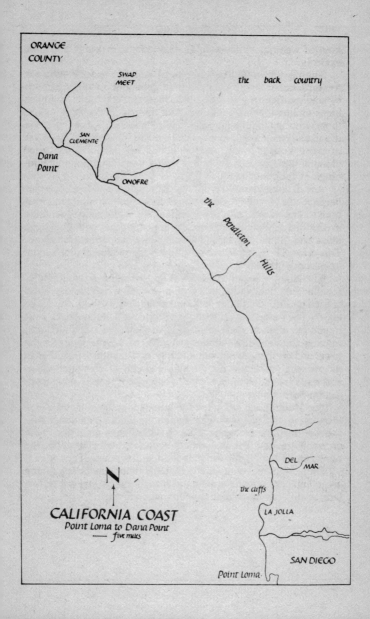

ORANGE
COUNTY

SWAP
MEET

the back country

SAN
CLEMENTE

Dana
Point

ONOFRE

the Pendleton Hills

DEL MAR

the cliffs

LA JOLLA

N

CALIFORNIA COAST
Point Loma to Dana Point
—— five miles

SAN DIEGO

Point Loma

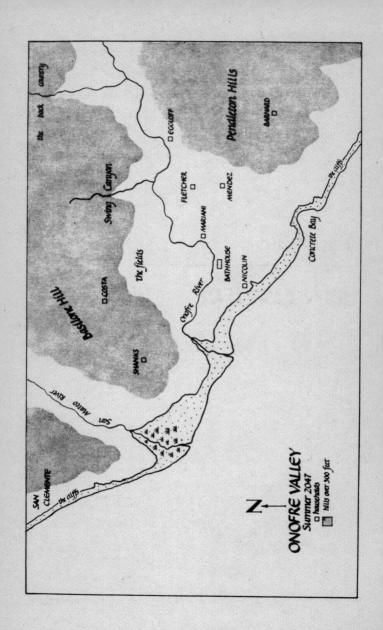

ONOFRE VALLEY
Summer 2047

N

□ households
▓ hills over 300 feet

SAN CLEMENTE

San Mateo River

the cliffs

Bastanchury Hill

□ COSTA

□ SHANKS

the fields

Swing Canyon

the back country

□ EGCLIFF

□ FLETCHER

□ MARIANI

Pendleton Hills

□ MENDEZ

□ BARNARD

Onofre River

BATHHOUSE

□ NICOLIN

Concrete Bay

the cliffs

Part One

SAN ONOFRE

Chapter One

    "It wouldn't really be graverobbing," Nicolin was explaining. "Just dig up a coffin and take the silver off the outside of it. Never open it up at all. Bury it again nice and proper—now what could be wrong with that? Those silver coffin handles are going to waste in the ground anyway."

The five of us considered it. Near sunset the cliffs at the mouth of our valley glow amber, and on the wide beach below tangles of driftwood cast shadows all the way to the sandstone boulders at the foot of the cliff. Each clump of wave-worn wood could have been a gravemarker, swamped and washed on its side, and I imagined digging under one to find what lay beneath it.

Gabby Mendez tossed a pebble out at a gliding seagull. "Just exactly how is that not graverobbing?" he demanded of Nicolin.

"It takes desecration of the body to make it graverobbing." Nicolin winked at me; I was his partner in these sorts of things. "We aren't going to do any such thing. No searching for cuff-

3

links or belt buckles, no pulling off rings or dental work, nothing of the sort!"

"Ick," said Kristen Mariani.

We were on the point of the cliff above the rivermouth— Steve Nicolin and Gabby, Kristen and Mando Costa, Del Simpson and me—all old friends, grown up together, out on our point as we so often were at the end of a day, arguing and talking and making wild plans . . . that last being the specialty of Nicolin and me. Below us in the first bend of the river were the fishing boats, pulled up onto the tidal flats. It felt good to sit on the warm sand in the cool wind with my friends, watching the sun leak into the whitecaps, knowing my work for the day was done. I felt a little drowsy. Gabby slung another pebble at the gulls, who ignored it and landed in a group near the boats, bitching over fishheads.

"Why, with that much silver we would be kings of the swap meet," Nicolin went on. "And queens," he said to Kristen, who nodded. "We'd be able to buy anything there twice. Or travel up the coast if we wanted. Or across the country. Just generally do what we pleased."

And not what your father tells you to, I thought to myself. But I felt the pull of what he said, I admit it.

"How are you going to make sure that the coffin you take the trouble to dig up has got silver on it?" Gab asked, looking doubtful.

"You've heard the old man talk about funerals in the old time," Nicolin scolded. "Henry, you tell him."

"They were scared of death in an unnatural way back then," I said, like I was an authority. "So they made these huge funeral displays to distract themselves from what was really happening. Tom says a funeral might cost upward of five thousand *dollars*."

Steve nodded at me approvingly. "He says every coffin put down was crusted with silver."

"He says men walked on the moon, too," Gabby replied. "That don't mean I'm going to go there looking for footprints." But I had almost convinced him; he knew that Tom Barnard, who had taught us to read and write (taught Steve and Mando and me, anyway), would describe the wealth of the old time, in detail, as quick as you might say, "Tell us—"

"So we just go up the freeway into the ruins," Nicolin went

on, "and find us a rich-looking tombstone in a cemetery, and there we have it."

"A tombstone with diamond earrings, eh?" said Gabby.

"Tom says we shouldn't go up there," Kristen reminded us.

Nicolin tilted his head back and laughed. "That's because he's scared of it." He looked more serious. "Of course that's understandable, given what he's been through. But there's no one up there but the wreckrats, and they won't be out at night."

He had no way to be sure of that, as we had never been up there day or night; but before Gabby could call him on it, Mando squeaked, "At *night?*"

"Sure!" Nicolin cried.

"I hear the scavengers will eat you if they can," Kristen said.

"Is your pa going to let you leave doctoring and farming during the day?" Nicolin asked Mando. "Well, it's the same with all of us, only more so. This gang has got to do its business at night." He lowered his voice: "That's the only time to be graverobbing in a cemetery, anyway," laughing at the look on Mando's face.

"Graverobbing at the beach you can do any time of day," I said, half to myself.

"I could get the shovels," Del said.

"And I could bring a lantern," Mando said quickly, to show he wasn't scared. And suddenly we were talking a plan. I perked up and paid more attention, a bit surprised. Nicolin and I had outlined a number of schemes before: trapping a tiger in the back country, diving for sunken treasure on the concrete reef, extracting the silver contained in old railroad tracks by melting them. But most of these proposals had certain practical difficulties to them that became apparent at some time or other in the discussion, and we let them slide. They were just talk. With this particular plan, however, all we had to do was sneak up into the ruins—something we always swore we really wanted to do—and dig. So we talked about which night the scavengers were least likely to be out and about (full moon, Nicolin assured Mando, when the ghosts were visible), who we might ask to come along, who it would have to be kept secret from, how we could chop the silver handles into tradeable discs, and so forth.

Then the ocean was lapping at the red rim of the sun, and

it got a good deal colder. Gabby stood up and kneaded his butt, talking about the venison supper he was going to have that night. The rest of us got up too.

"We're really going to do this one," Nicolin said intently. "And by God, I'm ready for it."

As we walked up from the point I took myself off from the rest, and followed the cliff's edge. Out on the wide beach the tidal puddles streaking the sand were a dark silver, banded with red—little models of the vast ocean surging beyond them. On the other side of me was the valley, our valley, winding up into the hills that crowded the sea. The trees of the forest blanketing the hills all waved their branches in the sunset on-shore wind, and their late spring greens were tinted pollen color by the drowning sun. For miles up and down the curving reach of the coast the forest tossed, fir and spruce and pine like the hair of a living creature, and as I walked I felt the wind toss my hair too. On the ravine-creased hillsides not one sign of man could be seen (though they were there), it was nothing but trees, tall and short, redwood and torrey pine and euca-lyptus, dark green hills cascading into the sea, and as I walked the amber cliff's edge I was happy. I didn't have the slightest inkling of a notion that my friends and I were starting a summer that would . . . change us. As I write this account of those months, deep in the harshest winter I have ever known, I have the advantage of time passed, and I can see that this excursion in search of silver was the start of it—not so much because of what happened, understand, but because of what didn't happen, because of the ways in which we were deceived. Because of what it gave us a taste for. I was hungry, you see; not just for food (that was a constant), but for a life that was more than fishing, and hoeing weeds, and checking snares. And Nicolin was hungrier than I.

But I'm getting ahead of my story. As I strolled the steep sandstone border between forest and sea, I had no premonition of what was to come, nor any heed for the warnings of the old man. I was just excited by the thought of an adventure. As I turned up the south path towards the little cabin that my pa and I shared, the smells of pine and sea salt raked the insides of my nose and made me drunk with hunger, and happily I imagined chips of silver the size of a dozen dimes. It occurred to me that my friends and I were for the very first time in our lives actually going to do what we had so often boastfully planned to do—and at the thought I felt a thrilling shiver of anticipation, I leaped from root to root in the trail: we were invading the territory of the scavengers, venturing north into the ruins of Orange County.

The night we picked to do it, fog was smoking up off the ocean and gusting onshore, under a quarter moon that gave all the white mist patches a faint glow. I waited just inside the door of our cabin, ignoring Pa's snores. I had read him to sleep an hour before, and now he lay heavily on his side, calloused fingers resting on the crease in the side of his head. Pa is lame, and simple, on account of tangling with a horse when I was young. My ma always used to read him to sleep, and when she died Pa sent me up to Tom's to carry on with my learning, saying in his slow way that it would be good for both of us. Right he was, I suppose.

I warmed my hands now and then over the gray coals of the stove fire, as I had the cabin door partway open, and it was cold. Outside, the big eucalyptus down the path blew in and out of visibility. Once I thought I saw figures standing under it; then a clammy puff of fog drifted onto the house, smelling like the rivermouth flats, and when it cleared away the tree stood alone. I wished the others would come. Except for Pa's snoring there was no sound but the quiet patter of fog dew, sliding off leaves onto our roof.

W-whooo, w-whooo. Nicolin's call startled me from a doze. It was a pretty good imitation of the big canyon owls, although the owls only called out once a year or so, it seemed, so it didn't make much sense as a secret call in my opinion. It did beat a leopard's cough, however, which had been Nicolin's first choice, and which might have gotten him shot.

I slipped out the door and hurried down the path to the eucalyptus. Nicolin had Del's two shovels over his shoulders; Del and Gabby stood behind him.

"We've got to get Mando," I said.

Del and Gabby looked at each other. "Costa?" Nicolin said.

I stared at him. "He'll be waiting for us." Mando and I were younger than the other three—me by one year, Mando by three—and I sometimes felt obliged to stick up for him.

"His house is on the way anyway," Nicolin told the others. We took the river path to the bridge, crossed and hiked up the hill path leading to the Costas'.

Doc Costa's weird oildrum house looked like a little black castle out of one of Tom's books—squat as a toad, and darker than anything natural in the fog. Nicolin made his call, and pretty soon Mando came out and hustled down to us.

"You still going to do it tonight?" he asked, peering around at the mist.

"Sure," I said quickly, before the others seized on his hesitation as an excuse to leave him. "You got the lantern?"

"I forgot." He went back inside and got it. When he returned we walked back down to the old freeway and headed north on it.

We walked fast to warm up. The freeway was two pale ribbons in the mist, heavily cracked underfoot, black weeds in every crack. Quickly we crossed the ridge marking the north end of our valley, and narrow San Mateo Valley immediately to the north of the ridge. After that, we were walking up and down the steep hills of San Clemente. We held close together, and didn't say much. On each side of us ruins sat in the forest: walls of cement blocks, roofs held up by skeletal foundations, tangles of wire looping from tree to tree—all of it dark and still. But we knew the scavengers lived up here *somewhere,* and we hurried along as silently as the ghosts Del and Gab had been joking about, a mile back where they'd felt more comfy. A wet tongue of fog licked over us as the freeway dropped into a broad canyon, and we couldn't see a thing but the broken surface of the road. Creaks emerged from the dark wet silence around us, as well as an occasional flurry of dripping, as if something had brushed against leaves, something following us, for instance.

Nicolin stopped to examine an offramp curving down to the right. "This is it," he hissed. "Cemetery's at the top of this valley."

"How do you know?" Gab said in his ordinary voice, which sounded awfully loud.

"I came up here and found it," Nicolin said. "How do you think I knew?"

We followed him off the highway, pretty impressed that he had come up here alone. Even I hadn't heard about that one. Down in the forest there were more buildings than trees, almost, and they were big buildings. They were falling down every way possible; windows and doors knocked out like teeth, with shrubs and ferns growing in every hole; walls slumped; roofs piled on the ground like barrows. The fog followed us up this street, rustling things so they sounded like thousands of scurrying feet. Wires looped over poles that sometimes tilted right down to the road; we had to step over them, and none of us touched the wires.

A coyote's bark chopped the drippy silence and we all froze. Was that a coyote or a scavenger? But nothing followed it, and we took off again, more nervous than ever. The street made some awkward switchbacks at the head of the valley, and once we got up those, we were on the canyon-cut plateau that once made up the top of San Clemente. Up here were houses, big ones, all set in rows by the street like fish out to dry, as if there had been so many people that there wasn't room to give each family a decent garden. A lot of the houses were busted and overgrown, and some were gone entirely—just floors, with pipes sticking out of them like arms sticking up out of a grave. Scavengers had lived here, and had used the houses one by one for firewood, moving on when their nest was burned; it was a practice I had heard about, but I'd never before seen the results first hand, the destruction and waste.

Nicolin stopped at a street crossing filled with a bonfire pit. "They sure set their streets out square," Del observed. "Up this one here," said Nicolin.

We followed him north, along a street that paralleled the ocean on the plateau's edge. Below us the fog was like another ocean, putting us on the beach again so to speak, with occasional white waves running up over us. The houses lining the street stopped, and a fence began, metal rails connecting stone piles. Beyond the fence the rippling plateau was studded with squared stones, sticking out of tall grass: the cemetery. We all stopped and looked. In the mist it was impossible to see where it ended; it looked like an awful big cemetery. Finally we stepped over a break in the fence and walked into the thick grass, between bushes and tombstones.

They had lined up the graves as straight as their houses. Suddenly Nicolin faced the sky and yowled his coyote yowl, *yip yip yoo-ee-oo-ee-oo-eeee*, yodeling as crazily as any bush dog.

"Stop that," Gabby said, disgusted. "That's all we need is dogs howling at us."

"Or scavengers," Mando added fearfully.

Nicolin laughed. "Boys, we're standing in a silver mine,

that's all." He crouched down to read a gravestone; too dark; he hopped over to another. "Look how big this one is." He put his face next to it and with the help of his fingers read it. "Here we got a Mister John Appleby. 1904–1984. *Nice* big stone, died the right time—living in one of them big houses down the road—rich for sure, right?"

"There should be a lot written on the stone," I said. "That's proof he was rich."

"There is a lot," Nicolin said. "Be-loved father, I think ... some other stuff. Want to give him a try?"

For a while no one answered. Then Gab said, "Good as any other."

"Better," Nicolin replied. He put down one shovel and hefted the other. "Let's get this grass out of the way." He started stabbing the shovel into the ground, making a line cut. Gabby and Del and Mando and I just stood and stared at him. He looked up and saw us watching. "Well?" he demanded quickly. "You want some of this silver?"

So I walked over and started cutting; I had wanted to before, but it made me nervous. When we had the grass pulled away so the dirt was exposed, we started digging in earnest. When we were in up to our knees we gave the shovels to Gabby and Del, panting some. I was sweating easily in the fog, and I cooled off fast. Clods of the wet clay squashed under my feet. Pretty soon Gabby said, "It's getting dark down here; better light the lantern." Mando got out his spark rasp and set to lighting the wick.

The lantern put out a ghastly yellow glare, dazzling me and making more shadows than anything else. I walked away from it to keep my night sight, and get my circulation going. My arms were spotted with dirt, and I felt more nervous than ever. From a distance the lantern's flame was larger and fainter, and my companions were black silhouettes, the ones with the shovels waist-deep in the earth. I came across a grave that had been dug up and left open, and I jumped and hustled back down to the glow of the lantern, breathing hard.

Gabby looked up at me, his head just over the level of the dirt pile we were making. "They buried them deep," he said in an odd voice. He tossed up more dirt.

"Maybe this one's already dug up," Del suggested, looking into the hole at Mando, who was getting up a handful of dirt with every shovel toss.

"Sure," Nicolin scoffed. "Or maybe they buried him alive and he crawled out by himself."

"My hand hurts," Mando said. His shovel stock was a branch, and his hands weren't very tough.

"'My hand hurts'," Nicolin whined. "Well get out of there, then."

Mando climbed out, and Steve hopped into the hole to replace him, attacking the floor of the hole until the dirt flew into the mist.

I looked for the stars, but there wasn't a one out. It felt late. I was cold, and ravenous. The fog was thickening; the area wrapped around us looked clear, but quickly the mist became more visible, until several yards away it was all we could see— blank white. We were in a bubble of white, and at the edges of the bubble were shapes: long arms, heads with winking eyes, quick sets of legs . . .

Thunk. One of Nicolin's two-handed shovel stabs had hit something. He stood with both hands on the stock, looking down. He jabbed tentatively, *tunk tunk tunk.* "Got it," he said loudly, and began to scrape dirt up again. After a bit he said, "Move the lantern down to this end." Mando picked it up and held it over the grave. By its light I saw the faces of my companions, sweaty and streaked with dirt, the whites of their eyes large. My arms were dirty to the elbows.

But that was just the start. Nicolin started to curse, and we quickly learned from him that our hole, a good five feet long by three feet wide, had just nicked the end of the coffin. "The damn thing's buried *under* the headstone!" It was still solidly stuck in the clay.

We argued a while about what to do, and the final plan— Nicolin's—was to scrape dirt away from the top and sides of the coffin, and haul it out into the hole we had made. After we had scraped away to the full reach of our arms, Nicolin said, "Henry, you've done the least digging so far, and you're long and skinny, so crawl down there and start pushing the dirt back to us."

I protested, but the others agreed I was the man for the job, so pretty soon I found myself *lying on top of that coffin,* with dripping clay an inch over my back and butt, tearing at the dirt with my fingers and slinging it out behind me. Only continuous cursing kept my mind off what was lying underneath the wood I was on, exactly parallel to my own body. The others yelled in encouragements, like "Well, we're going home now," or "Oh, who's that coming?" or "Did you feel the coffin shake just then?"—but I didn't think they were one bit funny. Finally I got my fingers over the far edge of the box, and I shimmied back out the hole, brushing the mud off me and muttering with disgust and fear. "Henry, I can always count on you," Steve said as he leaped into the grave. Then it was his and Del's turn to crawl around down there, tugging and grunting; and with a final jerk the coffin burst back into our hole, while Steve and Del fell down beside it.

It was made of black wood, with a greenish film on it that gleamed like peacock feathers in the lantern light. Gabby knocked the dirt off the handles, and then cleaned the gunk off the stripping around the coffin's lid: silver, all of it.

"Look at those handles," Del said reverently. There were six of them, three to a side, as bright and shiny as if they'd been buried the day before, instead of sixty years. I noticed the gash in the wood where Nicolin had first struck.

"Man," said Mando. "Will you look at all that silver."

We did look at it. I thought of us at the next swap meet, decked out like scavengers in fur coats and boots and feather hats, walking around with our pants almost falling off from the weight of all those big chips of silver. We shouted and yipped and yowled, and pounded each other on the back. Then we stood and looked at it some more, and yelled some more. Gabby rubbed a handle with his thumb; his nose wrinkled.

"Hey," he said. "Uh . . ." He grabbed the shovel leaning against the side of the hole, and poked the handle. *Thud*, it went. Not like metal on metal. And the blow left a gash in the handle. Gabby looked at Del and Steve, and crouched down to look close. He hit the handle again. Thud thud thud. He ran his hand over it.

"This ain't silver," he said. "It's cut. It's some kind of . . . some kind of *plastic*, I guess."

"God damn," said Nicolin. He jumped in the hole and grabbed the shovel; jabbed the stripping on the coffin lid, and cut it right in half.

Well, we stared at that box again, but nobody did any shouting this time.

"God damn that old liar," Nicolin said. He threw the shovel down. "He told us that every single one of those funerals cost a fortune. He said—" He paused; we all knew what the old man had said. "He told us there'd be silver."

He and Gabby and Del stood in the grave. Mando took the lantern to the headstone and put it down. "Should call this headstone a kneestone," he said, trying to lighten the mood a bit.

Nicolin heard him and scowled. "Should we go for his ring?"

"No!" Mando cried, and we all laughed at him.

"Go for his ring and belt buckle and dental work?" Nicolin repeated harshly, slipping a glance at Gabby. Mando shook his head furiously, looking like he was about to cry. Del and I laughed; Gabby climbed out of the hole, looking disgusted. Nicolin tilted his head back and laughed, short and sharp. He scrambled out of the grave. "Let's bury this guy and then go bury the old man."

We shoveled dirt back in. The first clods hit the coffin with an awful hollow sound, *bonk bonk bonk*. It didn't take long to fill the hole. Mando and I put the grass back in place as best we could. When we were done it looked terrible. "Appears he's been bucking around down there, don't it," Gabby said.

We killed the lantern flame and took off. Fog flowed through the empty streets like water up a steambed, with us under the surface, down among drowned ruins and black seaweed. Back on the freeway it felt less submerged, but the fog swept hard across the road, and it was colder. We hiked south as fast as we could walk, none of us saying a word. When we warmed up we slowed down a little, and Nicolin began to talk. "You know, since they had those plastic handles colored silver, it must mean that some time before that people were buried with real silver handles—richer people, or people buried before 1984, or whatever." We all understood this as a roundabout way of proposing another dig, and so no one agreed, although it appeared to make sense. Steve took offense at our silence and gained ground on us till he was just a mark in the mist. We were almost out of San Clemente.

"Some sort of God damned plastic," Gabby was saying to Del. He started to laugh, harder and harder, until he was leaning an elbow on Del's shoulder. "Whoo, hoo hoo hoo . . . we just spent all night digging up five pounds of plastic. Plastic!"

All of a sudden a noise pierced the air—a howl, a singing screech that started low and got ever higher and louder. No living creature was behind that sound; it was unlike anything I had ever heard. It reached a peak of height and loudness, and wavered there between two tones, rising and falling, *oooooo-eeeeee-oooooo-eeeeee-oooooo*, on and on and on, like the scream of the ghosts of every dead person ever buried in Orange County, or the final shrieks of all those killed by the bombs.

We all unstuck ourselves from our tracks and took off running. The noise continued, and appeared to follow us.

"What is it?" Mando cried.

"Scavengers!" Nicolin hissed. And the sound cranked up and down, closer to us than before. "Run faster!" Nicolin called over it. The breaks in the road surface gave us no trouble at all; we flew over them. Rocks began clattering off the concrete behind us, and over the embankment that the freeway ran on. "Keep the shovels," I heard Del exclaim. I picked up a good-sized rock by the road, relieved in a way that it was only scavengers after us. Nothing but fog behind me, fog and the howl, but rocks came out of the whiteness at a good rate. I threw my rock at a dark shape and ran after the others, chased by some howls that were at least animal, and could have been human. But over them was the blast, rising and falling and rising. "Henry!" Steve shouted. The others were down the embankment with him. I jumped down and traversed through weeds, behind the rest. "Get rocks," Nicolin ordered. We picked up rocks, then turned and threw them onto the freeway behind us all at once. We got screams for a reply. "We got one!" Nicolin said. But there was no way of knowing. We rolled onto the freeway and ran again. The screech lost ground on us, and eventually we were into San Mateo Valley, and on the way to Basilone Ridge, above our own valley. Behind us the noise continued, fainter with distance and the muffling fog.

"That must be a siren," Nicolin said. "What they call a siren. Noise machine. We'll have to ask Rafael." We threw the rocks we had left in the general direction of the sound, and jogged over the ridge into Onofre.

"Those dirty scavengers," Nicolin said, when we were onto the river path, and had caught our breath. "I wonder how they found us."

"Maybe they were out wandering, and stumbled across us," I suggested.

"Doesn't seem likely."

"No." But I couldn't think of a likelier explanation, and I didn't hear Steve offering one. It was no less likely than the existence of that ungodly noise, anyway.

"I'm going home," Mando said, a touch of relief in his voice. He sounded odd somehow—scared maybe—and I felt a chill run down me.

"Okay, you do that. We'll get those wreckrats another time."

Five minutes later we were at the bridge. We crossed, and Gabby and Del went upriver. Steve and I stood in the fork of the path. He started to discuss the night, cursing the scavengers, the old man, and John Appleby alike, and it was clear his blood was high. He was ready to talk till dawn, but I was tired. I didn't have his stamina, and I was still shaken by that noise. Siren or no, it had sounded deadly inhuman. So I said goodnight to Steve and slipped in the door of my cabin. Pa's snoring broke rhythm, resumed. I tore a piece of bread from the next day's loaf and stuffed it down, tasting dirt. I dipped my hands in the wash bucket and wiped them off, but they still felt grimy, and they stank of the grave. I gave up and lay on my bed, feeling gritty, and was asleep before I even warmed up.

Chapter Two

I was dreaming of the moment when we had started to fill in the open grave. Dirt clods were hitting the coffin with that terrible sound, *bonk bonk bonk;* but in the dream the sound was a knocking from inside the coffin, getting louder and more desperate the faster we filled in the hole.

Pa woke me in the middle of this nightmare: "They found a dead man washed up on the beach this morning."

"Huh?" I cried, and jumped out of bed all confused. Pa backed off, startled. I leaned over the wash bucket and splashed my face. "What's this you say?"

"I say, they found one of those Chinamen. You're all covered with dirt. What's with you? You out again last night?"

I nodded. "We're building a hideout."

Pa shook his head, baffled and disapproving.

"I'm hungry," I added, going for the loaf of bread. I took a cup from the shelf and dipped it in the water bucket.

"We don't have anything but bread left."

"I know." I pulled some chunks from the loaf. Kathryn's

17

bread was good even when a bit stale. I went to the door and opened it, and the gloom of our windowless cabin was split by a wedge of muted sunlight. I stuck my head out into the air: dull sun, trees along the river sopping wet. Inside the light fell on Pa's sewing table, the old machine burnished by years of handling. Beside it was the stove, and over that, next to the stovepipe that punctured the roof, the utensil shelf. That, along with table, chairs, wardrobe and beds, made up the whole of our belongings—the simple possessions of a simpleton in a simple trade. Why, folks didn't even really *need* to have Pa sew their clothes. . . .

"You better get down to the boats," Pa said sternly. "It's late, they'll be putting out."

"Umph." Pa was right; I was late. Still swallowing bread, I put on shirt and shoes. "Good luck!" Pa called as I ran out the door.

Crossing the freeway I was stopped by Mando, coming the other way. "Did you hear about the Chinaman washed up?" he called.

"Yeah! Did you see him?"

"Yes. Pa went down to look at him, and I tagged along."

"Was he shot?"

"Oh yeah. Four bullet holes, right in the chest."

"Man." A lot of them washed up like that. "I wonder what they're fighting about so hard out there."

Mando shrugged. In the potato patch across the road Rebel Simpson was chasing a dog with a spud in its mouth, yelling at it, her face red. "Pa says there's a coast guard offshore, keeping people out."

"I know," I said. "I just wonder if that's it." Big ships ghosted up and down the long coast, usually out near the horizon, sometimes nearer; and bodies washed ashore from time to time, riddled with bullets. But that was the extent of what we could say for sure about the world offshore, in my opinion. When I thought about it my curiosity sometimes became so intense that it shaded into something like fury. Mando, on the other hand, was confident that his father (who was only echoing the old man) had the explanation. He accompanied me out to the cliff. Out to sea was a bar of white cloud, lying on the horizon: the fog bank, which would roll in later when the onshore wind got going. Down on the river flat they were loading nets onto the boats. "I've got to get on board," I said to Mando. "See you later."

By the time I had descended the cliff they were launching the boats. I joined Steve by the smallest of them, which was still on the sand. John Nicolin, Steve's father, walked by and glared at me. "You two take the rods today. You won't be good for anything else." I kept my face wooden. He walked on to growl a command at the boat shoving off.

"He knows we were out?"

"Yeah." Steve's lip curled. "I fell over a drying rack when I snuck in."

"Did you get in trouble?"

He turned his head to show me a bruise in front of his ear. "What do you think?" He was in no mood to talk, and I went to help the men hauling the next boat over the flat. The cold water sluicing over my feet woke me up good for the first time that day. Out to sea the quiet *krrr, krrrrrr* of breaking waves indicated a small swell. The little boat's turn came and Steve and I hopped in as it was shoved into the channel. We rowed lazily, relying on the current, and we got over the breakers at the rivermouth without any trouble.

Once all the boats were out around the buoy marking the main reef, it was business as usual. The three big boats started their circling, spreading the purse net; Steve and I rowed south, the other rod boats rowed north. At the south end of the valley there is a small inlet, nearly filled by a reef made of concrete— Concrete Bay, we call it. Between the concrete reef and the larger reef offshore is a channel, one used by faster fish when the nets are dropped; rod fishing usually gets results when the nets are being worked. Steve and I dropped our anchor onto the main reef, and let the swell carry us in over the channel, almost to the curved white segments of the concrete reef. Then it was out with the rods. I knotted the shiny metal bar that was my lure onto the line. "Casket handle," I said to Steve, holding it up before I threw it over. He didn't laugh. I let it sink to the bottom, then started the slow reel up.

We fished. Lure to the bottom, reel it back up; throw it in again. Occasionally the rods would arc down, and a few minutes of struggling ended with the gaff work. Then it was back to it. To the north the netters were pulling up nets silver with fish flopping after their lost freedom; the boats tilted in under

the weight, until sometimes it seemed their keels would show
and they would turn turtle. Inland the hills seemed to rise and
fall, rise and fall. Under the cloud-filmed sun the forest was a
rich green, the cliff and the bare hilltops dull and gray.

Now five years before, when I was twelve and Pa had first
hired me out to John Nicolin, fishing had been a big deal. I
had been excited by everything about it—the fishing itself, the
moods of the ocean, the teamwork of the men, the entrancing
view of the land from the sea. But a lot of days on the water
had passed since then, a lot of fish hauled over the gunwale:
big fish and small, no fish or so many fish that we exhausted
our arms and wore our hands ragged; over steep slow swells,
or wind-blown chop, or on water flat as a plate; and under
skies hot and clear, or in rain that made the hills a gray mirage,
or when it was stormy, with clouds scudding overhead like
horses . . . mostly days like this day, however, moderate swell,
sun fighting high clouds, medium number of fish. There had
been a thousand days like this one, it seemed, and the thrill
was long gone. It was just work to me now.

In between catches I dozed, lulled by the swell. Slouching
down and resting my head on the gunwale worked fine for a
while, as did curling over on the seatboard, though my face
might get slapped by a twitching tailfin. The rest of the time
I just hunched over my rod, waking up when it jerked into my
stomach. Then I reeled the fish in, gaffed it, pulled it over the
side, smacked its head, got the lure out and tossed it over
again, and went back to sleep. I tried lying flat on my back
on the seat (all of three feet long), legs crisscrossed and feet
precariously placed on the gunwale, to sleep for ten minutes
more.

"Henry!"

"Yeah!" I said, sitting up and checking my rod automatically.

"We got quite a few fish here."

I glanced at the bonita and rock bass in the boat. "About a
dozen."

"Good fishing. Maybe I'll be able to get away this afternoon," Steve said wistfully.

I doubted it, but I didn't say anything. The sun was obscured, and the water was gray; it was getting chill. The fog
bank had started its roll in. "Looks like we'll spend it on shore,"
I said.

"Yeah. We've got to go up and see Barnard; I want to beat the shit out of that old liar."

"Sure."

Then we both hooked big ones, and we had a time of it keeping our lines clear. We were still working them when the blare of Rafael's bugle floated over the water from the netters. The nets were up, the fog was rolling in pretty quick; fishing was done for the day. We whooped and got our fish aboard without delay, slapped our oars into the oarlocks and beat it back to Rafael's boat. They parceled some fish out to us, as some of the boats were about foundering under their load, and we rowed into the rivermouth.

With the help of the Nicolin family and the others on the beach, we pulled the boat up onto the sand and took our fish over to the cleaning tables. Gulls soused us repeatedly, screeching and flapping. When the boat was empty and pulled up to the cliff, Steve approached his father, who was looking after the nets, shaking a finger at Rafael and lecturing him about some twists in the line.

"Can I go now, Pa?" Steve asked. "Hanker and I need to do our lessons with Tom." Which was true.

"Nope," old Nicolin said, bent over and still inspecting the net. "You're going to help us fix this net. And then you're going to help your ma and sisters clean fish."

At first John had made Steve go to learn to read from the old man, because he figured it was a sign of family prosperity and distinction. Then when Steve got to liking it (which took a long time), his father took to keeping him from it; it became another weapon in the battle between them. John straightened, looked at Steve; a bit shorter than his son, but a lot thicker; both of them with the same squarish jaw, brown shock of hair, light blue eyes, straight strong nose.... They glared at each other, John daring Steve to talk back to him with all the men wandering around. For a second I thought it was going to happen, that Steve was going to defy him and begin who knows what kind of bloody dispute. But Steve turned away and stalked over to the cleaning tables. After a short wait to allow his anger to lose its first bloom, I followed him.

"I'll go on up and tell the old man you're coming later."

"All right," Steve said, not looking at me. "I'll be there when I can."

Old Nicolin gave me three rock bass and I hauled them up

the cliff in a net bag I would have to return. The cluster of homes in the second bend of the river was nearly deserted. A gang of kids splashed clothes in the water, and farther upstream several women stood around the ovens at the Marianis'. Up away from the sea it seemed quiet; a dog's bark sounded clearly from across the placid stream.

I took the fish to Pa, who jumped up from his sewing machine hungrily. "Oh good, good. I'll get to work on these, one for tonight, dry the others." I told him I was going to the old man's and he nodded, pulling rapidly at his long moustache. "Eat this right after dark, okay?"

"Okay," I said, and was off.

The old man's home is on the steep ridge marking the southern end of our valley, on a flat spot just bigger than his house, about halfway to the peak of the tallest hill around. There isn't a better view from any home in Onofre. When I got up there the house, a four-roomed wooden box with a fine front window, was empty. I made my way through the junk surrounding the house carefully. Among the honey flats, the telephone wire cutters, the sundials, the rubber tires, the rain barrels with their canvas collecting funnels, the generator parts, the broken engines, the grandfather clocks and gas stoves and crates full of who knows what, there were big pieces of broken glass, and several varmint traps that he was constantly moving about, so that it was smart to watch out. Over at Rafael's house, machines like those scattered across Tom's little yard would be fixed and in working order, or stripped for their parts, but here they were just conversation pieces. Why have an automobile engine propped on sawhorses, and how had he gotten it up the ridge, anyway? That was just what Tom wanted you to wonder.

I kept going up the eroded path that ran the edge of the ridge. To the south forested spines rose from the beach cliff, one after another of them all the way down to Pendleton. Near the peak of the spine I was climbing the path turned and dropped into the crease south of it, a narrow canyon too small to hold a permanent stream, but there was a spring. The eucalyptus trees kept the ground clear of underbrush, and on a gentle slope of the crease the old man kept his beehives, a score of small white wooden domes. I spotted him standing among them, draped in his beekeeping clothes and hat so that he looked like a child in adult's clothing. But he moved pretty spryly—for a man over a hundred years old, I mean. He was ambling from dome to dome, pulling out trays and fingering them with a gloved hand, kicking another dome, wagging a finger at a third, and talking all the while, I could tell, despite the hat that hid most of his face. Tom talked to everything: people, himself, dogs, trees, the sky, fish on his plate, rocks he stubbed a toe on . . . naturally he talked to his bees. He shoved a flat back into a hive and looked around, suddenly wary; then he caught sight of me and waved. As I approached he went back to checking hives, and I observed his walk. His knees swung out to the sides when he stepped, as if his kneecaps were on the outsides of his legs. And his arms swung everywhere, for balance I guess, stiff and wild under his long sleeves.

"Get away from the hives, boy, you'll get stung."

"They aren't stinging you."

He took off his hat and waved a bee back toward its hive. "They don't have a lot of me to pick at, now do they. Besides they won't sting me; they know who's taking care of them." We got out from among the hives. The long white hair over his ears streamed back in the wind, mixing in my sight with the clouds; his beard was tucked into his shirt, "so I don't eat any of the little sweeties." The fog was rising, forming quick cloud streams. Tom rubbed his freckled pate. "Let's get out of the wind, Henry my boy. It's so cold the bees are acting like idiots. You should hear what nonsense they talk. Just like they've been smoked. Perhaps you'd have some tea with me."

"Sure." Tom's tea was so strong it was almost like having a meal.

"Have you got your lesson ready?"

"You bet. Say, did you hear about the dead man washed up?"

"I went down to look at him. Washed up just north of the rivermouth. A Japanese, I'd venture. We buried him at the back of the graveyard with the rest of them."

"What do you think happened to him?"

"Well . . . ." We turned onto the path to his house. "Someone shot him!" He cackled at my expression. "I guess he was trying to visit the United States of America. But the United States of America is *out of bounds*." He navigated his yard without paying the least bit of attention to it, and I followed him closely. We went into the house. "Obviously someone has declared us out of bounds, we are *beyond the pale*, boy, only in this case the pale is rather dark, those ships steaming back and forth out there are so black you can see them even on a moonless night, rather stupid of them if they wanted them truly invisible. I haven't seen a foreigner—a live foreigner, that is—those dead ones make mighty poor informants, hee hee—since the day. That's too long for coincidence, not that there aren't contributing indications. But that's the main fact; where are they?—since they *are* out there." He filled the teapot. "It's my hypothesis that declaring us off limits was the only way to avoid fighting over us, and destroying . . . but I've outlined this particular guess to you before, eh?"

I nodded.

"And yet I don't even know who we're talking about, when you get right down to it."

"The Chinese, right?"

"Or the Japanese."

"So you think they really are out there on Catalina just to keep folks away?"

"Well I know *someone's* on Catalina, someone not like us. That's one thing I *know*. I've seen the lights from up here at night, blinking all over the island. You've seen them."

"I sure have," I said. "It's beautiful."

"Yeah, that Avalon must be a bustling little port these days. No doubt something bigger on the backside, some Alexandrian causeway harbor, you know. It's a blessing to know something for sure, Henry. Surprisingly few things you can say that about. Knowledge is like quicksilver." He walked over to the fireplace. "But someone is on Catalina."

"We should go over and see who."

He shook his head, looking out his big window at the fast onshore streamers. "We wouldn't come back."

Subdued, he threw some twigs on the coals of the banked fire, and we sat before the window in two of his armchairs, waiting for the water to heat. The sea was a patchcloth, dark grays and light greys, with silver buttons scattered in a crooked line between us and the sun. It looked like it was going to rain rather than fog up; old Nicolin would be mighty annoyed, because you can fish in the rain. Tom pulled at his face, making a new pattern in the ten thousand wrinkles lining it. "Whatever happened to summertime," he sang, "yes when the living was eee-sy." I threw some more twigs on the fire, not bothering to respond to the little tune I had heard so often. Tom had told a lot of stories about the old time, and he was insistent that in those days our coastline had been a treeless, waterless desert. But looking out the window at the forest and the billowing clouds, feeling the fire warm the chill air of the room, remembering our adventure of the night before, I wondered if I could believe him. Half of his stories I could not confirm in his many books—and besides, couldn't he have taught me to read wrong, so that what I read would back up what he said?

It would be pretty difficult to make up a consistent system, I decided as he threw one of his packets of tea—made of plants he picked in the back country—into the pot. And I remembered once at a swap meet, when he came running up to Steve and Kathryn and me, drunk and excited, blabbing, "Look what I bought, look what I got!"—pulling us under a torch to show us a tatty old half an encyclopedia, opened to a picture of a black sky over white ground, on which stood two completely white figures and an American flag. "That's the *moon*, see? I *told* you we went there, and you wouldn't believe me." "I still don't believe you," Steve said, and nearly busted laughing at the fit the old man threw. "I bought this picture for four jars of honey to *prove* it to you skeptics, and you still won't believe me?" "No!" Kathryn and I were in hysterics at the two of them—we were pretty drunk too. But he kept the picture (though he threw away the encyclopedia), and later I saw the blue ball of the Earth in the black sky, as small as the moon is in our sky. I must have stared at that picture for an hour. So one of the least likely of his claims was apparently true; and I was inclined to believe the rest of them, usually.

"All right," Tom said, handing me my cup full of the pungent tea. "Let's hear it."

I cleared my mind to imagine the page of the book Tom had assigned me to learn. The regular lines of the poetry made them easy to memorize, and I spoke them out as my mind's eye read them:

> "'Is this the region, this the soil, the clime,'
>   Said then the lost Archangel, 'this the seat
> That we must change for Heaven?
>   —this mournful gloom
> For that celestial light?'"

I went on easily, having a good time playing the part of defiant Satan. Some of the lines were especially good for thundering out:

> " 'Farewell, happy fields,
> Where joy forever dwells! Hail, horrors! Hail,
> Infernal world! and thou, profoundest Hell,
> Receive thy new possessor—one who brings
> A mind not to be changed by place or time.
> The mind is its own place, and in itself
> Can make a Heaven of Hell, a Hell of Heaven.
> What matter where, if I be still the same,
> And what I should be, all but less than he
> Whom thunder hath made greater? Here at least
> We shall be free—' "

"All right, that's enough of that one," Tom said, looking satisfied as he stared out to sea. "Best lines he ever wrote, and half of them stolen from Virgil. What about the other piece?"

"I do that one even better," I said confidently. "Here you go:

> "Methinks I am a prophet new inspired,
> And thus expiring do foretell of him:
> His rash fierce blaze of riot cannot last,
> For violent fires soon burn out themselves.
> Small showers last long, but sudden storms are short;
> He tires betimes that spurs too fast betimes;
> With eager feeding, food doth choke the feeder—"

"That was us all right," Tom interrupted. "He's writing about America, there. We tried to eat the world and choked on it. I'm sorry, go on."

I struggled to remember my place, and started again:

> "This royal throne of kings, this sceptered isle,
> This earth of majesty, this seat of Mars,

This other Eden, demi-paradise,
This fortress built by Nature for herself
Against infection and the hand of war,
This happy breed of men, this little world,
This precious stone set in a silver sea
Which serves it in the office of a wall,
Or as a moat defensive to a house,
Against the envy of less happier lands,
This blessed plot, this earth, this realm, this England—"

"Enough!" Tom cried, chuckling and shaking his head. "Or too much. I don't know what I think. But I sure give you good stuff to memorize."

"Yeah," I said. "You can see why Shakespeare thought England was the best state."

"Yes . . . he was a great American. Maybe the greatest."

"But what does moat mean?"

"Moat? Why, it means a channel of water surrounding a place to make it hard to get to. Couldn't you figure it out by context?"

"If I could've, would I have asked you?"

He cackled. "Why, I heard that one out at one of the little back country swap meets, just last year. Some farmer. 'We're going to put a moat around the granary,' he said. Made me a bit surprised. But you hear odd words like that all the time. I heard someone at the swap meet say they were going to cozen up to someone, and someone else told me my sales pitch was a filibuster. Insatiate, simular—it's amazing, the infusion of words into the spoken language. Bad news for the stomach is good news for the tongue, know what I mean?"

"No."

"Well, I'm surprised at you." He stood up, stiff and slow, and refilled the teapot. After he got it set on the rack over the fire he went to one of his bookshelves. The inside of his house was a bit like the yard—junk everywhere, only smaller pieces of it: more clocks, a few of which actually worked, cracked china plates, a collection of lanterns and lamps, a machine for playing music (once in a while he'd put a record on it and turn it with one bony finger, commanding us to put our ears next to it, to hear scratchy songs whispering up and down, while he said "That's the Eroica! Listen to that!" till we told him to shut up and *let* us listen); but most of two walls were taken up by bookshelves, overflowing with stacks of mangy books. A lot of them he wouldn't let me read. But now he brought one over and tossed it in my lap. "Time for some sight reading. Start where I have the marker, there."

I opened the slim, mildewed book and began to read—an act that still gave me great trouble, great pleasure. "'Justice is in itself powerless: what rules by nature is *force*. To draw this over to the side of justice, so that by means of force justice rules—that is the problem of statecraft, and it is certainly a hard one; how hard you will realize if you consider what boundless egoism reposes in almost every human breast; and that it is many millions of individuals so constituted who have to be kept within the bounds of peace, order and legality. This being so, it is a wonder the world is on the whole as peaceful and law-abiding as we see it to be'"—this caused the old man to laugh for a while—"'which situation, however, is brought about only by the machinery of the state. For the only thing that can produce an immediate effect is physical force, since this is the only thing which men as they generally are understand and respect—'"

"Hey!"

It was Nicolin, busting into the house like Satan into God's bedroom. "I'm going to kill you right here and now!" he cried, advancing on the old man.

Tom jumped up with a whoop: "Let's see you try!" he shouted. "You don't stand a chance!"—and the two of them grappled a bit in the middle of the room, Steve holding the old man by the shoulders at just enough distance so that Tom's fierce blows missed him.

"Just what do you mean filling our heads with lies, you old son of a bitch?" Nicolin demanded, shaking Tom back and forth with genuine anger.

"And what do you mean busting into my house like that. Besides"—losing his pleasure in their usual sport—"when did I ever lie to you?"

Steve snorted. "When didn't you? Telling us they used to bury their dead in silver-lined caskets. Well now we know that one's a lie, because we went up to San Clemente last night and dug one up, and the only thing it had on it was plastic."

"What's this?" Tom looked at me. "You did what?"

So I told him about the gang's expedition into San Clemente. When I got to the part about the coffin handles he began to laugh; he sat down in his chair and laughed, heee, heeee, hee hee *heeee*, all through the rest of it, including the part about the scavengers' siren attack.

Nicolin stood over him, glowering. "So now we know you're lying, see?"

"Heeeeeee, hee hee hee hee hee hee." A cough or two. "No lies at all, boys. Only the truth from Tom Barnard. Listen here—why do you think that plastic on that coffin was silver-colored?" Steve gave me a significant look. "Because it usually *was* silver, of course. You just dug up some poor guy who died broke. His family bought him a cheap coffin. Now, what were you doing digging up graves for, anyway?"

"We wanted the silver," Steve said.

"Bad luck." He got up to get another cup, poured it full. "I tell you, most of them were buried wrapped in the stuff. Sit down here, Stephen, and have some tea." Steve pulled up a little wooden chair, sat down and commenced sucking on his tea. Tom curled in his chair and wrapped his knobby hands around his cup. "The really rich ones were buried in gold," he said slowly, looking down at the steam rising from his cup. "One of them had a gold mask, carved to look just like him, put over his dead face. In his burial chamber were gold statues of his wife, and dogs, and kids—he had on gold shoes, too, and little mosaic pictures of the important events of his life, made of precious stones, surrounding him on each wall of the chamber. . . ."

"Ah, come on," Nicolin protested.

"I'm serious! That's what it was like. You've been up there, now, and seen the ruins—are you going to tell me they didn't throw silver in the ground with their dead?"

"But why?" I asked. "Why that gold mask and all?"

"Because they were Americans." He sipped his tea. "That was the least of it, let me tell you." He stared out the window for a while, a faraway look in his brown eyes. "Rain coming." After another minute's silent sipping: "What do you want silver so bad for, anyway?"

I let Nicolin answer that one, because it was his idea.

"To trade for things," Steve said. "To get what we want at the swap meets. To be able to go somewhere, down the coast maybe, and have something to trade for food." He glanced at the old man, who was watching him closely. "To be able to travel like you used to."

Tom ignored that. "You can get everything you want by trading what you make. Fish, in your case."

"But you can't go anywhere! You can't travel with fish on your back."

"You can't travel anyway. They blasted every important bridge in the country, from the looks of it. And if you did manage to get somewhere, the locals would take your silver and kill you, like as not. Or if they were just, you'd still run out of silver eventually, and you'd have to go to work where you were. Digging shit ditches or something."

The fire crackled as we sat there and watched it. Nicolin let out a long sigh, looking stubborn. The old man sipped his tea and went on. "We travel to the swap meet in three days, if the weather allows. That's farther than we used to travel, let me tell you. And we're meeting more new people than ever."

"Including scavengers," I said.

"You don't want to get in any feud with those young scavengers," Tom said.

"We already are," Steve replied.

Now it was Tom's turn to let out a sigh. "There's been too much of that already. So few people alive these days, there's no reason for it."

"They started it."

Big drops of rain hit the window. I watched them run down the glass, and wished my home had a window. Even with the door closed and dark clouds filling the sky, all the books and crockery and lanterns and even the walls gleamed silvery grey, as if they all contained a light of their own.

"I don't want you fighting at the swap meet," Tom said.

Steve shook his head. "We won't if we don't have to."

Tom frowned and changed the subject. "You got your lesson memorized?"

Steve shook his head. "I've had to work too much. . . . I'm sorry."

After a bit I said, "You know what it looks like to me?"

"What what looks like," Tom asked.

"The coastline here. It looks like one time there was nothing but hills and valleys, all the way out to the horizon. Then one day some giant drew a straight line down it all, and everything west of the line fell down and the ocean came rushing in. Where the line crossed a hill there's a cliff, and where it crossed a valley there's a marsh and a beach. But always a straight line, see? The hills don't stick out into the ocean, and water doesn't come and fill in the valleys."

"That's a faultline," Tom said dreamily, eyes closed as if he were consulting books in his head. "The earth's surface is made up of big plates that are slowly sliding around. Truth! *Very* slowly—in your lifetime it might move an inch—in mine two, hee hee—and we're next to a fault where the plates meet. The Pacific plate is sliding north, and the land here south. That's why you get the straight line there. And earthquakes—you've felt them—those are the two plates slipping, grinding against each other. One time . . . one time in the old time, there was an earthquake that shattered every city on this coast. Buildings fell like they did on the day. Fires burned and there was no water to put them out. Freeways like that one down there pointed at the sky, and no one could get in to help, at first. For a lot of people it was the end. But when the fires were burned out . . . they came from everywhere. They brought in giant machines and material, and they used the rubble that was all that was left of the cities. A month later every one of those cities was built back up again, just as they had been before, so exactly that you couldn't even tell there had been an earthquake."

"Ah come on," said Steve.

The old man shrugged. "That's what it was like."

We sat and looked through the slant-lines of water at the valley below. Black brooms of rain swept the whitecapped sea. Despite the years of work done in the valley, despite the square fields by the river, and the little bridge over it, despite the rooftops here and there, wood or tile or telephone wire—despite all of that, it was the freeway that was the main sign that humans lived in the valley . . . the freeway, cracked and dead and half silted over and worthless. The huge strips of concrete changed from whitish to wet gray as we watched. Many was the time when we had sat in Tom's house drinking tea and looking at it, Steve and me and Mando and Kathryn and Kristen, during our lessons or sitting out one shower or another, and many was the time that the old man had told us tales of America, pointing down at the freeway and describing the cars, until I could almost see them flashing back and forth, big metal machines of every color and shape just flying along, weaving in and out amongst each other and missing dreadful crashes by an inch as they hurried to do business in San Diego or Los Angeles, red and white headlights glaring off the wet concrete and winking out over the hill, plumes of spray spiraling back and enveloping the cars following so that no one could see properly, and Death sat in every passenger seat, waiting for mistakes—so Tom would tell it, until it would actually seem strange to me to look down and see the road so empty.

But today Tom just sat there, letting out long breaths, looking over at Steve now and then and shaking his head. Sipping his tea in silence. It made me feel low; I wished he would tell another story. I would have to walk home in the rain, and Pa would have made the fire too small and our cabin would be chill, and long after our meal of bread and fish was done, I'd have to hunch over the coals to get warm, in the drafty dark.... Below us the freeway lay like a road of giants, gray in the wet green of the forest, and I wondered if cars would drive over it ever again.

Chapter Three

Swap meets brought out most of the people in Onofre, to get the caravan ready to go. A score of us stood on the freeway at the takeoff point on Basilone Ridge, some piling fish onto the boat trailers, some still running down to the valley and back again with forgotten stuff, others yelling at the dogs, who were for once useful, as they pulled the boat trailers. It was a real test getting them all into the halters. Around the trailers folks bickered over space. The trailers, light metal racks on a pair of wheels, were good wains, but there was a shortage of room on them. So there was old Tom threatening anyone who tried to change the wasteful stowing of his honey jars, and Kathryn defending her loaves of bread with the same threats and curses, and Steve commandeering whole trailers for the fish. Mostly we took fish to the swap meet—nine or ten trailers of them, fresh and dried—and my task was to help Rafael and Steve and Doc and Gabby to load the racks. Fish were slapping and dogs were yapping, and Steve was giving orders right and left to everyone but Kathryn, who would have kicked him, and overhead a flock of gulls screeched at us as they realized they weren't going to get a meal. It drove the dogs wild. It all reached a final pitch of excited yelling, and we were off.

On the coast the sky was the color of sour milk, but as we turned off the freeway and moved inland up San Mateo Valley, the one just north of ours, the sun began to break through here and there, and splashes of sunlight made the green hills blaze. Our caravan stretched out as the road got thinner—it was an ancient asphalt thing, starred by potholes that we had filled with stones to make our travel easier.

Steve and Kathryn walked at the end of the line of trailers, arms around each other. Sitting on the trailer end and letting one foot drag over asphalt, I watched them. I had known Kathryn Mariani for most of my life, and for most of my life I had been scared of her. The Marianis lived next to Pa and me, so I saw her all the time. She was the oldest of five girls, and when I was younger it seemed like she was always bossing us around, or giving someone a quick slap for trying to snatch bread or sneak through the cornfields. And she was big, too— after felling me with a kick of her heavy boot, as she had done more than once, her freckled ugly glare had inspected me from what seemed a tremendous height. I thought then that she was the meanest girl alive. It was only in the previous couple of years, when I grew as tall as her, that I got to the vantage point where I could see she was pretty. A snub nose doesn't look so good from below (looks like a pig snout, to tell the truth), nor a big wide mouth—but from level on she looked all right. And the year before she and Steve had become lovers, so that the other girls snickered and wondered how long it would be before they had to get married; we had become better friends as a result, and I got to know her as more than the scarecrow with a rolling pin that she had been to me. Now we kidded each other about the old times:

"Guess I'm going to lunch off that bread on the first trailer; I'm sure no one will mind."

"You do and I'll kick your butt back to Onofre like I used to, Henry dear." It made Nicolin laugh. He was a lot happier on these trips, with his family left behind, his father driving the men every day to get the catch in. When the dogs yelped he jogged up and tussled with them till they were grinning and simpering and slobbering over him again, ready to haul all day for the fun of it, because of the way Steve was laughing. A lot of the dogs belonged to the Nicolins, and spent most of their lives rat-catching on the cliffs. Steve had them well trained; they went quiet for him so he could sneak in and out at night without them barking hello. Pa and I didn't own any dogs—usually we were lucky just to be able to feed ourselves—but the Nicolins' dogs liked me well enough. "Good perro," I said to them as Steve went back to Kathryn.

We made the swap meet about midday. The site was a grassy-floored meadow, filled with well-spaced eucalyptus and ironwood trees. When we got there the sun was out, more than half the attending villages were already there, and in the dappled light under the trees were colored canopies and flags, trailers and car bodies and long tables, scores of people in their finest clothes, and plumes of woodsmoke, breaking through the trees from a number of campfires. The dogs went wild.

We held the dogs by the halters and wound our way through the crowd to our campsite. After we said hello to the cowmen from Talega Canyon who camped next to us, we moved all the cow dung scattered around our spot into the firepit, and unloaded the trailers, or set them around like tables. I helped Rafael put up awnings over the fish trailers. The old man, staring raptly at the white canopy over the cowmen, pointed to it and said to Steve and me, "You know in the old time people used to string those things from their backs, and jump out of airplanes thousands of feet up. They floated all the way to the ground under them."

"And fish played baseball," Steve said. "Celebrating the meet a bit early, eh Tom?" Tom protested, and we laughed. The dogs were a nuisance and we took them out to the back of our site and tied them to trees, calming them with fishheads. By the time we got back to the front of our camp the trading had already begun. We were the only seaside town at this meet, almost, so we were popular. "Onofre's here," I heard someone calling. "Look at this abalone," someone else said, "I'm going to eat mine right now!" Rafael sang out his call: "Pescados. Pescados." Even the scavengers from Laguna came over to trade with us; they couldn't do their own fishing even with the ocean slapping them in the face. "I don't want your dimes, lady," Doc insisted. "I want boots, boots, and I know you've got them." "Take my dimes and buy the boots from someone else; I'm out today. Blue Book says one dime, one fish." Doc grumbled and made the sale. After moving the campfire wood off a trailer, I was done with my work for the day. Sometimes I had clothes to trade: I got them all tattered and torn from the scavengers, and then sold them whole again after Pa had sewn them up. But this time he hadn't patched a thing, because we hadn't had anything to trade for old clothes last month. So the day was mine, though I would keep an eye out for wrecked coats—and see them, too, but on people's backs. I walked to the front of our camp and sat down in the sun, on the edge of the main promenade.

The promenade was busy. One woman in a long purple dress balanced a crate of chickens on her head as she walked by; she was trailed by two men in matching yellow and red striped pants, and blue long-sleeved shirts. Another woman in a group of colorfully dressed friends wore a rainbow-stained pair of pants so stiff they had a crease fore and aft.

It wasn't just the clothes that distinguished the scavengers. They all talked loudly, at the top of their voices, nearly all the time. Perhaps they did it to overcome the silence of the ruins, I thought as I listened to them. Tom often said that living in the ruins made the scavengers mad, every single one of them; and quite a few of them passing me had a look in their eye that made me think he was right—a look wild and wanton, as if they were searching for something exciting to do that they couldn't quite find. I watched the younger ones closely, wondering if the ones passing me were among those who had run us out of San Clemente. We had had small fights with a group of them before, at the swap meets and in San Mateo Valley, where rocks had flown like bombs—but I didn't see any of the members of that crowd, and couldn't be sure if they were the ones who had found us in San Clemente anyway. A pair of them walked by dressed in pure white suits, with white hats to match. I had to grin. My blue jeans had had their knees patched countless times, and all the blue was washed out of them. All the folks from new towns and villages wore the same sort of thing, back country clothes kept together by needle and prayer, sometimes new things made up of scraps of cloth, or hides; wearing them was like having a badge saying you were healthy and normal. I suppose the scavengers' clothes were another sort of badge, saying that they were rich, and dangerous. Right after a group of shepherds came a flock of scavenger women in dresses made of lace, each dress with more than six yards of cloth in it, I reckoned, of which two at least trailed on the ground. Wasteful.

Then I saw Melissa Shanks walking out of our camp, carrying a basket of crabs. I hopped up without a thought and approached her. "Melissa!" I said. When she looked at me I gave her a fool's grin. "Want some help bringing back what you get for those pinchers?"

She raised her eyebrows. "What if I was out to get a pack of needles?"

"Well, um, I guess you wouldn't need much help."

"True. But lucky for you I'm out in search of a barrel half, so I'd be happy to have you along."

"Oh good." Melissa spent some time working at the ovens; she was a friend of Kathryn's younger sister Kristen. Other than the times I'd seen her at the ovens, I didn't know her. Her father, Addison Shanks, lived on Basilone Hill, and they didn't have much to do with the rest of the valley. "You'll be lucky to get a half cask for that many crabs," I went on, looking in her basket.

"I know. The Blue Book says it's possible, but I'll have to do some fast talking." She tossed back her long black hair confidently, and it blazed in the sun, so glossy and perfectly kept that it seemed she wore jewelry. She was pretty: small teeth, a narrow nose, fine white skin. . . . She had a whole series of careful, serious, haughty expressions that her lips would hold, and that made her rare smiles all the sweeter. I stared at her too long, and bumped into an old woman going the other way.

"Carajo!"

"Sorry, mam, but I was made distract by this here young maiden—"

"Well get a grip!"

"Indeed I'll try mam, goodbye," and with a wink and a pinch on the butt (she slapped my hand) I rounded the crone, who was grinning. As Melissa was smiling too I took her arm in hand and we talked cheerily as we toured the meet on the main promenade, looking for a cooper. We eventually made for the Trabuco Canyon camp, agreeing that the farmers there were good woodworkers.

A plume of smoke rose from the Trabuco camp, floating through wedged sunbeams that turned the smoke seashell pink.

We smelled meat; they were roasting a steer half by half. A good crowd had gathered in their camp to join the feast. Melissa and I traded one of the crabs for a pair of ribs, and ate them standing, observing the antics of a slick trio of scavengers, who wanted six ribs for a box of safety pins. I was about to make a joke about them when I remembered Melissa's father's rumored dealings with scavengers. Addison did a lot of trading by night, to the north, and no one was sure how much he traded with scavengers, how much he stole from them, how much he worked for them. . . . He was sort of a scavenger himself, who preferred to live outside of the ruins. I chewed the beef in silence, aware all of a sudden that I didn't know the girl at my side very well. She gnawed her rib clean as a dog's bone, looking at the sizzling meat over the fire. She sighed. "That was good, but I don't see any barrels. I guess we should look in the scavenger camps."

I agreed, although that would mean a tougher trade. We walked over to the north half of the park, where the scavengers stayed—keeping a clear route back home, perhaps. The camps and goods for trade were much different here: no food, except for several women guarding trays of spices and canned delicacies. We passed a man dressed in a shiny blue suit, trading tools that were spread out over a blanket on the grass. Some of the tools were rusty, others brighter than silver, each a different shape and size. We tried to guess what this or that tool had been for. One that gave us the giggles was two pairs of greenish metal clamps at each end of a wire in a tube of orange plastic. "That was to hold together husbands and wives who didn't get along," Melissa said.

"Nah, they'd need something stronger than those. They're probably a doorstop."

She crowed. "A *what?*" But she wouldn't let me explain— she started to double over every time I tried, until I couldn't talk myself. We walked on, past large displays of bright clothing and shiny shoes, and big rusty machines that were no use without electricity, and gun men with their crowd of spectators, on hand to watch the occasional big trade or demonstration shot. The seed exchange, on the border between the scavengers' camps and ours, was hopping as usual. I wanted to go over and see if Kathryn was trading, because the way she traded for seeds was an art; but in the crowd of traders I couldn't see if she was there, and suddenly Melissa tugged on my arm. "There!" she said. Beyond the seed exchange was a woman in a scarlet dress, selling chairs, tables, and barrels.

"There you are," I said. I caught sight of Tom Barnard across the promenade. "I'm going to see what Tom's up to while you start your dealing."

"Good. I'll try the poor and innocent routine until you get there."

"Good luck." She didn't look all that innocent, and that was the truth. I walked over to Tom, who was deep in discussion with another tool trader. When I stopped at his side he clapped a hand on my shoulder and went on talking.

"—industrial wastes, rotting wood, animal bodies, sometimes—"

"Bullshit," said the tool trader. ("That too," the old man got in). "They made it from sugar cane and sugar beets; it says so right on the boxes. And sugar stays good forever, and it tastes just as good as your honey."

"There are no such things as sugar cane and sugar beets," Tom said scornfully. "You ever seen one of either? There are no such plants. Sugar companies made them up. Meanwhile they made their sugar out of sludge, and you'll pay for it with no end of dreadful diseases and deformities. But honey! Honey'll keep away colds and all ailments of the lungs, it'll get rid of gout and bad breath, it tastes ten times better than sugar, it'll help you live as long as me, and it's new and natural, not some sixty-year-old synthetic junk. Here, taste some of this, take a fingerful, I've been turning the whole meet on to it, no obligation in a fingerful."

The tool man dipped two fingers in the jar the old man held before him, and licked the honey off them.

"Yeah, it tastes good—"

"You bet it does! Now one God damned little lighter, of which you've got thousands up in O.C., is surely not much for two, twooooo jars of this delicious honey. Especially . . ." Tom cracked his palm against the side of his head to loosen the hinges of his memory. "Especially when you get the jars, too."

"The jars too, you say."

"Yes, I know it's generous of me, but you know how we Onofreans are, we'd give our pants away if people didn't mind our bare asses hanging out, besides I'm senile almost—"

"Okay, okay! You can shut up now, it's a deal. Give them over."

"All *right*, here they are young man," handing the jars to him. "You'll live to be as old as me eating this magic elixir, I swear."

"I'll pass on that if you don't mind," the scavenger said with a laugh. "But it'll taste good." He took the lighter, clear plastic with a metal cap, and gave it to the old man.

"See you again, now," Tom said, pocketing the lighter eagerly and pulling me away with him. Under the next tree he stopped. "See that, Henry? See that? A lighter for two little jars of honey? Was that a trade? Here, watch this. Could you believe my dealing? Watch this." He pulled out the lighter and held it before my face, pulled his thumb down the side. He let the flame stand for a second, then shut it off.

"That's nice," I said. "But you've already got a lighter."

He put his wrinkled face close to mine. "*Always* get these things when you see them, Henry. Always. They're about the most valuable thing the scavengers have to trade. They are the greatest invention of American technology, no question about it." He reached over his shoulder and rooted in his pack. "Here, have a drink." He offered me a small bottle of amber liquid.

"You've been to the liquor traders already?"

He grinned his gap-toothed grin. "First place I went to, of course. Have a drink of that. Hundred-year-old Scotch. Really fine."

I took a swallow, gasped.

"Take another, now, that first one just opens the gates. Feel that warmth down there?" I did. "Fine stuff."

I traded swallows with him and pointed out Melissa, who looked like she wasn't making much headway with the barrel woman. "Ahh," said Tom, leering significantly. "Too bad she ain't dealing with a man."

I agreed. "Say, can I borrow a jar of honey from you? I'll work it off in the hives."

"Well, I don't know . . ."

"Ah come on, what else are you going to trade for today?"

"Lots of stuff," he protested.

"You already have the most important thing the scavengers own, right?"

"Oh, all right. I'll give you the little one. Have another drink before you go."

I got back to Melissa with my stomach burning and my head spinning. Melissa was saying slowly, like for the fourth time, "We just pulled them out of the live pen this morning. That's the way we always do it, everyone knows that. They all eat our crab and no one's got sick yet. The meat's good for a week if you keep it cool. It's the tastiest meat there is, as you know if you've ever eaten any."

"I've eaten it," the woman snapped. "But I'm sorry. Crab is good all right, but there's never enough of it to make a difference. These barrel halves are hard to find. You'd have it forever, and I'd get a few tastes of crab for a week."

"But if you don't sell them you're going to have to cart them back north," I interrupted in a friendly way. "Pushing them up all those hills and then making sure they don't roll down the other side . . . why we'd be doing you a favor to take one of them off your hands for free!—not that we want to do that, of course. Here—we'll throw in a jar of Barnard honey with these delicious pinchers, and really make it a steal for you." Melissa had been glaring at me for butting in on her deal, but now she smiled hopefully at the woman. The woman stared at the honey jar, but looked unconvinced.

"Blue Book says a barrel half is worth ten dollars," I said. "And these sidewalks are worth two dollars apiece. We've got seven of them, so you're already out-trading us four dollars' worth, not counting the honey."

"Everyone knows the Blue Book is full of shit," the woman said.

"Since when? It was scavengers made it up."

"Was not—it was you grubs did."

"Well, whoever made it up, everyone uses it, and they only call it shit when they're trying to deal someone dirty."

The woman hesitated. "Blue Book really says crabs are two dollars each?"

"You bet," I said, hoping there wasn't a copy nearby, for crabs are only a dollar fifty.

"Well," said the woman, "I do like the way that meat tastes."

Rolling the barrel half back to our camp, Melissa forgot about my rudeness. "Oh Henry," she sang, "how can I thank you?"

"Ah," I said, "no need, yuk yuk." I stopped the barrel to let pass a crowd of shepherds with a giant table upside-down on their heads. Melissa wrapped her arms around me and gave me a good kiss. We stood there looking at each other before starting up again; her cheeks were flushed, her body warm against mine. As we started walking again she smacked her lips. "You been drinking, Henry?"

"Ah—old Barnard gave me a few sips back there."

"Oh yeah?" She looked over her shoulder. "Wouldn't mind some of that myself."

Back at camp Melissa went off to meet Kristen and I helped the end of the fish trading. Nicolin came by with a cigarette and under the sunbeams sparking the dust in the afternoon air we smoked it. Soon after that a fight started between a Pendleton cowboy and a scavenger, and it was broken up by a crowd of big angry men whose job was keeping things peaceful. These meet sheriffs didn't like their authority ignored, and people fighting were always going to lose, slapped around hard by this gang. After that I nodded off for an hour or two, back with the sleeping dogs.

Rafael woke me when he came back to feed scraps to the perros. Only the western sky was still blue; high clouds overhead still glowed with a bit of sunset light. I stood up too fast. When the blood got back to my head I walked over to our fire, where a few people were still eating. I crouched beside Kathryn and ate some of the stew she offered me. "Where's Steve?"

"He's already in the scavenger camps. He said he'd be in the Mission Viejo one for the next hour or two."

"Ah," I said, wolfing down stew. "How come you aren't with him?"

"Well, Hanker, you know how it is. First of all, I had to stay here and help cook. But even if I could've gone, I can't keep up with Steve for an entire night. You know what that's like. I mean I could do it, but I wouldn't have any fun at it. Besides, I think he likes being away from me at these things."

"Nah."

She shrugged. "I'm going to go hunt him down in a bit."

"How'd it go at the seed exchange?"

"Pretty good. Not like in the spring, but I did get a good packet of barley seed. That was a coup—everyone's interested in this barley 'cause it's doing so well in Talega, so the trading was hot, but our good elote did the trick. I'm going to plant that whole upper field with this stuff next week, and see how it does. I hope it's not too late."

"Your crew'll be busy."

"They're always busy."

"True." I finished the stew. "I guess I'll go look for Steve."

"It shouldn't be hard to find him." She laughed. "Just go for the biggest noise. I'll see you over there."

Among the new town camps on the south side of the park it was dark and quiet, except for the eerie, piercing cries of the Trabuco peacocks, protesting their cages. Small fires here and there made the trees above them flicker and dance with reflected light, and voices floated from the dark shapes blocking off the tiny flames. I stumbled over a root.

In the northern half of the park it was different. Bonfires roared in three clearings, making the colored awnings flap in the branches. Lanterns casting a mean white glare hung from the trees. I stepped onto the promenade and was shoved in the back by a large woman in an orange dress. "Sorry, boy." I walked over to the Mission Viejo camp. A jar flew past me, spilling liquid and smashing against a tree. The bright plastic colors of scavenged clothing wavered in the firelight, and every scavenger, man, woman and child, had gotten out their full collection of jewelry; they wore gold and silver necklaces, earrings, nose rings, ankle, belly, and wrist bracelets, and all of it studded with gems winking red and blue and green. They were beautiful.

The Viejo camp had tables set end to end in long rows. The benches lining them were jammed with people drinking and talking and listening to the jazz band at one end of the camp. I stood and looked for a while, not seeing anyone I knew. Then Nicolin deliberately struck me in the arm, and with a grin said, "Let's go hassle the old man, see he's over with Doc and the rest of the antiques."

Tom was set up at the end table with a few other survivors from the old time: Doc Costa, Leonard Sarowitz from Hemet, and George something from Cristianitos. The four of them were a familiar sight at swap meets, and were often joined by Odd Roger and other survivors old enough to remember what the old time was like. Tom was the senior member of this group by a long shot. He saw us and made a spot on the bench beside him. We had a drink from Leonard's jar; I gagged and sent half my swallow down my shirt. This put the four ancients in hysterics.

Old Leonard's gums were as clear of teeth as a babe's.

"Is Fergie here?" Doc asked George, getting back to their conversation.

George shook his head. "He went west."

"Ah. Too bad."

"You know how fast this boy is?" Tom said, slapping me on the shoulder. Leonard shook his head, frowning. "Once I threw him a pitch and he hit a iine drive past my ear—I turned around and saw the ball hit him in the ass as he slid into second."

The others laughed, but Leonard shook his head again. "Don't you distract me! You're trying to distract me!"

"What do you mean?"

"The point is—I was just telling him this, boys, and you should hear it too—the point is, if Eliot had fought back like an *American,* we wouldn't be in this fix right now."

"What fix is that?" Tom asked. "I'm doing okay as far as I can tell."

"Don't be facetious," Doc put in sourly.

"Back at it again, I see," Steve observed, rolling his eyes and going for the jar.

"Why, I don't doubt we would be the strongest nation on Earth again, by God," Leonard went on.

"Now wait a second," Tom said. "There aren't enough Americans left alive to add up to a nation at all, much less the strongest on Earth. And what good would it do if we had blown the rest of the world into the same fix?"

Doc was so outraged he cut Leonard off and answered for him: "What good would it do?" he said. "It would mean there wouldn't be any God damned Chinese boating off the coast, watching us all the time and *bombing* every attempt we make to rebuild! That's what good it would do. That coward Eliot put America in a hole for good. We're the bottom of the world now, Tom Barnard, we're bears in the pit."

"Raarrrr," Steve growled, and took another drink. I took the next one.

"We were goners as soon as the bombs went off," Tom said. "Makes no difference what happened to the rest of the world. If Eliot had decided to push the button, that just would've killed more people and wrecked more countries. It wouldn't have done a thing for us. Besides, it wasn't the Russians or the Chinese that planted the bombs—"

"You don't think," Doc said.

"You know it wasn't! It was the God damned South Africans. They thought we were going to mess with their slave system."

"The French!" George cried. "It was the French!"

"It was the Vietnamese," Leonard said.

"No it wasn't," Tom replied. "That poor country didn't even own a firecracker when we were done with it. And Eliot probably wasn't the man who decided not to retaliate, either. He probably died in the first moments of the day, like everyone else. It was some general in a plane who made the decision, you can bet your wooden teeth. And quite a surprise it must have been, too, even to him. Especially to him. Makes me wonder who he was."

Doc said, "Whoever it was, he was a coward and a traitor."

"He was a decent human being," said Tom. "If we had struck back at Russia and China, we'd be criminals and murderers. Anyway if we had done that the Russians would've sent their whole stockpile over here to answer ours, and then there wouldn't be a single damn *ant* left alive on North America today."

"Ants would still be alive," George said. Steve and I bent our heads to the table, giggling and pushing our fingers in each others' sides—"pushing the button," as the old men said. Odd that pushing a button could start a war. . . . Tom was giving us a mean look, so we straightened up and drank some more to calm ourselves.

"—over five thousand nuclear blasts and survived," Doc was saying. Every meet the number went up. "We could have taken a few more. Our enemies deserved a few of them too, that's all I'm saying." The bantering tone was gone from his voice; even though they had this argument every time they joined the other antiques, almost, Doc was still getting angry at Tom. Bitterly he cried, "If Eliot had pushed the button we'd all be in the same boat, and then we'd have a chance to rebuild. They won't let us rebuild, God damn it!"

"We are rebuilding, Ernest," Tom said jovially, trying to put the fun back in their argument. He waved at the surrounding scene.

"Get serious," Doc said. "I mean back to the way we were."

"I wouldn't want that," said Tom. "They'd likely blow us up again."

Leonard, however, was only listening to Doc: "We'd be in

a race with the Communists to rebuild, and you know who would win that one. We would!"

"Yeah!" said George. "Or maybe the French. . . ."

Barnard just shook his head and grabbed the jar from Steve, who gave him a struggle for it. "As a doctor you should never wish such destruction on others, Ernest."

"As a doctor I know best what they did to us, and where they're keeping us," Doc replied fiercely. "We're bears in the pit."

"Let's get out of here," Steve said to me. "They're going to start deciding whether we belong to the Russians or the Chinese."

"Or the French," I said, and we slithered off the bench. I took a last gulp of the old man's liquor and he whacked me. "Out of here, you ungrateful wretches," he cried. "Not willing to listen to history without poking fun."

"We'll read the books," Steve said. "They don't get drunk."

"Listen to him," said Tom, as his cronies laughed. "I taught him to read, and he calls me a drunk."

"No wonder they're so mixed up, with you teaching them to read," Leonard said. "You sure you got the books turned right way up?"

We wandered off to the sound of this sort of thing, and made our way with some stumbling to the orange tree. This was a giant old oak, one of a half dozen or so in the park, that held in its branches gas lanterns wrapped in transparent orange plastic. It was the mark of the scavengers from central Orange County, and our gang used it as the meeting place for later at night. We didn't see anyone from Onofre, so we sat on the grass under the tree, arms around each other, and made ribald comments on the passing crowd. Steve waved down a man selling jars of liquor and gave him two dimes for a jar of tequila. "Jars back without a crack, else we put the crack in your back," the man intoned as he moved on. On the other side of the orange tree a small bike-powered generator was humming and crackling; a group of scavengers was using it to operate a small instant oven, cooking slabs of meat or whole potatoes in seconds. "Heat it and eat it," they cried. "See the miracle microwave, the super horno! Heat it and eat it!" I took a sip of the tequila; it was strong stuff, but I was drunk enough to want to get drunker. "I am *drunk*," I told Steve. "I am *borracho*. I am aplastaaaa-do."

"Yes you are," Steve said. "Look at that silver." He pointed at one of the scavenger women's heavy necklaces. "Look at it!" He took a long swallow. "Hanker, those people are rich. Don't you think they could do just about anything they pleased? Go anywhere they pleased? Be anything they pleased? We've got to get some of that silver. Somehow we've got to. Life isn't just grunging for food in the same spot day after day, Henry. That's how animals live. But we're human beings, Hanker, that's what we are and don't you forget it, and Onofre ain't big enough for us, we can't live our whole lives in that valley like cows chewing cud. Chewing our cud and waiting to get tossed in some instant oven and *micro*-waved . . . um . . . give me another swallow of that, Hanker my best buddy, a powerful thirst for more has suddenly afflicted me."

"The mind is its own place," I remarked solemnly as I gave him the jar. Neither of us needed any more liquor, but when Gabby and Rebel and Kathryn and Kristen showed up, we were quick to help drink another jar. Steve forgot about silver for a while in favor of a kiss; Kathryn's red hair covered the sight. The band started again, a trumpet, a clarinet, two saxes, a drum and a bass fiddle, and we sang along with the tunes: "Waltzing Matilda," or "Oh Susannah," or "I've Just Seen a Face." Melissa showed up and sat down beside me. She'd been drinking and smoking, I could see. I put an arm around her, and over her shoulder Kathryn winked at me. More and more people crowded around the orange tree as the band heated up, and soon we couldn't see anything but legs. We played a game of guessing what town people were from by their legs alone, and then we danced around the tree with the rest of the crowd.

Much later we started our return to camp. I felt great. We pushed our way through singing people, gave our jars to the liquor man, and staggered onto the promenade, holding each other up and singing "High Hopes" all out of tune with the fading sound of the band.

Halfway home we collided with a group coming out of the trees, and I was roughly shoved to the ground. "Chinga," I said, and scrambled up. There were shouts and scufflings, a few others hit the ground and rolled back up swinging and shouting angrily. "What the—" The two groups separated and stood facing each other belligerently; by the light of a distant lantern we saw that it was the gang from San Clemente, decked out in identical red and white striped shirts.

"Oh," said Nicolin distinctly, his voice dripping with bored disgust, "it's them."

One of the leaders of their gang, a mean shot with a thrown rock, stepped into a shaft of light and grinned unpleasantly. His earlobes were all torn up from having on earrings in fights, but that hadn't stopped him; he still had two gold earrings in his left ear, and two silver ones in his right.

"Hello, Doll Grin," Nicolin said.

"Little people shouldn't come into Clemente at night," said the scavenger.

"What's Clemente?" Nicolin asked casually. "Nothing north of us but ruins, ruins on ruins."

"Little people might get scared. They might hear a *sound*," Doll Grin went on, and the guys behind him began to hum a rising tone, "uhnnnnnnn-eeeeeehhhhhhh," then falling, rising again: the sound of the siren we had heard that night. When they stopped their leader said, "We don't like people like you in our town. Next time you won't get away so easy. . . ."

Nicolin cracked his crazy smile. "Found any good dead bodies to eat lately?" he asked the scavengers innocently. With a rush they were on him, and Gabby and I had to come up on each side of him swinging hard, to keep him from being surrounded, although with his heavy boots he was doing quite well on their kneecaps. As the fight broke out in earnest he started shouting happily "Vultures! Buzzards! Wreckrats! Zopilotes!" and I had to look sharp because there were more of them than there were of us, and they seemed to have rings on every finger—

The sheriffs barged into us bellowing "What's this? Stop this—HEY!" I found myself on the dirt again, as did most of us. I started the laborious process of standing. "You kids get the fuck out of here," one of the sheriffs said. He was shaped like a barrel and was a foot taller than Steve, whom he held by the shirt. "We'll ban you all from swap meets forever if we have to break up these fights again. Now get out of here before we cave your faces in to make you think about it."

We rejoined the girls—Kristen and Rebel had been in the midst of the tussle, but the rest had stayed back—and trooped down the promenade. Behind us the Clemente gang started up the siren sound, "uhnnnnnneeeeeeeee-uhnnnnnneeeeeeeeeeeee-uhnnnnnnnnnnnneeeeeeee . . ."

"Damn!" Nicolin said, wrapping an arm around Kathryn. "We were going to pound those guys, too." Kathryn had been frowning, looking kind of disgusted, but at that she had to laugh.

"They had you two to one," she pointed out.

"Oh Katie, don't you know that's just the way we wanted it?" We all agreed we had had them in a tight spot, and walked back to camp in a fine humor. Melissa found me and slipped under my arm. As we approached the camp she slowed down and we fell behind the others. Sensing something to this, I steered us off the promenade into the grove. I stopped and leaned back against a laurel.

"You looked good fighting," she said, and then we were kissing. After some long kisses she sort of let her weight go on me, and I slid down the tree with her, scraping my back good on the bark. Once on the leaves I laid half on top, half beside her, a leg between hers, an awkward position, but it was making my blood pound. We were kissing without pause and I could feel her breathing fast, humming little gasps. I tried to get my hand down her pants but couldn't get it far enough, so I pushed it up under her shirt and held her breast. She bit my neck and a jolt ran down that whole side of my body. Someone with a lantern walked by on the promenade, and for a second I could see her shoulder: dirty white cotton twisted against pale skin, the swell of her breast pushed up by my hand . . . back to kissing, with the image clear in my closed eyes.

She pulled back. "Ohh," she sighed, "Henry. I told my dad I'd be right back. He'll start looking for me if I don't get back there pretty soon." She made a pout that I could just see in the dark, and I laughed and kissed it.

"That's okay. Some other time." I was too drunk to feel balked, why five minutes before I hadn't been expecting anything like this, and it was easy to slip back to that. Anything was easy. I helped her to her feet and took a piece of bark out of my back. And laughed.

I walked Melissa into camp and with a final quick kiss left her near her father's set-up. I went back out in the grove to take a leak. Off through the treetrunks I could still see the scavengers' camps, bouncing in the firelight, and faintly I could hear a group of them singing "America the Beautiful." I sang along under my breath, a perfect harmony part that only I could hear, and the old tune filled my heart.

Back on the promenade in front of our camp I saw the old man, talking with two strangers dressed in dark coats. The old man asked them questions, but I couldn't make out the words. Wondering who they were, I stumbled back to my sleeping spot. I laid down, head spinning, and looked up at the black branches against the sky, every pine needle clear as an ink stroke. I figured I'd be out in a second. But when I settled down there was a noise; someone was crushing leaves over and over again, *crick, crick, crick, crick* . . . from where Steve slept. I started listening and before long I heard breathing, and a soft, rhythmic expelling of breath, "Huh, huh, huh . . ." I knew it was Kathryn's voice. My hard-on was back; I wasn't going to be able to fall asleep. After a minute's listening I felt strange, and making some irritated noises, I got up and went out to the front of the camp, where the fire was a warm mass of coals. I sat watching them shift from gray to orange with every breath of wind, feeling horny and envious and drunk and happy.

All of a sudden the old man crashed into camp, looking drunker than I by a good deal. His scruff of hair flew around his head like smoke. He saw me and squatted by the fire. "Hank," he said, his voice uncommonly excited. "I've just been talking with two men who were looking for me."

"I saw you out there with them. Who were they?"

He looked at me, his bloodshot eyes gleaming with reflected firelight. "Hank, those men were from San Diego. And they came here—or up to just south of Onofre, actually—they talked to Recovery Simpson and followed us to the meet, to talk with me, ain't that nice—word gets around, you know, who a village elder is. Anyway . . ."

"The men."

"Yes! These men say they got from San Diego to Onofre *by train.*"

We sat there staring at each other over the fire, and some little flames popped up. Light danced on his wild eyes. "They came by train."

Chapter Four

A few days after we got back from the meet, Pa and I woke up to the sound of a hard rain drumming on the roof. We ate a whole loaf of bread and made a big fire, and sat down to needle clothes, but the rain fisted the roof harder and harder, and when we looked out the door we could scarcely see the big eucalyptus in the general gray. It looked like the ocean had decided to jump up and wash us down to it, and the young crops would be the first to go. Plants, stakes, the soil itself; they'd all be ripped away.

"Looks like we'll be putting the tarps down," Pa said.

"No doubt about it." We paced around the dark room in the firelight, got out our rain gear and paced some more, chattering with excitement. In a sheet downpour we heard Rafael's bugle faintly calling over the roar of the rain, hitting high-low-high-low-high-low.

We put on our gear and rushed out, and were drenched in seconds. "Whoo!" Pa cried, and ran for the bridge, splashing through puddles. At the bridge a few people were huddled under ponchos and umbrellas, waiting for the tarps to arrive. Pa and I ran to the bathhouse beside the river path, which was now a little creek bordering the foaming brown river. We had to dodge the occasional group of three or four trundling along awkwardly under the weight of one of the long tarps. At the bathhouse shed the Mendezes, Mando and Doc Costa, and Steve and Kathryn were hauling out tarps and lifting them onto the shoulders of whoever was there. I jumped under the end of a roll and followed it off, spurred by Kathryn's sharp voice. She had her whole crew jumping, no doubt of that. And it rained down on us like the world was under a waterfall.

I helped run three tarps over the bridge and out to the fields, and then it was time to get them down. Mando and I got on one end of a roll—loosely rolled plastic it was, once clear, now opaque with mud—and leaned over to get our arms around it. Rain poured onto my lower back and down my pants; my poncho was flying around my shoulders. Gabby and Kristen were on the other end of our roll, and the four of us maneuvered it into position at the downhill end of some rows of cabbage. We unrolled it one lift at a time, grunting and shouting directions at each other, walking up the furrows ankle deep in water. The field sloped ahead of us black and lumpy. Gray pools of water bounced under the rain's onslaught where the grading was not right. When we got to the end of the roll the last cabbages were just covered. Walking back I saw that under the tarps quite a few plants were getting bent into the furrows. It was a poor protection system, but the best we had. Below us small bowed figures were unfurling other tarps: the Hamishes, the Eggloffs, Manuel Reyes and the rest of Kathryn's farm crew plus Rafael and Steve. Beyond them the river churned, a brown flood studded with treetrunks and drowned shrubs. A thinner cloud rushed over and for a moment the light changed, so that everything glowed through the streaky veils of rain. Then just as suddenly it was twilight again.

The old man was at the bottom of the field helping to position the rest of the tarps, striding about under his shoulder umbrella, a plastic thing held over his head by two poles strapped to his back. I laughed and felt the rain in my mouth: "Now why can't he just wear a hat like everyone else?"

"That's just it," Mando said, hands clamped in his armpits for warmth. "He doesn't want to be like everyone else."

"He's already managed that without any such contraption on his head."

Gabby and Kristen joined us at the bottom. Gabby had fallen and was completely covered with mud. His sheepish grin was extra white by contrast. We got on another roll and began pulling it uphill. Wind hit the trees on the hill above and their branches bobbed and bent, as if the hillside were a big animal struggling under the storm, going *whoooo, whoooo,* and making the valley seem vast. Water poured down the tarps that were already laid. On the way back from the second tarp Gab and I paused to pull wrinkles out of it, and get it to sag properly into the furrows. The drainage ditch at the bottom of the fields was overflowing, but it all spilled into the river anyway.

Tom came over to greet us. His sheltered face was as wet as anyone's. "Hello Gabriel, Henry. And Armando, Kristen. Well met. Kathryn says she needs help with the corn." The four of us hurried up the riverbank to the cornfields, shivering and slapping our arms to our sides to drive out the chill. Kathryn was at their foot, running around getting groups together, booting reluctant rolls uphill, pointing out slack in the tarps already tied down. She was as black with mud as Gabby. She shouted instructions at us, and hearing that shrill tone in her voice we ran.

The shoots of corn were about two hands high, and we couldn't just lay the tarps right on them without breaking them. There were cement blocks every few yards, therefore, and the tarps had to be tied down to these through grommet holes. So the blocks had to be perfectly placed to match the holes. I saw that Steve and John Nicolin were working together, heaving blocks and tying knots. Everyone out there was dripping black. Kathryn had sent us to the upper end of the field, and when we got there we found her two youngest sisters and Doc and Carmen Eggloff, struggling with one of the narrowest tarps. "Hey Dad, let's get this thing rolling," Mando said as we approached them.

"Go to it," Doc replied wearily. We got them to continue unrolling, while we tied the sides of the tarp down to the blocks. Kathryn had set the blocks out a few weeks before, and I was amazed at how close they were to their correct positions, but still every one had to be shifted a bit. It took a lot of slipping around in the mud to get them right. Finally we got that tarp down, and hurried to start on another one.

A lot of time passed as we toiled up the slope again. Gusts of wind grabbed at the plastic and tore it away from my cold fingers. It hurt to hold on as hard as I had to. Tying the knots got almost impossible, and it was frustrating to watch my disobedient red and white fingers make mistakes again and again. My feet were long gone, of course. Thicker clouds flowed over, and it got darker. The spread tarps shone faintly. Kneeling in the muck and shivering, I looked up from a knot for a moment to see a field dotted with black figures, crouched or crawling or miserably bowed over, backs to the wind. I yanked the knot down grimly.

By the time we got our third tarp down—we were not much of a team for speed—most of the cornfields were covered. We sloshed around our last tarp and down to the riverbank and Kathryn. The river took a torrey pine past us and under the bridge; it looked forlorn, tumbling in the flood with its needles still green, its roots white and naked.

Almost the whole crew had gathered by the drowned drainage channel: twenty of us or more, watching the Mendezes and Nicolins run around the tarps and crawl under them, tightening and letting slack and generally fooling with the raised tarps so they'd drain properly. A few people made for the bathhouse; the rest of us stood around under umbrellas describing the unrolling to each other. The fields were now glistening, ridged plastic surfaces, and the rain hitting the tarps leaped back into the air, a score of droplets jumping up from each raindrop that fell, so that the plastic itself was almost invisible under a layer of wild droplet mist. Sheets of water poured off the lower ends of the tarps into the drainage ditch, free of mud and our summer crops. It was a satisfying sight.

When they were done adjusting the tarps we all trooped over the bridge to the bathhouse. Inside the big main room Rafael had been hard at work; it was already hot, and the baths were steaming. He was congratulated on his fire, "a nice controlled indoor bonfire," as Steve said. As I stripped my wet clothes off I admired for the hundredth time the complicated system of pipes and holding tanks and pumps that Rafael had constructed to heat the bath water. By the time I got in the dirt bath it was crowded. The dirt bath was the hotter of the two, and the air filled with the delighted moans and groans of scalded bathers. I couldn't feel my feet, but the rest of me burned.

Then the heat penetrated the skin of my feet and they felt like one of Pa's pin cushions. I hooted loudly. The sheet metal of the bath bottom was hot to the touch, and most of us floated, bumping and splashing and discussing the storm. Rafe pumped away harder than ever, grinning like a frog.

The clean bath had wooden seats anchored in it, and soon folks hopped over and gathered around those, talking and relaxing in the warmth. The boom of the rain on the corrugated metal roof washed over the chatter now and then; the pitch of the boom was an exact sign of how hard the rain was falling, and when it deepened enough people stopped talking and listened. Some of the group had gone out to help spread the tarps before their own gardens were covered, and they had to put their clammy clothes back on (unless they kept spares at the boathouse) and leave, promising all the while that they would hurry back. We believed them.

The firelight cast dancing shadows of the pipe system across the roof, and the plank walls glowed the color of the fire. Everyone's skin was ruddy. The women were beautiful: Carmen Eggloff putting branches on the fire, the ribs of her back sticking out; the girls diving like seals around one of the seats; Kathryn standing before me to talk, thick and rounded, beads of water gleaming on her freckled skin; Mrs. Nicolin twisting around and squealing, as John splashed her in a rare display of playfulness. I sat in my usual corner listening to Kathryn and looking around contentedly: we were a room of fire-skinned animals, wet and steaming, crazy-maned, beautiful as horses.

Most of us were getting out, and Carmen was handing around her collection of towels, when a voice called from outside.

"Hello there! Hello in there!"

Talk stopped. In the silence (roof drumming) we heard it clearer: "Hello in there, I say! Greetings to you! We're travelers from the south! Americans!"

Automatically the women, and most of the men, went for their towels or clothes. I yanked on my cold muddy pants, and followed Steve to the door. Tom and Nat Eggloff were already there; Rafael joined us still naked, holding a pistol in his hand. John Nicolin bulled his way through us, still pulling up his shorts, and pushed out the door.

"What brings you here?" we heard him ask. The answer was inaudible. A second passed, and Rafael opened the door again. Two men wearing ponchos entered before John; they looked surprised to see Rafael. They were completely drenched, which made them look weary and bedraggled. One was a skinny man with a long nose and a black beard that was no more than a thin strip around his jaw. The other was short and stocky, wearing a soaked floppy hat under his poncho. They took the ponchos off, revealing dark coats and wet pants. The shorter man saw Tom and said "Hello, Barnard. We met at the swap meet, remember?"

Tom said "Yes." They shook hands with him, and then with Rafael (a funny sight), John, Nat, Steve, and me. Without showing it much they looked around the room. All the women were dressed, or wrapped in towels, leaving a room filled with a fire, and steaming baths, and several naked men gleaming like fish among those of us with some cloth on. The shorter man did a sort of bow. "Thanks for taking us in. We're from San Diego, as Mr. Barnard here will tell you."

We stared at them.

"Did you get here by train?" Tom asked.

Both men nodded. The skinny one shivered. "We brought the cars within five miles of here," he said. "We left our crew there and walked the rest of the way. We didn't want to work on the tracks closer to you until we talked with you about it."

"We thought we'd get here sooner," the shorter one said, "but the storm slowed us."

"Why'd you hike in a storm in the first place?" John Nicolin asked.

After some hesitation the short one said, "We prefer to hike under cloud cover. Can't be seen from above, then."

John tilted his head and squinted, not getting it.

"If you want to jump in that hot water," Tom said, "go right ahead."

Shaking his head the taller one said, "Thank you, but . . ." They looked at each other.

"Looks warm," the short one observed.

"True," the other said, nodding a few times. He was still shivering. He looked around at us shyly, then said to Tom, "Perhaps we'll just warm up by your fire, if that's all right. It's been a wet walk, and I'd like to get dry."

"Sure, sure. Do what you like; the place is yours."

John didn't look too happy at Tom's wording, but he led the two men over to the fire, and Carmen threw on more wood.

Steve nudged me. "Did you hear that? A train to San Diego? We can get a ride down there!"

"I guess we might," I replied. The men were introducing themselves: the taller one was Lee, the short one Jennings. Jennings took off his cap, revealing straggly blond hair, then removed his poncho, coat, shirt, boots, and socks. He laid his clothes over the drying racks and stood with his hands stretched out to the fire.

"We've been working on the rails north of Oceanside for a few weeks now," he told us. Lee began to strip off his wet things as Jennings had. Jennings went on: "The Mayor of San Diego has organized a bunch of work forces of various sorts, and our job is to establish better travel routes to the surrounding towns."

"Is it true that San Diego has a population of two thousand?" Tom asked. "I heard that at a swap meet."

"About that." Jennings nodded. "And since the Mayor began organizing things, we've accomplished a good deal. The settlements are pretty well scattered, but we have a train system between them that works well. All handcars, you understand, although we do have generators providing a good supply of electricity back home. There's a weekly swap meet, and a fishing fleet, and a militia—all manner of things there weren't before. Naturally Lee and I are proudest of the exploration team. Why, we cleared highway eight all the way across the mountains to the Salton Sea, and shifted the train tracks onto it." Something in the way Lee moved before the fire caused Jennings to stop talking for a moment.

"The Salton Sea must be huge now," Tom said.

Jennings let Lee answer. Lee nodded. "It's fresh water now, too, and filled with fish. People out there were doing pretty good, considering how few of them there were."

"What brings you up here?" John Nicolin asked bluntly.

While Lee stared at John, Jennings looked around at his audience. Every face in the room was watching him closely, listening to what he had to tell. He appeared to like that. "Well, we had the rails going up to Oceanside," he explained, "and the ruined tracks extended north of that, so we decided to repair them."

"Why?" John persisted.

Jennings cocked his head to match the angle of John's.

"Why? I guess you'd have to ask the Mayor that one. It was his idea. You see"—he glanced at Lee, as if getting permission to speak further—"you're all aware that the Japanese are guarding us on the west coast here?"

"Of course," John said.

"You could hardly miss that," Rafael added. He had put his pistol away, and was sitting on the edge of the bath.

"But I don't mean from just the ships offshore," Jennings said. "I mean from the sky. From satellites."

"You mean cameras?" Tom said.

"Sure. You've all seen the satellites?"

We had. Tom had pointed them out, swiftly moving points of light that were like stars, cut loose and falling away as the universe moved on. And he had told us that there were cameras in them, too. But—

"Those satellites carry cameras that can see things no bigger than a rat," said Jennings. "They really got the eye on us."

"You could look up and say 'go to hell!' and they'd read your lips," Lee added with a humorless laugh.

"That's right," Jennings said. "And at night they have heat sensitive cameras that could pick up something as small as this roof, if you had the fire in here lit on a rainless night."

People were shaking their heads in disbelief, but Tom and Rafael looked as if they believed it, and as people noticed this there were some angry comments made. "I *told* you," Doc said to Tom. Nat and Gabby and a couple others stared at the roof in dismay. To think we were being watched that closely . . . it was terrible, somehow.

Strangers are good for news, they say, but these two were really something. I wondered if this was something Tom had known about all along, and had never bothered to tell us, or if he had been ignorant of it too. From his look I guessed he might have known. I wasn't sure that such surveillance made any difference in a practical way, but it sure felt awful, like a permanent trespass. At the same time it was fascinating. John looked to Tom for confirmation, and after a slight nod from him John said, "Just how do you know that? And what does that have to do with your coming this way, again?"

"We've learned some things from Catalina," Jennings said vaguely. "But that's not the end of it. Apparently the Japs' policy includes keeping our communities isolated. They don't want reunification on any scale whatsoever. Why, when we built the tracks on highway eight east"—he swelled indignantly at the memory—"we built some bridges big and strong as you please. One night around sunset, wham. They blew them up."

"What?" Tom cried. At the words *blew them up* he had jerked.

"They don't do it in any big way," Jennings said. Lee snorted to hear this. "It's true. Always at dusk—a red streak out of the sky, and *thunk*, it's gone. No explosions."

"Burnt up?" Tom asked.

Lee nodded. "Tremendous heat. The tracks melt, the wood incinerates instantly. Sometimes things around will catch fire, but usually not."

"We don't camp near our bridges much." Jennings cackled. "As you can imagine." But no one laughed with him. "Anyway, when the Mayor found out about this, he got mad. He wanted to complete the tracks, no matter the bombings. Communications with other Americans is a God-given right! he said. Since they got the upper hand for the time being, and will bomb us when they see us, we'll just have to see to it that they don't see us. That's what he said."

"We work real light," Lee said with sudden enthusiasm. "Most of the old pilings are still there for river bridges, and we just put beams across those and lay the rails across the beams. The handcars are light and don't need much support. After we've crossed we take the rails and beams across with us and hide them under trees, and there's no sign we've crossed. A few times for practice and we get so we can cross the easier rivers in a couple of hours."

"Of course sometimes it doesn't work," Jennings added. "Once near Julian we had bridge pilings burnt right to the water by those red streaks."

"Once they know we're at it, they may keep a closer watch," Lee said. "We don't know. They're not consistent. Mayor says there may be disagreements on how to deal with us. Or spotty surveillance. So we can't predict very well. But we don't camp near bridges."

The fact that these two men were struggling with the Japanese, even indirectly, silenced everyone in the room. They had a lot of eyes on them, and Jennings basked in it. Lee didn't notice. After a bit John pursued his question: "And now that you've managed to get up here, what might your mayor want with us?"

Lee was eyeing John sharper and sharper, but Jennings replied in a perfectly friendly way: "Why, to say hello, I reckon. To show that we can get to each other quick if we need to. And he was hoping we could convince you to send one of your valley's officials to come down and talk about trade agreements and such. And then there's the matter of extending the tracks farther north—we'd need your permission and cooperation to do that, of course. The Mayor is mighty anxious to establish tracks up to the Los Angeles basin."

"The scavengers in Orange County would be a problem there," Rafael said.

"Our valley doesn't have *officials*," John said belligerently.

"Someone to speak for the rest of you, then," Jennings said mildly.

"The Mayor wants to talk about these scavengers, too," said Lee. "I take it you folks don't have much use for them?" No one answered. "We don't fancy them either. Appears they are helping the Japs."

Steve had been nudging me so often that my ribs were sore; now he almost busted them. "Did you hear that?" he said in a fierce whisper. "I knew those zopilotes were up to no good. So that's where they get their silver!" Kathryn and I shushed him so we could hear the rest of the discussion.

Then there was an absence: the roof was silent. The rain had let up, at least for the moment. Those who wanted to go home dry inquired, and found that Lee and Jennings planned to stay for a day or two. So several people gathered their ponchos and boots and left. Tom invited the San Diegans to stay up at his place, and they quickly accepted. Pa came over to me.

"Is it okay with you if we go home and eat now?"

It looked like the talking was over, so I said, "Let's do it."

There was a sense of slowness and confusion to our departures. The strangers had told us so much we had never learned even at the swap meets that it filled our minds, and even finding the dry clothes that many kept at the bathhouse became difficult. I looked around; after all the projects Lee and Jennings had listed the bathhouse didn't seem like much anymore. Pa and I got back into our wet clothes, as we had none to spare for the bathhouse, and we hurried home along the hissing brown river. By the time we got home it was drizzling again. We got the fire going good and sat in our beds as we ate our dried fish and tortillas, gabbing about the San Diegans and their train.

"Maybe they'll bring the tracks up to our bridge," I said. "I bet it'd be strong enough, and there's no way they'll get over where the rail bridge used to be." Bent tracks sticking off the cliff over the river marked where that was. "The river's three times as wide as it used to be, Tom says."

"That's a good idea," Pa said admiringly. "You're a good one for the ideas, Hank. You should tell them that one."

"Maybe I will." I fell asleep thinking of trains, and of bridges made of nothing but train tracks.

The next morning I was fishing drowned greens out of our garden when I caught sight of Kathryn walking down the path, muddy once again, holding a bunch of scraggly young corn stalks in her hand. She'd been rolling up the tarps, and if they were up already, then she and her farm crew must have been at it since before first light, because they could never get as many people to help roll the tarps up as they could to put them down. Getting them back up was more or less their problem. And so of course Kathryn had just had a look at the damages. I could tell she was mad by the way she walked. The Mendezes' dog ran out barking playfully at her and she swung a foot at it with a curse. The dog slipped avoiding her boot and yelped, then ran back to its garden. Kathryn stood in the path cursing, and then kicked the base of the big eucalyptus with her heavy boot, *thump thump thump thump*. I decided to pass on saying good morning to her. I could talk to her some other time. She walked on, cursing still.

Tom appeared from the other direction. "Henry!" he called. I waved to him as he approached.

He stood looking down at me with a twinkle in his eye. "Henry, what would you say to a trip to San Diego?"

"What?" I cried. "Sure, you bet! What?"

He laughed and sat down on the barrel half in our yard. "I was talking with John and Rafe and Carmen and the San Diegans last night, and we decided I'd go down there and talk with 'this Mayor of theirs. I want to take someone along, and the older men will all be working. So I thought you might not mind."

"Wouldn't mind!" I stalked around him. "Wouldn't mind!"

"I figured not. And we can make some sort of deal with your pa."

"Oh yeah?" Pa said, looking around the corner of the house.

He grinned, came around the corner carrying two buckets of water. "What's this all about?"

"Well, Sky," Tom said, "I want to hire out your boy for a trip."

Pa put down the buckets and pulled his moustache while Tom told him about it. They wrangled over the value of a week of my work, both agreeing it wasn't much, but differing over just how little it was, until they'd worked out an agreement whereby Tom rented my services for whatever it took him to get a sewing machine that Pa had seen at the swap meet two months ago. "Even if the machine doesn't work—right, Sky?" said Tom.

"Right," Pa said. "I want Rafe to strip it for parts, mostly."

And Tom was to deal with John Nicolin concerning my absence from the fishing.

"Hey!" I said. "You got to ask Steve to come too."

Tom looked at me. Fingering his beard, he said, "Yes...I suppose I do, really."

"Ha," said Pa.

"Aye. I don't know what John will say, but you're right, if I ask you I have to ask Steve. We'll see what happens. When you're done fishing, ask John when I can come by to talk about the San Diegans. And don't say anything about this to Steve yet, else it will be him asking John and not me. And that might not be so good."

I agreed, and soon I was off running to the cliffs, singing San Diego, Sandy Dandy-ay-go. On the beach I shut up, and spent the afternoon fishing as usual. When we were back ashore I said to John, "Tom would like to talk with you about the train men, sir. He was wondering when it would be convenient for us to drop by and talk."

"Any time I'm not down here," John said in his abrupt way. "Tell him to come by tonight," he added. "Come eat a meal with us. You come too."

"Thank you, sir," I said. With a mysterious wink at Steve I was off up the cliff. I ran the river path home, splashing every puddle. To San Diego! To San Diego by train!

Chapter Five

Late that afternoon the old man and I walked down the river path to the Nicolins'. The valley cupped us like a green bowl, tilted to spill us into the sea. The air smelled of wet earth and wet trees. Overhead crows cawed and dipped and lazily flapped their ways home. Above them there wasn't a cloud in the sky; nothing but that pure dome of early evening blue. Naturally we were in high spirits. We skipped over puddles, cracked jokes, and described to each other the dinner we were headed for. "I'm starved," the old man declared. "Starved!" He waved at Marvin Hamish and Nat Eggloff, who were fishing over a pool across the river. "I haven't eaten a thing since you told me we were invited."

"But that was only a couple hours ago!"

"Sure, but I passed on tea time."

We turned off the river path and climbed the trail leading to the Nicolins' house. Once over the freeway we could see it through the trees.

It was the biggest house in the valley, set on a fine patch

of cleared land just behind the highest part of the beach cliff.
The yard around the house had been planted with canyon grass,
and the two-story, tile-roofed building stood on its green lawn
(well apart from the storage shed and the doghouses and the
chicken coop) like something left over from the old time. There
were shutters bracketing glass windows, big eaves over the
doors, and a brick chimney. Smoke lofted from this chimney
into the river-blue sky, and lamps glowed in the windows. Tom
and I gave each other a look, and went to pump the door
knocker.

Before we got there Mrs. Nicolin threw the door open,
crying, "It's a mess in here but you'll just have to ignore it,
come in, come in."

"Thanks, Christy," Tom said. "The house may be a mess,
but you're looking fine as always."

"Oh you liar," Mrs. Nicolin said, pulling back a loose strand
of her thick black hair. But Tom was telling the truth; Christy
Nicolin had a beautiful face, strong and kind, and she was tall
and rangy, even after bearing seven kids. Steve took a lot of
his features from her rather than from John: his height, his
sharp-edged nose and jaw, his mouth. Now she waved us in the
door past her, shaking her head at the ceiling to show us,
as she always did, that her day had been too harried to be
described or imagined. "They're cleaning up, they say. They've
been building a butterchurn all afternoon, and right in my dining
room."

Their house had a dozen or more rooms, but only the dining
room had a giant set of windows facing west, so despite Mrs.
Nicolin's protests it got used for everything that needed good
light, especially when the yard was wet. All of the rooms we
passed on our way through the front of the house had fine
furniture in them, beds and tables and chairs that John and
Teddy, Steve's twelve-year-old brother, had built in imitation
of old time stuff. To me the whole house looked like something
right out of books, and when I had said that to Tom he had
agreed, saying it was more like houses used to be than any
he'd ever seen: "Except they didn't have fireplaces in the kitchen,
nor rain barrels in the halls, nor wooden walls and floors and
ceilings in every single room."

When we got to the dining room the kids ran out of it yelling.
Mrs. Nicolin sighed and led us in. John and Teddy were sweeping up splinters and chunks of wood. Tom and John shook

hands, something they wouldn't do unless one was visiting the other in his home. Through the big west windows we had a good view out to sea. Sunlight slanted in and lit the bottom of the east wall, and the wood dust in the air. "Get this room clean," Mrs. Nicolin ordered. She pulled a hand through her hair, as if just standing in the room was making her dirty. John lifted his eyebrows in mock surprise, and tossed a scrap of wood in her direction. I left and went through the kitchen, which was stuffy with good smells, to find Steve. He was out back, cleaning the inside of the new churn.

"What's up?" he asked.

I decided to tell him, as I couldn't think of any way to avoid it. "Jennings and Lee asked Tom if he wanted to go back down with them to talk to that mayor. Tom's going to go, and he wants to take us along!"

Steve let the churn fall to the grass. "Take us along? You and me?" I nodded. "Wow! Why off we go!" He leaped over the churn, wiggled his arms in his victory shimmy dance. Suddenly he stopped and turned to examine me. "How long will we be gone?"

"About a week, Tom says."

His eyes narrowed, and his wide mobile mouth became straight and tight.

"What's the matter?"

"I just hope he'll let me go, that's all. Damn it! I'll just go anyway, no matter what he says." He picked up the churn again, and thumped the last chips out of it.

Soon Mrs. Nicolin called us all into the dining room, and got us seated around the big oak table: John and her at the head, her grandmother Marie, who was ninety-five and simple-minded, Tom, Steve and Teddy and Emilia, who was thirteen, and very quiet and shy; then me, and then the kids, Virginia and Joe the twins, and Carol and Judith, the babies of the family, back around the table next to Mrs. N. John lit the lamps on the table while Mrs. N. and Emilia brought in the food. The yellow lamplight was in sharp contrast to the blue evening outside. Faint reflections of us all sprang to in the big west window.

Emilia and Mrs. N. brought out plate after plate, until the tabletop was nearly invisible under them. Tom and I kicked each other under the table. Several of the plates were covered, and when John took off their tops steam puffed out, fragrant with the smell of chicken bubbling in a red sauce. There was a cabbage salad in a large wooden bowl, and soup in a porcelain tureen. There were plates of bread and tortillas, and plates covered with sliced tomatoes and eggs. There were jugs of goat's milk and water.

All of the smells made me drunk, and I said, "Mrs. N., this here's a feast, a *banquet,* why we're going to have to keep an eye out for Banquo's ghost, and likely I won't see him cause I'll be stuffing myself to the gills."

The Nicolins laughed at me, and Tom said, "He's right, Christy. The Irish would sing songs about this one." We passed the plates around following Mrs. Nicolin's orders, and when our plates were piled high we started eating, and it was quiet for a time, except for the clink of cutlery on plates and bowls. Soon enough Marie wanted to talk to Tom, for she just picked at her chicken and greens. Tom bolted his food so quickly— never stopping to chew, it seemed—that he had time to talk between bites, and while he refilled his plate. Marie was pleased to see Tom, who was one of the few people outside the family she regularly recognized. "Thomas," she piped loudly, "seen any good movies lately?"

Virginia and Joe giggled. Tom snapped down a chunk of chicken like it was bread, leaned over and spoke directly into Marie's nearly deaf ear: "Not lately, Marie." Marie blinked wisely and nodded, while across from Tom Virginia giggled again.

"But Tom, Gran's wrong, Gran's wrong, there aren't no movies—"

"Aren't *any* movies," Mrs. N. said automatically.

"Aren't any movies."

"Well, Virginia—" Tom gobbled down some of the fish soup. "Here, try this."

"Yooks, no!"

"Marie was talking about the old time."

"She gets the old time mixed up with now."

"Yes, that's true."

"What?" Marie cried, sensing the talk concerned her.

"Nothing, Marie," Tom said in her ear.

"Why does she do that, Tom?"

"Virginia," Mrs. N. warned.

"It's okay, Christy. You see, Virginia, that's an easy thing for us old folks to do, mixing things up like that. I do it all the time."

"You do not, but why?"

"We've got so much old time in our heads, you see. It crowds into the now and we mix it up." He swallowed some more chicken, licking the sauce out of his moustache luxuriously. "Here, try this; chicken's a special treat cooked in this wonderful way your mother cooks it."

"Yooks, no."

"Virginia."

"Maw-ummmmmmm."

"Eat your food," John growled, looking up from his plate. I saw Steve wince a little. He hadn't said a word since we came inside, even when his mother talked directly at him. It made me a little apprehensive, but to tell the truth I was distracted by the food. I had started too quickly, and now I slowed down, chewing each mouthful into nothing but its taste. There were so many different flavors, aromas, textures; each forkful of food had a different taste to it, and a mouthful of water after each swallow made my tongue fresh for more. I was getting full, but I couldn't stop. John began to slow down, and talked to no one in particular about the warm current that had hit the coast with the previous day's rain. Tom was still tossing it down, and Virginia said "No one's going to steal your plate, Tom." He heard that one a lot, but he smiled at Virginia all the same, and the kids laughed. "Have some more chicken," Mrs. N. urged me, "have more milk." "Twist my arm," I replied. Little Carol started to cry, and Emilia got up to sit by her and spoon some soup into her mouth, or try to. It was getting pretty noisy, and Marie noticed and cried, "Turn on the tee vee!" which she knew would get her a laugh. Meanwhile Steve continued to eat silently, and I saw John notice it. I took another swallow of milk to reassure myself that everything would go all right.

Over the remains of the meal we talked and nibbled equally. When Carol was calmed Emilia got up and started taking out dishes to the kitchen. "It's your night too," Mrs. N. reminded Steve. Without a word he got up and carried plates away. When the table was almost cleared they brought out berries and cream, and another jug of milk. Tom kicked me, and flapped his eyebrows like wings. "Looks wonderful, Christy," he said piously.

After we had feasted on berries and cream the kids were allowed to take Gran and scamper off, and John and Mrs. N.,

Steve and Emilia and Tom and I sat back in our chairs, shifting them around to face the window. John got a bottle of brandy from a cabinet, and we contemplated our reflections as we sipped. We made a funny picture. Steve wasn't talking tonight, and Emilia never talked, so the conversation was left to Tom and John, mostly, with an occasional word from Mrs. N. or me. John speculated some more about the current. "Seems the warm currents bring the coldest clouds—or the coldest clouds come when they do. Cold rain, and sometimes snow, when the water is forty degrees warmer than that. Now why should that be?"

None of us ventured a theory (I was surprised to see Tom pass on an opportunity to discuss the weather), and we sat in silence. Mrs. N. began to knit, and Emilia wordlessly moved over to hold the yarn. Suddenly John knocked back the rest of his brandy.

"So what do you think these southerners want?" he asked Tom.

The old man sipped his brandy. "I don't know, John. I guess I'll find out when I go down there. If what they say is true, they won't be able to do very much up here, since we're watched by the Asians. But...there's something they aren't telling us. When I mentioned the dead Asians washing ashore, Jennings almost said something, but Lee stopped him. Jennings knew something. But why they're up here? I'm not sure yet."

"Maybe they just want to see something new," Steve said darkly.

"Maybe," Tom replied. "Or it could be they want to see what they can do, test their power. Or trade with us, or go farther north. I don't know. They're not saying, at least not up here they're not saying. That's why I want to go down there and talk to this mayor of theirs."

John shook his head. "I'm still not sure you should go."

The corners of Steve's mouth went white. Tom said casually, "Can't do any harm, and in fact we need to do it, to know what's going on. Speaking of that, I'll need to take a couple people along with me, and I figure the young ones are easiest spared, so I wondered if Steve could be one of them. He's the kind I need along—"

"Steve?" John glared at the old man. "No." He glanced at Steve, looked back at Tom. "No, he's needed here, you know that."

"You could spare me for a week," Steve burst out. "I'm not needed here all that much. I'd work double time when I got back, please—"

"No," John said in his on-the-water voice. In the next room the sounds of the kids playing abruptly died. Steve had stood up, and now he jerked toward his father, who was still leaning back in his chair; Steve's hands were balled into fists, and his face was twisted up. "Steve," Mrs. Nicolin said quietly. John shifted in his chair to better stare up at Steve.

"By the time you get back the warm current will be gone. I need you here now. Fishing is your job, and it's the most important job in this valley. You can go south some other time, in the winter maybe when we aren't going out."

"I can pay someone to fill in for me," Steve said desperately. But John just shook his head, the grim set of his mouth shifting to an angry down-curve. I shrank in my chair, frightened. So often it came to this between them; they got right to the breaking point so fast that it seemed certain they would snap through one day. For a moment I was sure of it; Steve's hands clenched, John was ready to launch himself. . . . But once again Steve deferred. He turned on his heel and ran out the dining room. We heard the kitchen door slam open and shut.

Mrs. Nicolin got up and refilled John's glass. "Are you sure we couldn't get Addison Shanks to fill in for the week?"

"No, Christy. His work is here, he's got to learn that. People depend on that." He glanced at Tom, drank deeply, said in an annoyed voice, "You know I need him here, Tom. What are you doing coming down here and giving him ideas like that?"

Tom said mildly, "I thought you might be able to spare him."

"No," John said for the last time, putting his bulk into it. "I'm not gaming out there, Tom—"

"I know that. I know it." Tom sipped his brandy and gave me an uncomfortable look. I imitated Emilia and pretended I wasn't there, staring at the portrait of us all on the black glass of the window. We were a pretty unhappy looking group. The silence stretched on; we heard the kids laughing at the other end of the house. Steve was long gone, on the beach, I figured. I thought about how he felt at that moment, and the fine meal in my stomach turned lumpy. Mrs. Nicolin, face tight with distress, tried to refill our glasses. I shook my head, and Tom covered his glass with his hand. He cleared his throat.

"Well, I guess Hank and I'll get going, then." We stood. "Wonderful meal, Christy," Tom muttered to Mrs. N. She began to say goodbye as if nothing had happened; Tom cut her off with a pained expression and said, "Thanks for the meal, John. I'm sorry I brought all that up."

John grunted and waved a hand, lost in his thoughts. We all stood looking at him, a big man brooding in his chair, staring at his own colorless image, surrounded by all his goods and possessions. . . . "No matter," he said, as if releasing us. "I can see what caused you to do it. Come tell me what it's like down there when you get back."

"We will." Tom thanked Mrs. N. again and we backed out the door. She followed us out. On the doorstep she said, "You should have known, Tom."

"I know. Good night, Christy."

We walked up the river path full of food, but glum and heavy-footed. Tom muttered under his breath and took swings at branches near the path. "Should've known . . . nothing else possible . . . impossible to change . . . set like a wedge. . . ." He raised his voice. "History is a wedge in a crack, boy, and we're the wood. We're the wood right under the wedge, you understand, boy?"

"No."

"Ah . . ." He started muttering again, sounding disgusted.

"I do understand that John Nicolin is a mean old son of a bitch—"

"Shut up," Tom snapped. I did. "A wedge in a crack," he went on. Suddenly he stopped and grabbed my arm, swung me around violently. "See over there?" he cried, pointing across the river at the other bank.

"Yeah," I protested, peering into the dark.

"Right there. The Nicolins had just moved here, just John and Christy and John Junior and Steve. Steve was just a babe, John Junior about six. They came in from the back country, never said just where from. One day John was helping with the first bridge, in the start of winter. John Junior was playing on the bank, on an overhang, and . . . the overhang fell in the river." His voice was harsh. "Fell *plop* right in the river, you understand? River full of the night's rain. Right in front of John. He dove in and swam downstream all the way out into the sea. Swam nearly an hour, and never saw the kid at all. Never saw him again. Understand?"

"Yeah," I said, uneasy at the strain in his voice. We started walking again. "That still doesn't mean he needs Steve for fishing, because he surely doesn't—"

"Shut up," he said again, not as sharp as the first time. After a few steps he said quietly, as if talking to himself, "And then we went through that winter like rats. We ate anything we could find."

"I've heard about those times," I said, irritated that he kept going back to the past. That was all we heard about: the past, the past, the God damned past. The explanation for everything that happened was contained in our past. A man could behave like a tyrant to his son, and what was his excuse? History.

"That don't mean you know what it was like," he told me, irritated himself. Watching him in the dark I saw marks of the past on him: the scars, the caved-in side of his face where he had no teeth left, his bent back. He reminded me of one of the trees high on the hills above us, gnarled by the constant onshore winds, riven by lightning. "Boy, we were hungry. People *died* 'cause we didn't have food enough in the winters. Here was this valley soaked with rain and growing trees like weeds, and we couldn't grow food from it to stay alive. All we could do was hunker down in the snow—snow *here,* damn it—and eat every little hibernating creature we could find. We were just like wolves, no better. You won't know times like those. We didn't even know what day of the year it was! It took Rafe and me four years to figure out what the date was." He paused to collect himself and remember his point. "Anyway, we could see the fish in the river, and we did our best to get them into the fire. Got some rods and lines and hooks out of Orange County, tackle from fishing stores that should have been good stuff." He snorted, spat at the river. "Fishing with that stupid sport gear that broke every third fish, broke every time you used it . . . it was a damned shame. John Nicolin saw that and he started asking questions. Why weren't we using nets? No nets, we said. Why weren't we fishing the ocean? No boats, we said. He looked at us like we were fools. Some of us got mad and said how are we going to find nets? Where?

"Well, Nicolin had the answer. He went up into Clemente and looked in a *telephone* book, for God's sake. Looked in the God damned yellow pages." He laughed, a quick shout of delight. "He found the listing for commercial fishing warehouses, took some men up there to look for them. First one we found was empty. Second one had been blown flat on the day. The third one we walked into was a warehouse full of nets. Steel cables, heavy nylon—it was great. And that was just the start. We used the phone book and map to find the boatyards in Orange County, because all of the harbors were clean empty, and we hauled some boats right down the freeway."

"What about the scavengers?"

"That was when there weren't too many scavengers, and there wasn't any fight in the ones that were there."

Now there I knew he was lying. He was leaving himself out of the story, as he always did. Almost everything I knew of Tom's history I had heard from someone else. And I had a lot of stories about him; as the oldest man in the valley legends naturally collected around him. I had heard how he had led those foraging raids into Orange County, guiding John Nicolin and the others through his old neighborhoods and beyond. He had been death on scavengers in those days, they said. If ever they were hard pressed by scavengers Tom had disappeared into the ruins, and pretty soon there weren't any scavengers around to bother them anymore. It was Tom, in fact, who introduced Rafael to guns. And the tales of Tom's endurance— why, they were so numerous and outlandish that I didn't know what to think. He must have done some of those things to get such a reputation, but which ones? Had he gone for a week without sleep during the forced march from Riverside, or eaten the bark from trees when they were holed up in Tustin, surrounded? Or walked through fire and held his breath under water for a half hour, to escape? Whatever he had done, I was sure he had run ragged every man in the valley, and him over seventy-five years old at the time. I had heard Rafael declare that the old man must have been radiated on the day, and mutated so that he was destined never to die, like the wandering Jew. "One thing's for sure," Rafe said, "I walked with him by one of the scavengers' geiger counters at a swap meet once, and that machine almost busted its bell. Scavengers took off...."

"Anyway," Tom was saying to me now, "John Nicolin did or directed everything that had to do with fishing, and doing it was what brought the people in this valley together, and made us a town. The second winter after he arrived was the first one no one died from hunger. Boy, you don't know what that means. We ate dried fish till we were dead sick of it, but no one was dead dead. There's been hard times since, but none to match those before Nicolin arrived. I admire him. So if he's got fish on the brain, if he won't let his son leave it for a week or even a day, then that's too bad. That's the way he is now, and you've got to understand it."

"But it doesn't matter how well fed he is, if he makes his son hate him."

"Aye. But that's not his intention. I know he doesn't intend that. Remember John Junior. Could be, even if John himself doesn't know it, he just wants to keep Steve where he can see him. To try and keep him safe. So that even the fishing is just a cover. I don't know."

I shook my head. It still wasn't fair, keeping Steve at home. A wedge in a crack. I understood a little better what Tom had meant, but it seemed to me then that we were the wedges, stuck so far in history that we couldn't move but one way when we were struck by events. How I wished we could be clear and free to move where we would!

We had walked to my home. Firelight shone through the cracks around the door. "Steve'll make it another time," said Tom. "But us—we'll be off to San Diego on the next cloudy night."

"Yeah." Right then I couldn't rouse much enthusiasm for it. Tom hit my shoulder and was off through the trees.

"Be ready!" he called as he disappeared in the forest gloom.

The next cloudy night didn't come for a while. For once the warm current brought clear skies with it, and I spent my evenings impatiently cursing the stars. During the days I kept fishing. Steve was ordered by John to stay on the net boats, so off in my rowboat I wasn't faced with him hour after hour, but I did feel lonesome, and odd—as if I was betraying him somehow. When we did work together, unloading fish or rolling nets, he just talked fishing, not meeting my eye, and I couldn't find anything to say. I felt tremendously relieved when three days after the dinner he laughed and said, "Just when you don't want clear days they come blaring down. Come on, let's use this one for what it was meant to be used for." Fishing was done, and with the hours of day left we walked out the wide beach to the rivermouth, where waves were slowly changing from blue lines to white lines. Gabby and Mando and Del joined us with the fins, and we waded out over the coarse tan sand of the shallows into the break. The water was as warm as it ever got. We took a fin each and swam out through the soup to the clear water outside the waves' breaking point. Out there the water was like blue glass; I could see the smooth sheet of sand on the bottom perfectly. It was a pleasure just to tread water out there, to let the swells wash over my head and to look back at the tan cliffs and the green forest, edged by the sky and the eye-blue ocean under my chin. I drifted back in and rode the waves with the others, happy they didn't resent me, too much, for getting the chance to go to San Diego.

We only talked waves, however, as we waited for the bigger sets, and none of them mentioned my coming trip even indirectly. And when we got back on the beach, the others said goodbye to me, and left in a group. I sat in the sand, feeling strange.

A figure appeared walking down the riverside, in the narrow gap in the cliffs where the river rolled through to the sea. When it got closer I saw that it was Melissa Shanks. I stood and waved; she saw me and made her way around the pools on the beach to me.

"Hello, Henry," she said. "Have you been out body surfing?"

"Yeah. What brings you down here?"

"Oh, I was looking for clams up on the flats." It never occurred to me that she didn't have any rake or bucket with her. "Henry, I hear you're going down to San Diego with Tom?"

I nodded. Her eyes got wide with excitement.

"Why, you must be thrilled," she said. "When are you going?"

"The next cloudy night. Seems like the weather doesn't want me to go."

She laughed, and leaned over to kiss my cheek. When I raised my eyebrows she kissed me again, and I turned and kissed back.

"I can't believe you're going," she said dreamily, between kisses. "It's just so—well, you're the best man to do it."

I began to feel better about going on this trip of mine.

"How many of you are going?"

"Just me and Tom."

"But what about those San Diegans?"

"Oh they're going too. They're taking us down."

"Just those two who came up here?"

"No, they have a whole crew of men waiting down the freeway where they stopped fixing up the tracks." I explained to her how the San Diegans ran their operation. "So we have to go on a cloudy night, so the Japs won't see us."

"My God." She shivered. "It sounds dangerous."

"Oh no, I don't think so." I kissed her again, rolling her back onto the sand, and we kissed for so long that I had her half out of her clothes. Suddenly she looked around and laughed.

"Not here on the beach," she said. "Why, anyone on the cliff could see us."

"No they couldn't."

"Oh yes they could, you know they could. Tell you what." She sat up and rearranged her blue cotton shirt. I looked through her black hair to the late afternoon sun, and felt a surge of happiness pulse through me. "When you get back from San Diego, maybe we could go up Swing Canyon and take some swings."

Swing Canyon was a place where lovers went; I nodded eagerly, and reached for her, but she stood up.

"I have to be off now, really, my pa is going to be wondering where I got to." She kissed her forefinger and put it to my lips, skipped off with a laugh. I watched her cross the wide beach, then stood up myself. I shook myself, laughed out loud. I looked out to sea; were those clouds, out there?

Just after sunset my question was answered. Clouds streamed in like broken waves, and the sky was blue-gray and starless when it got dark. I took my coat off its hook and got a thick sweater from our clothes bag, chattering with Pa. Late that night Tom rapped at the door. I was off to San Diego.

Part Two

SAN DIEGO

Chapter Six

Out by the big eucalyptus Jennings and Lee stood waiting. "Short partner you got there," Jennings joked to Tom, but I thought Lee was frowning at me. "He's as good as any you've got!" Pa called from the door, sounding upset. "Let's be off," Lee said roughly.

We went to the freeway and headed south. Soon we passed the steep bank at the back of Concrete Bay, and were out of the valley and onto the Pendleton shore. The freeway was in pretty good shape; though the surface was cracked a bit, it was clear of trees and shrubs, except for an occasional line of them filling a big crack like a fence. But most of the way the road was a light slash through dark, overhanging forest. The level country it crossed was a narrow strip between steep hills and the sea cliff, cut often by deep ravines. Usually the freeway spanned these ravines, but twice it fell into them, and we were forced to descend their sides and cross the gurgling black creeks at their bottoms, on big blocks of concrete. Lee led the way over these breaks without a word. He was anxious to be in San Diego, it seemed.

A short distance beyond the second break in the freeway Lee stopped. I looked past him and saw a cluster of ruined buildings in the trees. Lee raised his hands to his mouth and made a passable imitation of a gull cry three times in a row, then three again, and from the buildings a shrill whistle replied. We approached the largest of the buildings, and were met halfway there by a group of men who greeted us loudly and happily. They led us into the building, where a small fire gave off little light and lots of smoke. The men from San Diego—seven of them—surveyed Tom and me.

"You sure took a piece of time to get two specimens no better than these," a short man with a large belly said. He pulled on his beard and barked a laugh, but his little reddened eyes didn't look amused.

"Ain't San Onofre serious about talking to the Mayor?" the man next to him said. It was the first time I had ever heard *San* put in front of Onofre; folks at the swap meet called us plain Onofre, like we did.

"Now enough of that," Jennings said. "This here is Tom Barnard, one of the oldest living Americans—"

"Granted," said the short man.

"*And* one of Onofre's leaders. And this boy here is his most able assistant."

Tom didn't even flinch during all this; he stared calmly at the short man, head tilted to the side like he was contemplating a new sort of bug. Lee hadn't stopped to listen. He was gathering rope under one arm, and he only paused to look up and say, "Get that fire out and get on the cars. I want to be in San Diego by sunup."

The men sounded like that was fine with them. They got their gear together and doused the fire, and we left the building and the freeway, striking out into the forest behind Lee, in the direction of the ocean. We had only walked twenty or thirty paces when Lee stopped and lit a lantern.

In the gleam of light I saw their train: a platform on metal wheels, with a long bar set on a block in the middle of it. The men started throwing their stuff on the train, and behind the first I saw a second one. Approaching it I stepped over the rails. They were just like the rails that crossed our valley—

bumpy and corroded, with spongy beams set every few feet under them. Tom and I stood watching as sledgehammers and axes, bundles of rope and bags of clanking metal stakes were stowed on the two platforms.

Quickly everything was aboard, and we climbed on the front train behind Lee and Jennings. Two of the men stood at the ends of the crossbar; one pulled on the high end, assisted by Lee, and with a crunch we were rolling over the rusty rails. When that end of the crossbar was low, the short man with the belly hauled down with all his weight on the other end. The two men traded pulls, and away we went, followed by the other car.

We rolled out of the copse of trees that had hidden the trains, onto a brush-covered plain. Here the hills lifted a few miles inland, rather than directly from the coast, and what trees there were grew mostly in the ravines. The rails ran just to the sea side of the freeway, and I could see the ocean from time to time when we topped a rise, silvered gray under low clouds. We passed a headland that had taken Nicolin and me half a day to walk to; it was as far south as I had ever been. From there on I was in new territory.

The car's wheels ground over the tracks with a sound like a rasp cutting metal, and we picked up speed until we were going faster than a man could run. The four idle men on our car were seated around the center block, or lying flat on their stomachs, looking ahead. Rolling down a slope we moved even faster, and I felt that I had to stand to feel it right, so I did. I just couldn't sit down any longer. A cold wind struck me, the rotten ties flashed under the car so fast I couldn't make out any individual ties! The men looked at me like I was a fool, but I didn't care. Tom's beard was blowing back over his shoulders like a flag, and he grinned at me. "The only way to travel, eh?" I nodded vigorously, too excited to speak. It felt like we were flying, no matter the crunch and rattle from below. "How f-fast are we going?" I stammered out.

Tom looked over the side, put his hand up to the wind. "About thirty miles an hour," he said. "Maybe thirty-five. It's been a good long while since I've gone this fast, I'll tell you."

"Thirty miles an hour!" I cried. "Yeee-*ow!*"

The men laughed at me, but I didn't care. So far as I was concerned, they were the fools; we were going thirty miles an hour, and they sat there trying to avoid the wind!

"Want to pull?" Jennings said from the back end of the crossbar. At that the men laughed again.

"Do I!" I said. Jennings stepped aside and I took the T at the end of the pole on its upswing. When I pulled down on it I could feel the car surge forward, all out of proportion to the force I had exerted, and I whooped again. I pulled hard, and saw the white grin of the man pulling across from me. He pulled just as hard, and we made that car fly down Pendleton like we were in a dream. Through eyes made all watery by the whipping wind I watched the ties flash under us, and all of a sudden I *knew* what it had been like to live in the old time, I *knew* that power they had wielded, that marvelous extension of man's natural abilities. All Tom's stories and all his books had told me of it, but now I felt it in my muscles and my skin, I could see it flying all by me, and it was exhilarating. We *pumped* that car down those tracks. Behind us the men on the following car hooted and hollered: "Hey up there! Who you got on the bar?" "We know it ain't Jennings doing that!" The men on both cars laughed at that. "It *is* Jennings," one of them said. "I didn't know you missed your wife that much!" "What are you worried she's up to?" "Better not waste all your *pumping* up here!" "Throw us a tow rope if you feel that good!"

"Slow it down some," Lee said after a while. "We got a ways to go, don't want to tire out those poor men back there."

So we slowed a bit. Still, when one of the men took my place, I was sweating from the effort, and standing there I chilled fast. I sat down and huddled in my coat. The white ends of newly cut brush flashed by, lit by the sparks our wheels threw out from time to time. The land got hillier. On the up slopes we all had to get up and help pump the bar; on the downs we rolled so fast I wouldn't have stood up for silver.

We passed a bit of white cloth, hanging from a pole planted on the side of the mound that the tracks ran on. Lee stood and pulled the brake lever, and we came to a halt blasting red sparks over the trackbed, with a screech that made me shudder, it hurt my ears so.

"Now comes the complicated part," Jennings said, and jumped off the car. In the sudden silence I could hear running water ahead of us. Tom and I got off the train and followed the rest of the men down the tracks. There in a dip lay a considerable stream, about half the width of our valley's river. Black posts stuck out of the surface in a double line, all the way across. Beams and planks connected some of the posts, and extended to the banks on either side, but there were big gaps as well, and all in all it was a wreck. Each post knocked up a little circle of foam from the river, showing it was a fast stream.

"That's our bridge foundation," Jennings said to Tom and me, while Lee directed the men on the bank. "It's all that's left of the old bridge, which must have burned when the water was high."

"More likely the Pendleton bomb knocked it down," Tom suggested. "I doubt the river was ever higher than it is now."

"You've got a point there," Jennings said. "Anyway, the pilings are in pretty good shape. We leveled them, and brought up some beams that sit over the pilings sideways, like lintels. Then we set rail over the beams at the right gauge, and roll the cars over, and haul all the beams and rail to the other bank after us. It's a lot of work, but with the material hidden no one can tell we're crossing this bridge."

"Very ingenious," Tom said.

Three or four more lanterns had been lit, and their light was directed at the pilings by metal reflectors. The men hustled about in the dark, cursing at manzanita and brambleberry, and pulling the beams out of the brush down to the bank. They hooked these beams onto a thick length of rope that they had fished out of the shallows upstream from the bridge. This rope extended across the river under the water, was threaded through a large pulley, and came back under the stream to our side. Jennings continued to describe the system to us, with the pride of a designer: the ten crossbeams, or ties, were hauled out into the river upstream from the pilings, and then the rope was slackened till the ties floated between the pilings. Men balancing on the pilings—they got out to them on the narrow planks and slats that were left permanently in place—would then fish the ties up and secure them atop the pilings.

Jennings' description ended with a chorus of cursing from the men on the bank. The rope was stuck, and wouldn't move through the pulley. They argued over what to do, but Lee cut it short:

"Someone's going to have to swim over and clear that pulley. We can't mess with carrying the beams out; they're too heavy to carry."

The men were not cheered by this pronouncement. One of

them, a man from the second car, kind of snickered and yanked a thumb in my direction. "Why not let young power-pull do it?"

There were snorts of amusement from the short fat guy, and Tom began to protest in my behalf, but I interrupted him. "Sure I'll do it," I said. "I'm probably the best swimmer here, anyway."

"He's right about that," Tom admitted. "He and his friends go out swimming in surf higher than your head."

"Good man," Jennings said heartily. "You see, Henry, we've swum this river many times, but it's not easy. You're best off pulling yourself over with the rope; that way you won't be carried downstream. Just get over there and clear that pulley, and we'll have this bridge up in no time."

So I stripped, and before I got too cold I plunged into the river, holding on to the thick slimy rope. The water was colder than the ocean had been in the last week, and my heart pounded so I could hardly catch my breath. Holding on to the rope meant I couldn't really swim, and the rope was so slick that I had to be very careful pulling myself hand over hand. And the swift current pulled my feet downstream, so that kicking wasn't very effective either. It took a lot longer than I would have guessed to cross, but eventually my knees rammed into soft mud, and I walked out onto the other bank. When I stood on firm mud I shouted back to the men that the swim had been no trouble, and followed the rope to the pulley.

A mass of water weed had grown on the rope, and when I pulled it free the rope ran cleanly and the system was working again. I was pleased with that, and the men on the other bank called out their congratulations. But watching their silhouetted forms walk delicately over bending planks to the pilings, I realized it would be a while before they were finished. Meanwhile I was standing wet and cold, with the river between me and a stitch of clothing. Jennings had probably known I would have to swim back across, but he kindly hadn't made that clear. There was nothing for it but to get back in the water and pull to the other side. I cursed Jennings briefly, yelled my intentions to the men, squished through the mud until the water was up to my chest, and started pulling again.

What I hadn't counted on were the ten ties, now pulled out into the river and floating downstream from the rope, exactly in my way. Around each beam I had to kick myself upstream, or dive under, all the while keeping a hold on the wet rope. Still, I would have been okay; but out of the gloom upstream rolled a full torrey pine tree, floating low in the water. It barged right over me, and then got hung up in the rope, and all of the sudden I was thrust well under the surface, caught in a thicket of twisted branches and poking needles. I was barely able to hold on to the rope, and I hadn't had time to get a good breath; chill water shoved at my mouth and nose. Tearing with my free hand at the branch above me, I considered letting go and diving under the tree to freedom, but then there would be the pilings to deal with, and I was scared of ramming into one of them. The tree wouldn't let me up. The rope bowed under the new pressure. Desperately I shoved my face up between two branches and got a quick mouthful of air. I shifted hands on the rope and seized the trunk of the tree in my left hand, pulled it over and the rope under. The tree flipped over; it was still caught on the rope, but now I could tread water beside it, still holding the rope. "Chinga!" I gasped. "Shit! Pinché buey!"

"Hey!" they were calling from the bank. "Anything wrong out there?" "Henry!" Tom was yelling.

"Nothing!" I yelled back. "I'm okay!" But now they were hauling the rope back in, pulling me across. That was fine by me. I realized why none of the men had been anxious to swim across. If the branch had knocked me free I could have swum to the bank downstream, no doubt, but getting through the pilings would have been dangerous, and walking up the bank to the bridge miserable. I took a couple hand-over-hand grabs, but they were pulling faster and soon I squished into mud. Two of the men waded knee deep to pull me out. On shore they wrapped me in a wool blanket, and after I had dried off with it they gave me another to sit in. I huddled over the lanterns and told them it had been no problem. They didn't have much to say to that, and Tom gave me his suspicious eye.

While I warmed up they got the bridge assembled. The ties were placed on the pilings, the rails were slid over the ties, and spikes were driven through gaps in the rail flange, into already existing holes in the ties. The rails were closer together than the two rows of pilings, but not by much. Black figures crawled back and forth over the structure, silhouetted by the lantern light in a variety of precarious positions; once I saw a standing figure drop a plank he had been lowering onto an isolated beam, and fall to his hands and knees to avoid falling in. The plank swirled away. Shouts from Lee punctuated the sounds of hammering.

"The first time they did this it must have been a lot of trouble," Tom said to me, crouched by my side with his hands around the lantern glass. "I guess it must hold those cars, but I sure wouldn't have wanted to be the first to take one across."

"They look like they know what they're doing," I said.

"Yeah. Tough work in the dark. Too bad they can't just build a bridge and leave it there."

"That's what I was thinking. I can't believe the . . ." I didn't know what to call them. "That they'd actually bomb a little bridge like this one."

"I know." In the dim glow Tom's expression was somber. "But I don't think these folks are lying, or going to all this trouble for nothing. I guess whoever's up there is keeping the existing communities separated, like Jennings said. But I wasn't aware of it. It's a bad sign."

Jennings walked nonchalantly along one rail and jumped onto the bank to approach us. "Just about done," he announced. "You men should walk across now. We take the cars over as empty as we can get them, although it's just a precaution, you understand."

"That we do," said Tom. He helped me to my feet, and I put on my clothes. I wrapped the blankets around my shoulders, for I was still cold. We crossed the downstream rail standing up, walking very carefully and ready at any moment to drop to the rail and hang on. The ties felt solid when I walked on them, but they were a touch warped, and the rail didn't lay directly on a few of them. I pointed this out to Jennings, who seemed very much at ease on the rail.

"It's true. We can't keep those ties perfectly flat. It makes for a little yaw when you cross, but nothing worse than that. At least not so far. We'll see if Lee has to go for a swim like you did when he brings the first car over. I hope not—it's still a fair walk to San Diego."

On the south bank we gathered by the lanterns and the men holding them directed their light at the first car. Lee and another man cranked it slowly across. The rails squeaked and squealed as the car went over a tie; the rest of the time they were ominously silent, giving under the car's weight. It was an odd sight in the middle of the stream, hanging over both sides of the rails, a big black mass on two spindly strips, like a spider walking across its web strands. When they pumped it up the other bank the men said "All right," and "That was a good one," in low, satisfied voices.

They walked the equipment over, and pumped the second car across, and then pulled up the spikes and hauled the rails to the south side. Lee was a terror for keeping them arranged in order, so that it would be easy to set up the next time they came north. "Very ingenious," said Tom. "Very clever, very dangerous, very well done." "Looked simple enough to me," I replied. Soon the rope was rigged through a pulley on the other shore, and the platforms of the two cars were stacked with equipment again. We got on the front one with the other men, and were off rolling. "The next one's a lot easier," Jennings told us as we pumped up the slope and away.

I volunteered to pump, because I was still cold. This time I pulled at the front end, and watched the hills course away from us (an odd sight) with the wind at my back. Once again I felt exuberant at the speed of our grinding flight over the land, and I laughed aloud.

"This kid swims and pumps like a good resistance man," Jennings said. I didn't know what he meant, but the other men on the car agreed with him, those who bothered to speak, anyway.

But when I warmed up I was tired. I was quickly relieved by the short man with the belly, who gave me a friendly slap on the shoulder and sent me to the rear of the platform. I sat down under my blanket, and after a while I drowsed off, still half aware of the train, the wind, the men's low voices.

I woke when the car stopped. "We at the next river?"

"No," Tom said quietly. "Look there." He pointed out to sea.

A completely hidden moon was making the clouds glow a little, and under them the ocean's surface was a patchy gray. I saw immediately what Tom was pointing at: a dim red light in the middle of a black lump. A ship. A big ship—a huge ship, so big that for a second I thought it was just offshore, when actually it was halfway between the cliffs and the cloud-fuzzed horizon. It was so difficult to reconcile its distance from us and its immense size that I felt I could be dreaming.

"Kill the lanterns," Lee said.

The lanterns were put out. No one spoke. The giant ship

ghosted north soundlessly, and its movement was as wrong as its size and position. It was fast, very fast, and soon it slipped below a hill we had come over, and out of sight.

"They don't come so close to the land in inhabited areas," Jennings told us in a voice filled with bravado. "That was a rare sighting."

Presently we started up again, and passing another white flag by the trackbed, we came to the banks of another river. This one was wider than the first, but the pilings extended right up both banks, and there was a platform across most of it. The San Diegans went to work laying track over the rickety old-time platform, and Tom and I stayed on the car by the lanterns. It had gotten colder through the night, and we were tucked under blankets and breathing little plumes of frost. Eventually we got up to help carry equipment over, just to stay warm. When the cars were across the river, and the bridge pulled apart, I got between two stacks of rope, out of the wind, and fell asleep.

Intermittently rough spots in the track jarred and woke me, and I cursed myself for missing part of my trip. I would poke my head up to look around, but it was still dark, and I was still tired, and I would fall asleep again. The last time I woke it was getting light, and all the men were up to help pump us over a steep rise. I forced myself to get up, resolved to stay awake, and I helped pump when a spot opened.

We were among ruins. Not ruins like in Orange County, where tangles of wood and concrete marked crushed buildings in the forest—rather there were blank foundations among the trees, and restored houses or larger buildings here and there. Cleaned up ruins. The short man pointed out the area where he lived and we passed inland of it. The bluffs we were traveling over alternated with marshes that opened onto the beach, so our tracks rose and fell regularly. We crossed the marshes on giant causeways, with tunnels under them to let the marsh's rivers reach the sea. But then we came on a marsh that didn't have a causeway. Or if it had, once upon a time, it was long gone. We were separated from the bluff to the south by a wide river, snaking through a flat expanse of reeds. It broke through the beach dunes to the sea in three places.

The San Diegans stopped the cars to look. "San Elijo," Jennings said to Tom and me. The sun was poking through clouds, and in the dawn air, thick with salt, hundreds of birds were flapping out of the dull green reeds and skimming the brassy pools and bands of the meandering river. Their cries floated lazily over the sound of the surf breaking, out on the fringe of the broad tawny beach.

Tom said, "How do you cross it? Pretty long bridge to build, wouldn't you say?"

Jennings chuckled. "We go around it. We've set rails on the roads permanently. Down here *they*"—thrusting a thumb skyward—"don't seem to mind."

So we rode the tracks around the north side of the marsh, and crossed the river back in the hills where it was no more than a deep creek, on a permanent bridge like ours back home.

"Have you been able to determine how far away from San Diego you can build without disturbing them?" Tom asked as we crossed this bridge.

Lee opened his mouth to reply, but Jennings got there first, and Lee squeezed his lips together with annoyance. "Lee here has a theory that there are very strict and regular limits to what we can do before they intervene—a matter of isolating each of the old counties, to the extent they can. Isn't that what you said, Lee?"

With a roll of his eyes Lee nodded, grinning at Jennings despite himself.

"Me, I'm not so sure I don't agree more with the Mayor," Jennings went on, oblivious to Lee's amusement. "The Mayor says there is no rhyme nor reason to what they do; madmen watch us from space, he says, and control what we can and can't do. He really gets upset. We're like flies to the gods, he says."

"'Like flies to wanton boys are we to the gods,'" Tom corrected.

"Exactly. Madmen, looking down on us."

Lee shook his head. "There's more to it than that. It's a question of how much they see. But their reaction is governed by rules. I imagine it's a charter from the United Nations or some such thing, telling the Japs out there what to do. In fact—" But there he stopped himself, frowning as if he felt he had gone on too long.

"Oh, no question they've got cameras that can image a man," Jennings disagreed complacently. "So it's not a question of how much they can see. The question is, how much they will notice. Now, we've made changes on that rail line north that can't be hid. The bridges are the same, but we've cleared some brush off the tracks, for instance. So hiding the bridge work may be a waste of time. We're not invisible, like I told the Mayor, though I'm not sure he listened. We're just unobtrusive. Now the watchers may pore over every photograph they take, or they may have machines scanning for major changes, we don't know. This line north should be a good test of their attention, if you ask me."

We were rolling through a thick forest of torrey pine. The sun split the shadows and sparked the dew. The air warmed and I felt drowsy again, despite my fascination with the new country we were passing through. Among the trees were groups of houses from the old time, many of them restored and occupied; smoke rose from many a chimney. When I saw this I nudged Tom, powerfully disturbed. These San Diegans were nothing else but scavengers! Tom saw what I meant, but he just shook his head briefly at me. It wasn't the time to discuss it, that was sure. But it made me uneasy.

The tracks led to a village somewhat like ours, except there were more houses, and they were placed closer together, and many of them had been built in the old time. The screech of our brakes sent chickens cackling and dogs howling, and it made me grind my teeth. Several men and women emerged from a big house across the clearing from the tracks. The San Diegans jumped off the cars and greeted the locals. In the light of day they looked filthy and red-eyed and whiskery, but no one seemed to mind.

"Welcome to San Diego!" Jennings said to us as he helped Tom off the car. "Or to University City, to be more exact. Care to join us for breakfast?"

We agreed heartily to that, and I realized I was as hungry as I was tired, or even more so. We were introduced to the group who had come from the big house to greet us, and we followed them into it.

Inside the front door was an entryway two stories tall, carpeted red, with red and gold wallpaper on the walls, and a glass candle holder hanging from the ceiling. The staircase against one wall was carpeted as well, and it had a bannister of carved and varnished oak. Wide-eyed, I said, "Is this the Mayor's house?"

The San Diegans erupted with laughter. I felt my cheeks burn. Jennings put his arm around my shoulders with a whoop.

"You've proved yourself tonight, Henry my boy. We aren't laughing *at* you; it's just... well, when you see the Mayor's place, you'll understand why. This here is my house. Come on in and clean up and meet the wife, and we'll have a good meal to celebrate your arrival."

Chapter Seven

    After breakfast Tom and I slept for most of the day, on old couches in the Jennings' front room. Late in the day Jennings bustled in and woke us, saying, "Quick now, quick. I've been to talk to the Mayor—he's invited you to a dinner and a conference, and he doesn't like to be kept waiting."

    "Shut up and let them get ready," Jennings' wife said as she looked over his shoulder at us. She looked remarkably like him, short, thick and cheerful. "When you're ready I'll show you to the bathroom." Tom and I followed her to it, and relieved ourselves in a working water toilet. When we were done Jennings hustled us outside. Lee and the short man were already on one of the train cars. We joined them, and they pumped us south. Apparently in the light of day the tubby man felt more sociable, and he introduced himself as Abe Tonklin.

    We rattled over tracks laid on the cracked concrete of another freeway, under a canopy of torrey pine and eucalyptus, red-wood and oak. The car crunched swiftly through alternating shadows and slanted beams of sunlight, and now and then we passed a big clearing in the forest, packed with crops, usually corn. Once I waved at a man standing in one of these yellowy green expanses, and then realized he was a scarecrow.

Over the roar of wheel on rail Jennings shouted, "We're almost there." We topped a rise and below us was a narrow lake, stretching right to left in front of us. It was as if a marsh similar to the ones to the north had flooded. Scattered on the lake's surface were towering buildings, *skyscrapers,* at least a dozen of them. One of them, to the left, was a giant circular wall. And in the middle of the lake stood a piece of freeway, up on concrete pilings above the water. A white house stood on this platform. Flying above this house I could make out a little American flag, snapping in the breeze. I looked at Tom, my mouth hanging open in amazement. Tom's eyes were big. I took in the sight again. Flanked by forested hills, lit by the low sun, the long lake and its fantastic collection of drowned and ruined giants was the most impressive remnant of the old time I had ever laid eyes on. They were so big! Once again I had that feeling—like a hand squeezing my heart—that I *knew* what it had been like. . . .

"Now *that's* the Mayor's house," Jennings said.

"By God, it's Mission Valley," Tom said.

"That's right," Jennings replied, as proudly as if he'd made it all himself. Tom shook his head and laughed in a dumbfounded way. The tracks came to an end, and Lee braked the car with the usual nerve-jangling screech. We got off and followed the San Diegans down the freeway. It led right into the lake and disappeared. The piece of freeway standing on stilts in the lake's center was on a line with it, and in a notch of the hills forming the opposite shore I saw the gray concrete rising out of the lake again. All at once I understood that the section of freeway on stilts in the lake was all that was left of a bridge that had spanned the whole valley. Rather than have their road dip into the valley and rise again, they had placed it on towers for well over a mile, from hillside to hillside—just to avoid a drop and rise for their *cars!* I was stunned; I stared at it; I couldn't get a grasp on the sort of thinking that would even imagine such a bridge. It was unbelievable.

"You okay?" Lee asked me.

"Huh? Yeah, sure. Just looking at the lake."

"Quite a sight. Maybe we can take a sail around it in the morning." This was as friendly as Lee had been to me, and I saw that he appreciated my astonishment.

Where the road plunged into the lake a large floating dock moored a score of rowboats and small catboats. Lee and Abe led us to one of the larger rowboats. We got in, and Abe rowed us toward the freeway island. As we got closer Jennings answered Tom's questions about the lake: "The rains washed mountains of dirt down to the rivermouth, which was bracketed by a pair of long jetties and crossed by several roads—just generally obstructed. So the dirt stuck there and formed a plug. A big dam. What? There's still a channel through to the ocean, but it's on top of the plug, so we got the lake back here. It's well above sea level. Runs all the way to El Cajon."

Tom laughed. "Ha! We always said a good rain would flood this valley, but *this*. . . . What about the overpass out here?"

"The first floods were pretty violent, they say, and the sides of the hills got ripped away, so the towers holding the road fell. Only the center ones held. We blasted the wreckage hanging from the center section so it would look cleaner. More planned, you know."

"Sure."

As we rowed under it I could see the broken end of the freeway, yellow in the late sun. Rusted metal rods stuck out from the pocked concrete, twisting down at their ends. The platform was about fifteen feet thick, and its bottom was twenty feet or so above the sunbeaten lake surface. We rowed between the slender concrete pillars holding up the platform, and our bow waves slapped against them.

The platform over us had been part of an intersection, and narrow ramps branched from the main north-south fragment to descend to the valley floor. Now these curving side roads served as convenient boat ramps for us. We glided to the eastern ramp, and were moored by a few men who were there to greet us. We stepped from the front of the boat onto a small wooden ledge, and from there onto the concrete ramp. The red sun gleamed between two towers, and the breeze ruffled our hair. From the dwellings above we heard laughter and voices, and a tinkling of crockery.

"We're late," Lee said. "Let's go." As we ascended the ramp I noticed that it tilted side to side, as well as up. Tom told me, when I mentioned it, that this had been done to keep the cars coming down the ramp at high speed from skidding off the side. I looked over the edge at the water below and thought that the old Americans must have been fools, or crazy, to take such risks.

Up on the wide and level north-south platform we could see the houses built on it. The big house stood at the north end, and the cluster of smaller buildings, each about the size of my home, were arranged in a horseshoe at the south end. Half of the big house was only one story tall, and on the roof of this part, facing us, was a porch with a blue railing. Over the railing leaned several men, watching us. Jennings waved to them as we approached. I walked next to Tom, suddenly nervous.

Abe left us to join a group of men standing at the west railing of the road, a fat metal thing. The sun was dropping into the crease where the hills met at the west end of the lake. Lee and Jennings led Tom and me into the big house. Once inside Jennings took a comb from a pocket and ran it through his hair. Lee grinned sardonically at this grooming, and pushed past Jennings to lead us up a broad staircase. On the upper floor we walked down a dim hallway to a room containing a lot of chairs and a piano. Large glass doors in the south wall of this room opened onto the roof porch, and we walked through them.

The Mayor stood in a group of men by the railing, watching us approach. He was a big man, tall, wide-shouldered and deep-chested. His forearms were thick with muscle, and under his plaid wool pants I could see his thighs were the same. One of his men helped him to shrug into a plain blue coat. His head looked too small for his body. "Jennings, who are these men?" he said in a high, scratchy voice. Underneath his black moustache was a small mouth, a weak chin. But as he adjusted his collar he looked us over with sharply intelligent, pale blue eyes.

Jennings introduced Tom and me.

"Timothy Danforth," the Mayor said in reply. "Mayor of this fine town." There was a little American flag in the lapel of his jacket. He shook hands with each of us; when I shook I squeezed as hard as I could, but I might as well have been squeezing rock. He could have squashed my hand like bread dough. As Tom said later, his handshake alone could have made him mayor. He said to Tom, "I am told you are not the elected leader of San Onofre?"

"Onofre doesn't have an elected leader," Tom said.

"But you hold some sort of authority?" the Mayor suggested.

Tom shrugged and walked past him to the porch rail. "Nice view you've got here," he said absently, looking west, where the sun had been halved by the darkening hills. I was shocked at Tom's rudeness; I wanted to speak up and tell the Mayor that Tom had as much authority as anyone in Onofre—and that he didn't mean any disrespect. But I kept my mouth shut. Tom kept looking at the sunset. The Mayor watched him out of narrowed eyes.

"Always good to meet another neighbor," the Mayor said, in a hearty voice. "We'll celebrate with a meal out here, if you like. It should be a warm enough evening." He smiled and his moustache waggled, but all the time his eyes kept that sharp look. "Tell me, are you one who lived in the old time?" His tone seemed to say, are you one of those who used to live in Paradise?

"How did you guess?" Tom said.

The dozen men on the porch laughed, but Danforth just stared at Tom. "It's an honor to meet you, sir. There aren't many of you left, especially in such good health. You're an inspiration to all of us."

Tom lifted his bushy eyebrows. "Really?"

"An inspiration," the Mayor repeated firmly. "A monument, so to speak. A reminder of what we're striving for in these most difficult of times. I find that old timers like you understand better what we're striving for."

"Which is?" said Tom.

Luckily, or perhaps deliberately, the Mayor was still attending to the memory of his little speech, and he didn't hear Tom's question. "Well, come sit down," he said, as if we had been refusing to. There were several round tables on the porch, among small trees in big buckets. As we sat around one next to the rail Danforth's little eyes peered at Tom, with a sideways glance of great penetration. Tom innocently stared at the flag, which ruffled limply from a pole sticking out of the roof.

Twenty-five or thirty tables were set up on the freeway below, and more boats were arriving in the gloom of the early evening. The hills to the south were a brilliant green at their very tops, but that was the last of the light. From somewhere in the house a generator started to hum, and electric lights snapped on all over the island. The little buildings at the south end, the freeway railings, the rooms of the house behind us: all blazed with a white light. Girls my age or younger moved around the porch, bringing plates and silverware out from inside. One of the girls set my plate before me and gave me an inviting smile. Her hair shone gold under the glare of the lights, and I smiled back. Men and women appeared at the top of the east ramp, dressed like scavengers in bright coats and colorful dresses, but I didn't care. In San Diego things were obviously not the same. Down here they combined the best of scavenger and newtowner, I thought. One of the brighter lights shone on the flag, and everyone on the island stood at attention as the limp folds of red white and blue were lowered. Tom and I stood with them, and I felt a peculiar glow flushing my face and the chinks of my spine. . . .

Around our table were Tom and me, Jennings, Lee, the Mayor, and three of his men, who were quickly introduced to us. Ben was the only name I remembered. Jennings told the Mayor about their trip north, describing the two bridges and all the major breaks in the track. He made the repair work sound difficult, and I guessed that they had come home behind schedule. Or maybe Jennings just exaggerated out of habit. He certainly did when telling them about my swim across the creek, and I blushed, pleased that the blond serving girl was hovering between our table and the next to hear the tale. Jennings made it a tall tale indeed, and as the San Diegans congratulated me Tom nudged me under the table. "It was nothing," I told them. "I was anxious to get down here and see this town." The Mayor nodded his approval of the sentiment, sinking his chin into his neck until it looked like there was nothing but folds of skin between his Adam's apple and his mouth.

"What's the shortest time it would take you to train up to Onofre?" the Mayor asked Lee. Tom and I nudged each other again this time: first of all, the Mayor had shifted from calling our valley San Onofre to Onofre, after hearing Tom say it just once; and secondly, he knew which of his men to ask when he wanted a straight answer. Of course if he couldn't figure out Lee and Jennings he'd scarcely be able to mayor a doghouse. But it was a sign.

Lee cleared his throat. "Last night it took about eight hours, from our stopping point up there to University City. That's about as fast as it could be done, unless we left the bridges up."

"We can't do that." Danforth's mobile face was grim.

"I guess not. Anyway, another fifteen minutes to Onofre. The track's in good shape to there."

"And beyond as well," Jennings added, which made Tom look up. The Mayor scowled.

"Let's talk about that after dinner," he said.

After the girls had set the tables, with plates and glasses and cloth napkins and silverware that looked like real silver, they brought out big glass bowls filled with salads made of lettuce and shrimp. Tom examined the shrimp with interest, forking one to get it closer to his eyes. "Where do you get these?" he inquired.

The Mayor laughed. "Wait till after the grace, and Ben here will tell you."

All the serving girls came out and stood still, and the Mayor stood and walked to the rail, so he could be seen from below. He had a limp, I noticed; his left foot wouldn't bend. We all bowed our heads. The Mayor declaimed the prayer: "Dear Lord, we eat this food you have provided us in order to make us strong in the service of you and of the United States of America. Amen." Everyone joined in on the amen, which covered the little choking sounds Tom was making beside me. I ribbed him hard.

We started in on the salad. From below voices chimed with the sounds of clinking dishes. Between bites Ben said to Tom, "We get the shrimp from the south."

"I thought the border was closed."

"Oh, it is. Definitely. Not the old border, though. Tijuana is no more than a battleground for rats and cats. About five miles south of that is the new border. It's made of barbed wire fences, and a bulldozed strip on each side of it three hundred yards wide. And guard towers, and lights at night. I've never heard of a single person that got over it." As he took a bite the other men at the table nodded their agreement with this. "There's a jetty where the fence hits the beach, too, and beyond that guard boats. But they're Mexican guard boats, you see. The Japanese have the coast right down to the border, but beyond that the Mexicans take over. They don't do too good a job."

"Neither do the Japs," Danforth said.

"True. Anyway, the Mexican guard boats are there, but it's easy to get past them, and once past them the fishing boats will sell you anything they have or can get. We're just another customer as far as they're concerned. Except they know they have us over a barrel, so they squeeze us every trade. But we get what we want."

"Which is shrimp?" said Tom, surprised. His salad was gone.

"Sure. Don't you like it?"

"What do the Mexicans want?"

"Gun parts, mostly. Souvenirs. Junk."

"Mexicans love junk," Danforth said, and his men laughed. "But we'll sell them something different someday. Put them back where they belong, like it used to be." He had been watching Tom wolf his food; now that Tom was done, he said, "Did you live around here in the old time?"

"Up in Orange County, mostly. I came down here to school."

"Changed, hasn't it?"

"Sure." Tom was looking around for the next course. "Everything's changed." He was still being rude, apparently on purpose; I couldn't figure out what he was up to.

"I imagine Orange County was pretty built up in the old time."

"About like San Diego. Or a little more so."

The Mayor breathed a whistle, looking impressed.

When everyone had finished the salads the bowls were taken away, and replaced with pots of soup, plates of meat, stacks of bread, dishes of vegetables, pyramids of fruit. The plates just kept on coming, giving me chance after chance to smile at the blond girl: chicken and rabbit, pork pie and frog legs, lamb and turkey, fish and beef, abalone in big slabs—plate after plate after plate was set down, and the covered ones were opened for our inspection. By the time the girls were done, there was a feast on those tables that made Mrs. Nicolin's dinner look like the ones Pa and me ate every night. Nearly overwhelmed, I tried to decide where to start. It was hard. I had a little clam chowder while I thought it over.

"You know," said Danforth after we were well into it, "the Japanese are landing up there in your old home territory, these days."

"That so?" Tom said, shoveling abalone onto his plate. The amount of food on the table didn't seem to have impressed him. I *knew* he was interested in this stuff about the Japanese, but he refused to show it.

"You haven't seen any of them in Onofre? Or any signs?"

Tom appeared reluctant to take his attention from his food, and he did no more than shake his head as he chewed, and then give the Mayor a quick glance.

"They're interested in looking at the ruins of old America," the Mayor said.

"They?" Tom mumbled, his mouth full.

"Mostly Japanese, although there are other nationalities too. But the Japanese, who were given the charter to guard our west coast, make up most of them."

"Who guards the other coasts?" Tom said, as if testing how much they claimed to know.

"Canada was assigned the east coast, the Mexicans the Gulf Coast."

"They're supposed to be neutral powers," Ben added. "Although in the world today the very idea of a neutral power is a joke."

The Mayor went on: "Japanese own the offshore islands here, and Hawaii. It's easiest for the rich Japanese to get to Hawaii, and then here, but we're told tourists of all nationalities want to try it."

"How do you know all this?" Tom said, barely able to disguise his interest.

Proudly Danforth said, "We've sent men to Catalina to spy it out."

Tom couldn't help himself, no matter how much he ate: "So what happened? Have we been quarantined?"

With a disgusted stab of his fork the Mayor said, "The Russians did it. So we've been told. Of course it's obvious. Who else was going to come up with two thousand neutron bombs? Most countries couldn't even afford the vans those things were hidden in when they went off."

Tom squinted, and I thought I knew why; this was the same explanation he had given us in his story Johnny Pinecone, which I was pretty sure he had made up. It was odd.

"That was how they got us," the Mayor said. "Didn't you know? They hid the bombs in Chevy vans, drove the vans into the centers of the two thousand largest cities, and parked them there. Then the bombs all went off at once. No warning. You know, no missiles coming or anything."

Tom nodded, as if a mystery had finally been cleared for him.

"After the day," Ben went on, as it seemed the Mayor was too upset to go on, "the U.N. reconvened in Geneva. Everyone was terrified of the Soviet Union, especially the nations with nuclear weapons, naturally. Russia suggested we be made off limits for a century, to avoid any conflict over us. A world preserve, they said. Clearly punitive, but who was going to argue? So here we are."

"Interesting," Tom said. "But I've heard a lot of speculation in the last fifty years." He started forking again. "Seems to me we're like the Japanese themselves were after Hiroshima. They didn't even know what hit them, did you know that? They thought maybe we had dropped manganese on the electric train tracks, and started a fire. Pitiful. And we're no better."

"What's Hiroshima?" the Mayor asked.

Tom didn't reply. Ben shook his head at Tom's doubts. "We've had men on Catalina for months at a time. And—well, I'll send you over to Wentworth's tomorrow. He'll tell you. We know what happened, more or less."

"Enough history," said the Mayor. "What's important is the here and now. The Japanese in Avalon are getting corrupt. Rich Japanese want to visit America and do some sight-seeing. It's the latest adventure. They come to Avalon and contact people who will take them to the mainland. Those people, some of them Americans, sail them in past the coastal patrol at night, into Newport Beach or Dana Point. We've heard there are hundreds of them in Hawaii waiting to do it."

"That's what you said." Tom shrugged.

An exasperated scowl appeared on the Mayor's face and was gone. As dishes were cleared from the tables he stood up and leaned over the rail. "Tell the band to play!" he called down. The people below shouted to him, and he limped past us into the house. Over the railing I saw the big white-clothed tables below, piled with food and crockery. From above the San Diegans looked wonderfully groomed, their hair neatly cut and combed, their shirts and dresses bright and clean. Again I saw them as scavengers. From down the freeway a bit a small brass band started to play some stodgy polkas, and the Mayor appeared, moving from table to table. He knew everyone down there. As the people below finished their meals they got up and walked in front of the band to dance. All around us the water and the shores of the lake were dark: we were an island of light, propped up over the gloom. Below they were having a good time, but with the Mayor gone, the group on the porch looked bored.

Then Danforth reappeared between the tall glass doors, and laughed at the sight of us. "All done stuffing yourselves? Why don't you get down there and dance? This is a celebration! Get down there and mingle with the folks, and Ben and I will talk further with our guests from the north."

Happily the men and women seated around our tables stood and filed into the house. Jennings and Lee went with them, and only Ben stayed upstairs with the Mayor to talk with us.

"I have an excellent bottle of tequila in my study," Danforth said to us. "Let's go in there and give some a try."

We followed him in, down a hall to a wood-paneled room that was dominated by a large desk. Drapes covered a window, and bookcases covered the wall behind the desk. We sat in plush armchairs that were arranged in a half-circle facing the desk, and Tom tilted his head to the side in an attempt to read the book titles. Danforth got a long slim bottle from a shelf jammed with bottles, and poured us each a glass of tequila. Nervously he paced behind the desk, back and forth, back and forth, looking down at the carpet. He switched on a lamp that glared off the surface of the desk, lighting his face from below. It was quiet, no sound from the party outside. Solemnly he proposed a toast: "To the friendship of our two communities."

Tom lifted his glass and drank.

I tried a few sips of the tequila. It was harsh. My stomach felt like I'd put an iron ball in it, I'd eaten so much. I balanced the glass on the arm of my chair and sat back, ready to watch Tom and the Mayor go at it again—though what kind of contest it was, I couldn't figure.

The Mayor had a thoughtful, brooding expression. He continued to slowly pace back and forth. He lifted his glass and looked through it at Tom. "So what do you think?"

"Of what?" Tom said.

"Of the world situation?"

Tom shrugged. "I just heard about it. You folks know a lot more than we did. If it's all true. We know there are Orientals out there on Catalina. Their bodies wash up on our beach occasionally. Beyond that, all we've heard is swap meet talk, and that changes every month."

"You've had Japanese bodies washing up?" Danforth asked.

"We call them Chinese."

The Mayor shook his head. "Japanese."

"So that coast guard is shooting up some of the illegal landing parties?" Tom ventured.

Again the Mayor shook his head. "The coast guard is paid off. It wasn't them." He took a sip from his glass. "It was us."

"How's that?"

"It was us!" the Mayor said, suddenly loud. He limped to the window, fiddled with the drapes. "We sail up off Newport and Dana Point, on foggy nights or nights when we've been tipped off that they're coming, and we ambush them. Kill as many as we can."

Tom looked at the glass in his hand. "Why?" he said finally.

"Why?" The Mayor's chin melted into his neck. "You're an old timer—you ask me why?"

"Sure."

"Because we aren't a zoo here, that's why!" He began to pace again, bobbing around behind his desk, around and behind our chairs, behind the desk again. Without warning he slammed his right palm onto the desktop, *smack!* I jumped in my chair. "They blew our country to pieces," he said in a strangled, furious high voice, completely unlike the one he had been using just a moment before. "They killed it." He cleared his throat. "There's nothing we can do about that now. But they can't come sight-seeing in the ruins. *No.* Not while there are Americans left alive. We aren't animals in a cage to be looked at. We'll make them learn that if they set foot on our soil, they're dead." He took up the tequila bottle in a trembling hand and refilled his glass. "No stepping into the cages in this zoo. When word gets around that no one ever comes back from a visit to America, they'll stop coming. There won't be any more customers for that scum north of you." He drank hastily. "Did you know there are scavengers in Orange County arranging to give guided tours to the Japs?"

"I'm not surprised," Tom said.

"Well I am. Those people are scum. They are traitors to the United States." He said it like a death sentence. "If every American joined the resistance, no one could land on our soil. We'd be left alone, and the rebuilding could get on. But we all have to be part of the resistance."

"I didn't know there was a resistance," Tom said mildly.

Bang! The Mayor's hand hit the desk again. He leaned over it and cried, "That's what we brought you here to tell you about!" He straightened up, sat down in his chair, held his forehead in his hand. Suddenly it seemed hushed and quiet again. "Tell him, Ben."

Ben leaned forward in his chair enthusiastically. "When we got to the Salton Sea we learned about it. The American resistance. Although usually they just called it the resistance.

The headquarters are in Salt Lake City, and there are military centers in the old Strategic Air Command quarters under Cheyenne, Wyoming, and under Mount Rushmore."

"Under Mount Rushmore?" Tom said.

Head still cradled in one hand, face shadowed, the Mayor peered at him. "That's right. That's where the secret military headquarters of the United States always was."

"I didn't know," Tom said, eyebrows gently arched.

Ben went on. "There are organizations all across the country, but it's all one group really, and the goal is the same. To rebuild America." He rolled the phrase over his tongue.

"To rebuild America," breathed the Mayor. I felt that flush in my face and spine begin again. By God, they were in contact with the east coast! New York, Virginia, Massachusetts, England. . . . The Mayor reached for his glass and sipped; Ben jerked down two swallows as if it were a toast, and Tom and I likewise drank. For a moment there seemed a shared feeling in the room. I could feel the alcohol going to my head, along with the news of the resistance, this dream of Nicolin's and mine come to life. It made a heady mixture. Danforth stood again and looked at the framed map on the side wall of the study. Passionately he said, "To make America great again, to make it what it was before the war, the best nation on Earth. That's our goal." He pointed a finger through the shadows at Tom. "We'd be back to that already if we had retaliated against the Soviets. If President Eliot—traitor, coward!—hadn't refused to defend us. But we'll still do it. We'll work hard, we'll pray hard, we'll hide our weapons from the satellites. They're inventing new ones in Salt Lake and Cheyenne, we're told. And one day . . . one day we'll spring out on the world again like a tiger. A tiger from the depths of the pit. . . ." His voice shifted up to a scratchy strangled mutter that I couldn't make out. He was half turned away from us, and he went on like that for a while, talking to himself in a voice that moaned and sighed. The lamp on his desk flickered, flickered again. Ben jerked out of his chair and went to a corner to get a kerosene lamp.

With a tap of the knuckles on the desk the Mayor raised his voice again, sounding relaxed and reasonable. "That's what I wanted to talk to you about, Barnard. The largest resistance group on this coast is centered around Santa Barbara, we've heard. We met some of them out at the Salton Sea. We need to connect with them, and present a unified opposition to the

Japanese on Catalina and the Santa Barbara islands. The first part of that task is to rid Orange County and Los Angeles of all Japanese tourists, and the traitors who guide them. So we need you. We need Onofre to join the resistance."

"I can't speak for them," Tom said. I almost protested, and my mouth moved: *Of course we'll join.* I bit my lip and stayed silent. Tom was right; it would have to be voted. Tom waved a hand. "It sounds . . . well, I don't know if we'll want in or not."

"You've got to want in," the Mayor said fiercely, fist held over the desk. "This is more important than what you want. You tell them they can make this country what it used to be. They can help. But we all have to work together. The day will come. Another Pax Americana, cars and airplanes, rockets to the moon, telephones. A unified country." Suddenly, without anger or whispery passion, he said, "You go back up there and tell your valley that they join the resistance or they oppose it."

"Not a very neighborly way of putting it," Tom observed, his eyes narrowed.

"Put it any way you please! Just tell them."

"I'll tell them. But they'll want to know just exactly what you want of them. And I can't guarantee what they'll say to it."

"No one's asking you to guarantee anything. They'll know what's right." The Mayor took a long look at Tom, his little eyes bright. "I would have thought an old timer like you would be hopping with joy to hear of the resistance."

"I don't hop much these days," Tom said. "Bad knees."

The Mayor circled the desk and bent over Tom's chair, looked at Tom. With both hands he trapped one of Tom's. "Don't lose your feel for America, old man," he said hoarsely. "It's the best part of you. It's what kept you alive for so long, whether you know it or not. You've got to fight to keep that feeling, or you're doomed."

Tom pulled his hand away. The Mayor straightened up and limped back around the desk. "Well, Ben! These gentlemen deserve to enjoy a little of the partying outside before they retire, don't you agree?" Ben nodded and smiled at us. "I know you men had a hard night last night," Danforth said, "but I hope you'll have enough energy to join the folks outside for at least a short while."

We agreed that we did.

"Before we go back out, then, let me show you a little secret." We stood and followed him out of the room. He bobbed down the hallway to another door, and pulled a key from his vest. "In here is the key to a whole new world." He unlocked the door, and we followed him into the room, which contained nothing but machine parts, scattered over three tables. On the biggest table was a metal box as big as a boat locker, covered with knobs and dials and gauges, with wires trailing out of it from two openings.

"Short wave radio?" Tom said.

"Exactly," said Ben, beaming with approval at Tom's good guess.

"We've got a man coming from the Salton Sea to fix this thing," the Mayor whispered. "And when we do that, we'll be in touch with the whole country. Every part of the resistance. It will be the start of a new age."

So we stood there and stared at it for a while, and then tiptoed out of the room. When the Mayor was done locking the door we went outside onto the freeway, where the band was still playing. Instantly the Mayor was surrounded by young women who wanted a dance with him. Tom wandered off toward the west railing, and I went for the drink table. The man behind the table recognized me; he had helped dock our boat when we arrived at the island. "Drink's on the house," he declared, and poured me a cup of tequila punch. I took it and walked in circles around the dance floor. The women dancing with the Mayor held close to him and danced in slow circles, unlike the polka dancing going on around them. I was feeling the drink. The music, the electric lights glaring off the concrete, the bright rugs thrown here and there, the cool breeze, the night sky, the eerie ruined skyscrapers rising blackly from the murk around us—the incredible news of the American resistance—it all combined to put me in a blaze of excitement. I was on the edge of a new world, truly. I twisted through the crowd to Tom, who was leaning against the fat railing, looking down at the water. "Tom, isn't it grand? Isn't it wonderful?"

"Let me think, boy," he said quietly.

So I walked back over to the band, subdued for a moment. But it didn't last. The girl dancing with the Mayor was the blond who had served our table at the feast. When she gave way to another girl I hurried out among the dancers and swept her into a hug.

"Dance with me too," I asked her. "I'm from the north."

"I know," she said, and laughed. "You sure aren't one of the boys from around here, and that's a fact."

"From the icy north," I said as I awkwardly swept her into the polka. It made me a little dizzy. "From over glaciers and crevasses and great expanses of snow have I come to your fair civilized town."

"What?"

"Here from the barbarous north, to see your Mayor, the prophet of a new age."

"He is like a prophet, isn't he? Just like from church. My father says he's made San Diego what it is."

"I believe it. Did he make a lot of changes when he took office?"

"Oh, he's been mayor since before I can remember. Since I was two, I think Daddy said."

"Long time ago."

"Fourteen years . . ."

I kissed her briefly, and we danced three or four songs, until my dizziness returned and I had trouble with my bearings. She accompanied me to the tables, and we sat and talked. I chattered on like the most extravagant liar in California; Nicolin himself couldn't have beat me that night, and the girl laughed and laughed. Later on Jennings and Tom came by, and I was sorry to see them. Jennings said he was taking us to our night's lodgings on the other end of the platform. Reluctantly I said goodnight to the girl, and followed them drunkenly down the freeway south, singing to myself, "Oomp-pah-pah," and greeting most of the people we passed. Jennings installed us in one of the bungalows at the south end of the platform, and I chattered at the silent Tom for two or three minutes before I passed out. "A new age, Tom, I'm telling you. A new world."

Chapter Eight

Shotgun blasts woke us up the next morning. Jumping up to look out the door of our little bungalow, we discovered that the Mayor and several of his men were taking target practice, shooting at plates that one of them was throwing out over the lake. The man threw—the plate arched out—the shooter aimed—*bam!*—a flat sound like two wet planks slapping together. About one in every three plates burst into white splinters. The rest clipped the sparkling surface of the lake and disappeared. Tom shook his head disdainfully as he regarded this exercise. "They must have found a lot of ammunition somewhere," he said. Jennings, standing to one side and watching the action, turned and saw us in our doorway. He came over and led us to one of the tables set outside the big house. There in the tangy clouds of gunpowder smoke we had a breakfast of bread and milk. Between the bangs of the gun I could hear the American flag snapping smartly in the fresh morning breeze. I watched it waving over the house; I watched the target practice. Every time a plate exploded the men hooted and talked it over. The Mayor was a good shot; he seldom missed, which may have been the result of taking his turn often. The rest of his men might as well have been dumping those plates into the lake by the boxful.

When we were done eating the Mayor gave his shotgun to one of the men around him, and clumped over to us. He looked a bit smaller in the sunlight than he had under the lanterns and electric lights.

"I'm going to send you back to Jennings' house by way of La Jolla, so you can talk to Wentworth."

"Who's he?" Tom asked, without any pretense of politeness.

"He's our bookmaker. He can tell you more about the situation Ben and I described to you last night. After you've talked to him, Jennings and Lee and their crew will take you back north on the train." He sat down across from us and leaned his thick forearms on the table. "When you get there, you tell your folk just what I said last night."

"Let me understand you clearly," Tom said. "You want us to join this resistance effort you've heard of."

"That we're part of. That's right."

"Which means what, in actual terms?"

Danforth stared steadily at Tom's face. "Every town in the resistance has to do its share. That's the only way we'll achieve victory. Of course we've got a much larger population down here, and we'll be providing most of the manpower on this coast, I'm sure. But we need to get through your valley on the tracks, for one thing. And you folks could make raids up the coast a lot easier than we can, living where you do. Or we could base our raids in your river, depending on how we decide to work it. See, there is no set way, you should understand that. But we need you to sign up."

"What if we don't want to?"

The Mayor's jaw tightened. He let Tom's question hang in the air for a while, and the men around us (target practice being over for the moment) grew silent. "I can't figure you, old man," Danforth complained. "You just take my message to the people in your valley."

"I'll tell them what you've told me, and we'll let you know our decision."

"Good enough. I'll be seeing you again." He pushed back his chair, stood up and limped into the gleaming white house.

"I think he's done talking to you," Jennings said after another long silence. "We can be off." He led us back to our bungalow, and when Tom had gotten his shoulder bag we walked down the tilted ramp to the boats. Lee and Abe were waiting on the floating dock, and we all got in a boat and cut over the blue water to the lake's north shore. It was a fine day, sky free of clouds and not much wind. We climbed up to a different train than the one we had arrived on, set on different tracks, ones that took us west along the shore of the lake. "Quite a terminal you have there," Tom remarked, breaking his silence. Jennings began to describe every mile of the rail system, but since none of the names he mentioned meant anything to me I stopped listening and kept a lookout for the sea. We came to a big marsh just when I expected to spot it, and turned north to skirt the marsh's edge. A heavily forested hill marked the northern end of the marsh, and we clattered along on a freeway that snaked through a crease to the east of the hill. Before we had left the crease Lee braked the car—I had learned to stick my fingers in my ears when he did that. "We have to walk to La Jolla," Jennings said. "No tracks from here."

"Nor roads neither," Lee added.

We slid off the side of the handcar, and started up a trail that was the only passage through thick forest. It was more like what Tom called a jungle: ferns and creepers and vines wove the densely set trees together, and every lichen-stained branch was locked in a struggle for sunlight with ten other branches. Knots of torrey pine competed with trees I'd never seen the likes of before. There was a damp smell to the spongy trail, and fungus or bright green ferns grew on every log that had fallen across our path. Behind me Tom muttered as he walked, thumping his shoulder bag against his side. "Mount Soledad just another wet north face now. All the houses washed down. All fall down, all fall down." Lee, striding ahead of me, turned and gave Tom a funny look. I knew just what the look meant: it was hard to believe Tom had been alive when these ruins had stood whole. Tom cursed as he kicked a root and mumbled on, unaware of Lee's glance. "Flood and mud, rain and pain, lightning blast and fire burn, all fall down. And all that terrible construction. Ah ha, there's a foundation. Was that one Tudor? Chinese? Hacienda? California *ranch?*" "What's that?" Jennings called back, thinking he had heard a question. But Tom talked on: "This town was everything but itself. Nothing but money. Paper houses; this hill sure looks better with all that shit washed away. I wish they could see it now, hee hee hee."

On the ocean side of the hill it was a different story. Where the hillside leveled off, forming a point that thrust out from the coast on either side, all the trees had been cleared away. In this clearing a few old buildings were surrounded by small wooden houses. The concrete walls of the old buildings had been repaired with redwood, and the new houses had been put together with fragments of the old, so that some had massive roof beams, others wide chimneys, others an orange tile roof. Most of the houses had been painted white, and the old concrete had been painted pale shades of blue or yellow or orange. As we descended the west side of the hill we caught sight of the clearing through the leaves, and the little village in it shone against the backdrop of the dark blue ocean. We came out of the overhanging branches of the forest, and the trail widened into a straight street paved with thick grass.

"Paint," Tom observed. "What a good idea. But all the paint I've seen lately has been hard as rock."

"Wentworth has a way to liquefy it," Jennings said. "Same way he liquefies old ink, he tells me."

"Who is this Wentworth?" I said.

"Come and find out," said Jennings in reply.

At the far end of the street of grass, just above a small cove, was a low building made of tan blocks of stone. A wall made of the same sort of blocks surrounded the place, and torrey pines stood against the wall on both sides. We walked through a big wooden gate that had a tiger carved into it, a green tiger with black stripes. Inside the wall, grass alternated with patches of flowers. Jennings looked in the open door of the building, and waved us in after him.

The first room had big glass windows in one wall, and with its door open it was as sunny as the courtyard. A half dozen kids and three or four adults were at work on low tables, kneading a pure white dough that by its smell could not be bread. A man with black-rimmed spectacles and a salt and pepper beard looked up from a table where he was giving instructions to the workers, and walked over to us.

"Jennings, Lee," he said, wiping his hands dry on a cloth tied around his waist. "What brings you out here today?"

"Douglas, this here is Tom Barnard, a . . . an elder of Onofre Valley, up the coast. We brought him down on the new tracks.

Tom, this is Douglas Wentworth, San Diego's bookmaker."

"Bookmaker," Tom repeated. He shook Wentworth's hand. "I'm happy to meet a bookmaker, sir."

"You take an interest in books?"

"I surely do. I was a lawyer once, and had to read the worst kind of books. Now I'm free to read what I like, when I can find it."

"You have an extensive collection?" Wentworth asked, knocking his glasses up his nose with a finger to see Tom better.

"No sir. Fifty volumes or so, but I keep trading them with our neighbors for others."

"Ah. And you, young man—do you read?" His eyes were the size of eggs behind his spectacles, and they held my gaze with ease.

"Yes, sir. Tom taught me how, and now that I can I enjoy it more than almost anything."

Mr. Wentworth smiled briefly. "It's refreshing to hear that San Onofre is a literate community. Perhaps you'd like to take a tour of our establishment? I can take a few moments from the work here, and we do have a modest printing arrangement that might be of interest."

"We'd be delighted," Tom said.

"Lee and I will go get some lunch," Jennings said. "Back shortly."

"We'll wait for you," Tom said. "Thanks for bringing us here."

"Thank the Mayor."

"Keep kneading until you get a perfect consistency," Wentworth was saying to his students, "then begin to roll out the water. I'll be back before the pressing."

He led us to another room with good windows, one filled with small metal boxes set on tables. A woman was turning a handle on the side of one of these machines, rotating a drum on which a piece of print-covered paper was clamped. More pages covered by print were ejected from the bottom of the box.

"Mimeograph!" Tom cried.

The woman working the machine jerked at Tom's shout, and glared at him.

"Indeed," said Wentworth. "We are a modest operation, as I said. Mimeographing is our principal form of printing here.

Not the most elegant method, or the most long lasting, but the machines are reliable, and besides, they're about all we've got."

"What about ditto masters?" Tom asked.

Wentworth, pleased at the question, asked the woman to step aside. She did so with a frown. "We had a good supply of ditto masters, and we've learned how to make more, using the mimeo ink and this paper. Still, it's the weak link in our chain." He pulled a page out of a basket in the side of the machine and showed it to us. "Because of that we have to conserve, by single spacing and small margins. Difficult to read, rather ugly—"

"I think it's beautiful," Tom said, taking up the page to read it.

"It suffices."

"Pretty color ink, too," I put in; the ink was a bluish purple, and the page was thick with it.

Wentworth let out a short, sharp laugh. "Ha! Do you think so? I would prefer black, myself, but we must work with what we have. Now over here is our true pride. A hand letter press." He gestured at a contraption of bars holding a big screw, which took up most of the far wall.

"Is that what that is," Tom said, putting the sheet of paper back in its basket. "I've never seen one."

"This is what we do our fine work on. But there isn't enough paper, and none of us knew, at first, how to set type. So it goes very slowly. We have had some successes, however. Following Gutenburg, here is our first one." He hauled a big leather-bound book off the shelf beside the machine. "King James version, of course, although if I could have found a Jerusalem, it would have been a difficult choice."

"Wonderful!" Tom said, taking the book. "I mean—" He shook his head, and I laughed to see him at a loss for words at last—it took a pile of words to do it. "That's a lot of typesetting."

"Ha!" Wentworth took the book back from Tom. "Indeed. And all for the sake of a book we already have. That's not really the point, is it."

"You print new books?"

"That occupies at least half our time, and is the part I'm most interested in, I confess. We publish instruction manuals, almanacs, travel journals, reminiscences...." He looked at Tom, his eyeballs swimming in the glass of his spectacles. "As a matter of fact, we invite all survivors of the war to write their story down and submit it to us. We're almost certain to print it up. As our contribution to historical record."

Tom raised his eyebrows, but said nothing.

"You ought to do it," I urged him. "You'd be perfect for it, all those stories you've got about the old time."

"Ah, a storyteller?" said Wentworth. "Then indeed you should. My feeling is, the more accounts we have of that period, the better."

"No thank you," Tom said, looking uncomfortable.

I shook my head, perplexed once again that such a talky old man would so stubbornly refuse to discuss his own life story—which is all some people can be gotten to talk about.

"Consider it further," Wentworth said. "I think I could guarantee the readership of most of the San Diego residents. The literate residents, I mean to say. And since the Salton Sea people have contacted us—"

"They contacted you?" Tom interrupted.

"Yes. Two years ago a party arrived, and since then your guides Lee and Jennings, very industrious men, have supervised the reconstruction of a rail line out there. We've shipped books to them, and they tell us they've sent them even farther east. So distribution of your work, though uncertain, could very well span the continent."

"You agree that communication extends that far?"

Wentworth shrugged. "We see through a glass darkly, as you know. I have in my possession a book printed in Boston, rather well done. Beyond that, I cannot say. I have no reason to disbelieve their claims. In any case, a book by you might just as easily reach Boston as that book reached me."

"I'll think about it," Tom said, but in a tone that I knew meant he was just killing the subject.

"Do it, Tom," I objected.

He just looked at the big press.

"Come see what we have printed so far," Wentworth added by way of encouragement, and led us out of the printing room to a corner room, again a chamber bright with sun, its windows overlooking the point break below. This was the library: tall bookcases alternated with tall windows, and held books old and new.

"Our library," said Wentworth. "Not a lending library, unfortunately," he added, interpreting perfectly the greedy smack-

ing of Tom's lips. "This case contains the works printed here."
Tom began to examine the shelves of the bookcase Wentworth
indicated. Most of the books on them were big folders, filled
with mimeographed pages; one shelf held leather-bound books
the size of the old ones.

Wentworth and I watched Tom pull out book after book.
*"Practical Uses of the Timing Device From Westinghouse
Washer-Dryers,* by Bill Dangerfield," Tom read aloud, and
laughed.

"It looks like your friend might take a while," Wentworth
said to me. "Would you like to see our gallery of illustrations?"

What I really wanted to do was look at the books along
with Tom, but I saw Wentworth was being polite so I said yes
sir. We went back into the hall, and continued down it. Before
a long window made of several large panes of glass the hall
widened, and against the wall opposite the window were pictures of all sorts of animals, drawn in bold strokes of black
ink.

"These are the originals of illustrations for a book describing
all the animals seen in the back country of San Diego." I must
have looked surprised, for the pictures included some animals
I had seen only in Tom's tatty encyclopedia: monkeys, ante-
lopes, elephants. . . . "There were very extensive zoos in San
Diego before the war. We assume that all the animals in the
main zoo were killed in the downtown blast, but there was an
annex to the zoo in the hills, and those animals escaped, or
were freed. Those who survived the subsequent climatic
changes—I suppose some were actually helped—have pros-
pered. I myself have seen bears and wildebeest, baboons and
reindeer."

"I like the tiger here," I said. I knew it was a tiger from
one of the first books Tom had ever given me to read, the one
about Sambo.

"I did that one myself, thanks. That was quite an encounter.
Shall I tell you about it?" He spoke his questions funny, letting
them fall rather than rise at the end.

"Sure."

We sat down in wicker chairs placed before the windows.

"We were on a trek beyond Mount Laguna. Do you know
Mount Laguna? It is a considerable peak twenty miles inland,
and the snowpack lies heavy on it nearly all the year round.
In the spring the streams in the surrounding hills gush with the

melt, and in their steeper sections they can be quite impassable.

"Our expedition to Julian was dogged by bad luck every step of the way. The radio equipment we had been told of was demolished. The library of Western literature I had hoped to relocate was nowhere to be found. One of the members of our expedition broke an ankle in the ruins of the town. Lastly, worst of all, on our return we were discovered by the Cuyamuca Indians. These Indians are exceedingly jealous of their territory, and parties traveling in the area have reported fierce attacks at night, when the Indians are least afraid of firearms. All in all, it was a bad day's march, our injured friend between us in a sling, and Cuyamucans on horseback observing us from every other open hilltop.

"As nightfall approached I struck out ahead of my party, to scout possible camps, for our slow progress meant we would be spending the night in Indian territory. I found nothing very suitable for night defense, and as it was getting near sundown I retraced my path. When I got to the small clearing where I had left my friends, however, they were not there. Their tracks were confusing, but seemed to lead north, and over the sounds of the rushing streams in the area I imagined I heard gunfire in that direction as well.

"While I was pursuing my friends the sun went down, and as you know the forest begins immediately upon that departure to get very dark. I came to a steep creek; I had no idea where my party had gotten to; I looked at the creek, momentarily at a loss. Staring through the dusk at the tumbling water I became aware of the presence of another pair of eyes, across the creek from me. They were huge eyes, the color of topazes."

"What are topazes?" I asked.

"Yellow diamonds, I should have said. As I met the gaze of those unblinking eyes, the tiger who owned them stalked out of a clump of torrey pine to the bank of the stream directly across from me."

"You're kidding!" I exclaimed.

"No. He was a fully grown Bengal tiger, at least eight feet long, and four feet high at the shoulders. In the dim light of that glade his winter fur seemed green to me, a dull green banded by dark stripes.

"He appeared from the clump so suddenly that at first I was merely appalled at the catastrophic proportions my bad luck had reached. I was sure I was living out the last moments of

my existence, and yet I could not move, or even take my eyes
from the unblinking gaze of that beautiful but most deadly
beast. I have no notion of exactly how long we stood there
staring at each other: I know it was one of the central minutes
of my life.

"Then the tiger stepped over the creek with a fluid little
jump, as easy as you would step over that crack in the floor.
I braced myself as he approached—he lifted a paw as wide as
my thigh, and pressed it down on my left shoulder—right here.
He sniffed me, so close I could see the crystalline coloring of
his irises, and smell blood on his muzzle. Then he took his
paw from me and with a nudge of his massive head pushed
me to my right, upstream. I stumbled, caught my balance. The
tiger padded past me, turned to look, as if to see if I were
following. I heard a rasp from its chest—if it was a purr, it
was to a cat's purr as thunder is to a doorslam. I followed it.
My astonishment had gone outside itself, and prevented all
other thought. I kept my hand on the tiger's shoulder, where
I could feel the big muscles bunch and give as it walked, and
I stayed at its side as it wound between trees on a path of its
own. Every minute or two it would turn its head to look into
my eyes, and each time I was mesmerized anew by its calm
gaze.

"Much later the moon rose, and still we walked through the
forest together. Then I heard gunshots ahead, and the beast's
purring stopped, its shoulder muscles tensed. In a clearing
illumined by moonlight I made out several horses, and around
them men—Indians, I guessed, for my party had no horses
with it. More gunshots sounded from trees on the other side
of the clearing, and I surmised that my friends were there, for
just as we had no horses, the Cuyamuca Indians had no guns.
The tiger shrugged off my hand with a twitch of his fur, a
twitch that no doubt usually removed flies, and strode ahead
of me, down toward the clearing."

"Hey!" Tom cried, hurrying around the corner of the hallway. He held one of the books printed on the hand letter press
firmly before him, and gestured with it at Wentworth.

"Which one have you found?" Wentworth inquired. He didn't
seem disturbed by the interruption of his story, but I was
squirming.

"An American Around the World," Tom read. *"Being an*

Account of a Circumnavigation of the Globe in the Years 2030 to 2039. By Glen Baum."

Wentworth uttered his sharp, spontaneous laugh. "Very good. You have found the masterpiece of our line, I believe. Besides being an intrepid adventurer, Glen can tell a tale."

"But is it true? An American went around the world and returned just eight years ago?" Put that way, I understood why Tom was so flabbergasted—I had been stuck with the tiger in the back country—and I got out of my chair to have a look at this book. Sure enough, there it was: *An American Around the World,* right there on the cover.

Wentworth was smiling at Tom. "Glen sailed to Catalina in 2030, that is certain. And he reappeared in San Diego one night in the fall of 2039." His egg eyes flickered and something passed between the two men that I didn't catch, for Tom laughed out loud. "The rest you have between those covers."

"I had no idea this kind of stuff was still being written," Tom said. "How wonderful."

"It is, isn't it."

"Where is this Glen Baum now?"

"He took off for the Salton Sea last fall. Before he left he told me the title of his next book: *Overland to Boston.* I expect it will be as interesting as the one you hold." He stood up. Down the hall I could hear the voice of Jennings, joking with the woman in the mimeograph room. Wentworth led us back into the library.

"So what happened to you and the tiger?" I asked.

But he was rooting in a box on the bottom shelf of one case. "We have a lot of copies of that book. Take one with you back to San Onofre, courtesy of the New Green Tiger Press." He offered one of the leather-bound books to Tom.

Tom said, "Thank you sir, thank you very much. This means a lot to me."

"Always glad to get new readers, I assure you."

"I'll make all my students read it," said Tom, grinning as if he'd just been handed a block of silver.

"You won't have to make us," I said. "But what about the tiger that time—"

Jennings and Lee entered the room. "Lunch time," Jennings cried. Apparently it was the habit in San Diego to eat a meal in the middle of the day. "Have a good tour?" Tom and I told him that we had, and showed him our book.

"Another thing," Wentworth said, groping in a different box. "Here is a blank book, in case you decide to write that memoir." He riffled the pages of a bound book, showing them to be blank. "Give it back to us full, and we will set about the task of reproducing it."

"Oh, I couldn't," said Tom. "You've given us enough already."

"Please, take it." Wentworth held it out to him. "We have plenty of these. No obligation to write—but if you decide to, then the materials will be at hand."

"Well, thanks," Tom said. After a moment's hesitation he put the two volumes in his shoulder bag.

"Shall we have lunch out on their lawn?" Jennings asked, holding aloft a long loaf of bread.

"I must return to my class," Wentworth said. "But feel free to enjoy the courtyard." And to Tom, as he led us to the door: "Remember what I said about that memoir, sir."

"I will. You're doing great work here."

"Thank you. Keep teaching people to read, or it will all go to naught. Now I must get back. Goodbye, thank you for visiting, goodbye." He turned and went into the front room, where his students were still kneading the paper pulp.

After lunch in the sun-filled salt air of the courtyard, we hiked back over Mount Soledad to the tracks, and pumped the car northward up and down steep hills. A few miles up the tracks Tom had Lee apply the brakes. "Mind if we go out to the cliffs for a look around?"

Jennings looked doubtful, and I said, "Tom, we can look off cliffs when we get home."

"Not like these." Tom looked at Jennings. "I want to show him."

"Sure," Jennings said. "I told the wife we'd be back for supper, but she won't have that ready till after dark anyway."

So we got off the car again, and made our way westward to the coast, through a dense forest of torrey pine and brambleberry. Pretty soon we came upon an outcropping of tall stone crags. When we got in among them I saw they were concrete. They were buildings. The walls that remained—some of them as high as our beach cliff—were surrounded by piles of concrete rubble. Blocks as big as my house rose out of the ferns and brambleberries. Jennings was talking a streak about the place, and Tom held me by the arm and told the two San Diegans to go on ahead of us to the cliff. "He's got it all wrong," he said sourly when Jennings was out of earshot.

After they were gone I wandered in the ruins. A bomb had gone off nearby, I reckoned; the north side of every standing wall was black, and as soft and crumbly as sandstone. In the rubble and weeds I saw shards of glass, angled bits of metal both rusty and shiny, strips of plastic, a ribcage from a skeleton, melted glass tubes, metal boxes, slate boards.... Rafael would have loved it. But after a time I felt oppressed, like I had in San Clemente. This was no different from that: the ruins of the old time, the signs of a giant past that was now shattered bits of rock covered by weeds, a past so big that not all our efforts would ever get us back to it, or to anything like it. Ruins like these told us how little our lives were, and I hated them.

I saw Tom in the outbreak of concrete crags to the north, wandering aimlessly from ruin to ruin, tripping over blocks and then staring down at them like they'd jumped into his path. He was tugging on his beard as if he wanted to pull it out. Unaware of my presence, he was talking to himself, uttering short violent phrases that all ended with a sharp tug on the beard. As I got closer I saw that all the thousand lines in his face drooped down. I'd never seen him look so desolate.

"What was this place, Tom?"

I thought he wouldn't answer. He looked away, pulled his beard. Then he let out his breath. "It was a school. My school."

One time a couple of summers before, we had all gathered under the torrey pine in Tom's junkyard, Steve and Kathryn, Gabby and Mando and Kristen, Del and little Teddy Nicolin, all talking at once under sunny skies, we were, and fighting over who got to read *Tom Sawyer* next, and plotting to tickle Kristen till she cried, and the old man sitting with his back against the treetrunk, laughing and laughing. "All right, shut up you kids, shut up now, school's in session."

I let Tom be and walked west across the faint remains of a road, into trees where little tangles of rotted beams marked the sites of old buildings. Buildings you could believe people had once put up, had once inhabited. I sat at the edge of a canyon that dropped to the sea. I could tell that the cliffs were going to be big ones, because I was still far above the water, and the canyon was short. The sun got lower. I dashed a tear from my eye and wished I was home, or at least away from this place.

Tom walked through the trees a distance away, looking for me. I stood and called out, walked over to him. "Let's go out to the cliff and find those guys," he said. He still looked low, and I fell in beside him without a word. "Here, around this way," he said, and led me to the south rim of the canyon.

The trees gave way to shrubs, then to knee high weeds, and then we were on the cliff's edge. Far below lay the ocean, flat and silvery. The horizon was really out there—it must have been a hundred miles away. So much water! A stiff wind hit me in the face as I looked down the pocked tan cliff, which fell down and down and down in nearly vertical ravines, to a very broad beach, strewn with seaweed. Jennings and Lee were a few hundred yards down the cliff edge, just tiny figures on top of that cliff, throwing rocks down at the beach, though they hit the middle of the cliff instead. Looking at the rocks fall I suddenly knew what the gulls saw, and I felt I was soaring in the sky, high above the world.

To the left Mount Soledad and La Jolla stuck out into the sea, blocking the view farther south. To the north the cliff curved away, until in the distance little cliffs like dirt clods broken in half alternated with blank bluish spots, which were like marshes. The tiny cliffs and marshes extended in a curve all the way up to the green hills of Pendleton, and up there where the hills met the sea and sky was our valley, our home. It was hard to believe I could see that far. The waves below broke in long curves, leaving their white tracery on the water with just a whisper, a faint *kkkkkkkkkkk, kkkkkkkkkkk.* Tom was sitting down, his feet swinging over the edge. "The beach is at least twice as wide," he said in a strangled voice. Talking to himself. "They shouldn't let the world change so much in one life. It's too hard." I moved to get out of earshot, so he could talk without being overheard. But he looked up at me; he was talking to me: "I spent hours down there when time could have stopped, and I wouldn't have minded." He tugged his beard. "These cliffs are all different now."

I didn't know what to say to him. The setting sun lit the cliffs, so that they threw off an orange light that filled the air. Our shadows stretched far across the field behind us, and the wind was cold. The world seemed a big place, a big, windy,

dusky place. Uneasily I paced up and down the cliff edge,
looking and looking. The old man stayed where he sat, a little
bump on the cliff. The sun sank into the water, drowning bit
by bit, paring away until only the emerald wink of the green
flash was left. The wind picked up. Jennings and Lee came
along the cliff toward us, tiny figures waving their arms.

"Better be getting back," Jennings called when they got
closer. "Elma will be having dinner on the table."

"Give the old man a minute more," I said.

"She'll be mad if dinner has to wait too long," Jennings
said more quietly. But Lee said "Let him be," and Jennings
stood quietly, looking down at the tapestry left by broken waves.

Eventually Tom stirred, walked down to us as if he'd just
woken up. The evening star glowed like a lantern in the ocean
sky.

"Thanks for bringing us out here," Tom said.

"Our pleasure," Jennings replied. "But we'd better head
back now. It's going to be a hell of a walk through those ruins
in the dark."

"We'll skirt them to the south," Lee said, "down that road
that . . ." He sucked in his breath hard.

"What's wrong?" Jennings exclaimed.

Lee pointed north, toward Pendleton.

We all looked, saw nothing but the dark curve of the coast,
the first faint stars above—

A white streak fell out of the sky, plunged into the hills far
to the north and disappeared.

"Oh, no," Jennings whispered.

Another streak from the sky. It fell just like a shooting star,
except it didn't slow down or break into pieces; it fell in a
straight line, like lightning set against a straightedge, taking
no more than three blinks of the eye from the time it appeared
high above to the time it silently disappeared into the coastline.

"Pendleton," Lee said. "They're busting up our track." He
began to curse in a heavy, furious low voice.

Jennings kicked at a shrub till he cracked its trunk. "Shit!"
he shouted. "*Shit!* God damn those people, God *damn* them.
Why can't they leave us alone—"

Three more streaks fell from the sky, one after another,
landing farther and farther north, defining the curve of the
coast. I closed my eyes and red bars swam around in the black.
I opened them to see another streak burst into the world up

there among the stars, plummeting down instantly onto the land.

"Where are they coming from?" I asked, and was surprised to hear my voice shake. I was afraid, I think, that they would be bombs like those that had fallen on the day.

"Airplane," Jennings said grimly. "Or satellite, or Catalina, or halfway around the world. How the fuck would we know?"

"They're hitting all over Pendleton," Lee said in a bitter voice. Jennings commenced kicking shrubs out of the ground and throwing them over the cliff, cursing all the while.

"They've stopped," Tom pointed out. In the dark I couldn't read his expression, and after Lee's and Jennings' shouts his voice was calm. We watched the sky for another one. Nothing.

"Let's go," Lee finally croaked. Slowly we crossed the weed field on the edge of the cliff in single file. Then into the forest. Halfway back to the train Jennings, walking ahead of me, said, "The Mayor ain't going to like this one little bit."

Chapter Nine

Jennings was right. The Mayor didn't like it. He went north himself to inspect the damage, and when he returned to Jennings' home leading his little crew of assistants, he told us how much he didn't like it. "I've been to look, and the rails where those bombs hit are melted," he shouted, stretching the seams of a tight blue coat to pound on the dining table. Limping around the room, pausing to shout in the impassive faces of Lee and Jennings, waving his fists overhead as he cursed the Japanese . . . oh, he was in a state all right. I stayed behind Tom and took care to keep quiet. "Puddles of iron! And the dirt around it like black brick. Trees burnt to a crisp." He stumped over to Lee and waved a finger in Lee's face. "You men must have left some sign that you were working on those tracks, something that could be seen in the satellite pictures. I hold you responsible for that."

Lee stood with his mouth clamped tight, staring angrily past the Mayor. Behind that I noticed that a couple of the Mayor's men (Ben for one) looked pleased at Lee's chastisement, and gave each other sneering glances. Jennings, bold in his own home, stepped up to protest.

"Most of that line goes through forest, Mayor, and it's under trees so it can't be seen from above. You saw that. In the open patches we didn't touch a thing, even if we had to work the cars through brush. And the bridges look exactly like they did before. Not a thing had been changed except the track, and we *had* to change that to make it passable. There was nothing that could be seen from above, I swear."

Jennings went on spouting lies and contradictions like that for a while, and when he had convinced the Mayor of his point, the Mayor got even angrier. "Spies," he hissed. "Someone in Onofre must have told the scavengers in Orange County, and they told the Japs." He tested the strength of Jennings' table again, *wham*. "We can't have that. That sort of thing *has to be stopped.*"

"How do you know the spies aren't here in San Diego?" Tom asked.

Danforth and Ben and the rest of the Mayor's men glared at Tom. Even Jennings and Lee looked shocked.

"There are no spies in San Diego," Danforth said, his chin tucked into his neck. His voice made me feel like I did when the brake was pulled on the train. "Jennings, you get hold of Thompson and have him sail you and Lee and these two up the coast. Get off at Onofre with them, and hike back down the tracks and survey the damage. I want to know how long it's going to take to get that route open again."

"Melted track will be hard," Jennings replied. "We'll have to replace it like we did on the Salton Sea line, and it'll be impossible to do without leaving signs. Maybe we could follow three ninety-five up to Riverside, then turn back to the coast—"

Wham. "I want the coastal tracks working. You get Thompson and do as I tell you."

"Yes, sir."

Soon after that the Mayor and his men left the house, without any kind of farewell to Tom and me. Jennings sighed, and made an apologetic face at his wife, who was in the entrance to the kitchen looking discouraged. "Lee, I wish *you'd* talk back to him sometimes. He just gets madder when you don't answer like that." But Lee was still angry, and he said no more to Jennings than he had to Danforth. Tom jerked his head and

I followed him out of the room. "Looks like it's back by the sea," he said with a shrug.

The next day a heavy wall of clouds moved onshore. Jennings and Lee had already made the arrangements with Thompson, so quickly we got our bags filled and said goodbye to Mrs. Jennings. We pumped our handcar over steep hills back to the coast, and north to the Del Mar River. From the bluff bordering the south side of the marsh we could see the hundred wandering streams that the river made through the grass and cattails, iron streams through solid green. The main channel of the river snaked back on itself in big S's, and came very close to a narrow plateau of ground beneath the bluff we were on. There against the bank, curving with it, was a long wooden dock against which were moored several sailboats, and a number of rowboats. We began to roll faster down the tracks, which led us all the way to the sea beach before making a half-circle and coming back to the dock. Even so the incline was steep, and we flew down the rails and made the turn above the beach with a wicked screech, like we were strangling a thousand gulls at once. Then it was down a gentler incline to the dockside, where Lee brought the car to a scratching halt.

For a moment the setting sun poked through the black wall of cloud, and sent a pencil of light up the marsh, brightening the gloom of the dusk. In the muted green light I saw a couple of men working on a big sloop moored at the downstream end of the dock, attaching a jib to the bowsprit halyard. The sloop was a long one, nearly thirty feet I reckoned, wide-beamed and shallow-keeled, with canvas decking before the mast, and open plank seats aft of it. As we walked onto the dock a whiff of fish in the general salt smell reminded me of home in a powerful way. The clouds came together again, and we were back in the murk.

"Looks like we'll be sailing in a storm," I observed, for the wind was picking up, and the clouds clearly held rain.

"That's the way we want it," said Jennings.

"Too much of a storm and we'd be in trouble."

"Maybe. But we've got anchorages up the coast, and Thompson has done this a thousand times. In fact it should be easier than usual, with no Jap landing parties to intercept. You'll be home almost as fast as if we'd gone by train. Well not really, but once we had a strong wind from the south on the way up, and from the north on the way—"

"Let's be under way," a man hallooed from the sloop. "Tide's turning!"

Jennings introduced us to the speaker, who turned out to be Thompson, and to his two sailors, Handy and Gilmour. We stepped down into the sloop. Tom and I sat on the plank just aft of the box stepping the mast, and leaned back against the box's cross supports—struts that extended to each gunwale, and also held up the back end of the canvas decking. We stowed our bags under the canvas, while Jennings and Lee sat down on the plank aft of ours. The two sailors lifted short oars from the bottom of the boat and fitted them in oarlocks. The men on the dock unmoored us and pushed us into the stream. The sailors rowed lazily, keeping us pointed downstream and letting the current do the work. A dinghy tied to the stern of the sloop weaved behind us, pushed this way and that by the stream. We looped through the marsh; grass grew half as tall as the mast on either bank, and scores of bobbing ducks paddled into the reeds as we passed. After passing a mound of concrete wreckage we made a final bend to the left, where the river poured over a shallow break in the beach, beside the bluff on the north side of the marsh. We spilled over this bar and the rowers pulled like madmen to get us through the violent soup, and over some big waves. When we were outside the break they shipped the oars, and pulled up the two sails. Jennings shifted to the windward side so he wouldn't be sitting under the boom. Thompson trimmed the sails from his seat at the tiller in the stern, and we heeled over and sailed up the coast, paralleling the swells so that we rolled heavily. The wind was from the southwest, so we clipped along at a very good speed.

We stayed about a mile offshore, and before darkness fell we had a fine view of the beach cliffs, and the forested hills rising behind them. But soon the sun must have set, for the murk turned to night darkness, and the black bulk of the land was scarcely visible under the edge of the clouds. Over the hissing of our wake and the creaks of the boom rubbing the mast, Jennings told Thompson and Handy and Gilmour the story of how we had seen the bombing of the railroad tracks. Tom and I sat against the mast, huddled in every stitch of clothing we had with us. The swells riding under us smoked a little, and the clouds got lower and lower, till we sailed through a narrow layer of clear windy air, sandwiched between thick slices of water and cloud. Tom dozed from time to time, head lolling on the foredeck.

After a couple hours I stretched out on a pile of rope between two planks, and tried to imitate Tom and get some sleep. But I couldn't. I lay on my back and watched the gray sail, almost the color of the clouds above it, suck and fill in an unpredictable way. I listened to the voices of Jennings and the others in the stern, without making out half of what they said. I shut my eyes, and thought about things we had seen on our journey south: the Mayor pounding Jennings' table till the salt shaker bounced, the dial and gauge-filled front of the broken radio in the Mayor's house, the face of the pretty girl I had danced with. We were in a new world now, I thought. We were in a world where Americans could freely pursue their destiny, or fight for it when they were opposed . . . a world altogether different from our little valley's world, with its ignorance of anything beyond the swap meets. Nicolin would be ecstatic to hear of it, and to read the book Wentworth had given us—to learn how an American had traveled all over the world . . . to join the resistance with the rest of the valley, and fight our hidden enemies on Catalina. . . . Oh, I'd have news for the gang, all right, and tales to tell that would make their eyes bug out like frogs'. How would I describe the Mayor's island house, so unlike anything known in Onofre? . . . All those electric lights, reflected in that black lake with all its ruined towers . . .

I must have succeeded in falling asleep for a while, because when I opened my eyes again we were sailing in fog. Not a complete white out, but the sort of fog that is dense in patches and clear in others. Sometimes there was clear air for a man's height above the water, and then a solid white ceiling of cloud; other times the cloud came right down and mixed with the smoking surface of the water. I stuck my hand over the side, and found that the water was considerably warmer than the air. I burrowed my cold feet into the pile of rope I'd been lying on. Tom still sat beside me, awake now, looking off to starboard.

"How do they know where we are?" I asked, sucking salt off my chilled fingers.

"Jennings says that Thompson stays close enough to shore to hear the waves break." I cocked an ear landward and heard a faint crack and rumble.

"Big swell."

"Yeah. He says the sound changes when we pass a river-mouth, and Thompson knows which rivermouth is which."

"He must come up this way a lot to be able to do that."

"True."

"Let's hope he doesn't lose track and run us onto the Pulgas River delta."

"We're past that, he says. I believe we're ten or fifteen miles down from Onofre."

So I had slept a long time, which was a blessing, as it meant I had missed a few hours of being cold. The men aft were still talking quietly among themselves, all of them awake and leaning back against the gunwales, their coats buttoned up and their necks wrapped in wool scarves. We sailed into a white patch, and Thompson, alert at the tiller, steered us seaward so that we slapped over the swells as we gained leeway. I couldn't fall asleep again, and for a long time everything remained the same: the fog, the hiss of the swells sliding under the boat, the creaking of the boom, the cold. The wind blew in fits and starts, and I could hear Thompson and Lee discussing the possibility of running in to one of the rivermouths and spending the coming day there. "Hard to do," Thompson said in an unconcerned way. "Damned hard to do with this fog, and the wind dying down. And the swell is picking up, whoah, see what I mean? These'll make pretty damn big waves, I'd say." The mast creaked as if in agreement, and the way the steep and smoking swells lifted and dropped, lifted and dropped, without us ever being able to properly see them, made them seem especially big. Swell after swell lifted the boat and slid away from it, and the rhythm of it almost had me asleep again, when Tom sat up suddenly.

"What's that noise?" he said sharply.

I didn't hear anything unusual, but Thompson opened his mouth to hear better, and nodded. "Japanese cruiser. Getting closer."

Long moments passed while the rest of us heard the low muffled grumble of an engine. Thompson put the tiller over—

A curling white wave washed over the bow and stopped us dead. The mainsail flapped and then backed. Foaming water dripped over the canvas decking into my lap; Tom snatched up his shoulder bag to keep it from getting soaked. A cone of white light appeared in the fog. Our boat rocked at the bottom of this blinding cone, and one edge of the lit fog revealed the bulk of a tall ship, a black shape rumbling beside us, hardly seeming to move with the swell. My heart raced as I took all this in, standing up; I braced myself against Tom, looking at him fearfully. We were caught!

"Radar," Tom whispered.

"Put down your sail," a voice shouted. *"Everyone stand with hands on head."* The voice was mechanically amplified (as I learned later) and it had a metallic ring to it that made me cringe with fear. *"You are under arrest."*

I looked aft. Lee, all glare and black shadow in the searchlight's powerful whiteness, was aiming a rifle at the top of the cone. *Crack!* The light above us burst and went dark in a tinkling of glass. Immediately the stern of our boat was spitting fire, for every man back there was shooting up at the Japanese ship. Tom pulled me down, the gunfire was a continuous banging, overwhelmed by a great BOOM, and suddenly the front of the sloop was gone. Broken planks and cold seawater poured up the boat over us. "Help!" I cried, freeing my feet from the tangle of rope. I was making my way over the canted gunwale when the mast fell on me.

After that, I don't remember much. Searchlights breaking inside my eyelids. Choking on brine. Confused shouts, rough hands pulling me and hurting my armpits. Being hauled up metal steps and bumping my knees painfully. Choking and gasping, vomiting water. A metal deck, a coarse dry blanket.

I was on the Japanese ship.

When I realized this—it was the first thought I had, as I regained consciousness and saw the studded gray metal decking under my nose—I struggled to escape the hands holding me. Nothing doing. Hands restrained me, voices spoke nonsense at me: *mishi kawa tonatu ka,* and the like, on and on. "Help!" I cried. But my head was clearing, and I knew there was no help for me there. The suddenness of it all kept me from feeling it properly. I shivered and choked as if I'd been walloped in the stomach, but the real extent of the disaster was just sinking in as the Japanese sailors began to strip my wet clothes from me and wrap me in blankets. One was pulling my shirt sleeve down my arm; I twisted my hand out of it and fisted him in the nose. He squawked with surprise. I took a good swing and caught another one on the side of the head, and then started kicking wildly. I got some of them pretty good. They ganged up on me and carried me through a doorway into a glass-walled room at the back of the bow deck. Put me down on a bench that followed the curve of the hull. I sat back against the hull and cried.

Up in the bow I could see sailors still searching the water, shining a new searchlight this way and that, and shouting into an amplifying box. Two of them stood behind a giant gun on a thick stand—no doubt the gun that had demolished our sloop. The ship vibrated with the hum of engines, but we drifted over the swells, going nowhere. At our height above the water the fog was impenetrable. They had little motor dinghies down there searching, puttering about in the murk, but I could tell by their voices that they weren't finding anything.

They had killed my old friend Tom. The thought made me cry, and once I started I sobbed and sobbed. All those years he had survived everything, every danger imaginable—only to get drowned by a miserable shore patrol. And all so fast.

After what seemed a long time, the men searching the water were ready to quit. I had pretty well recovered my wits, and some of my warmth, for the blankets were thick. I felt cold inside, though, cold in my heart. I was going to make these men pay for killing Tom. Tom hadn't seemed too sure about the American resistance, but I was definitely part of it now, I thought to myself—starting right then and there, and for the rest of my life. In my cold heart I made a vow.

A door in the back wall of the glassed in room opened, and through it walked the captain of the ship. Maybe he was the captain and maybe he wasn't, but there were gold tags on the shoulders of his new brown coat, and the coat had gold buttons. So I'm going to call him the captain, because it's certain he was important. His face and hands were a shade darker than the coat, and his face looked like the faces of the bodies that washed up on our beach. Japanese, I had learned to call him. Two more officers, wearing brown suits without the gold shoulder tags or the buttons, stood behind him, their faces like masks.

Murderers, all of them. I stared fiercely at the captain, and he looked back, his eyes expressionless behind hanging upper eyelids. The room pitched gently, and fog pressed against the dripping salt-encrusted windows, fog that looked red because of the little red light set over the door.

"How do you feel?" the captain said in English that was clear, but lilting in a way I'd never heard before.

I stared at him.

"Have you recovered from the blow to your head?"

I stared at him some more.

After a time he nodded. I've seen his face more than once since then, in dreams: his eyes dark brown, almost black; deep lines in his skin, extending from the outside corners of his eyes in fans around the side of his head; black hair cut so close to his scalp that it had the texture of a brush. His lips were thin and brown, and now they were turned down with displeasure. He looked devilish, taken all together, and I struggled to look unconcerned as I stared at him, because he scared me.

"You appear to have recovered." One of his officers gave him a thin board, to which sheets of paper were clipped. He took a pencil from the clip. "Tell me, young sir, what is your name?"

"Henry. Henry Aaron Fletcher."

"Where do you come from?"

"America," I said, and glared at each of them in turn. "The United States of America."

The captain glanced at his officers. "Good show," he said to me.

A gang of regular sailors in blue coats came in from the bow and jabbered at him. He sent them back to the bow, and turned to me again.

"Do you come from San Diego? San Clemente? Newport Beach?" I didn't answer, and he continued: "San Pedro? Santa Barbara?"

"That's way north," I said scornfully. Shouldn't have spoken, I thought. But I wanted to tear into him so bad I was shaking—shaking with fright, too—and I couldn't help talking.

"So it is. But there is no habitation directly onshore, so you must come from north or south."

"How do you know there isn't a habitation onshore?"

He smiled just like we do, though the results were ugly. "We have observed your coastline."

"Spies," I said. "Sneaking spies. You should be ashamed. You're a sailor, mister. Don't you feel ashamed for attacking unarmed sailors on a foggy night and killing them all—sailors who weren't doing you any harm?" I had to be careful or I would start crying again. I was mighty close as it was, but I held to my anger.

The captain pursed his lips as if he'd bitten into something sour. "You were hardly unarmed. We took quite a few shots from you, and one of our men was hurt."

"Good."

"Not good." He shook his head. "Besides—I suspect your companions may have swimmed to shore. Otherwise we would have found them."

I thought of the dinghy we had been pulling, and thought a prayer.

"I must have an answer, please. You come from San Diego?"

I shook my head. "Newport Beach."

"Ah." He wrote on his paper. "But you were returning from San Diego?"

As long as I lied, it was okay to tell him things. "We were on our way to San Clemente and missed it in the fog."

"Missed San Clemente? Come now, we are several miles south of that town."

"I told you, we missed it."

"But you had been headed north for some time."

"We knew we had gone too far, and we were headed back. It's hard to tell where you are in the fog."

"In that case, why were you at sea?"

"Why do you think?"

"Ah—to avoid our patrols, you mean. Yet we don't interfere with coastal traffic. What was your business in San Clemente?"

I thought fast, looking down so the captain wouldn't see me doing it. "Well . . . we were taking some Japanese down there to hike in and look at the old mission."

"Japanese don't land on the mainland," the captain said sharply.

So I had startled him! "Of course they do," I said. "You say that because it's your job to see that they don't. But they do it all the time, and you know it."

He stared at me, then conferred with his officers in Japanese. For the first time I took notice of that fact that I was hearing someone talk in a foreign tongue. It was peculiar. It sounded like they were repeating four or five sounds over and over again, too fast to actually be saying anything. But obviously they were, for the officers gestured and nodded agreement, the captain gave orders, all in a rapid gibberish. More than their skin or their eyelids, their meaningless speech brought it to me

that I was dealing with men from the other side of the world—
men a lot different from me than the San Diegans had been.
The idea scared me, and when the captain turned and spoke to
me in English it sounded unreal, as if he were just making
sounds he didn't understand.

Scribbling on the page clipped to the board, he said, "How
old are you?"

"I don't know. My pa can't remember."

"Your mother can't remember?"

"My father."

This struck him as odd, I could see. "No one else knows?"

"Tom guesses I'm sixteen or seventeen." Tom . . .

"How many people were on your boat?"

"Ten."

"How many people live in your community?"

"Sixty."

"Sixty people in Newport Beach?" he said, surprised.

"Hundred and sixty, I mean." I was getting tangled in my
lies.

"How many people live in your house or dwelling?"

"Ten."

His nose wrinkled, and he lowered the board. "Can you
describe the Japanese you met in Newport Beach?"

"They looked just like you," I said truculently.

He pursed his lips. "And they were with you tonight on
the boat we sank?"

"That's right. And they came over here on a ship as big as
this one, so why didn't you stop *them?* Isn't that your job?"

He waved a hand impatiently. "Not all landings can be
stopped."

"Especially when you're paid not to try, eh?"

He pursed his lips again into that bad-taste look.

Shaking more and more, I cried, "You say you're here to guard
the coast, but all you really do is bomb our tracks and kill us when
we're just sailing—when we're just sailing home—" and all of
a sudden I was crying again, bawling and crying. I couldn't help
it. I was cold, and Tom was dead, and my head hurt something
fierce, and I couldn't stand up to this stranger and his questions
any longer.

"Your head is still painful?" I was holding my head between
my arms. "Here, stretch out on this bench and rest. We need
to get you to hospital." His hands took me by the shoulders,

and helped me lie out against the curving metal of the ship's tall gunwale. The officers lifted my legs up and wrapped them in the blankets, moving the clipboard from where the captain had put it down. I was too dispirited to kick them. The captain's hands were small and strong; they reminded me of Carmen Eggloff's hands, strangely enough, and I was about to burst into sobs again, when I noticed the ring on the captain's left ring finger. It was a big darkened gold ring that held a cut red jewel in the top of it. Letters were carved into the gold around the jewel, curving around the stone so they were hard to read. But the hand wearing the ring stilled for a moment right before my nose, and I could make out the words. *Anaheim High School 1976.*

I jerked back and bumped my head against the gunwale. "Be peaceful, young sir. Don't agitate yourself. We'll talk further of these things in Avalon."

He was wearing an American ring. A class ring, like those many of the scavengers wore during the evenings at the swap meets, to show which of the ruins they came from. I quivered in the scratchy blankets as I thought about what that meant. If the captain of the ship assigned to keep foreigners from coming to our coast was himself visiting Orange County—visiting it regularly, and wearing a ring that a scavenger must have given him—then no one was guarding the coast in earnest. It was all a sham, this quarantine—a sham that had gotten Tom killed. Tears pooled in my eyes, and I squeezed them back, furious at the injustice, the corruption of it—furious and confused. It was all happening too fast. It seemed just moments ago I had been dozing, eyes shut, in the San Diegans' sloop. And now—what had he said?—"We'll talk further of these things *in Avalon.*"

I sat up. They were taking me to Catalina to be questioned. Tortured, maybe. Thrown in prison, or made a slave—kept away from Onofre for the rest of my life. The more I thought of it the more frightened I became. Up to that point I hadn't stopped to think what they were going to do with me—I was confused, and that's a fact—but now it was obvious I should have; they weren't going to take me up the Onofre river and drop me off. No sir. They were going to take me with them. The idea made my heart thump so hard I thought my ribs would bust, they hurt so much. Blood pushed through me like water crashing down creekbeds after a downpour; I could feel my hands swelling with it. Even my feet got warm, and my breathing was so quick and choppy I thought I might faint. Catalina! I was terrified of going to Catalina—I would never see home again! Though it was selfish of me (and the rest of my story will tell you how selfish I have been, time and time again), I felt worse about that than I had about Tom's death.

The captain and his officers stood under the little red light over the door in the back wall. Salt crusts marred the dim red reflections of them in the big windows. The reflection of the captain's face was looking at me, which meant, I decided, he was watching my reflection. He was keeping an eye on me.

Out on the bow deck a couple of sailors still stood by the searchlight. It looked like they were fixing it. Otherwise, the deck was empty. Fog swept over us, cold and white. The sea was invisible, but by the sound I judged that we were fifteen or twenty feet off the water. The ship vibrated ever so slightly, but we still hadn't gone anywhere.

They had taken every stitch of clothing off of me, to get me dry. All the better.

The captain walked back to me. "Are you feeling better?"

"Yes. I'm getting sleepy, though."

"Ah. We will take you into one of the berths."

"No! Not yet. I'd be sick if I had to move. I just want to rest here a minute more." I slumped down and did my best to look exhausted.

The captain watched me. "You said something about tracks being bombed?"

"Who, me? I never said anything about tracks."

He nodded doubtfully.

"Why do you do it?" I asked despite myself. "Why do you come halfway around the world to patrol here?"

"We have been given the responsibility by the United Nations. I don't believe you would understand all the details of the matter."

So it was true, what they had told us in San Diego. Part of it, anyway. "I know about the United Nations," I said. "But there isn't a person from America there to tell our side. Everything they do is illegal." I spoke drowsily, to put him off his guard. I shouldn't have spoken at all, but my curiosity got the better of me.

"They're all we've got, young sir. Without them, perhaps war and devastation would come to us all."

"So you hurt us to help yourselves."

"Perhaps." He stared at me, as if surprised I could argue at all. "But it may be that it is the best policy for you as well."

"It isn't. I live there. I know. You are holding us back."

He nodded briefly. "But from what? That is the part that you have not experienced, my brave young friend."

I feigned sleep, and he walked back to his officers under the red light. He said something to them and they laughed.

Up and down the room pitched, up and down, up and down, smooth and gentle. I jumped out of the blankets and ran toward the open doorway to the bow. The captain had been watching for me to make such a move: "Ha!" he yelled, leaping after me. But he had miscalculated. I just caught the astonished look on his face as I flashed out the door ahead of him—I was too fast for him. Once outside I raced for the gunwale, and dove past the startled sailors into the fog.

Chapter Ten

After a long fall my arms and face smacked the sea, and my body walloped them home. When I felt the water's chill I thought *Oh, no,* sure I had made a serious mistake. The air had been knocked out of me, and ten feet under I had to breathe something awful. When I popped back to the surface to suck in air a swelltop rolled over me and I breathed water instead. I was certain my hacking and gasping would give me away to the Japanese, who shouted after me. Undoubtedly they were lowering boats to search for me. The water was freezing, it made my whole body cry out for air.

I struck out swimming away from the shouts and the dim glow of the searchlight, and was rammed by an approaching swell. Damned if I hadn't jumped off the seaward side of the ship. I would have to swim around it. And I had been sure I was leaping off the landward side. How had I gotten so turned around? My confidence in my sense of direction disappeared, and for a minute I panicked, afraid I wouldn't be able to find my way to shore. I sure wasn't going to see it. But the swell was a reliable guide, as I quickly realized when it shoved me time after time in the same direction. It was coming a bit out of the south, I had noted in the sloop, and I only had to swim in with it, maybe angling a bit to the right as it propelled me, and I would be on the straightest course to shore.

So that was all right. But the cold shocked me. The water might still have been from that warm current we had enjoyed the previous week, but now, with the storm wind whipping across the surface and chilling my head and arms, it didn't feel warm in any way. Already the cold ate into me, and I almost shouted to the Japanese to come to my rescue. But I didn't do it. I didn't want to face the captain again. I could imagine his face as I explained, yes, sir, I *did* want to escape, but, you see, the water was too cold. It wouldn't do. If they were to haul me out, that was fine—part of me hoped they would, and soon, too. But if they didn't, I was stuck with it.

To combat the cold I swam as hard as I could, trusting that I was around the bow of the ship and putting distance between us. It would be a nasty shock to clang into its hull unexpectedly, and it still seemed possible, because in the fog I couldn't see ten feet. As swell after swell passed under me, however, it became less likely. Too bad, part of me thought. You're in for it now. The rest of me got down to the business of getting to shore, the sooner the better. I settled into a rhythm and began working.

Only once did I see or hear the ship again, and it was soon after I had made the final decision to swim for it. Usually the fog does not convey sound better than the open air, no matter what some folks will have you believe. It tends to dampen sound as it limits sight, though not as drastically. But it is funny stuff, and sometimes, caught fishing by a fog bank, Steve and I have heard the voices of other fishermen talking in low tones and sounding as if they were about to collide with us, when they were half a mile away. Tom could never explain it, nor Rafael neither.

It happened again on this night. After a while on my own I was frightened by Japanese voices chattering at each other. The voices were behind me, and far enough above me that I guessed they came from the ship. I groaned, thinking that I had been confused in my swimming, and that I was still in the vicinity of the ship; but then a cold swirl of wind caught their voices midsentence, and blew them away for good. It was just me and the fog and the ocean, and the cold.

I only know three ways to swim. Or call it four. Crawl, backstroke, sidestroke, and a frog kick. Crawl was the fastest by far, and did the most to keep me warm, so I put my face in the brine—which scared me somehow, but keeping my head up was too tiring—and swam for it. I could feel the swells pick me up feet first, give a welcome shove, and pass under, leaving me floundering in the trough. Other than that, all I felt was the wind cutting into my arms as I stroked. The cutting got so bad that I switched to the frog kick just to keep my arms under water. The water was still cold, but I had gotten used to it a little, and it was better than my wet arms in the wind. Working hard was the best solution, so after a few frog strokes I went back to the crawl and swam hard. When I got tired or my arms got too cold, I switched to frog kick or sidestroke, and let kicking and the swell carry me along. It was a matter of shifting the discomforts from spot to spot, and then bearing them for as long as I could.

The thing about swimming is it leaves you a lot of time to think. In fact there is little to do but think, unlike when hiking through the woods, for instance, when there are rocks to look out for, and the path of least effort to be found. In the sea all paths are the same, and at night in the fog there's not much to look at. This is what I could see: the black swells rising and sinking under me; the white fog, which was becoming low clouds again as the wind unfortunately picked up; and my own body. And even these things were only visible when I had my head up and my eyes open, which wasn't very often. So I had nothing to do but worry about my swimming. Mostly I swam with my head in the brine and my eyes closed, feeling my muscles tire and my joints ache with cold, and though my thoughts raced wildly they never got too far from this vital *feeling*, which determined the stroke I used from moment to moment.

Kicking hard on my back warmed my feet some, and they needed it. I could barely feel them. But kicking was slow, and effortful too. I sure wished I had a pair of Tom's fins at that moment, the ones he lent us to body surf with. I loved those fins—old blue or green or black things that made us walk like ducks and swim like dolphins. What I wouldn't have done for a pair of them right then and there! It almost made me cry to think of them. And once they occurred to me I couldn't get them out of my mind. Now to my little assortment of thoughts was added, if only I had those fins. If *only* I had them.

I flopped back on my stomach and started the crawl again. The backs of my upper arms were getting stiff and sore. I wondered how long I had been at it, and how much longer I had to go. I tried to calculate the distance. Say the ship had been a mile offshore. That would be about half the length of our valley's beach. If I had started swimming at Basilone Hill, then by this time I'd be about to . . . well, I couldn't say. There was no way to tell. I was sure I had swum a good distance, though, from the way my arms hurt.

Stroke, stroke, stroke, stroke, stroke. Sometimes it was easy to blank the mind and just swim. I changed strokes at the count of a hundred; hundred after hundred slipped by. A lot of time passed. When I did the frog kick I noticed that the fog was lifting, becoming the low cloud bank that had rushed overhead when we were sailing north in the sloop. Perhaps that meant I was getting close to land. The clouds were very white against the black sea; probably the moon was now up. The surface of the water was a rolling obsidian plain. Swirling into it were little flurries of snow, flying forward over me as much as they were falling. When they hit the water they disappeared instantly, without a splash. The sight of them made me feel the cold more than ever, and again I almost started to cry, but couldn't spare the effort. I was crying miserable, though. If only I had those fins.

I put my head down and doggedly crawled along, ordering myself to think of something besides the cold. All the times I had looked out over a peaceful warm sea, for instance. I recalled a time when Steve and Tom and I were lazing up at Tom's place, looking for Catalina. "I wonder what it would look like if the water was gone," Steve had said. Tom had jumped on the notion with glee. "Why, we'd think we were on a giant mountain. Offshore here would be a plain tilted away from us, cut by canyons so deep we wouldn't be able to see the bottom of them. Then the plain would drop away so steeply we wouldn't be able to see the lowlands beyond. That's the continental shelf I've told you about. The lowland would rise again to foothills around Catalina and San Clemente islands, which would be big mountains like ours." On he had rambled, pulling up imaginary hipboots to lead us on an exploration of the new land, through mud and muck that was covered with clumps of seaweed and surprised-looking fish, in search of wrecked ships and their open treasure chests. . . .

It was the wrong time to remember that discussion. When I thought of how much water was underneath me, how far away the bottom was, I got scared and pulled my feet closer to the surface. All those fish, too—the ocean was teeming with fish, as I well knew, and some of them had sharp teeth and voracious appetites. And none of them went to bed at night. One of those ugly ones with its mouth crammed with teeth could swim up and bite me that very moment! Or I might blunder into a whole school of them, and feel their slick finny bodies colliding with mine—the sandy leather of a shark, or the spikes of a scorpion fish. . . . But worse than the fish was just being out there at all, with *all* that water below, down and down and colder and darker, all the way to the slimy bottom so *far* below. I thrashed with panic for a while, terrified at the thought of where I was, of how deep the sea was.

But several rushes of panic passed, and I was still there floundering. There was nothing I could do to change things. And more and more as time passed the real danger, the cold, reasserted itself and made me forget my fears of the imagination. It couldn't be escaped, I couldn't swim hard enough now to ward it off, and the water felt icy, no longer any refuge from the snowy wind. The cold would kill me soon. I could feel that in my muscles. It was more frightening than the size of the sea by far.

My thoughts seemed to chill, becoming slothful and stupid. My arms hurt so I could barely move them. Backstroke was hard, crawl was hard, frog stroke was hard. Floating was hard. If only I had those fins. Such a long way to the bottom. My arms were as stiff and heavy as ironwood branches, and my stomach muscles wanted a rest. If they cramped I would drown. Yet I had no choice but to keep them tensed, and go on swimming. I put my numbed face in the water and plowed along in a painful crawl, trying to hurry.

There was a rhythm I could keep to if I could ignore the pain, and grimly I stuck to it. My sense of time left me. So did the notion of a destination. It was not so much a matter of getting somewhere, as it was avoiding death then and there. Left arm, right arm, breath; left arm, right arm, breath. And so on. Each motion a struggle against the cold. The few times I bothered to look up, nothing had changed: low white clouds, flakes of snow swirling ahead and disappearing into the sea with a faint *ssss, ssss, ssss*. I couldn't feel my hands and feet, and the cold moved up my limbs and made them less and less obedient to my commands. I was getting too cold to swim.

The time came when it seemed I would have to give up. All my fine stories for the gang were going to go to waste, told only to myself in a last rush of thought on the way to the distant bottom. A waste, but there it was. I couldn't swim any more. If only I had those fins. Still, each time I thought to myself, Hanker, this is it, time to sink—I found the energy to slap along a few strokes more. It felt like swimming in cold butter. I couldn't go on. Again I decided to give up, and again I found a few more kicks in me. I imagine that most of the people who drown at sea never do decide to give up; their bodies stop obeying, and make the decision for them.

On my back I could frog kick, and flap my arms at my sides. It was the only way left to me, so I kept at it, anxious to postpone the moment of letting go, though I knew it wasn't far away. The thought of it was terrifying, sickening. Like nothing else I'd ever felt. Being taken to Catalina was *nothing* compared to it, and now I knew for sure I had made a fatal mistake by jumping overboard. Swells swept up out of the dark, becoming visible as they lifted me. Maybe they could do the work for me, if I could stay afloat. I didn't want to die. I wasn't willing to quit. But I was too cold, too weak. On my back like I was, I had to work to avoid swallowing water when the crests of the swells passed over me, for one mouthful would have sunk me as fast as a hundred pounds of iron. Only dimly, at first, did I notice that the swells were getting taller. That's all I need, I thought. A bigger swell, how wonderful. Still— didn't that mean something? I was too cold, I wasn't thinking anymore in the way that we usually think, silently talking to ourselves. I had only the simplest sort of thoughts: sensations, a repeated refusal to sink, instructions to my feeble limbs.

Cold fingers brushed my back and legs, and I squealed.

Seaweed, slick and leafy. I struggled around the floating clump, granted a bit of strength by the scare. Then on top of a swell I heard it. *p-KKkkkkkkkk . . . p-KKkkkkkkkkk*. Waves breaking. I had made it.

Suddenly I had some energy. I couldn't believe I hadn't heard the sound of the waves before, it was so plain. At the crest of the next swell I looked landward, and sure enough there it was, a black mass big and solid under the clouds. "Yeah!" I said aloud. "Yeah!"

I ran into another clump of seaweed, but I didn't care. Disentangling myself from it I crested another swell, and from there the clear sound of the breaking waves told me my troubles weren't over. Even from behind, the long irregular *crack* of the waves falling was louder than the Mayor's shotgun had been. And following the crack was a low roaring *krrkrrkrrkrrkrrkrrkrrkrr*, that faded away just enough to make the next break noticeable. All the sounds joined together in a fierce trembling boom; it was hard to believe I hadn't heard it earlier. Too tired.

I swam on, and now at the crests of the swells I could see the waves breaking ahead of me. As each wave broke water sucked over the back of it like it was the edge of the world; white water exploded into the fog, and the whole churning mass tumbled in to the beach. There was going to be a problem getting to shore.

The swells kept pushing me in until one larger than the rest picked me up and carried me along with it, getting steeper and steeper as it went along. I was caught under the crest, and slowly it dawned on me that it was going to pitch over and throw me with it. I took a deep breath and plunged into the wave, felt it pulling me up as I struggled through the thick lip and out the back side. Even so I was almost taken over the back of the break, and into the churning soup. The next swell was nearly as big, and I had to swim as fast as I could to get over it before it broke. I breasted its top while it stood vertical, and looked back down at the foam-streaked water some fifteen feet below. Had that black area down there been rock? Was there a reef under me?

Whimpering miserably I swam out a good distance, so I wouldn't get caught inside by a wave bigger than the two that had almost drowned me. The idea of a reef was horrifying. I was too tired for such a thing, I wanted to swim straight in to the beach. It was so close. It was possible that what I had seen was a patch of black water in the foam, but I couldn't be sure, and if I was wrong I would pay for it with my life. I treaded water for a time and studied the waves as they broke and sucked water over behind them. The place where they consistently broke first marked the shallowest water, and if there were rocks they probably were there. So I swam parallel to the beach a

ways, to the spot where the waves consistently broke last. The
cold was in my thoughts again, and my fear grew. I decided
to start in.

I attended to the swells, because if a wave broke before it
reached me, it would roll me under and never let me up. No,
I needed to catch a wave and ride it in, just like we did for
fun in the waves off Onofre. If I caught one right, I might take
it all the way onto the sand. That was what I wanted. I needed
a big wave—not too big, though: medium big. Waves usually
came in sets of threes, a big one followed by two littler ones,
but floating over them in the dark I couldn't get any sense of
that. Looking back and forth I accidentally swallowed a mouthful of water, and it almost sent me to the bottom. I saw I
couldn't afford to be picky, and I struck out backstroking,
determined to catch the very next wave. If I ran into rocks that
would be it, but I didn't have a choice. I had to take the chance.

As a swell picked me up I suddenly didn't feel tired at all,
though I still couldn't swim well. I turned on my stomach as
the wave tilted my feet up, and swam for it. What I would
have given for a pair of Tom's fins, kicking as I was to match
the growing speed of the wave! But I caught it anyway, just,
and felt it pick me up and carry me along. I was high on the
steep face as it pitched over, so that I dropped through the air
and smacked my chest into the water. If it had been reef that
would have been the end of me, but it wasn't, and I skidded
over the water at the front edge of the broken wave, my head
alone out of the white water, barreling over the suds at a
tremendous speed.

The wave petered out too soon, however, and left me gasping in the soup. I stood and felt for the bottom—no bottom—
sank, and hit sand with my feet almost immediately. I pushed
back to the surface and saw another wave steaming in. Rolling
myself into a ball I let the wave tumble me shoreward—a
standard body surfing trick, but one inappropriate to my weakness. I barely struggled back to the surface when my forward
motion stopped. But now I could stand, heaving, on good
smooth sand! Walking cramped my legs and I collapsed. All
of the water that had been pushed onto the beach by the last
few waves chose that moment to sluice back down, and I knelt
and clawed the coarse flowing sand as the torrent rushed over
me. Then it was past, and I hobbled out of the water.

As soon as I got up the steep wash and beyond the high

water mark, I fell down. The beach was covered with a gritty layer of melting hail. My stomach muscles relaxed at last, and I started to throw up. I had swallowed more water than I knew, and it took a while to get it all out. I didn't mind. It was the most triumphant retching I ever did.

So I had made it. All well and good. But there was no chance to celebrate, because now there was a new set of problems. The snowing had stopped for a moment, but there was still a wind which cut me most distinctly. I crawled up the beach to the cliff backing it. Narrow beach, cliff three times my height—it could have been anywhere on the Pendleton shore. At the base of the cliff there was less wind, and I hunkered down behind a sandstone boulder, among other clumps of fallen cliff. I started wiping myself dry with my fingers, and while doing that looked around.

Out to sea moonlit clouds obscured the view. The beach stretched away in both directions, covered by black blobs of seaweed. I was beginning to shiver. One of the blobs of seaweed had a more regular shape than the rest. Standing up to look at it better I felt the onshore wind blow right through me. Still, that clump of weed—I stumbled around my boulder and walked toward it, being careful not to hurry and fall.

A break I had not noticed in the cliff was the mouth of a deep ravine, spilling its creek onto the beach to cut through the sand to the sea. I sat and slid down the sloping sand to the creek, stopping to drink some of its water—I was thirsty, strangely enough. When I stood again it was a struggle to make my way up the three foot embankment on the other side; I kept slipping, and finally, cursing and sniffling, I had to crawl up it and then stand.

Back on the plateau of the beach I could see the black blob clearly, and my suspicion was confirmed. It was a boat, pulled almost to the cliff. "Oh, yes," I said. Careful not to hurry, I thought, you'll fall. It was farther away than it looked, but at last I staggered to its side, and sat in the lee of it. Held the gunwale with my numb hands.

There were two oars in it and nothing else, so there was no way to be positive, but I was sure it was the dinghy we had been trailing behind our sloop. They had made it to shore! Tom was (most likely) alive!

I, on the other hand, was nearly dead. Presumably my companions were somewhere in the area—up the ravine was a good guess—but I couldn't follow them. I was too weak and cold to stand. In fact my head banged the dinghy's side while I was just sitting there. I knew I was in bad shape. I didn't want to die after taking the trouble to swim all that way, so I got to my knees. Too bad they hadn't left something in the boat besides the oars. Since they hadn't . . . I considered it at a snail's pace, as if very drunk. One thought per minute, as slow and stumbling as my walk down the beach. "Should get . . . out of . . . the wind . . . yeah." I crawled to a big clump of seaweed and pulled off the top layers. They were all tangled and didn't want to come. I got angry—"Stupid seaweed, let loose!"—blubbering like that until I got to the middle of the clump, which was still dry. Dryness felt like warmth. I pulled as many of the black leafy strands as I could carry out of the clump, and staggered back to the boat with them. Dropped the weed.

I pushed at the side of the dinghy. It might as well have been set in stone. I groaned. Pushing on the gunwale I could rock it a bit. "Turn over, boat." I was amazed and frightened by my lack of strength; normally I could have flipped that dinghy with one hand. Now it became the great struggle of my life to overturn the damn thing. I got out the oars, slid one under the keel, lifted the wide end, and balanced it on the handle end of the other one, which had its wide end jammed in the sand. That tilted the boat, and on the other side I stepped on the low gunwale and pulled at the high one, all at once and with all my might. The boat flipped and I had to fall away from it flat on my face to avoid being crushed.

I spit out sand and regained my feet. Carried a sandstone clod to the bow. Lifting the bow was not that hard, and I rolled the clod under it to keep it up. If I had had the sense to put the seaweed in the boat I would have been set, but at this point I wasn't thinking that far in advance. The seaweed just fit under the gap, and I stuffed it under, strand after strand, until all that I had dragged over with me was under the boat. Getting myself under was more difficult—I scraped my back, and finally pushed up with my head until the bow was lifted far enough to get my butt in.

Once under the boat I was tempted to just lie there, because I was beat. But I was still shivering like a dog, so I felt around in the blackness and pulled all the seaweed together. It made a pretty thick mat, and when I had crawled on it there was still a lot of weed left to pull over me, in a sort of blanket. I pulled the sandstone clod under the boat with me and was out of the wind, in a dry bed.

I started to shiver in a serious way. I shivered so hard my jaw hurt, and the seaweed around me cracked and rustled. Yet I didn't feel any warmer for it. Flurries of rain or slushy snow hit the bottom of the boat, and I was pleased with myself for being sheltered. But I couldn't stop shivering. I twisted around, put my hands in my armpits, gathered seaweed closer to me— anything to get warmer. It was a fight.

There passed one of those long hours that you seldom hear about when people are telling their tales—a cold, fearful time, spent entirely in the effort to warm up. It went on and on and on, and eventually I did warm a little. I was not toasty, you understand, but after the cold sea and the open windy beach my bed of dry seaweed under the boat felt pretty good. I wanted to stay there forever, just huddle up and fall asleep and never have to move again.

But another part of me knew I should locate Tom and the San Diegans before they got out of my reach. I figured they would be waiting out the night in some sort of shelter, like I was, and that they would take off in the morning. Pushing up the bow of the dinghy I saw a thin slice of the dawn: sand, broken cliff bottom, dark cloud. The darkest and most miserable day ever to dawn, without a doubt. The wind whistled over the boat, but I decided it was time to find them, before they took off and left me.

Getting out from under the boat was easier than slipping beneath it had been; I lifted the bow, setting the sandstone block under it, and slithered through the gap. Returning to the wind was a shock. All my precious warmth was blown away in an instant. In the dawn I could see down the beach much farther than before. It was bare and empty, a desolate gray reach. Moving the boat to one side exposed the seaweed, and I tied strands of it around me and looped them over my shoulders until I was fairly well covered by the crackly black leaves. It was better wind protection than I would have guessed, and far better than nothing at all.

The ravine had cut a V in the cliff almost to the level of the beach, so that I could walk right up it, in the streambed to avoid brush. I was beyond caring what might happen to my feet in the creekbed, and luckily the bottom was rounded stones.

A branch scratched my leg and I took my gaze from the sides of the ravine to watch what I was doing. After climbing a short waterfall I found myself among trees, and the brush became less dense. The ravine took a sharp bend to the right, then bent back again; after that the air was almost still. Overhead the treetops swayed and their needles whistled. Flurries of snow drifted among them, blurring their sharp black lines. I groaned at the sight and hiked on.

Taller waterfalls fell when the ravine got steeper, and to ascend them I had to put my head down to climb through mesquite, ignoring my skin's suffering and losing my seaweed coat strand by strand. I was so weak that when I came to the third of these tiny cliffs I cried. I didn't think I could make it up such a face. When I had reconciled myself to it I climbed on hands and knees, crawling right up the creek itself to avoid the brush to either side. That was stupid, maybe, because I started shivering again, but at that point I wasn't going to win any prizes for thinking. I'm not sure there was any other way to get up the cliff anyway. Near the top I slipped and fell right under the water—I almost drowned in a knee-deep creek, after surviving the deep sea. But I managed to pull my head out, and to make it up the cliff a bit later. Once on top I was almost too tired to walk. If only I had Tom's fins, I thought. When I realized what I had thought I choked out a laugh, and then started to cry. I waded the pool at the top of the little falls and continued on beside the stream, hunched over and trailing seaweed behind me, snuffling and crying, sure I was about to die of the cold.

That was the state I was in when I stumbled into their camp. I rounded a thicket and almost walked into the fire, blink-brilliant yellow among all the grays and blacks.

"Hey!" someone cried, and suddenly several men were on their feet. Lee had a hatchet cocked at his ear.

"Here you are," I said. "It's me."

"Henry!"

"Jesus—"

"What the hell—"

"*Henry!* Henry Fletcher, by God!" That was Tom's voice. I located him. Right in front of me.

"Tom," I said. Arms held me. "Glad to see you."

"You're glad to see *me?*" He was hugging me. Lee pulled

him away to get a wool coat around me. Tom laughed, a cracked joyous laugh. "Henry, Henry! Hank, boy, are you okay?"

"Cold."

Jennings was throwing wood on the fire, grinning and talking to me or someone else, I couldn't tell. Lee pulled Tom off me and adjusted the coat. The fire began to smoke, and I coughed and almost fell.

Lee took me under the arms and put me by the fire. The others stared at me. They had a little lean-to made of cut branches, floored with firewood. In front of it the fire blazed, big enough to burn damp wood.

"Henry—did you *swim* to shore?"

I nodded.

"Jesus, Henry, we rowed around out there for the longest time, but we never saw you! You must have swum right by us somehow."

I shook my head, but Lee said, "Shut up, now, and start rubbing his legs. This boy could die right here if we don't get him warm, can't you see how blue he is? And he can't talk. Lay him down here by the fire. He can tell us what happened later."

They laid me down at the open edge of the shelter, next to the fire. Pulled my seaweed from me and dried me with shirts. I was all sandy and I could tell the drying was scraping me, but I didn't feel it much. I was relieved, very relieved. I could relax at last. The fire felt like an opened oven. The heat struck me in pulses, wave after wave of it washing over me, slowly penetrating me. I'd never felt anything so wonderful. I held my hand just over some side flames, and Tom pulled it up a bit and held it there for me. Lee wrapped a thick wool blanket around my legs when they were fully dry.

"W-where'd you get all the c-clothes?" I managed to say.

"We had quite a bit of stuff in the dinghy," Jennings replied.

Tom put my arm back at my side and lifted the other one. "Boy, you don't know how happy I am to see you. Whoo!"

"No lie," Jennings said. "You should have seen him moaning. He sounded terrible."

"I felt terrible, I mean to tell you. But now I feel just fine. You have no *idea* how glad I am to see you, boy! I haven't been this happy in as long as I can remember."

"Too bad we missed you in the dark," Jennings said. "You

could have rowed in with the rest of us and saved a lot of trouble, I bet. We had lots of room." Thompson and the rest laughed hard at that.

"I got picked up by the Japanese," I said.

"What's this?" cried Jennings.

I told them as best I could about the captain and his questioning. "Then he said we were going to Catalina, so I jumped over the side."

"You jumped over the side?"

"Yes."

"And swam in?"

"Yes."

"Whoah! Did you see the dinghy on the beach?" "How did you get in with the swell breaking so high?"

I sorted the questions with difficulty. "Swam in. Saw the boat on the beach, and rested under it. I figured you must be up here." I looked at the men curiously. "How'd you get the boat in?"

Jennings took over, naturally. "When the sloop went down we all stepped in the dinghy, all except Lee who fell overboard. So we didn't even get wet. We rowed off a ways and pulled Lee out of the drink and waited for you. But we couldn't find you, and Thompson said he saw you go down under the mast. So we figured you'd drowned, and rowed ashore."

"How'd you get the boat in?" I asked again.

"Well, that was Thompson's doing. With all of us in that little boat we had about an inch clearance, so when he found where that little creek was pouring out and breaking the swell a bit, he booted Lee and me overboard, and we had to swim in. That was something, I tell you—although I guess you'd know. Anyway they caught one of the smaller waves and rode it right onto the beach. A nicer piece of seamanship you'll never see."

Thompson grinned. "Lucky we caught that wave right, actually."

"So except for Lee, and me at the end there, we didn't even get wet! But you, boy. That must have been one hell of a swim."

"Long way," I agreed. I lay on my side, curled so that all of me was equally close to the fire. I could feel the wool gathering all the heat and holding it around me, and I was happy—content to listen to the men's voices, without bothering any longer to decipher what they were saying.

Several times through that day Tom roused me to see if I was doing all right, and when I mumbled something he would let me go to sleep again. The first time I woke on my own, my right arm had gone to sleep, and I needed to shift on my bed of boughs. Shaking my arm awake I felt twinges all up and down it. Both arms were sore. I shifted onto an elbow and looked around. It was near dark. Wet snow was gusting down, filtering through the branches around us. The men were under the lean-to behind me, lying down or sitting on branches Lee had cut for the night's fire. Lee was scraping his hatchet's edge with a whetstone; he saw I was awake, and tossed another branch on the blaze. Thompson and his men were asleep. My back was cold. I rolled so it faced the fire, and felt the heat finger me. Tom and Jennings stared into the flames, looking morose.

Our camp was in a little bend in the creek, in a hollow created where a big tree had fallen and torn out its roots. Beside our lean-to the roots still poked at the sky, adding to our shelter. The trees around the fallen one were tall enough to stick above the ravine, and their tops bobbed and swayed. I turned to the fire and nestled down again. The stream gurgled, the fire snapped and hissed, the treetops hooted as loudly as their broken voices would let them. I fell asleep.

The next time I woke it was night. The snow appeared to have stopped. We got the fire roaring, and stood and stretched around it. The last loaf of bread was pulled out of Thompson's pack, and divided among the seven of us. Kathryn's bread never tasted any better than this damp stale stuff. Tom pulled some sticks of dried fish from his shoulder bag and passed them around, and Lee handed us each his cup after he had heated some water in it. Noticing Tom's bag when he reached in it I said, "Did you save those books Wentworth gave you?"

"Yes. They never even got wet."

"Good."

Over the ravine the wind was strengthening, and I could make out low clouds racing overhead. The San Diegans discussed their plans, dragging it out to pass the time. They got me to tell the story of my swim in detail. After that they went back to their considerations, and decided that unless the storm got worse or went away altogether, they would abandon the dinghy and hike down the rail line. They had food cached along the way, and seemed to feel there would be no trouble returning overland. Tom and I could come with them, or head north; Onofre, Lee assured us, was just a few miles away. Tom nodded at that. "We'll head home." Silence fell. Jennings asked me to describe the Japanese captain again, and I told them everything I could remember. When I mentioned the captain's ring the San Diegans were disgusted, and in a way pleased. It was another sign of corruption. Tom frowned, as if he didn't like me giving them any more signs like that. The San Diegans began to tell us tales of the life on Catalina. I was interested, but couldn't keep awake. I sat down and nodded off.

Despite the cold and wet, I slept for several hours. I came to about midnight, however, and quickly found I had slept my fill. I took a branch from beneath me and laid it on the fire. We had a good bed of coals by that time, and the branch caught fire almost immediately. By its light I could see the other men, lying back in the lean-to or on their sides across the fire from me. To my surprise, firelight glinted off their eyes. Except for Thompson and Jennings, every one of them was awake, waiting for day to arrive. My feet were cold, I was stiff and sore all over, and there wasn't a chance I was going to fall asleep again. I shifted and struck my feet on the edge of the coals. The hours passed ever so slowly—cramped, stiff, hungry, boring, miserable hours—another of those stretches that are skipped over when adventure tales are told, although if mine is any example, a good part of every adventure is spent in just such a way, waiting in great discomfort to be able to do something else. Lee tossed another branch on the fire beside mine, and we watched it give off steam until flames appeared and got a purchase on it.

A lot of branches turned to ash before the ghostly light of a storm dawn slowly created distances between all the black shapes in the ravine. It was snowing again, fitfully, snowing slush that melted as soon as it touched anything. I could see, looking at the whiskery lined faces of the men, that they were as stiff and cold and hungry as I was. Lee rose and went to cut some more firewood. The rest of the men stood up as well, and walked away to take a leak or stretch out sore muscles. When Lee came back, he threw the wood he had gathered on the coals, and cursed at the smoke. "We might as well get going," he croaked. "Weather isn't going to get any better for a good while, I don't believe. And I don't want to spend another day waiting it out."

Thompson and the sailors weren't so sure, I could tell. Jennings said to them, "When we get to Ten Post River there's a box of food and clothing. We can put up a shelter like this one here if we need to, and we'll have some food."

"How far away is that?" Thompson asked.

"Five miles, maybe."

"Pretty far in this weather."

"Yeah, but we can do it. And these two can be back up in Onofre by midday."

Thompson agreed to the plan, and without further ado we got ready to leave. Jennings laughed at my woeful face and gave me his underpants, thick white things that hung past my heels, and were still a trifle damp. "With these and that coat you should be okay."

"Thanks, Mr. Jennings."

"Say nothing of it. We're the ones who got you dumped in the drink. You've had a wild one, I'd say."

"It's not over yet," Tom said, looking up at the flying snow.

We hiked up the ravine until it was only a dip in the plain of the forest, and then stopped. Water dripped from the branches around us, and the wind swirled. Fearfully I felt the cold climb past my numb bare feet and up my legs; I'd had enough of that.

We said a hasty farewell to the San Diegans. "We'll be back to Onofre soon, so I can collect my clothes," Jennings told me.

"And the Mayor will want to hear from you," Lee said to Tom.

We promised to be ready for them, and after some awkward shuffling of the feet they were off through the trees. Tom and I turned and walked north. Soon we came upon the torn remains of a narrow asphalt road, and Tom declared we should follow it.

"Shouldn't we go up to the freeway?"

"Too exposed. The wind will be howling in the open stretches."

"I know, but there are open stretches here too. And it would be easier walking."

"Maybe so. Your feet, eh? But it's too cold up there. Besides, this road has a whole string of little cinderblock restrooms from when it was a beach park. We can stop in them if we have to, and I've got a couple of them stocked with wood."

"Okay."

The road was just patches of asphalt on the forest floor, broken pretty regularly by little ravines. We made slow going of it, and soon I couldn't feel my feet at all. Walking seemed exceptionally hard work. Tom kept on my windward side, and occasionally held me up with his right arm. I lost track of our surroundings until we came to a long stretch of treeless land, covered with waist-high brush that flailed in the wind. Here we could see far out to sea, and the wind struck us full force.

"Tom, I'm cold."

"I know. There's one of the old restrooms ahead; we'll stop there. See it?"

But when we got there we found that the opposite side of it was smashed, and the roof was gone. It was filling with slush.

"Damn," said Tom. "Must be the next one."

On we went. I couldn't seem to shiver. "Tengo sueño," I muttered. "Ten-go suen-yo." The cold: I know I've mentioned it many times here. But not enough to indicate its power, its deadly influence—the way it hurts even when you're numb, and the way that the pain saps your strength, and the way that a part of your mind stays awake, scared to death that other parts are as asleep as your fingers. . . .

"Henry!"

". . . What."

"Here comes the next one. Put your arm around me. Henry! Put your arm around me. Like so." He held me up, and we stumbled toward the next little block pile—the only building from the old time I had ever seen that was smaller than my home.

"That's it," Tom assured me. "We'll just pop in there and get warmed up, and then take off again. It can't blow this hard all day. We're not more than two miles from home, I'd guess, but this wind is too much. We got to take shelter."

The shrubs bounced against the ground again and again, and upslope the trees howled. Snow obscured the view to sea, it kept striking me in the eyes. We reached the block building, and Tom looked in the open doorway warily. "Oh good," he said. "This is the one. And no beasties in it either."

He pulled me inside, helped me sit down against one block wall. The doorway was on the inland side, so the wind shelter was complete. That in itself was a blessing. But in the corner across from me was a big pile of branches, wood long dead and perfectly dry. Tom leaped to the pile with cries of self-congratulation, and began shifting it into the doorway. When he had it all arranged to his satisfaction he dug around in his shoulder bag and pulled out a lighter. He snapped it; as if he had said a magic spell a tall flame stood off the end of it. Behind the little orange flame his face gleamed, a grin splitting it in two, showing his half-dozen remaining teeth. Water dripped down his pate into the complicated delta system of his wrinkles, his beard and hair were tangled, and his eyes were wide open so that the whites showed over the iris. His hand shook, and he laughed like an animal. He flicked the flame off and on twice, then crouched down and applied it to the smaller branches and twigs at the bottom of his pile. In hardly any time at all the whole pile was blazing. The air in the little room cooked. I held my feet in my hands, and shifted across the floor to put them closer to the flames. Tom saw me move on my own and he hopped around the fire cheerfully.

"Now if we had food we'd be set. A castle wouldn't beat it. My own *house* wouldn't beat it. Man, look at that wind. Tearing it up. But the snow seems to be stopping. When we get nice and warm we should probably make a quick run for home and get a meal, eh? Specially if it stops snowing."

From inside our tiny fortress the waterfall roar of the wind was loud. I got warm enough to start shivering again, and my feet pricked and burned. Tom put more wood on. "Whoo-eee! Look at that wind. Boy, this is it. This is *it,* you understand me?"

"Uh." I thought I did understand him, but this wasn't *it* for me. *It* was treading water at night outside a giant swell breaking, not knowing whether there are rocks between you and the shore. I'd had my fill of *its,* at least temporarily and maybe for good. I wanted nothing more to do with them.

We got warm enough to take off our clothes and scorch a little water out of them. Then Tom urged me to get ready to leave. "It ain't snowing, and the day won't last forever." I was ravenous so I agreed with him, though I was unhappy to leave our shelter. In what sounded like a lull in the wind we left our blockhouse and hurried along the asphalt road. The wind instantly cooled our clothes back down, as I knew it would, and I could feel how wet my coat and pants were. The clouds galloped overhead, but for the moment the snow had stopped.

"Snow in July," Tom muttered with a curse. He took the windward side again and matched me step for step. Both of us had our faces turned away from the wind. "This area never used to get snow. Never. Barely got rain. And the ocean temperature bouncing around like that. Crazy. Something severely screwed up with the world's weather, Hank, I tell you that with the utmost certainty. I wonder if we've kicked off another ice age. Boy, wouldn't that teach them? Sure would teach them, damn it. If they did it with the war, serves them right and amen to that. If we kicked it off before they got us, then that would be funny. Posthumous revenge, right Henry? Eh?" On and on he puffed with his nonsense, trying to distract me. "You learnt a passage once that fits our situation here, didn't you Hank? Didn't I assign you something like this? Tom's a-cold, boy you said it. Freezing! I never did learn it by memory myself. Blow, winds! Hail, hurricanoes! Something like that. Surely good casting, if I say so myself . . ." and so on, until the cold got to him too, and he put his head down and his arm around my waist and we trudged it out. It seemed to go on forever. Once I glanced up, and saw the sea as green as the forest, gray clouds massed over it, whitecaps breaking out everywhere on its surface, so that it was almost as white as it was green. Then I put my head down again.

Finally Tom said, "There's my house ridge up there. We've almost made it."

"Good."

Then we were back among trees, and crossing that ridge. Past Concrete Bay and up to the freeway. It was snowing again and we could hardly see any distance at all. Trees appeared like ghosts out of the falling slush. I wanted to hurry but my feet were gone again and I kept stumbling on things. If it weren't for the old man I would have fallen a dozen times.

"Let's go to my house," I said. "Can't climb to yours."

"Sure. Your pa will want to see you anyway."

Even the valley seemed to stretch out, and it took hard walking to cross it. We weaved past the big eucalyptus at the corner, up to my door. I've never been happier to see that shack in my life. White slush slid down the roof as we pounded the door and burst in like long lost voyagers. Pa had been asleep. Looking surprised he gave me a hug, tugged his moustache. "You look terrible," he said. "What happened to your clothes?" Tom and I laughed; we began to talk. I put my feet right on the stove and felt the skin scorch. Tom was talking fast as Jennings, and laughing every other sentence. I ransacked the shelves and threw Tom a half loaf of bread, saving a chunk for myself. "Got anything else?" Tom inquired, mouth full. Pa got out some jerky for us, and we wolfed it down. We ate every scrap of food in the place, and stoked up the fire in the stove higher than it had been since my ma died. Talking all the while. "I didn't know *what* I was going to tell you," Tom was saying. "He was gone for good!" Pa's eyes were wide. I took out the wash bucket and washed myself with a rag, getting all the sand out of my crotch and armpits. My feet burned something fierce. We both kept telling Pa our story, confusing him no end. Finally we both shut up at the same time.

"Sounds like you had a time," Pa said.

"Yes," Tom said, and cackled loudly, almost hysterical with relief. He jammed a last chunk of bread in his mouth, nodded, swallowed. "That was something."

Part Three

THE WORLD

Chapter Eleven

After Tom went home I slept like a dead man for the rest of the day and all that night. When I woke up the next morning I was annoyed to see that the storm was over. The sun streamed in the door like it had never left. Why, if we had held on one more day in our shelter, we could have waltzed home easy as you please! Pa heard me moan and he stopped sewing. "Want me to get the water this morning?"

"No, I'll do it. I'm sore is all." Actually my arms were blocks of wood, and my legs scissors, and I was unhappy to discover a host of scratches and scrapes and bruises that hurt practically every time I breathed. But I had an urge to get out and look around, so I got off the bed with more groans.

When I got outside and started down the path (buckets jerking my poor arms every step) the sunlight stung my eyes. There were still some clouds but mostly it was sunny, everything steaming. The Costas' drum house looked like it was on fire it was steaming so. I creaked down the path staring and staring.

Have I described the valley yet? It is in the shape of a cupped hand, and filled with trees. Down in the crease of the palm is the river winding to the sea, and the fields of corn and barley and potatoes. The heel of the hand is Basilone Hill, and up there is the Costas' place, and Addison's tower, and Rafael's rambling house and workshop. Across from that, the spiny forested fingers of Tom's ridge. All of the oldest houses were eccentric, I noticed; I had never thought of it that way before, but it was so. Rafael kept adding rooms to store machinery and things, and they followed the contour of the hillside, so that in time, if you were to try and draw a plan of it, it would look like an X written on top of a W. Doc Costa had made his house of oil drums, as I've said, to hold in the heat in the winter and the cool in the summer. Probably he hadn't counted on the house whistling like a banshee in the least little breeze; he said it didn't bother him any, but I thought it might be the reason Mando scared so easily. The Nicolins had their big old time house on the beach cliff, and the Eggloffs had their home burrowed back into the hillside where thumb and finger would meet, if you were still thinking of the valley as a cupped hand; they lived like weasels in there, and by the graveyard too, but they claimed to have Doc all beat as far as warmth in the winter and cool in the summer were concerned. And then there was Tom, up on his ridge where he was bound to get frozen by storms and baked by the sun, but did he care? Not him—he wanted to see. So did Addison Shanks, apparently, set up on Basilone Hill in a house built around an old electric tower; but maybe he was there because it was nice and close to San Clemente, where he could conduct his dealings with no one the wiser. The newer houses, now, were all down in the valley next to the fields, convenient to the river, and everybody had helped build them, so that they looked pretty much the same: square boxes, steel struts at the corners, old wood for walls, wood or sheet metal, maybe tiles, for a roof. The same design twice as long and you had the bathhouse.

When I got to the river I sat gingerly and continued to look around at it all. I couldn't get enough of it. It all looked so familiar and yet so strange. Before my trip south Onofre was just home, a natural place, and the houses, the bridge and the paths, the fields and the latrines, they were all just as much a part of it as the cliffs and the river and the trees. But now I saw it all in a new way. The path. A broad swath of dusty dirt cutting through the weeds, curving here to get around the corner of the Simpsons' garden, narrowing there where rocks cramped it on both sides. . . . It went where it did because there had been agreement, when folks first moved to the valley, that this was the best way to the river from the meadows to the south. People's thinking made that path. I looked at the bridge— rough planks on steel struts, spanning the gap between the stone bases on each bank. People I knew had thought that bridge, and built it. And the same was true of every structure in the valley. I tried to look at the bridge in the old way, as part of things as they were, but it didn't work. When you've changed you can't go back. Nothing looks the same ever again.

Walking back from the river, arms aching with the weight of the full buckets, I was grabbed roughly from behind.

"Ow!"

"You're back!" It was Nicolin, teeth bared in a grin. "Where you been hiding?"

"I just got back last night," I protested.

He took one of my buckets. "Well, tell me about it."

We walked up the path. "Man, you're all dinged up!" Steve said. "You're hobbling!" I nodded and told him about the train ride south, and the Mayor's dinner. Nicolin squinted as he imagined the Mayor's island house, but I thought, he's not getting it right. There was nothing I could do about it by talking, either. When I told him about the trip home, my swim and all, he put his bucket down in Pa's garden and took me by the shoulders to shake me, laughing at the clouds. "Jumped overboard! And in a storm! Good work, Henry. Good work."

"Hard work," I said, rubbing my arm as he danced around the bucket. But I was pleased.

He stopped dancing and pursed his lips. "So these Japanese are landing in Orange County?"

I nodded.

"And the Mayor of San Diego wants us to help put a stop to it?"

"Right again. But Tom doesn't seem real fond of the idea."

There were snails on the cabbage, and I stooped carefully to knock them off. Down close I could see the damage pests had done to every head. Miserable cabbage it was, and I sighed, thinking of the salads at the Mayor's dinner.

"I *knew* those scavengers were up to no good," Nicolin said, staring north. "But helping the Japanese, that's despicable. We'll make them pay for it. And we'll be the American resistance!" He swung a fist at the sky.

"Part of it, anyway."

The idea took him into regions of his own, and he wandered the garden insensible to me. I yanked some weeds and inspected the rest of the cabbages. Gave it up as a bad job.

Casually Steve said, "Going out fishing today?"

"I don't think so. My arms are so stiff I can hardly move them. I wouldn't be any good on the boats."

"Well, I've got to get down there soon." Steve frowned. "But tell me more about this Mayor."

So we passed some time talking about the trip, and Pa joined us in the garden to listen. Soon Steve had to leave, and I spent the rest of the day napping or stretching around in the garden, trying to loosen up. Again I slept the night without stirring.

The next morning Steve dropped by to walk with me down to the rivermouth. The men there stopped launching the boats long enough to greet me and ask some questions. When John walked by we all shut up and looked busy until he passed. Eventually we got the boats off, and getting them outside the swell took all our attention. The men were impressed that I'd managed to swim in through such a swell at night, and to tell the truth so was I. In fact I was scared all over again, though I tried not to show it. Far to the south I could see the long curving lines of the swell sweep toward the land, crash over, tumble whitely to shore. For a display of raw power there was nothing to match it. I was lucky to be alive, damned lucky! I gulped my heart back down to where it belonged, clenched my hands to stop them shaking.

Rafael wanted to hear everything he could about the Japanese, so all the time we were getting the nets out I talked, and he questioned me, and I had a good time. John rowed by and ordered Steve to get out and do the rod fishing—told me to stay with the nets. Steve got in the dinghy and rowed off south, with a resentful glance over his shoulder at us.

And then it was fishing again. The boats tossed hard in the swell, the spray gleamed in the sun, the green hills bounced to the horizons north and south. We cast the nets (my arms complaining with every pull or throw), and rowed them into circles and drew them up again heavy with fish. I rowed, pulled on nets, whacked fish, caught my balance on the gunwale, talked, kneaded my arms, and, looking up once at the familiar sight of the valley from the sea, I figured my adventure had ended. Despite all I was sorry about that.

When the fishing was done and the boats on the flat, Steve and I found the whole gang waiting for us on the top of the cliff. Kathryn hugged me and Del and Gabby and Mando slapped my sore back, and oohed and aahed over my cuts and bruises. Kristen and Rebel joined us from the bread ovens, and they all demanded that I tell my story to them. So I sat and began to tell it, excitement filling my voice with creaks and long "and *thennnnns.*"

Now this was the third time I'd told the tale in two days, and I had latched on to certain turns of phrase that seemed to tell it best. But it was also the third time that Nicolin had heard it, and I could tell by the tightness in the corner of his mouth, and the way he looked off into the trees, that he was getting tired of it. He recognized all my phrases, and it slowed me down. I found new ways to describe what had happened, but that didn't make much difference. I found myself passing over events as fast as I could, and Gab and Del jumped in to pepper me with questions about the details. I answered the questions, and I could see that Nicolin was listening, but he kept looking into the trees. Even though I was just telling the facts I began to feel like I was bragging. Kathryn braided her disobedient hair and encouraged me with an exclamation here and there; she saw what was going on, and I caught her giving Steve a hard look. We got back on the subject of San Diego, and I told them about La Jolla, thinking that Nicolin hadn't yet heard about that part of the trip. I described the ruined school, and the place where they printed books, and sure enough Nicolin's mouth relaxed and he looked at me.

". . . And then after he'd shown us the whole place he gave Tom a couple of books, a blank one to write in, and another one they just printed, called"—I hesitated for effect—"*An American Around the World.*"

"What's this?" Steve said. "A book?"

"An American around the world," Mando said, savoring the words, his eyes fish-round.

I told them what I knew. "This guy sailed to Catalina, and from there he went all the way around the world, back to San Diego."

"How?" Steve asked.

"I don't know. That's what the book tells, and I haven't read it. We didn't have time."

Said Steve, "Why didn't you tell me about this book before?"

I shrugged.

"Do you think Tom is done reading it yet?" Mando asked.

"I wouldn't be surprised. He reads fast."

Everyone nodded. "Faster than anyone *I* know," Mando declared.

Nicolin stood up. "Henry, you know I've already heard about your swim, so you'll excuse me if I go try and pry that book out of the old man's hands for us."

"Stephen," Kathryn said impatiently, but I cut her off, saying, "Sure."

"I got to read that book. If I get hold of it we can read it together in the morning."

"By that time you'll be done with it," Gabby said.

"Steve," Kathryn said again, but he was already on his way and he waved her off without looking back.

We all sat there and watched him hurry up to the freeway. I went on with my story, but even though Steve had been putting a crimp in my style, it suddenly wasn't as much fun.

It was near sunset when I finished. Gabby and Del took off. Mando and Kristen followed; at the freeway Mando sidled up to Kristen and took her hand. I raised my eyebrows, and seeing it Kathryn laughed.

"Yeah, something's going on there."

"Must have happened while I was gone."

"Earlier, I think, but they're bolder now."

"Anything else happen?"

She shook her head.

"What was Steve like?"

"Oh . . . not so good. It bothered him, you and Tom being off. Things were tight between him and John. Those two . . ."

"I know."

"I was hoping he would calm down when you got back."

"Maybe he will."

She shook her head, and I guessed she was right. "Those San Diegans will be coming this way again, right? And that book. I don't know what will happen when he reads that." She looked afraid, and it surprised me. I couldn't remember ever seeing Kathryn look afraid.

"Just a book," I said weakly.

She shook her head and gave me a sharp look. "He'll end up wanting to go around the damn world, I know it."

"I don't think he could."

"Wanting is enough as far as I'm concerned." She sounded so bitter and low that I wanted to ask her what was going on between her and Steve. Surely it was more than the book. But I hesitated. It was none of my business, no matter how well I knew them and no matter how curious I was. "We'd best be home," she said. Sun slipping under the hills. I followed her to the river path, watching her back and her wild hair. Across the bridge she put her arm around my shoulders and gave me a squeeze that hurt me. "I'm glad you didn't drown out there."

"I know the feeling."

She laughed and took off. Once again I wondered what went on between her and Steve—what their talk was like, and all. It was like anything else: I was most curious about the things I couldn't know. Even if one of them were willing to tell me about it, they couldn't—there wasn't the time for it, nor the honesty.

That night Nicolin came by fuming. "He wouldn't give me the book! Can you believe it? He says come back tomorrow."

"At least he's going to let us read it."

"Well of course! He sure better! I'd punch him if he didn't and take it away from him! I can't wait to read it, can you?"

"I want to bad," I admitted.

"Do you suppose the author went to England? That would tell us more about the east coast; I hope he did." And we discussed possible routes and travel problems, without a fact to base our speculation on, until Pa kicked us out of the house, saying it was his bedtime. Under the big eucalyptus tree (its leaves all burnt by the storm) we agreed to go up to Tom's next day after fishing, and beat the book out of him if we had to, for we were fiercely determined to dent our ignorance of the world, and this book seemed likely to do it.

By the time we got up to Tom's place the following day, all winded by our run up the ridge, Mando and Kristen and Rebel were already there. "Give it over," Nicolin gasped as we burst in the door.

"Ho ho," Tom said, tilting his head and staring at Steve. "I was thinking I might give it to someone else first."

"If you do I'll just have to take it away from them."

"Well, I don't know," Tom drawled, looking around the room. "By rights Hank here should get first crack at it. He saw it first, you know."

This was touching a sore spot; Nicolin scowled. He was dead serious, but Tom met his black gaze blinking like a lamb.

"Ha," Tom said. "Well, listen here, Steve Nicolin. I got to go and work the hives for a while. I'll lend you the book, but since these others want to read it too, you read a chapter or three aloud before you go. In fact, read until I get back, and we'll talk about our lending agreement then."

"Deal," Nicolin said. "Give it over."

Tom went into his bedroom and reappeared with the book in hand. Nicolin whooped and pounced on him, and they yelled and pounded each others' shoulders until Nicolin had it. Tom gathered his beekeeping gear, saying, "You be careful of those pages now," and "Don't bend the back too hard," and the like.

When he was gone Steve sat by the window. "Okay, I'm gonna read. Sit down and be quiet."

We sat, and he read.

AN AMERICAN AROUND THE WORLD

Being an Account of a Circumnavigation of the Globe in the Years 2030 to 2039, by GLEN BAUM.

I was born in La Jolla, the son of a ruined country, and I grew up in ignorance of the world and its ways; but I knew it was out there, and that I was being kept from it. On the night of my twenty-third birthday I stood on the peak of Mount Soledad and looked out at the ocean's wide waste. On the horizon to the west faint lights blinked like red stars, clustered together constellationlike on the black lump in the blackness that was San Clemente Island. Under those red pricks of light strode the never seen foreigners whose job it was to guard me from the world, as if my country were a prison. Suddenly I found the situation intolerable, and I resolved then and there, kicking the rocks of the summit into a cairn as a seal of my pledge, that I would escape the constraints put upon me, and wander the globe to see what I would. I would discover what the world was really like; see what changes had occurred since the great devastation of my country; return, and tell my countrymen what I had seen.

After some weeks of thought and preparation I stood on the stub of Scripps pier with my tearful mother and a few friends. The little sloop that had been my father's bobbed impatiently over the waves. I kissed my mother good-bye, promising to return within four years if it was within my power, and climbed down the pier's ladder into my craft. It was just after sunset. With some trepidation I cast off and sailed away into the night.

It was a clear night, the Santa Ana wind blowing mildly from my starboard rear quarter, and I made good time northwest. My plan was to sail to Catalina rather than San Clemente Island, for Catalina was rumored to have ten times as many foreigners as San Clemente, and it also had the major airport. In my boat I carried a good thick coat, and a pack filled with bread and my mother's cheese; nothing else I could obtain in La Jolla would have been any use to me, I reckoned. I crossed the channel in ten hours, on the same reach the entire way.

To the east blues were leaking into blacks by the time I approached the steep side of Catalina Island. Its black hills, ribbed by lighter black ridges, were starred by lights red and white and yellow and blue. I sailed around the southern end of the island, planning to land on a likely looking beach and walk to Avalon. Unfortunately for my plan, the west side of Catalina appeared to be very sheer, beachless rock cliffs, unlike any similar stretch of the San Diego coast; and it was now that time of the dawn when everything is distinguishable but the colors of things. Through that gray world I coasted (in the island's lee the wind was slack), when to my surprise a sail was hauled up on a mast I hadn't seen before, against the cliff. Immediately I tried to veer back out to sea, but the boat tacked slowly out ahead of me and intercepted my course. I was contemplating steering into the cliff and taking my chances there, when I saw that the only person aboard the other boat was a black-haired girl. She put her boat on a parallel course after crossing ahead of me, and brought her boat next to mine, staring all the while at me.

"Who are you?" she called.

"A fisherman from Avalon."

She shook her head. "Who are you?"

After a moment's indecision I chose boldness and cried,

"I come from the mainland, travelling to Avalon and the world!"

She gestured for me to pull down my sail; I did, she did likewise, and our boats came together. Though her skin was white, her features were Oriental. I asked her if there was a beach I could land on. She said there was, but that they were patrolled, like all the island's shore, by guards who either saw your papers or took you to jail.

I had not foreseen this difficulty, and was at a loss. I watched the water lap between our boats, and then said to the girl, "Will you help me?"

"Yes," she replied. "And my father will get you papers. Here, get in my boat; we must leave yours behind."

Reluctantly I clambered over the gunwales, pack in hand. My father's boat bucked emptily. Before we cast off from it, I took a hatchet from the bottom of the girl's boat, reached over and knocked a hole in the bottom of mine. Surreptitiously I wiped a tear from my eye as I watched it sink.

When we rounded the southern point and approached Avalon the girl—her name was Hadaka—instructed me to get under the fish in the bottom of her boat. She had been night fishing, and had a collection on her keel that I was unhappy to associate with: eels, squid, sand sharks, rockfish, octopus, all thrown together. But I did as she said. I lay smothering, still as the dead fish over me, as she stopped to be questioned in Japanese at the entrance to Avalon harbor; and I sailed into Avalon with an octopus on my face.

When Hadaka had docked the boat I quickly jumped up and acted as her assistant. "Leave the fish," she said when they were covered. "Quick, up to my house." We walked up a steep street past markets just opening. I felt conspicuous, for my smell if for no other reason, but no one paid any untoward attention to us, and high on the hill surrounding the town we slipped through a gate and were in her family's little yard garden. To the east the sun cracked the floor of America and shone on us. I had left my country behind; I was on foreign soil for the first time in my life.

"Well, that's Chapter One," Steve said. "He's on Catalina!"
"Read some more!" Mando cried. "Keep going!"

"No more," Tom said from the door. "It's late, and I need some peace and quiet." He coughed, and put his bee gear down in a corner. He waved us out: "Nicolin, you can keep the book for as long as it takes you to read it—"

"*Yow!*"

"Wait a minute! For as long as it takes you to read it aloud to the others here."

"Yeah!" said Mando as he hungrily eyed the book.

"That would be fun," Kristen said, glancing at Mando.

"Okay," Steve agreed. "I like it that way anyway."

"Well then, get home to supper. All of you!" Tom shooed us out the door with some dire warnings to Steve about what would happen if the book should come to harm. Steve laughed and led us down the ridge path, holding the book up triumphantly. I looked out in the direction of Catalina with whetted curiosity, but clouds obscured it from view. Americans were on that island! How I longed to travel there myself. My battered toe thumped a rock and with a howl I returned my attention to the ground beneath me. Down where the trail divided we stopped and agreed to meet the following afternoon to read some more.

"Let's meet at the ovens," Kristen said. "Kathryn wants to do a full batch tomorrow."

"After the fishing." Steve nodded, and skipped down the beach path, swinging the book overhead.

But the next day after fishing he wasn't so cheerful. John was on him for something or other, and when we got the boats pulled out of the river Steve was ordered to help sort and clean the fish. He stood still as a rock staring at his pa, until I sort of nudged him and got him to walk away. "I'll tell them you'll be late," I said, and beat it up the cliff before he took his frustration out on me with more than a glare.

Up at the ovens Kathryn had the girls at work: Kristen and Rebel were pumping the bellows, all flushed with the effort, their hair streaked with flour. Kathryn and Carmen Eggloff were shaping the tortillas and loaves and arranging them on the trays. The air above the brick ovens shimmered with heat. Around behind the corner of the Marianis' house Mrs. M. was helping some of the other girls knead barley dough. Kathryn stopped bossing Kristen and Rebel long enough to greet me. "Go ahead and sit down," she said when I told them Steve would be late. "Mando and Del aren't here yet anyway."

"Men are always late," Mrs. M. said around the corner. It was her great pleasure to hang out with the girls and gossip. "Henry, where's your friend Melissa?" she asked, hoping to embarrass me.

"Haven't seen her since I got back," I replied easily.

Rebel and Carmen were arguing. "I can't believe Jo would be so stupid as to get pregnant again," Carmen said. "It's a shame."

"Not if she has a good one," said Rebel.

"She's had four bad ones in a row. I think that's a sign she should heed."

Rebel said, "But it's hard to be pregnant all that time and nothing to show for it."

"They were bad ones," Carmen said. "Real bad."

"God made the bad ones too," Rebel said, pursing her lips.

"He didn't make them bad," Carmen countered. "It was radiation that did that, and I'm sure God doesn't approve. Those that are born bad, it's a blessing to them to send them back to God and let Him try with them again. If we let them live they'd be a burden on themselves as much as on us. I can't see how you don't see that, Reb."

Rebel shook her head stubbornly. "They're all God's children."

"But they would be a burden," Kathryn put in practically. "You have to figure you're not about to have a kid until after its Name Day."

"We don't have the right," Rebel said. "What if you had been born with only one arm, Kate? You'd still have had the brains and drive to bring bread back to this valley. Your gift isn't in your body."

"It was yeast brought bread back, not me," Kathryn said, trying to lighten things.

"But if we let them live," Carmen said, "half the valley would be crippled. And the generation after that might not survive."

"I don't believe that," Rebel said. Her mom had had three bad ones after Del and her, and she was pretty touchy about it. I think she missed those little tykes. But Carmen was just as firm the other way. She and Doc made the decisions, and I don't think she liked the matter discussed at all. Kathryn saw they were getting wrought up, and noticed my interest, and I don't think she wanted it happening with me around. She said,

"Maybe Jo didn't plan to get pregnant."

"I bet she didn't," Mrs. M. said with a smirk. "Marvin Hamish is not one to watch the moon too close." They laughed, even Rebel and Carmen. Then Mando and Del arrived, and the conversation shifted to the quality of the grain this season. Kathryn was depressed about it; the storm that had almost killed me had succeeded with a good portion of her crop.

Then Steve arrived. He swung Kathryn off the ground with a hug, and dusted the flour off his hands.

"Katie, you're a mess!" he cried.

"And you smell like fish!" she cried back.

"Do not. All right, it's time for Chapter Two of this fine book."

"Not until we get these trays into the ovens," Kathryn said. "You can help."

"Hey, I finished my day's work."

"Get over there and help," Kathryn commanded. Steve shambled over, and we all got up to get the trays in.

"Pretty tough boss," Steve scoffed.

"You shut up and watch what you're doing," Kathryn said.

When we got the trays in we all sat, and Steve pulled the book from his coat pocket, and started the story again.

Chapter II. The International Island.

Between two rosebushes thick with yellow blooms stood a tall white woman holding a pair of garden shears. Though they did not look much alike, she was Hadaka's mother. When she saw me she snapped the shears angrily.

"Who is this?" she cried, and Hadaka hung her head. "Have you brought home another one, foolish girl?"

"So that's how she gets her boyfriends," Rebel interjected, to hoots from the girls. "Not a bad method!"

"That's what you call fishing for men all right," Carmen said.

"Quiet!" Steve ordered, and went on.

"I saw him sailing to the forbidden shore, mother, and I knew he came from the mainland—"

"Quiet! I've heard it all before."

I put in, "I am deeply grateful to your daughter and yourself for saving my life."

"This only encourages your father," Hadaka's mother fumed. Then to me: "They wouldn't have killed you unless you tried to escape."

"See," Kathryn said to me, "they might have killed you when you jumped off their ship. You were in a more dangerous position than you've let on."

I began "Umm, well—"

"Stow it," said Steve. He was tired of hearing about my adventure, that was sure. Mando added, *"Please."* Mando was desperate to hear the story; he really loved it. Steve nodded approvingly and started again.

Her shears snipped the air. "Come in and get yourself cleaned up." She wrinkled her nose as I passed her, and beslimed and bewhiskered as I was I could hardly blame her; I felt like a barbarian. Inside their tile-walled bathing room I washed under a shower that provided water from freezing to boiling, depending on the bather's desire. Mrs. Nisha (for such, I found, was their family name) brought me some clothes and showed me how to use a buzzing shaver. When all was done I stood before a perfect mirror in gray pants and a bright blue shirt, a cosmopolitan.

When he arrived home Hadaka's father was less upset by my presence than his wife had been. Mr. Nisha looked me up and down and shook my hand, invited me in harsh English to sit with the family. He was Japanese, as I may not have said, and he looked much like Hadaka, although his skin was dark. He was a good deal shorter than Mrs. Nisha.

"Must procure you papers," he said after Hadaka told him the story of my arrival. "I get you papers, you work for me a little while. Is it a deal?"

"It's a deal."

He asked a hundred questions, and after that a hundred more. I told him everything about me, including my plans. It seemed I had been even luckier than I yet knew, having Hadaka intercept me, for Mr. Nisha was a worker in the Japanese government of the Channel Islands, in the department supervising the Americans living there. In this

work he had met Mrs. Nisha, who had crossed the channel
as I had some twenty years before. Mr. Nisha also had a
hand in a dozen other activities at least, and most of them
were illegal, although it took me a week or two to realize
this fully. But from that very night I saw that he was quite
an entrepreneur, and I took pains to let him know I would
serve him in any way I could. When he was done questioning
me all three of them showed me to a cot in their garden
shed, and I retired in good spirits.

Within the week I had papers proving I had been born
on Catalina and had spent my life there, serving the Japanese. After that I could leave the Nishas' house freely, and
Mr. Nisha put me to work fishing with Hadaka and weeding
their garden. Later, after this trial period was done, he had
me exchange heavy brown packages with strangers on the
streets of Avalon, or escort Japanese from the airport on the
backside of the island into town, without of course sub-
jecting them to the inconveniences of the various check-
points.

It should not be imagined that these and the other clan-
destine activities Mr. Nisha assigned to me were at all unusual in Avalon. It was a town teeming with representatives
of every race and creed and nation, and as the United
Nations had declared that the island was to be used by the
Japanese only, and only for the purpose of quarantining the
American coast, it was obvious that many visitors were there
illegally. But officials like Mr. Nisha existed in great numbers, at all levels, both on Catalina and in the Hawaiian
Islands, which served as the entry point to western America.
Almost everyone in town had papers authorizing their presence, and it was impossible to tell whose were forged or
bought; but wandering the streets I saw people dressed in
all manner of clothing, with features Oriental, or Mexican,
or with skin as black as the night sky; and I knew something
was amiss in the Japanese administration.

I was happy to try conversing with any or all of these
foreigners, employing my few words of Japanese, and listening to some peculiar versions of English. The only per-
sons I was wary of talking to were those who looked American,
and I noticed that they were not anxious to talk with me
either. Chances were too good that they were refugees as
I was, employed in some desperate enterprise to stay in

Avalon; it was rumored that quite a few worked for the police. In the face of such dangers it seemed best to ignore any fellow feeling.

The old part of Avalon stood much as it had in the old time, I was told: small whitewashed houses covering the hillsides that fell into the little bay that served as the harbor. Jetties had been built to enlarge the harbor, and new construction spilled over the hills to the north and west, hundreds of buildings in the Japanese style, with thick beams and thin walls, and peaky tile roofs. The whole of the island had new concrete roads, lined with low stone walls that divided the grounds of parklike estates, on which were giant mansions that the Japanese called *dachas*. Here officials of the U.N. and the Japanese administration made their homes. The dachas on the west side of the island were smaller; the really big ones faced the mainland, as the view of America was greatly prized. The biggest dachas of all, I heard, were on the east side of San Clemente Island; it was their lights I had seen on the night I decided to circumnavigate the globe.

A few weeks passed. I travelled in a car over the white roads, drove once and nearly crashed into a wall; when one drives there is a gale created merely by one's passage over the road, and everything moves a bit too fast for the reflexes.

"Isn't that what you said you felt when you were on the trains?" Rebel interrupted to ask me.

"That's true," I said. "You go so fast that you're ripping through the air. I'm glad we didn't have to drive that train; we would've crashed a hundred times."

"Quiet!" Mando exclaimed, and Steve nodded and went on, too absorbed in the story to even look up from the page.

I saw the giant flying machines, *jets*, land at the airport like pelicans, and take off with roars that almost burst the ears. And all the while I pursued various tasks for the gain of Mr. Nisha. When I had fully obtained his trust, he asked me if I would guide a night expedition to San Diego, consisting of five Japanese businessmen who were visiting Catalina expressly for that purpose. I was extremely reluctant to return to the mainland, but Mr. Nisha proposed to split the fee he charged for such a trip with me, and it was enormous. I weighed the advantages, and agreed to it.

So one night I found myself motorboating back to San Diego, giving instructions to the pilot, Ao, the only other person aboard who spoke English. Ao knew where the coast patrol ships were to be that night, and assured me there would be no interference from them. I directed him to a landing site on the inside of Point Loma, took them up to the ruins of the little lighthouse, and walked them through the lined-up white crosses of the naval cemetery—a cemetery so vast it might have been thought to hold all of the dead from the great devastation. At dawn we hid in one of the abandoned houses, and all that day the five businessmen clicked their huge cameras at the spiky downtown skyline, and the blasted harbor. That night we returned to Avalon, and I felt reasonably happy about it all.

I led four more expeditions to San Diego after that, and they were all simple and lucrative but for the last, in which I was convinced against my better judgement to lead the boat up the mouth of the Mission River at night. My readers in San Diego will know that the mouth of the Mission is congested with debris, runs over an old pair of jetties and a road or two, changes every spring, and is in general one of the most turbulent, weird, and dangerous rivermouths anywhere. Now on this night the ocean was as flat as a table, but it had rained hard the day before, and the runoff swirled over the concrete blocks in the rivermouth as over waterfalls. One of our customers fell overboard under the weight of his camera (they have cameras that photograph at night), and I dove in after him. It took a lot of effort from myself and Ao to reunite us all, and escape to sea. In a sailboat we would have drowned; and I was used to sailboats.

After that I was not so pleased with the notion of guiding further expeditions. And I had accumulated, through Mr. Nisha's generosity, a good quantity of money. Two nights after the disaster trip, there was a big party at one of the plush dachas high on the east flank of the island, and the man whose life I had saved offered, in his dozen words of English, to hire me as a servant and take me with him to Japan. Apparently Ao had told him of my aspiration to travel, and he hoped to repay me for saving his life.

I took Hadaka out into the shaped shrubbery of the

garden, and we sat over a lighted fountain that gurgled onto the terrace below. We looked at the dark bulk of the continent, and I told her of my opportunity. With a sisterly kiss (we had shared kisses of a different nature once or twice

"I'll bet they had!" Rebel crowed, and the girls laughed. Kathryn imitated Steve's reading voice:

"And I prepared to tell my dear mother back home that her grandchildren would be one-quarter Japanese. . . ."

"No interruptions!" Steve shouted, but we were in stitches now. "I'm going to go right on!" He read,

(we had shared kisses of a different nature once or twice, but I did not feel an attraction strong enough to risk Mr. Nisha's anger).

"Oooh, coward!" Kristen cried. "What a chicken!"

"Now wait a minute," said Steve. "This guy has a goal in mind; he wants to get around the world. He can't just stop on Catalina. You gals never think of anything but the romance part of the story. Quiet up now or I'll stop reading."

"Pleeeeeease," Mando begged them. "I want to know what happens."

Hadaka informed me that it would be best for all if I took the chance and departed, though the Nishas had not made me aware of it, my staying with them was not entirely safe, as my papers could be proved counterfeit, which would immerse Mr. Nisha in all kinds of trouble. It occurred to me that this was why he had shared so much of the profit of our mainland trips with me—so I could eventually leave. I decided that they were a most generous family, and that I had been exceedingly lucky to fall in with them.

I went back inside the dacha, therefore, and avoiding the naked American girls who pressed drinks and cigarettes on everybody, I told my benefactor Mr. Tasumi that I would take up his offer. Soon afterward I bade a sad farewell to my Catalina family. When I had left my mother and friends in San Diego, I could truthfully say to them that I would try to return; but what could I say to the Nishas? I kissed mother and daughter, hugged Mr. Nisha, and in a genuine conflict of feelings was driven to the airport, there to embark on a seven thousand mile flight over the great Pacific Ocean.

"That's Chapter Two," Steve said, closing the book. "He's on his way."

"Oh read some more," Mando said.

"Not now." He gave a sour glance at the women, who were getting the trays out of the ovens. "It's about time for supper, I guess." Standing up, he shook his head at me and Mando. "These gals sure are hard on a story," he complained.

"Oh come on," Kathryn said. "What's the fun of reading it together if we can't talk about it?"

"You don't take it seriously."

"What does that mean? Maybe we don't take it *too* seriously."

"I'm off home," Steve said, sulking. "You coming, Hank?"

"I'm going back to my place. I'll see you in the morning."

"Tom wants a town meeting at the church tomorrow night," Carmen told us. "Did you know?"

None of us did, and we agreed to try to get together before the meeting, and read another chapter.

"What's the meeting about?" Steve asked.

"San Diego," said Carmen.

Steve stopped walking away.

"Tom'll bring up the question of helping the San Diegans fight the Japanese," I said. "I told you about that."

"I'll be there," Steve assured us sternly, and with that he was off. I helped Kathryn scrape the new loaves off the trays, and took one home to Pa, gnawing at one end of it and wondering how many days it would take to fly across the sea.

Chapter Twelve

Usually our big meetings were held in Carmen's church, but this time she and Tom had been nagging every person in the valley to come—Tom had even gone into the back country to roust Odd Roger—so the church, which was a narrow barnlike building in the Eggloffs' pasture, wasn't going to be quite big enough, and we were meeting at the bathhouse. Pa and I got there early and helped Tom start the fire. As I carried in wood I had to dodge Odd Roger, who was inspecting the floor and walls for grubs, one of his favorite foods. Tom shook his head as he eyed Roger. "I don't know if it was worth the trouble dragging him here." Tom seemed less excited about the meeting than I'd expected him to be, and unusually quiet. I myself was really hopping around; tonight we were going to join the resistance, and become part of America again, at long last.

Outside the evening sky was streaked with mare's tail clouds still catching some light, and a stiff wind blew onshore. People talked and laughed as they approached the bathhouse, and I saw lanterns sparking here and there through the trees. Across the Simpsons' potato patch their dogs were begging with pathetic howls to join us. Steve and all his brothers and sisters arrived, and we sat down on the tarps. "So I saw that the shark had his big mouth open and was about to swallow me," Steve was telling them, "and I stuck my oar between his jaws so he couldn't bite me. But I had to hang on to the oar to keep from being sucked down whole, and I was running out of air too. I had to figure something out."

Then John and Mrs. Nicolin rounded the bend in the river path, and their kids got inside quick. Marvin and Jo Hamish ambled across the bridge, Jo in a white shift that billowed away from her quickening belly. I remembered the conversation at the ovens, and wondered what she had growing in her this time. And then people were coming from everywhere, descending on the bathhouse from every direction. A gaggle of Simpson and Mendez kids appeared around the side of the grain barrows, leading their fathers, who conferred heads together as they walked. Rafael and Mando and Doc came down the hill across the river, and behind them were Add and Melissa Shanks. I waved at Melissa and she waved back, her black hair flying downwind. A bit later Carmen and Nat Eggloff trooped out of the woods, carrying a heavy lantern between them and arguing, while Manuel Reyes and his family hurried behind them to stay in the lantern light. It sounded like a swap meet was crammed into the bathhouse, and when the Marianis arrived I thought we might have more than a capacity crowd. But it was cold outside, so Rafael took over and sat everyone down: the men against the walls, the little kids in their mothers' laps, our gang in one of the empty bathing tubs. When we were done the whole population of the valley was packed in like fish in a box, ready to go to market. Lanterns were hung on the walls and some big logs in the fire caught, and the room blazed like it never did during baths. The chattering was so loud off the sheet metal roof that the babies started to shriek and cry, and the rest of us were nearly as excited, because we never got together in such a way except for Christmas, and the rare valley meeting.

Tom moved about the room slowly, talking with folks he hadn't seen in a while. He called the meeting to order as he went, but the visiting continued despite his announcements, and others had begun to circulate and argue behind him. Lots of people had nothing but questions, however, and when Marvin said to Tom, "So what's this all about?" the question was repeated, and the room grew quieter.

"All right," Tom said hoarsely. He started to tell them about our trip to San Diego. Sitting on the tub edge I looked around at all the faces. It seemed like an awful long time since Lee and Jennings had walked into this same room out of the rain, to tell us of their new train line. So much had happened to me since then that it didn't seem possible a few weeks could hold it all—could make that many changes in me. I felt like a different person than the one who had listened to Lee and Jennings tell their tales; but I didn't know exactly how I was different, or what it meant for me. It was just a feeling, a discomfort, or an uncertainty, or an ignorance—as if I had to learn everything over again. I didn't like it.

The way Tom told it, the San Diegans kept looking to be fools or wastrels, no better than scavengers. So I had to interrupt him from time to time and add my opinion of it—tell them all about the electric batteries and generators, and the broken radio, and the bookmaker, and Mayor Danforth. We were arguing in front of everybody, but I thought they needed to know my side, because Tom was against the southerners. He disagreed with me sharply when I went on about the Mayor. "He lives in style, Henry, because he's got a gang of men doing nothing but help him run things, that's all. That's what gives him the power to send men off east to contact other towns."

"Maybe so," I said. "But tell them what they found out east."

Tom nodded and addressed the others. "He claims that his men have been as far as Utah, and that all the inland towns are banded together in a thing called the American resistance. The resistance, they say, wants to unify America again."

That hushed everyone. From the wall near the door John Nicolin broke the silence. "So?"

"So," Tom continued, "he wants us to do our part in this great plan, by helping the San Diegans fight the Japanese on Catalina." He told them about our long conference with the Mayor. "Now we know why dead Orientals have been washing onto our beach. But apparently they haven't stopped trying to land, and now the San Diegans want our help getting rid of them for good."

"What exactly do they mean by help?" asked Mrs. Mariani.

"Well . . ." Tom hesitated, and Doc cut in:

"It means they'd want our rivermouth as an anchorage to base attacks from."

At the same time Recovery Simpson, Del and Rebel's pa, said, "It means we'd finally have the guns and manpower to do something about being guarded like we are."

Both of these opinions got a response from others, and the discussion split into a lot of little arguments. I kept my mouth shut, and tried to listen and find out who was thinking what. I could see that even a group as small as ours could be divided into even smaller groups. Recovery Simpson and old man Mendez led the families who did the bulk of their work in the back country, hunting or trapping or sheep herding; Nat and Manuel and the shepherds were quick to follow Simpson's lead, usually. Then there were the farmers; everyone did a little of that, but Kathryn directed all the women who grew the big crops. Nicolin's fishing operation was the third big group, including all the Nicolins, the Hamishes, Rafael and me; and lastly there were the folks who didn't fit into any one group, like Tom, and Doc, and my pa, and Addison, and Odd Roger. These groupings were false in a way, in that everyone did a bit of everything. But for a while I thought I noticed something; I thought that the hunters, whose work was already like fighting, were going for the resistance, while the farmers, who needed things to be the same from year to year (and who were mostly women anyway), were going against it. That made sense to me, and I bet to myself that the way Nicolin went would decide the issue; but then all around me I saw that there were as many exceptions to my pattern as there were examples of it, and I lost the momentary feeling that I understood what was happening.

Doc was one of the first to defy my expectations. Here he was as old as Tom, almost, and always arguing at the ancients' table at the swap meet that America had been betrayed by those who wouldn't fight. It had seemd obvious to me that he would be disagreeing with Tom again, and arguing for joining the San Diegans in their fight. But here he stood saying, "I remember once when Gabino Canyon folks were asked by the Cristianitos Canyon people to join them when they were fighting with Talega Canyon over the wells at the Four Canyon Flat. They did it, but when the fight was over there wasn't any Gabino Canyon at the swap meet anymore. It was just Cristianitos. The thing is, bigger towns tend to eat up the littler ones around them. Henry will tell you there's hundreds of people down there—"

"But we're not just the next canyon over from them," Steve objected. "There's miles and miles between us and them. And we *should* be fighting the Japanese. Every town should be part of the resistance, otherwise it's hopeless." He was vehement, and several people nodded, ignoring the talk around them. Steve had a presence, all right. His voice turned people's ears.

"Miles aren't going to matter if the train works," Doc answered. So he was against joining. Shaken, I was about to ask him how he could drop all his swap meet talk just when the chance for action had arrived, when Tom said real loudly, "Hey? Let's go it one at a time now."

Rafael jumped in the gap. "We should fight the Japanese every chance we get. Face it, they're hemming us in. We're like fish in a big purse net. And they're not only keeping us from the world, they're keeping us from each other, by bombing tracks and bridges."

"We only have the San Diegans' word for those attacks," Doc said. "How do we know they're telling the truth?"

"Of course they're telling the truth," Mando said indignantly. He waved a fist at his pa: "Henry and Tom *saw* the bombs hit the tracks."

"That may be so," Doc admitted. "But it doesn't mean everything else they said is true. Could be they want us scared and looking for help. That Mayor of San Diego will start thinking he's Mayor of Onofre the moment we join him."

"But what could he do to us?" Recovery said. The other hunters nodded, and Recovery stepped forward to take the argument from Doc and Mando. "All it means is that we'll be dealing with one more town, just like we deal with all the towns that come to the swap meet."

Doc dropped on Cov's argument like a pelican flopping on a fish. "Exactly not! San Diego's a lot bigger than us, and they don't just want to trade. Like you said, Cov, they've got a lot of guns."

"They ain't going to shoot us," Cov said. "Besides, they're fifty miles away."

"I agree with Simpson," old man Mendez said. "An alliance like this is part of knitting things up again. Those folks don't want anything we have, and they couldn't do anything to us if they did. They just want help in a fight that's our fight too, whether we join it or not."

"That's what I say," Rafael added firmly. "They're holding us down, those Japanese! We've got to fight them just to stand up."

Steve and I nodded our heads like puppets in a swap meet puppet show. Gabby stuck his fist between us and shook it triumphantly. I hadn't known Rafe felt so strongly about our situation, because it wasn't something he talked about. The gang was impressed. I felt Steve shifting in the tub, twitching catlike as he nerved himself to stand up and pitch in with those who wanted to fight. But before he did his father stepped out from the wall he had been leaning against, and spoke.

"We should be working. That's what we should be doing. We should be gathering food and preserving it, building more shelter and improving what we got, getting more clothes and medicines from the meets. Getting more boats and gear, firewood, all of that. Making it all work. That's your job, Rafe. Not trying to fight people out there who have a million times the power we do. That's a dream. If we do anything in the way of fighting, it should be right here in this valley, and for this valley. Not for anybody else. Not for those clowns down south, and sure not for any idea like *America.*" He said it like the ugliest sort of curse, and glared at Tom as he said it. "America's gone. It's dead. There's us in this valley, and there's others in San Diego, Orange, behind Pendleton, over on Catalina. But they're not us. This valley is the biggest country we're going to have in our lives, and it's what we should be working for, keeping everyone in it alive and healthy. That's what we should be doing, I say."

The bathhouse was pretty quiet after that. So John was against it. And Tom, and Doc. . . . I felt like the wind had been taken out of our sails by John, but Rafael rose to speak. "Our valley isn't big enough to think that way, John. All the people we trade with depend on us, and we depend on them. We're all countrymen. And we're all being held down by the guards on Catalina. You can't deny that, and you got to agree that working for us in this valley means being free to develop when we can. The way it is, we don't have that freedom."

John just shook his head. Beside me Steve hissed. He was

near boiling over—his hands were clenched into white fists as he tried to hold himself in. This was nothing new. Steve always disagreed with his father at meetings. But John wouldn't abide Steve crossing him in public, so Steve always had to stay shut up. The usual meeting ended with Steve bursting with indignation and resentful anger. I don't know that this meeting would have been any different, but for Mando speaking up earlier, and arguing with Doc. Steve had noted that; and could he stand by silent, not daring to do what little Armando Costa had? Not a chance. And then I had been arguing with Tom all night. There were too many fires under Steve at once, and all of a sudden he popped up, face flushed and fists trembling at his sides. He looked from person to person, at anybody but his pa.

"We're all Americans no matter what valley we come from," he said rapidly. "We can't help it and we can't deny it. We were beat in a war and we're still paying for it in every way, but some day *we'll be free again*." John stared at him fiercely, but Steve refused to back down. "When we get there it'll be because people fought every chance they could get."

He plopped back down on the tub edge, and only then did he look across the room at John, challenging him to reply. But John wasn't going to reply; he didn't deign to argue with his son in public. He just stared at him, his color high. There was an uncomfortable pause as everyone saw what was happening—saw John denying Steve's right to join the discussions.

Tom looked up from warming his hands at the fire, and saw what was going on. "What about you, Addison?" he said.

Add was against the wall, Melissa seated at his feet; he stroked Melissa's glossy hair from time to time, and watched the rest of us carefully as we argued. Now Melissa looked down, her lower lip between her teeth. If it were true that Add dealt with scavengers, then he would likely have problems if we joined raids in Orange County. But he shrugged and met our stares boldly, as if it didn't matter a damn to him. "I don't care much one way or the other."

"Pinché!" old Mendez said. "You must have some opinion."

"No," drawled Add, "I don't."

"That helps a lot," said Mendez. Gabby looked surprised to see his father speak; old Mendez was a silent man.

"Yeah, Add, what did you come for, anyway?" Marvin said.

"Wait a minute." It was my pa, scrambling to his feet. "Ain't a crime to come here without an opinion one way or other. That's why we talk."

Addison gave Pa a polite nod. That was just like Pa; the only time he spoke was to defend silence.

Doc and Rafael ignored Pa and went at it again, getting heated. There were arguments breaking out all over, so they could say angry things without embarrassing the other. "You're always wanting to play with those guns of yours," Doc said scornfully. Eyes flashing under his thick black brows, Rafael came back: "When you're the only medical care in the valley, we ain't doing so well you must admit." No one who heard them liked such talk, and I waved a hand between them and said, "Let's not get personal, eh?"

"Oh we're just talking about our *lives* is all," Rafe snapped sarcastically. "We wouldn't want to get *personal* about it. But I tell you, the doctor here is going to kiss snake's butt if he thinks I mess with guns for the fun of it."

"But you guys are friends—"

"Hey!" Tom cried, sounding weary. "We haven't heard from everyone yet."

"What about Henry?" Kathryn said. "He went to San Diego too, so he's seen them. What do you think we should do?" She gave me a look that was asking for something, but I couldn't tell what it was, so I said what I was thinking and hoped it would do.

"We should join the San Diegans," I said. "If we feel like they're trying to make us part of San Diego, we can destroy the tracks and be rid of them. If we don't, we'll be part of the country again, and we'll learn a lot more about what's going on inland."

"I learn all I want to know at the swap meet," Doc said. "And wrecking the tracks isn't going to stop them coming in boats. If there's a thousand of them, as they say, and we number, what, sixty?—and most of them kids?—then they can pretty much do what they want with this valley."

"They can whether we agree or not," Cov said. "And if we go along with them now, maybe we can get what we want out of it."

John Nicolin looked especially disgusted at that sentiment, but before he could speak I said, "Doc, I don't understand you. At the swap meets you're always grousing for a chance to get back at them for bombing us. Now here we got the chance, and you—"

"We *don't* got the chance," Doc insisted. "Not a thing's changed—"

"Enough!" Tom said. "We've heard all that before. Carmen, it's your turn."

In her preaching voice Carmen said, "Nat and I have talked a lot about this one, and we don't agree, but my thoughts are clear on the matter. This fight the San Diegans want us to join is useless. Killing visitors from Catalina doesn't do a thing to make us free. I'm not against fighting if it would do some good, but this is just murder. Murder is never the means to any good end, so I'm against joining them." She nodded emphatically and looked to the old man. "Tom? You haven't told us your opinion yet."

"The hell he hasn't," I said, annoyed at Carmen for sounding so preacherly and commonsensical, when it was just her opinion. But she gave me a look and I shut up.

Tom roused himself from his fireside torpor. "What I don't like about this Danforth is that he tried to make us join him whether we want to or not."

"How?" Rafael challenged.

"He said, we're either with them or against them. I take that as a threat."

"But what could they do to us if we didn't join?" Rafe said. "Bring an army up here and point guns at us?"

"I don't know. They do have a lot of guns. And the men to point them."

Rafael snorted. "So you're against helping them."

"I guess so," Tom said slowly, as if uncertain himself what he thought. "I guess I'd like to have the choice of working with them or not, depending on what they had in mind. Case by case, so to speak. So that we're not just a distant section of San Diego, doing what they tell us to."

"The point is, they can't *make us* do what they say," Recovery said. "It's just an alliance, an agreement on common goals."

"You hope," said John Nicolin.

Cov started to argue with John, and Rafael was still pressing Tom, so the discussion broke up again, and pretty soon every adult in the room was jawing it, and most of the kids too. "Do you want them in our river?" "Who, the Japs or the San Diegans?" "You'll risk your life for nothing." "I'm damned if I want those cruisers setting the border on my whole life." On it went, arguments busting in on neighboring arguments as the participants heard something they liked or disliked. Fingers were waved under noses, curses flew even around Carmen, Kathryn had Steve by the front of the shirt as she made a point. . . . It sounded like we were evenly split, too, so that neither side could win on the volume of their voices. But I could see that we joiners were in trouble. The old man, John Nicolin, Doc Costa, and Carmen Eggloff—all four of them were against, and that was the story right there. Rafael and Recovery and old Mendez were important in the valley, and they had a strong voice in things, but they didn't wield the same sort of influence that the others did. John and Doc circulated around the room arguing and conferring on the sly with Pa and Manuel, Kathryn and Mrs. Mariani; and I knew which way things were shifting for the vote.

At the height of the arguing Odd Roger stood and waved his arms with an absurd gleam of comprehension in his eye. He squawked loudly, and Kathryn scowled. "He's lucky he wasn't born in this valley," she muttered; "he'd never have made it to Name Day." A lot of people were like that, upset that Tom had brought Roger at all. But suddenly Roger broke into English, in a shrill reedy voice:

"Kill every scavenger on the land, kill them! Scavenger poisons the water, breaks the snares, eats the dead. Unless the corruption be cut from the body the body dies! I say kill them all, kill them all, kill them all!"

"All right, Roger," Tom said, taking his arm and leading him to his corner. When he returned to the hearth Tom shouted the arguments down, vexed at last. "Shut up! Nobody's saying anything new. I propose we have the vote. Any objections?"

There were plenty of those, but after a lot of bickering over the wording of the proposition we were ready.

"All those in favor of joining San Diego and the American resistance to fight the Japanese, raise their hands."

Rafael, the Simpsons, the Mendezes, Marvin and Jo Hamish, Steve, Mando, Nat Eggloff, Pa and me: we raised our hands and helped Gabby's little brothers and sisters to raise theirs. Sixteen of us.

"Now all those against?"

Tom, Doc Costa, Carmen; the Marianis, the Shankses, the

Reyes; and John Nicolin went down the line of his family, pulling up the arms of Teddy and Emilia, Virginia and Joe, Carol and Judith, and even Marie, as if she were one of the kids, which in mental power she was. Little Joe stood at attention, hand high, black hair falling over his face, belly and tiny pecker sticking out under a snot-smeared shirt. Mrs. N. sighed to see that shirt. "Oh, man," Rafael complained; but that was the rule. Everyone voted. So there were twenty-three against. But among the adults it was a lot closer, and in the strained silence after Carmen finished counting there were some hard stares exchanged. It was like nothing I had ever seen in the valley. A coming fight can feel good, say at the swap meet when facing off with a scavenger gang; but in the valley, with no one there but friends and neighbors, it felt bad. Everyone was affected the same way, I think; and no one thought of a way to patch this one up.

"Okay," Tom said. "When they show up again I'll tell Lee and Jennings we aren't going to help them."

"Individuals are free to do what they want," Addison Shanks said out of the blue, as if he were stating a general principle.

"Sure," Tom said, looking at Add curiously. "As always. We aren't making any alliance with them, that's all."

"That's fine," Add said, and left, leading Melissa out.

"It's not fine by me," Rafael declared, looking around at us, but especially at John. "It's wrong. They're holding us down, do you understand? The rest of the world is getting along, making good progress with the help of machines, and medicines for the sick, and all of that. They *blasted* that away from us, and now they're *keeping* it away from us. *It isn't right.*" His voice was as bitter as I'd ever heard it; not really Rafael's voice at all. "We should be fighting them."

"Are you saying you aren't going to go along with the rest of us?" John asked.

Rafael gave him an angry look. "You know me better than that, John. I go with the vote. Not that I could do much by myself anyway. But I think it's wrong. We can't hide in this valley like weasels forever, not sitting right across from Catalina like we do." He took in a big breath and let it out. "Well, shit. I don't guess we can vote it away anyway." He threaded his way through the folks still sitting, and left the bathhouse.

The meeting was done. I crossed the bathhouse with Steve and Gabby. Steve was doing his best to avoid his pa. In all the milling around we saw Del gesture at us, and with a nod to Mando and Kathryn we followed them out.

Without a word we trailed up the river path, following someone else's lanterns. Then over the bridge, to the big boulders at the bottom of the barley field. The boulders were wet, so we couldn't sit on them. The wind pushed the trees, and after the bathhouse it was cold enough to give me goosebumps. In the blustery dark my companions were no more than shapes, like knobs on the boulders. Across the river lanterns blinked through the trees, stitching the trails that our neighbors were taking home.

"Could you believe all that talk?" Gabby said scornfully.

"Rafael was right," Nicolin said bitterly. "What will they think of us in San Diego, and across the country, when they hear about this?"

"It's over now," said Kathryn, trying to soothe him.

"Over for you," Steve said. "It turned out the way you wanted. But for us—"

"For everyone," Kathryn insisted. "It's over for everyone."

But Steve wouldn't have it. "You'd like that to be true, but it isn't. It won't ever be over."

"What do you mean?" Kathryn said. "The vote was taken."

"And you were mighty happy with the results, weren't you," Steve accused her.

"I've had enough of this for one night," Kathryn said. "I'm going home."

"Why don't you go ahead and do that," Nicolin said angrily. Kathryn stopped stepping off her boulder to glare at him. I was glad I wasn't Steve at that moment. Without a word she was off toward the bridge. "You don't run this valley!" Steve shouted after her, his voice hoarse with tension. "Nor me neither! You never will!" He paced off the boulder into the barley field. I could just make out Kathryn as she crossed the bridge.

"I don't know why she was being such a bitch tonight," Steve whined.

After a long silence, Mando said, "We should have voted yes."

Del ha-ha'd. "We did. There weren't enough of us."

"I meant everybody."

"We should have joined," Nicolin shouted from the barley.

"So?" Gabby said—ready as always to egg Steve on. "What are you going to do about it?"

Across the river dogs yapped. I saw the moon for a wisp

of time, above the scudding clouds. Behind me barley rustled, and I shivered in the cold wind. Something in the shifting shadows made me remember my miserable, desperate hike up the ravine to find Tom and the San Diegans, and the fear came on me again, rustling through me like the wind. It's so easy to forget what fear feels like. Steve was pacing around the boulders like a wolf caught in a snare. He said,

"We could join them ourselves."

"What?" Gab said eagerly.

"Just us. You heard what Add said at the end there. Individuals are free to do as they like. And Tom agreed. We could approach them after Tom tells them no, and tell them we'd be willing to work with them. Just us."

"But how?" Mando asked.

"What kind of help do they want from us, hey? No one in there could say, but I know. Guides into Orange County, that's what. We can do better at that than anyone else in Onofre."

"I don't know about that," Del said.

"We can do it as well as anybody!" Steve revised, for it was true that his pa and some others had spent a good bit of time up north in years past. "So why shouldn't we if we want to?"

Fearfully I said, "Maybe we should just go along with the vote."

"Fuck that!" Steve cried furiously. "What's with you, Henry? Afraid to fight the Japanese, now? Shit, you go off to San Diego and now you tell us what to do, is that it?"

"No!" I protested.

"You scared of them now, now that you've had your great voyage and seen them up close?"

"No." I was shocked by Nicolin's anger, too confused to think how to defend myself. "I want to fight," I said weakly. "That's what I said in the meeting."

"The meeting doesn't mean shit. Are you with us or not?"

"I'm with you," I said. "I didn't say I wasn't!"

"Well?"

"Well . . . we could ask Jennings if he wants some guides, I guess. I never thought of it."

"*I* thought of it," Steve said. "And that's what we're going to do."

"After they talk to Tom," Gabby said, clearing things up, pushing Steve on.

"Right. After. Henry and I will do it. Right, Henry?"

"Sure," I said, jumping at his voice's prod. "Sure."

"I'm for it," Del said.

"Me too," cried Mando. "I want to too. I've been in Orange County as much as any of you."

"You're in it too," Steve assured him.

"And me," Gabby said.

"And you, Henry?" Steve pressed. "You're with us too?"

Around us nothing but shadows, windblown in the darkness. The moon slid into a cloud crease and I could see the pale blobs of my friends' faces, like clumps of dough, watching me. We put our right hands together above the central boulder, and I could feel their calloused fingers tangle with mine.

"I'm with you," I said.

Chapter Thirteen

The next time I saw the old man I gave him hell, because it was very possible that if he had come out on the side of the resistance the vote would have been different. And if the valley had voted to join the resistance, then Steve wouldn't have come up with his plan to join the San Diegans secretly, and I wouldn't have caved in and gone along with it. To avoid admitting to myself that I had caved in to Steve, I decided his plan was a good one. So in a way it was all the old man's fault. It was too bad we had to sneak off to help the San Diegans, but we had to be part of the resistance. I remembered vividly how it felt to be staring at the metal deck of the Japanese ship, crying because I thought Tom and the others were dead, and vowing to fight the Japanese forever. And it was no thanks to them that Tom had survived, either. He just as well could have died, and so could have I. I told Tom as much as I stood berating him for his vote in the meeting. "And any time we go out there, the same thing could happen," I concluded, shaking a finger under his nose.

"Any time we sail out on a foggy night and shoot guns at them, you mean," he said, through a mouth jammed with honeycomb. We were out in his yard, sweltering under high filmy clouds, and he was scorching the slats of several boxlike supers from an unsuccessful hive. Hive stands and smokers and supers lay strewn about us on the weeds. "It may be that the jays ate every bee in this hive," he mumbled. "This one scrub jay was popping down ten at a meal. I set one of Rafael's mousetraps on top of the post he was landing on, and when he landed the trap knocked him about fifteen feet. Was he mad! He cursed me in every language known to jays."

"Ah, shit," I said, yanking some of his long white hair out of the corner of his mouth before he chewed it down. "All our lives you've been telling us about America. How great it was. Now we've got a chance to fight for it, and you vote against the idea. I don't get it. It's contrary to everything you've taught us."

"Is not. America was great in the way that whales are great, see what I mean?"

"No."

"You've gotten remarkably dense lately, you know that? I mean, America was huge, it was a giant. It swam through the seas eating up all the littler countries—drinking them up as it went along. We were eating up the world, boy, and that's why the world rose up and put an end to us. So I'm not contradicting myself. America was great like a whale—it was giant and majestic, but it stank and was a killer. Lots of fish died to make it so big. Now haven't I always taught you that?"

"No."

"The hell I haven't! What about all those arguments at the swap meet with Doc and Leonard and George?"

"There you're different, but just to rile Doc and Leonard. Here at home you always make America sound like God's own country. Besides, right in the here and now there's no doubt we're being held down, just like Rafe said. We have to fight them, Tom, you know that."

He shook his head, and sucked in his cheek on the caved-in side of his mouth, so that from my angle it looked like he only had half a face. "Carmen hit the nail hardest, as usual. Did you listen to her? I didn't think so. Her point was, murdering those dumb tourists doesn't do a thing to change the structure of the situation. Catalina will still be Japanese, satellites will still be watching us, we'll still be inside a quarantine. Even the tourists won't stop coming. They'll just be better armed, and more likely to hurt us."

"If the Japanese are really trying to keep people away, we could kill all the visitors who sneak in."

"Maybe so, but the structure remains."

"But it's a start. Anything as big as this can't be done all at once, and the start will always look small. Why, if you'd been around during the Revolution, you'd have been against ever starting it. 'Killing a few redcoats won't change the *structure*,' you'd have said."

"No I wouldn't, because it wasn't the same structure. We aren't being occupied, we're being quarantined. If we joined San Diego in this fight the only result would be that we'd be part of San Diego. Doc was right just like Carmen was."

I thought I had him on the run, and I said, "The same objection could have been made in the Revolution. People from Pennsylvania or wherever could have said, if we join the fight we'll become part of New York. But since they were part of the same country, they worked together."

"Boy, it's a false analogy, like historical analogies always are. Just 'cause I taught you your history don't mean you understand it. In the Revolution the British had men and guns, and we had men and guns. Now we still have men and guns like in 1776, but the enemy has satellites, intercontinental missiles, ships that could shell us from Hawaii, laser beams and atom bombs and who knows what all. Think about it logically for a bit. A tiger and a titmouse would make a better fight."

"Well, I don't know," I grumbled, feeling the weight of his argument. I wandered through the dismantled hives, the sundials and rain barrels and junk, to regroup. Below us the valley was a patchwork, the fields like gold handkerchiefs dropped on the forest, with gliding patches of sunlight making even larger fields of brilliant green. "I still say that every revolution starts small. If you had voted for the resistance, we could have thought of something. As it is, you've put me in a tough spot."

"How so?" he asked, looking up from the supers.

I realized I'd said too much. "Oh, in talk, you know," I floundered. Then I hit on something: "Since we aren't going to help the resistance, I'll be the only one of the gang who got to go to San Diego. Steve and Gabby and Del don't like that much."

"They'll get there some day," he said. I breathed a sigh of relief to have him off the track. But I felt bad to keep something from him; I saw that I would be lying to him regularly, from then on. I walked back over to him, and as I watched him work I scraped mud off my heels uneasily. His arguments had a sense that couldn't be denied, even though I was sure his conclusions were wrong. Because I wanted his conclusions to be wrong.

"You got your lesson ready?" he asked. "Other than the history of the United States?"

"Some of it."

"You're getting to be as bad as Nicolin."

"I am not."

"Let's hear it then. 'I know you. Where's the king?'"

I called the page up before my mind's eye, and against a fuzzy gray mental field appeared the yellow crumbly page, with the rounded black marks that meant so much. I spoke the lines as I saw them.

"'Contending with the fretful elements;
   Bids the wind blow the earth into the sea,
   Or swell the curled waters 'bove the main,
   That things might change or cease; tears his white hair,
   Which the impetuous blasts, with eyeless rage,
   Catch in their fury and make nothing of;
   Strives in his little world of man to outscorn
   To to-and-fro-conflicting wind and rain.
   This night, wherein the cub-drawn bear would crouch,
   The lion and the belly-pinched wolf
   Keep their fur dry, unbonnetted he runs,
   And bids what will take all.'"

"Very good!" Tom cried. "That was our night, all right. 'All-shaking thunder, strike flat the thick rotundity of the world, crack nature's molds, all germens spill at once that make ingrateful man.'"

"Wow, you memorized two whole lines," I said.

"Oh hush. I'll give you lines from *Lear*. You listen to this.

"'The weight of this sad time we must obey;
   Speak what we feel, not what we ought to say.
   The oldest hath borne most; we that are young,
   Shall never see so much, nor live so long.'"

"*We* that are young?" I inquired.

"Hush! O sharper than a serpent's tooth indeed. The oldest hath borne most, no lie." He shook his head. "But listen, ungrateful wretch, I gave you those lines to help you to *remember* our trip back up here in that storm. The way you've been carrying on up here since then, it's like you've already forgotten it—"

"No I haven't."

"—Or you haven't been able to believe in it, or fit it into your life. But *it happened to you.*"

"I know that."

Those liquid brown eyes looked at me hard. Quietly he said, "You know that it happened. Now you have to go on from there. You have to learn from it, or it might as well not have happened."

I didn't follow him, but all of the sudden he was scraping the super resting on his knees. And saying, "I hear they're reading that book we brought back, down at the Marianis'—how come you're not down there?"

"What?" I cried. "Why didn't you tell me?"

"They weren't going to start until the bread was done. Besides, it was time for your lesson."

"But they would have finished baking midafternoon!" I said.

"Isn't that what time it is?" he asked, looking at the sky briefly.

"I'm gone," I said, snatching a dripping honeycomb from the flat behind him.

"Hey!"

"See you later." Off I ran, down the ridge trail, through the woods on a shortcut of my own, and through the potato patches to the Mariani herb garden. They were all out on the grass between the ovens and the river: Steve, Kathryn, Kristen, Mrs. Mariani, Rebel, Mando, Rafael, and Carmen. Steve was reading, and the others barely glanced at me as I sat down, huffing like a dog. "He's in Russia," Mando whispered. "Well shit!" I said. "How'd he get there?" Steve never looked up from the page, but kept on reading, from about here as I recall:

"In the first year after the war they were very open with the U.N., to show they had nothing to do with the attack. They gave the U.N. a list of all the Americans in Russia, and after that the U.N. was adamant about knowing where we were and what was happening to us. If it weren't for that

I wouldn't be speaking English. They would have assimilated us. Or killed us."

Johnson's tone made me look more closely at the heavily clad, harmless-looking Soviets who were crowded in with us. Some of them glanced at us furtively when they heard our foreign speech; most slumped in their seats and slept, or stared dully out the compartment window. The smell of tobacco smoke was powerful, masking to a certain extent other smells: sweat, cheese, the raw alcohol odor of the drink *vodka*. Outside the huge gray city of Vladivostok was replaced by rolling forest, mile after hilly mile of it. The train rolled along the tracks at a tremendous clip, and we crossed scores of miles every hour; still, Johnson assured me that our journey would take many days.

We had done little more than shake hands before walking under the eyes of the train guards, and playing our parts. Now I asked him about himself; where he lived, what his history had been, what his occupation was.

"I'm a meteorologist," he said. Seeing my look, he explained, "I study the weather. Or rather, I did study it. Now I watch a Doppler screen used to predict weather and give severe storm warnings. One of the last fruits of American science, the Doppler systems, as a matter of fact. But they're old now, and it's a minor position really."

Naturally I was interested in this. I asked him if he could tell me why the weather had become so much colder on the California coast since the war. This was several hours into our trip, and the Soviets around us filled the compartment with an air of utter boredom; at the prospect of talking about his specialty, Johnson's face brightened somewhat.

"It's a complicated question. It's generally agreed that the war did alter the world's weather, but how it effected the change is still debated. It's estimated that three thousand neutron bombs exploded on the continental United States that day in 1984; not too much long term radiation was released, luckily for you, but a lot of turbulence was generated in the stratosphere—the highest levels of air—and apparently the jet stream altered its course for good. You know about the jet stream?"

I indicated that I did not. "I have flown on a jet, however."

He shook his head. "At the upper levels of the air the

wind is constant, and strong. Big rivers of wind. In the northern hemisphere the jet stream circles around west to east, and zigzags up and down as it goes around the world, about four or five zigs and zags for every trip around." He made a ball of his fist and traced the course of the jet stream with a finger of his other hand. "It varies a little every time, of course, but before the war there was one anchor point, which was your Rocky Mountains. The jet stream invariably curved north around the Rockies, and then back south across the United States, like this." He pointed out the knuckle that had become the Rockies. "Since the war, that anchoring point has been gone. The jet stream has cut loose, and now it wanders—sometimes it's sweeping straight down from Alaska to Mexico, which is why you in California get Arctic weather occasionally."

"So that's it," I said.

"That's part of it," he corrected me. "Weather is such a complex organism, you can never point to any single thing and say, that's it. The jet stream is on the loose, but tropical storm systems are changed as well—and which caused which? Or are they causally related? No one can say. The Pacific high, for instance—this would affect you in southern California—there was a high pressure system, very stable, that sat off the west coast of North America. In the summer it would shift north and sit off California, keeping the jet stream pushed north; in the winter it would descend to an area below Baja California. Now it doesn't move north in the summer anymore, and so you aren't protected by it. That's another big factor; but again, cause or effect? And then there's the dust thrown into the stratosphere by the bombs and the fires, dropping world temperatures by a couple of degrees—and the permanent snowpack that resulted in the Sierra Nevada and the Rockies, generating glaciers that reflect the sunlight and cool things even more . . . and the shifting of Pacific currents . . . lots of changes." Johnson's expression was a curious mixture of gloom and fascination.

"It sounds as if California's weather has changed most of all," I said.

"Oh, no," Johnson said. "Not at all. California has been strongly affected, no doubt about it—like moving fifteen degrees of latitude north—but a few other parts of the world have been just as strongly affected, or even more so. Lots of rain in northern Chile!—and my, is that washing all that sand off the Andes into the sea. Tropical heat in Europe during the summer, drought during the monsoon—oh, I could go on and on. It has caused more human misery than you can imagine."

"Don't be so sure."

"Ah. Yes. Well, it isn't only the Soviets' gray empire that has made the world such a sad place since the war; the weather has had a large part in it. Happily Russia itself has not gone unaffected."

"How so?"

He shook his head, and wouldn't elaborate.

Two days later—still in Siberia, despite our speed—I saw what he meant.

We spent the morning out in the corridor of our car, exhibiting our travelling papers to a trio of suspicious conductors. The fact that I spoke not a word of Russian was a real stumbling block to their acceptance of us, and I chattered at them in Japanese and fake Japanese in a nervous attempt to assure them I was from Tokyo as my papers declared me to be, hoping they would not know how unlikely that was. Luckily our papers were authentic, and they left satisfied.

When they were gone Johnson was too upset to return to our compartment. "It's those stupid busybodies in there who got the conductors on us. They heard us speaking a foreign language and that was enough. That's the Soviets for you all over. Let's stay out here for a while. I can't stand the stink in there anymore anyway."

We were still out in the corridor, leaning against the windows, when the train came to a halt, out in the middle of the endless Siberian forest, with not a sign of civilization in sight. Tree-covered hills extended away in every direction for as far as the eye could see; we crossed a rolling green plane, under a low blue hemisphere filled with even lower clouds. I stopped my description of California, which Johnson could not get enough of, and we leaned out the window looking toward the front of the train. To the west the clouds, which had been low and dark, were now a solid black line. When Johnson saw this he leaned far out of the window, saying, "Hold my legs. Hold me in by the legs." When he slid back in there was a fierce grin on his usually dour face. Leaning close to me he whispered, "Tornado."

Within a few minutes conductors arrived in our car and instructed everyone to get off.

"Won't do a bit of good," Johnson declared. "In fact, I'd rather be on the train." Nevertheless we joined the crowd before the door.

"Why do they do it, then?" I asked, trying to keep an eye on the clouds to the west.

"Oh, once a whole train got picked up and flung all over the countryside. Killed everyone on it. But if you'd been standing right next to it you'd have been just as dead."

This was not very reassuring to me. "These tornadoes are common, then?"

Johnson nodded with grim satisfaction. "That's the weather change in Russia I mentioned. Warmer midcontinent, but they get tornadoes now. Before the war ninety-five percent of the world's tornadoes occurred in the United States."

"I didn't know that."

"It's true. They were the result of a combination of local weather conditions, and the specific geography of the Rockies, the Great Plains, and the Gulf of Mexico—or so they deduced, tornadoes being another meteorological mystery. But now they're common in Siberia." Our fellow travellers were staring at us, and Johnson waited to continue until we were off the train. "And they're big. Big like Siberia is big. Several towns have been torn off the map by them."

The conductors herded us to a clearing beside the track, at the very end of the train. Black clouds covered the sky, and a cold wind made a ripping sound in the trees. The wind grew stronger in a matter of minutes; leaves and small branches fell almost horizontally through the air above us, and by drawing just a few feet apart from the rest of the passengers, we could talk without being overheard; indeed, we could barely hear ourselves.

"Karymskoye is just ahead, I think," Johnson said. "Hopefully the tornado will hit it."

"You hope it will?" I said in surprise, thinking I had misunderstood, for to tell the truth Johnson's English was accented somewhat.

"Yes," he hissed, his face close to mine. In the muted green light he suddenly looked wild, fanatical. "It's retribution, don't you see? It's the Earth's revenge on Russia."

"But I thought it was South Africa that set the bombs."

"South Africa," he said angrily, and grabbed me by the arm. "How could you be so naive? Where did they *get* the bombs? Three thousand neutron bombs? South Africa, Argentina, Vietnam, Iran—it doesn't matter who actually put them in the United States and set them off, I doubt we'll ever know for sure—perhaps they all did—but it was *Russia* that made them, Russia that arranged for their use, Russia that profited most from them. The whole world knows it, and notes how these monstrous tornadoes plague them. It's *retribution*, I tell you. Look at their faces! They all know it, every single one of them. It's the Earth's punishment. *Look! There it is.*"

I looked in the direction he was pointing and saw that the black cloud to the west now sank to the earth at a certain point, in a broad, swirling black funnel of cloud. The wind howled around us, tearing at my hair, and yet I could still hear a low grinding noise, a vibration in the ground, as if a train many times larger than ours was speeding along distant tracks.

"It's coming this way," Johnson shouted in my ear. "Look how thick it is!" On his bearded, craggy face was an expression of religious rapture.

The tornado now slimmed to a black column, spinning furiously on itself. At its base I could make out whole trees flying away from it, scores of them. The bass roar of it grew; some of the Russians in the clearing fell to the ground, others knelt and prayed, raising twisted faces to the black sky; Johnson waved a fist at them, shouting soundlessly in the roar, his face contorted. The twister must have struck Karymskoye, because the flying trees were replaced by debris, pieces of a city reduced to rubble in an instant. Johnson danced a little tilted jig, leaning into the wind.

I myself kept an eye on the unearthly storm. It was moving from left to right ahead of us, approaching at an angle. The condensed spinning column was so solidly black that it might have been a tower of whirling coal. The bottom of this tower bounced off the ground from time to time; it touched down on a hill past the stricken town, blasted trees away from it, bounced into the air almost up to the black cloud above it, extended and touched down again, moved on. To my considerable relief it appeared that it would pass to the north of us by three or four miles. When I was sure of that, some of Johnson's strange elation spilled into me. I had just seen a town destroyed. But the Soviet Union was responsible for my country's destruction—thousands of towns—so Johnson had said, and I believed him. That made this storm retribution, even revenge. I shouted at the top of my lungs, felt the sound get torn away and carried off. I screamed again. I had not known how much I would welcome a blow struck against the murderers of my country —how much I needed it. Johnson pounded my shoulder and wiped tears from his eyes, we staggered against the wind across the clearing and into some trees, where we could scream and point and laugh and kick trees, and cry and shout curses too terrible to be heard, lamentations too awful to be thought. Our country was dead, and this poor exile my guide felt it as powerfully as I did. I put my arm around him and felt that I held up a countryman, a brother. "Yes," he hissed again and again. "Yes, yes, yes." Within twenty minutes the tornado bounced back up into the cloud for good, and we were left in a stiff cold wind to compose ourselves. Johnson wiped his eyes. "I hope it didn't tear up much track," he said in his slightly guttural accent, "or we'll be here a week."

A shadow fell across the book, and Steve stopped reading. We all looked up. John Nicolin stood there, hands on hips.

"I need your help replacing that bad keel," he said to Steve.

Steve was still in the forests of Siberia, I could tell by the distant focus of his eyes. He said, "I can't, I'm reading—"

John snatched the book from him and closed it, *thud*. Steve jerked up, then stopped himself. They glared at each other. Steve's face got redder and redder. I held my breath, disoriented by the abrupt removal from the story.

John dropped the book on the grass. "You can waste your time any way you want when I don't need your help. But when I need it, you give it, understand?"

"Yes," said Steve. He was looking down at the book now. He stretched to pick it back up, and John walked away. Steve kept inspecting the book for grass stains, avoiding our gazes. I wished I wasn't there to see it. I knew how Steve felt about having such scenes observed. And here were Kathryn, Mando, Kathryn's mother and sister and the others. . . . I watched John's wide back disappear down the river path and cursed him in my thoughts. There was no call for that sort of showing it over Steve. That was pure meanness—no past could excuse it. I was glad he wasn't my father.

"Well, so much for reading," Steve said in his joking tone, or close to it. "But how about that tornado, eh?"

"I got to get home to supper anyway," Mando said. "But I sure want to hear what happens next."

"We'll make sure you're at the next reading," Kathryn said, when it became clear that Steve wasn't going to respond. Mando said goodbye to Kristen and scampered off toward the bridge. Kathryn stood up. "I'd best see to the tortillas," she said. She bent over to kiss Steve's head. "Don't look so glum, everybody's got to work sometime."

Steve gave her a bitter glance and didn't reply. The others wandered off with Kathryn, and I stood up. "I'm off too, I guess."

"Yeah. Listen Hank, you're still seeing Melissa, aren't you?"

"Now and then."

He eyed me. "But you make good use of the time, I bet."

I shrugged and nodded.

"The thing is," he went on, "if we offer to guide these San Diegans into Orange County, we've got to know more than how to follow the freeway north. Anyone can figure that out. They might not want to have anything to do with us if that's all we can offer them. But if we knew where the Japanese were going to land, and when, they'd be bound to take us along, don't you see."

"Maybe."

"Sure they would! What do you mean maybe?"

"Okay, but so what?"

"Well, since you're friends with Melissa, why don't you ask Addison if he could help us out like that?"

"*What?* Oh, man—I barely know Add. And his business in Orange County is his own, no one ever asks him anything about that."

"Well," Steve said, looking at the ground despondently, "it sure would help us out."

I winced to hear him sound like that. We looked at the ground for a while. Steve thwacked the book against his thigh. "Wouldn't hurt to try, would it?" he pleaded. "If he doesn't want to tell us something like that, he can just say so."

"Yeah," I said doubtfully.

"Give it a try, okay?" He still wasn't looking me in the eye. "I really want to do something up north—fight 'em, you know?"

I wondered who he really wanted to fight, the Japanese or his pa. There he stood, looking down, frowning, hangdog, still smarting from his pa's lording it. I hated to see him look that way.

"I'll ask Add and see what he says," I said, letting my reluctance sound clear in my voice.

He ignored my tone. "All right!" He gave me a brief smile. "If he tells us something, we'll be guiding the San Diegans for sure."

It felt odd to receive gratitude from Steve. I hadn't seen it very often. Before, what we had done for each other was part of being friends—brothers—and it was regarded as such, as nothing remarkable. Before...oh, it was all changed now, changed past repair. Before when I disagreed with him, it was no big deal; we argued it out, and whatever the result, it was no challenge to his leadership of the gang. But now if I argued with him in front of the group, he wouldn't abide it, he'd get furious. Now questioning him was questioning his leadership, and all because I had been to San Diego and he hadn't. I was beginning to wish I'd never taken that stupid trip.

And now, to add to the mess, I was the one who was friendly with Melissa and Addison Shanks, so just when he least wanted to, Steve had to ask me to act, while he stood on the sidelines again and watched; and he had to be grateful in the bargain! And me—I couldn't argue with him without endangering our friendship; I had to go along with his every plan, even the ones I didn't like; and now, I had to go at his request and do something he would have loved to do himself, that I had *no* taste for. Things were...out of my control. (Or so it felt. We lie to ourselves a lot with that one.)

All of this occurred to me in a single snap of understanding—one of those moments when a lot of things I'd seen but not comprehended came together, as bits in the pattern of someone else's behavior, which now made sense. It was something that had happened to me more and more often that summer, but it still took me aback. I blinked and glanced at Steve again in a quick evaluation. "You'd better get down there and help your pa," I said.

"Yeah, yeah," he said, pissed again. "Back to the pit. All

right, see you soon, okay buddy?"

"See you," I replied, and walked up to the river path. When I got home I realized I hadn't seen a thing along my way.

Chapter Fourteen

I was out in Pa's garden one clear evening, enjoying the still sky and its arched range of blues, when I saw the fire on the ridge. A bonfire at Tom's place, blinking bright yellow in the dusk. I stuck my head in the door—"Off to Tom's," I said to Pa—and was gone. In the forest birds squeaked as I navigated my shortcut. It wasn't really visible at night, but I knew it by the feel of the ground and the shapes of the shadows, and even without the voices of the trees to guide me I almost ran. Through certain openings in the branches the bonfire winked at me, urging me along.

Up on the ridge I ran into Rafael, Addison and Melissa, the Basilone neighbors, standing in the trail and drinking a jar of wine. Tom's bonfires drew people. Steve and Emilia and Teddy Nicolin were already in the yard, tossing pitchy wood on the blaze. Tom led Mando and Recovery out of his house, coughing and laughing. The Simpson kids were popping around the junk in the yard, trying to scare each other. "Rebel! Deliverance! Charity! Get your asses out of there!" Recovery shouted. I grinned. It was a welcome sight, Tom's bonfire on the hill in the evening. We greeted each other and arranged the stumps and chairs a comfortable distance from the fire, and cheered a little when John and Mrs. Nicolin showed up with a bottle of rum and a big chunk of butter wrapped in paper. By the time Carmen and Nat and the Marianis showed up the party was in full swing. No one referred to the meeting, of course, but looking around I couldn't help thinking of it. This party was the antidote, so to speak. The idea of the gang bucking the vote made me uneasy, and I tried to forget it, but Steve kept jerking his head in Melissa's direction, already impatient for me to work on the Shankses.

Melissa was gulling with the Mariani girls, so I took my cup of hot buttered rum and sucked on it cautiously before the fire. Watched the flame spurt out of the beads of pitch. Mando was trying to make tripods of branches over the hottest part of the fire, playing with it (he learned that from me). Fire dazzles the mind into a curious sort of peace. It commands the eye's attention like no other sight. Yellow transparent banners, flicking up from wood and vanishing: what is that stuff, anyway? I asked Tom, but it was about the lamest of his explanations, and that's saying a lot. What it came down to was, if things got hot enough they burned; and burning was the transformation of wood to smoke and ash by way of flame. Rafael nearly strangled on his rum laughing when Tom finished.

"Very enlightening," I hooted, and dodged Tom's blows. "That's the lamest—hooo, heee—the lamest explanation you've ever made!"

"Wha—what about lightning?" Raphael cackled.

"What about why dolphins are warm-blooded?" Steve nodded. Tom waved us off like mosquitoes and went for more rum, and we settled down to giggling.

But Tom knew why fire so captured the eye and mind, or so it seemed to me. One time I had ventured that fire made a good image of the mind—thoughts flickering like flames, eventually exhausting the wood of our flesh. Tom had nodded but said no, it was the other way around. The mind, he said, was a good image of fire—at least in this respect: for millions of years, humans had lived even more humbly than we did. Right on the edge of existence, for literally millions of years. He swore to that length of time, and made me try to imagine that many generations, which of course I couldn't. I mean, think about it. Anyway, back at the beginning fire only appeared to humans as lightning and forest infernos, and they scorched a path from the eye to the brain. "Then when Prometheus gave us control of fire—" Tom said.

"Who's this Prometheus?"

"Prometheus is the name for the part of our brains that contains the knowledge of fire. The brain has growths like tubers, or boles on a tree, where knowledge of certain subjects accumulate. As the sight of fire caused this particular bole to evolve it got bigger, until it was named Prometheus and the human animal was in control of fire." So, he went on, for generation after generation to a number beyond counting men had sat around fires and watched them. To these ice-bitten ancestors fire meant warmth; to them, who bolted the flesh of smaller creatures every third day or so, it meant food. Between the eye and Prometheus grew a path of nerves like a freeway, and fire became a sight to turn the head and make one rapt. In the last century of the old time, civilized humanity had lost its dependence on simple fires, but that was no more than a blink of the eye in the span of human time; and now the blink was over, and we stared at fires hypnotized again. For the blink of time had done nothing to the road of nerves—every brain still had one—and it led fiery sensation to the dormant Prometheus as quickly as ever, rousing that old bole from his dreams and symbols and bright lost thoughts.

"Let's have a story," Rebel Simpson said.

"Yes, tell us one, Tom," Mando said.

The others joined me around the fire, and we sat in a semicircle sipping and contemplating, the kids darting to adjust firefly twigs in the coals. All agreed Tom should tell a story. He rocked in his outdoor rocking chair that threatened to flop backwards on every rock, and cleared his throat and grumbled about what work it would be. Patiently we waited him out, faces ruddy before the blaze.

"Tell us Johnny Pinecone," Rebel pleaded. "I want to hear Johnny Pinecone."

I nodded at that. It was one of my favorite things, to hear how in the last seconds of the old time Johnny had stumbled on one of the hidden atom bombs in the back of a Chevy van, and had thrown himself on it like a Marine on a grenade, to use Tom's expression, hoping to protect his fellow citizens from the blast—how he had survived in the bubble of still air at ground zero, but been blown miles high and rearranged by cosmic rays, so that when he floated down like a eucalyptus leaf he was loony as Roger, and immortal as well. And how he had hiked up into the San Bernadino Mountains and up San Gorgonio, and gathered pinecones and taken them back to the coastal plains, planting them on every new riverbank "to put a cloak of green over our poor land's blasted nakedness"— back and forth, back and forth for year after year after year, until the trees sprang up and blanketed the countryside, and Johnny sat down under a redwood growing like Jack's beanstalk and fell asleep, where he snores to this day, waiting for the time when he's needed again.

It was a fine story. But others objected that Tom had told it last season. "Don't you know more than three stories, Tom?" Steve ragged him. "Why don't you ever tell us a new one? Why don't you ever tell us a story about the old time?"

Tom gave him his mock glare and hacked. Rafael and Cov chimed in with Steve. "Give us one about you in the old time." I sucked rum and watched him closely. Would he do it this time? He looked a touch worn and out of sorts. He glanced at me, and I think he recalled our argument after the meeting, when I told him how great he always made America seem to us.

"Okay," he decided. "I'll give you a story of the old time. But I warn you, nothing fancy. This is just something that happened."

We settled back on our stumps and in our rain-warped chairs, satisfied.

"Well," he said, "back in the old time I owned a car. God's truth. And at the time of this story I was driving that car from New York to Flagstaff. A drive like that would take about a week, if you hurried. I was near the end of the trip, on Highway Forty in New Mexico. It was about sunset, and a storm was coming. Big black clouds looked like a wave rolling off the Pacific, pale blue sky still above and behind me, and the land below was desert floor littered with mesas. Nothing on it but shrubs and the two lines of the road. Ghost country.

"First thing I noticed was two sunbeams breaking over the top of the cloud front. You've seen that happen, but these two were like beacons, fanning out to left and right of me, like signs of some sort. Just think of those sunbeams—they had come *that close* to the earth" (holding up thumb and forefinger) "and yet missed, so they would proceed on all the way across the universe. But first they gave me a sign.

"Second thing that happened, the old Volvo puffed over a big rise, and a sign on top said *Continental Divide*. I should have known. Before the downslope there was a hitchhiker by the side of the road.

"Now at the time I was a lawyer, and I valued my solitude. For a whole week I didn't have to talk, and I liked that. Even though I owned a car I had hitchhiked in my time, and I had known the hitchhiker's despair, made of a whole bunch of little disappointments in humanity, slowly adding up. And it was about to rain, too. But I still didn't want to pick this guy up, so as I drove by I was kind of looking off to the left so I wouldn't have to meet his eye. But that would have been cowardice. So at the last second I looked at him. And believe me the moment I recognized him I put the car on the shoulder and skidded over the gravel to a halt.

"That hitchhiker was me. He was me myself."

"Oh you liar," Rebel said.

"I'm not lying! That's what it was like in the old time. I mean to tell you, stranger things than that happened every day. So let me get on with it.

"Anyway. We both knew it, this guy and me. We weren't just lookalikes, like the ones friends tell you about and then you meet them and they don't look anything like you. This guy was the one I saw in the mirror every morning when I shaved. He was even wearing an old windbreaker of mine.

"I got out of the car, and we stared at each other. 'So who are you?' he said, in a voice I recognized from tape recordings of myself.

"'Tom Barnard,' I said.

"'Me too,' says he.

"We *stared* at each other.

"Now as I said, at this time I was a lawyer, working winters in New York City. So I was a pretty slight little guy, with a bit of a gut. The other Tom Barnard had been doing physical work, I could tell; he was bigger, tough and fit, with a beard starting and a dark weathered color to his skin.

"'Well, do you want a ride?' I said. What else could I say? He nodded a bit hesitantly, picked up his backpack and walked to my car. 'So the Volvo is still hanging in there,' he said. We got in. And the two of us sitting there, side by side in the car, made me feel so strange I could hardly start the engine. Why, he had a scar on his arm where I once fell out of a tree! It was too uncanny. But I took off down the road anyway.

"Well, sitting there silent gave us both the willies, and we started to talk. Sure enough, we were the same Tom Barnard. Born in the same year to the same parents. By comparing pasts all through the years we quickly found the time we had separated or broken in two or whatever. One September five years before, I had gone back to New York City, and he had gone to Alaska.

"'You went back to the *firm?*' he asked. With a wince I nodded. I had thought of going to Alaska, I remembered, after my work with the Navaho Council was done, but it hadn't seemed practical. And after much deliberation I had returned to New York. In the end we pinned down the moment exactly: the morning I left for New York, driving before sunrise in the raw dawn silence, there was a moment getting on Highway Forty when I couldn't remember if the onramp was a simple left turn, or a cloverleaf circle to the right; and while I was still thinking about it I came to, already on the freeway headed east. The same thing had happened to my double, only he had gone west. 'I always knew this car was magical,' he said. 'There's two of it, too —but I sold mine in Seattle.'

"Well—there we were. The storm crashed over us, and we drove through little flurries of rain. Wind pushed the car around. After a time we got over our amazement, and we talked and talked. I told him what I had done in the last five years— mostly lawyering—and he shook his head like I was crazy. He told me what he had done, and it sounded great. Fishing in Alaska, mapping rivers in the Yukon, collecting animal skeletons for the fish and game service—hard work, out in the world. How his stories made me laugh! And from him I heard my laugh like other people heard it, and it only made me laugh the harder. What a crazy howl! Has it ever occurred to you that other people see you in the same way you see them, as a collection of appearances and habits and actions and words— that they never get to see your thoughts, to know how wonderful you really are? So that you seem as strange to them as they all appear to you? Well, that night I got to look at myself from the outside, and he sure was a funny guy.

"But the life he had lived! As we drove on, it gave me a sinking feeling in my stomach. See, he had lived a life right close to the one I had imagined living, there every winter in my little New York apartment. My life there—well, it was just sitting in boxes, one after the next, and watching people talk or talking myself. That was my life. But this Tom! He had gone and done what I wanted to do. And he didn't know what the rest of his life was going to be like, laid out for him like the road in front of us. I realized that I loved my cross-country drives because I *crossed country*—that during the times when I wished that I could turn the car around in New Mexico and head back to New York, there to turn and come west again, and keep on like that, as if the Volvo were on a pendulum hanging from the North Pole—it was because I wanted to stay in the country, to be out in it. I began to feel the emptiness of my life, the emptiness I had felt when I looked in the shaving mirror in my apartment in New York, looking at the lines under my eyes and thinking I could have lived a different life, I could have made it better.

"I got to feeling so low that eventually I suggested to my double that maybe I was no more than a hallucination he was having. It seemed to make sense. He had made the strong choice, I the weak—didn't it make sense that I was no more than a ghost come to haunt him, a vision of what would have happened if he had made the mistake of returning to New York?

"'I don't think so,' he answered. 'It's likelier I'm a hallucination of yours, that you stopped and picked up along the way. You'd have to be a hell of a hallucination to ferry me all the way across New Mexico, after all. No, we're both here all right.' He punched me lightly in the arm, and the spot he hit got very warm.

"'I guess we're both here,' I admitted. 'But how?'

"'There was too much of us for any one body to hold!' he said. 'That was why we had trouble sleeping.'

"'I still get insomnia,' I said. And I knew why—I had lived my life wrong, I had chosen to live in boxes.

"'Me too,' he said, surprising me. 'Maybe from sleeping on the ground so much. But maybe from living such a life as mine.' For a moment he looked as discouraged as I felt. He said, 'I don't feel like I'm doing anything real sometimes, 'cause no one else does. I'm against the grain, I guess. It can cut into your sleep all right.'

"So he had his troubles too. But they sounded like nothing compared to mine. He was healthier and happier than I, surely.

"The storm picked up and I put on the windshield wipers, adding their squeak to the hum of the engine and the hiss of the wet tires. Our headlights lit up gusts of rain, and on the other road trucks trailing long plumes of spray roared by, going east. We put Beethoven's Third on the tape deck; the second movement was up, sounding like noises made by the storm. We sat and listened to it, and talked about when we were a kid. 'Do you remember this?' 'Oh, yeah.' 'Do you remember that?' 'Oh man, I never wanted anyone else to find out about *that*.' And so on. It was pretty friendly, but it wasn't comfortable. We couldn't talk about our different lives anymore, because there was something wrong there, a tension, a disagreement even though neither of us was satisfied.

"It was starting to rain harder, and the car was buffeted hard by wind. Very little was visible outside the cones of light from the headlights—the black mass of the earth, the black clouds above. The march from the second movement, music grander than you folks can imagine, poured out of the speakers, matching the storm stroke for stroke. And we talked and laughed, and we filled with feeling and howled and pounded on the roof of the car, overwhelmed by all that was happening—because the two of us being there meant we were special, you see. It meant we were magical.

"But right in the middle of our howling the Volvo sputtered, at the top of another rise. I pressed on the gas, but the engine died. I coasted onto the shoulder and tried to start it. No luck. 'Sounds like water in the distributor,' my double said. 'Didn't you ever get that fixed?'

"I admitted I hadn't. After some discussion we decided to try and dry it off. That wasn't going to be easy, but it beat sitting in the car all night. We got out our ponchos, and luckily the rain diminished to a steady falling mist. By the time I got my poncho on, my companion had the hood up and was leaning over the engine. He had a small flashlight in one hand, and was pulling at the distributor with the other. I reached in and three Barnard hands went to work on it, taking the distributor cap off, pulling it apart, drying it, getting everything back together dry. My double ran to get a plastic bag while I hunched over the engine, feeling its warmth, my poncho extended like a cape. My double returned—we were working at emergency speed, you understand—and he leaned over the engine, and then all four of our hands were working on the distributor with uncanny coordination. When we were done clamping it down he dashed to the driver's seat and started the engine. It caught and ran, and he revved it. We had fixed it! As I closed the hood my double got out of the car grinning. 'All right!' he cried, and slapped my hand, and suddenly he leaped up and spun in the air, howling out the vowel-y Navaho chant we had learned as a boy—and there I was spinning with him, swirling my poncho out like a Hopi dancing cape, screaming my lungs out. Oh it was a strange sight, the two of us dancing in front of that car, on that high ridge, hollering and spinning and stomping in puddles, and I felt—oh there isn't the *word* for the way I felt at that moment, truly.

"The rain had stopped. On the horizon to the south little lines of lightning flashed from low clouds into the earth. We stood side by side and watched them, two or three every second. No thunder.

"'My life feels like this,' one of us said, but I wasn't sure who. And my right arm was hot, where it touched his left arm. I looked at it—

"And saw our arms met to enter a single hand. We were becoming one again. But it was a left hand—his hand. Then I noticed our legs came down to the same boot, a right boot. My foot.

"On the forearm wavering between us I could make out the reddish tissue connecting our arms, like burn-scar tissue. And I could feel the hot pulling and plucking. We were melting together! Already we shared part of the upper arm, and soon we would be joined at the shoulder like Siamese twins, and I felt the same burning in my right leg, oh, our time was up! First arms and legs, then torso then *heads!*

"I looked in his face and saw my mirror image, twisted with horror. I thought, that's what I look like, that's who I am, our time is over. Our eyes met.

"'*Pull,*' he said.

"We pulled. He grabbed the fender with his right hand, and I stepped out with my left foot, trying for traction in the muddy gravel. I leaned out and pulled like I had never pulled before. That forearm stuck out between us like a claw. We gasped and grunted and pulled, and the scar tissue above the elbow burned, and stretched, and gave us back a little of our arms. It was as painful as if I held onto something and deliberately tried to pull my arm off. But it was working. We both had elbows of our own now.

"'Hold on tight,' I gasped, and dove for the road! Boom! *Rip!*—an instant of agony, and I crashed onto wet asphalt. I pushed myself up with both hands. My feet were both there. I shook my right hand violently, grabbed my right boot. I was whole again.

"I looked at my double. He was leaning against the car, holding his left forearm in his right hand, shaking. Seeing it I felt my own trembling. He was staring at me with a furious expression, and for a second I thought he would attack me. For a second I had a vision, and saw him leap on me and pummel me, fists sinking into me and never coming out, so that we struggled and bit and kicked and melded into each other with every blow, until we became a single figure hitting itself, prone on the gravel, jerking and twitching.

"But that was a vision I had. In actuality, he shook his head hard, his lip curled into a bitter look.

"'I'd better go,' he said.

"Said I, 'I think you better.' As I got to my feet he walked to the passenger door, and got his backpack out. He pulled his poncho off to get the pack on his back.

"'Back to home for you, eh Thomas?' he said. There was contempt in his voice, and suddenly I was angry.

"'And you can hit the road again,' I said. 'And I'm glad to see you go. You had me feeling like my whole life was a mistake, like you did it right and I did it wrong. But I'm not doing it wrong! I'm living with people the way a human being should, and you're just taking the escape, wandering the road. You'll burn out quick enough.'

"He glared at me, and said, 'You've got me wrong, *brother*. I'm trying to live my life the best I know how. And I'm not going to burn out, ever.' He put his poncho back on. 'You take the name,' he said. 'I don't know if we live in the same world or not, but someone might notice. So you keep the name. I have the feeling you're the real Tom Barnard, anyway.'

"So we had traded curses.

"He looked at me one last time. 'Good luck,' he said. Then he walked away from the road, up the ridge. Through the mist, under that poncho, he looked inhuman. But I knew who he was. And as I watched him fade into the dark and the shrubs my spirit sank, and I was filled with despair. That was my own self disappearing there; I was watching my own true self walk away in the rain. No one should have to watch that.

"When I couldn't see him anymore I drove off in a panic. Creaks in the car made me jump into the steering wheel, and I was too scared to look back and see what it was. I drove faster and faster, and prayed the distributor would stay dry. The valleys of east Arizona rolled on and on, and for the first time, I think, I realized how gigantic the country really was. I couldn't stop thinking of what had happened. Things we had said seemed to ring aloud in the air. I wished that we had had more time—that we had parted friends—that we had allowed the joining to take place! Why were we so afraid of wholeness? But I was afraid; the fear of that union washed over me, and I drove ever faster, as if he might be running down the highway after me, wet and exhausted, miles behind."

Tom coughed a few times, and stared into the fire, remembering it. We watched him open mouthed.

"Did you ever see him again?" Rebel asked anxiously. That broke the spell and most of us laughed, including Tom. But then he frowned at her and nodded.

"Yes, I did see him again. And more than that."

We settled back; the older folks, who had heard this story before, I guessed, looked surprised.

"It was several years later when I next saw him; you'll know what year I mean. I was still a lawyer, older and slouchier and tubbier than ever. That was life in the old time—the years in the boxes took it out of you fast." At that point Tom looked at me, as if to make sure I was listening. "It was a stupid life really, and that's why I can't see it when people talk about fighting to get back to that. People back then struggled at jobs in boxes so they could rent boxes and visit other boxes, and they spent their whole lives running in boxes like rats. I was doing it myself, and it made no sense.

"Part of me knew that it made no sense, and I fought back in a weak sort of way. At this time I was out west doing that again, hiking a little. I decided to hike to the top of Mount Whitney, the tallest mountain in the United States. Weak as I was it was a killer task just to get up that ten mile trail, but after a couple days' hard work I made it. Mount Whitney. Right before sunset, this was—again—so that I was the only person on the peak, which was rare.

"So I was walking around the top, which was broad, nearly an acre. The trail goes up the west side, which is nice and gradual. But the eastern face is almost sheer, and looking down it into the shadows made me feel funny. Then I noticed a climber. He was coming up that sheer face alone, up one of the cracks in the face. Old John Muir had climbed the face alone like that, but he was crazy for risks, and few climbers since had exposed themselves to such danger. It made me dizzy to look at this guy's exposure, but I watched all the same, naturally. As he got higher he kept looking up, and at one point he saw me and waved. And I felt funny. The closer he got the more familiar he looked. And then I recognized him. It was my double, in climbing gear and full beard, looking as strong an animal as you could ask for. And there on that granite face!

"Well, I thought about hightailing it down the trail, but at one point when he looked up at me, I saw that he recognized me too, and I realized we would have to say hello. Or something. So I waited.

"It seemed to go on forever, the last part of that climb, and him in mortal danger the whole time. But when he crawled over the top, the sun was still over that distant western horizon, out over the Pacific way out there in the haze. He stood up, and walked toward me. A few feet away he stopped and we stared at each other wordlessly, in an amber glow of light like you only get in the Sierras at dusk. There didn't seem anything to say, and it was like we were frozen.

"And then it happened." Here Tom's voice took on a hoarse, harsh quality, and he leaned forward in his lame chair, stopping its rocking, and stared into the fire refusing to look at any of us. He hacked three or four coughs and spoke rapidly: "The sun was about half an orange ball lying out on the horizon, and—and one bloomed beside it, and then a whole bunch of others, up and down the California coast. Fifty suns all strung out and glowing for sunset. The mushroom balls as tall as us, and then taller. Little haloes of smoke around each column. It was the day, folks. It was the end.

"I saw what it was, and then I knew what it was; I turned to look at my double, and saw he was crying. He moved to my side and we held hands. So simple. We melted together as easy as that—as easy as agreeing to. When we were done, I was up there all alone. I remembered both of my pasts, and felt my brother's strength. The mushroom clouds blew toward me, coming on a cold wind. Oh I felt all alone, believe me, shivering and watching that horrible sight—but I felt, well . . . healed somehow, and . . . Oh, I don't know. I don't know. I got down off of there somehow."

He leaned back and almost rocked too far in his chair. We all took a deep breath.

Tom stood and prodded the fire with a stick. "You see, you couldn't live a whole life in the old time," he said, his voice relaxed again, even peevish. "It's only now that we're out by a fire, in the world—"

"No morals if you please," Rafael said. "You've told us enough of those lately, thank you." John Nicolin nodded at that.

The old man blinked. "Well, okay. Stories shouldn't have morals anyway. Let's get some more wood on that fire! This story's over, and I need something to drink."

With a cough he went to get the drink himself, and released us. Some stood and threw wood on the fire, others asked Mrs. N. if there was more butter—all a bit subdued, but satisfied. "How the old man talks," Steve said. Then he took my arm and indicated Melissa, over on the other side of the fire. I shrugged him off, but after a bit I walked around the fire and joined her. She put her arm around me. Feeling that small hand over my hip made the rum in me jump. We wandered out in the junk of the yard, and kissed hungrily. I was always surprised at how easy it was with Melissa. "Welcome home," she said. "You still haven't told me about your trip—I've heard it all second hand! Will you come over to my house later and tell me about it? Daddy will be there of course, but maybe he'll go to bed."

I agreed quickly, thinking more about her kisses than the information I was supposed to get from Add. But when it occurred to me (while nuzzling Melissa's neck, so beautiful in the firelight), I was pretty pleased with myself. It was going to be easier than I thought. "Let's see if there's more rum," I said.

A while later we had found the rum and downed it, and Addison had found us. "Let's be off," he said to Melissa gruffly.

"It's early yet," she said. "Can we bring Henry with us? I want to hear about his trip, and show him our house."

"Sure," Add said indifferently. I waved goodbye to Steve and Kathryn behind Melissa's back, and felt pretty slick when I saw Steve's startled expression. The three of us took off down the ridge trail. Add led Melissa and me across the valley without a word or a look back, so he didn't see Melissa's arm around my waist, nor her hand in my pocket. The pocket had a hole convenient to her, but I was none too comfortable with Add right in front of us, and I didn't respond except with a kiss on the bridge, where I could trust my footing. Stumbling along the path up Basilone I could feel the rum in my blood, and Melissa's fingers groping in my pants. Whew! But at the same time I was thinking, how am I going to ask Add about the scavengers and the Japanese? The rum sloshed my thoughts when I considered it, but it was more than the drink. There wasn't a good way, that was all there was to it. I would have to cast without bait and hope for the best.

The Shanks house was one of the old ones, built by Add before hardly anybody lived in Onofre. He had used an electric wire tower as the framework of the place, so it was small but tall, and strong as a tree. The shingled walls sloped inward slightly, and the four metal struts of the tower protruded from the corners of the roof, meeting in a tangle of metal far above it.

"Come on in," Add said hospitably, and took a key from his pocket to unlock the door. Once inside he struck a match and lit a lantern, and the smell of burnt whale oil filled the room. Boxes and tools were stacked against the walls, but there wasn't any furniture. "We live upstairs," Melissa said as Add led us up a steep plank staircase in one corner. She giggled and pushed my butt as she followed me up, and I almost banged into one of the thick metal struts of the old electric tower.

Nobody from Onofre Valley had ever been on the second floor, as far as I knew. But it was nothing special: kitchen in one corner, blond wood tables, an old couch and some chairs. Scavenger stuff all. A stairway leading to a trapdoor indicated another floor above. Add set the lantern on the stove, and commenced opening windows and throwing back the shutters guarding them. There were a lot of shutters. When he was done we had a view in all four directions: dark treetops, every way.

"You've got a lot of windows," I said, rum-wise. Add nodded. "Have a seat," he said.

"I'm going to change clothes," Melissa said, and went up the stairway to the floor above.

I sat in one of the big upholstered chairs, across from the couch. "Where'd you get all this glass?" I asked, hoping that would be a start on my ultimate subject. But Add knew that I knew where the glass came from, and he gave me a crooked smile.

"Oh, around. Here, have another glass of rum. I've got rum better than the Nicolins'."

I was fine on rum already, as I've mentioned, but I took a glass from him.

"Here, sit on the couch," Add said, and took back the glass while I moved. "It's got the better view. If the air's clear you'll see Catalina. If not, then the great sea. Getting to be your second home, I hear."

"My last home, almost."

He laughed long and loud. "So I hear. So I hear. Well." He sipped from his glass. "Quite a pleasant evening, this. I like Tom's stories."

"So do I." We both drank again, and for a moment it looked like we had run out of things to say. Luckily Melissa came back down the stairs, in a white house dress that pinched her breasts together. Smiling at us, she got a glass of rum for herself, and sat right beside me on the couch, pressing against my arm and leg. It made me nervous, but Add gave us his crooked smile (so different from Tom's crooked smile, which came of a busted mouth—Add only pulled back one side of his), and nodded, seeming satisfied with how cozy we were. He leaned back and balanced his glass on the worn arm of his chair.

"Good rum, isn't it?" Melissa said. I agreed that it was.

"We traded two dozen crabs for it. We only trade for the best rum available."

"I wish we were going to be trading with San Diego," Add said peevishly. "Was San Diego as big as Tom said it is?"

"Sure," I said. "Maybe bigger."

Melissa rested her head on my shoulder. "Did you like it down there?"

"I guess so. It was quite a trip, I'll say that."

They began to ask me about the details of it. How many little towns were there? Were there railroad tracks to all of them? Was the Mayor popular? When I told them about the Mayor's morning target practice they laughed. "And he does that every morning?" Add asked, rising to get us refills.

"So they said."

"That must mean they have a lot of ammunition," he said to himself in the kitchen. "Hey, this bottle's polished."

"You bet they do," I said. It seemed like there would be a way to get the conversation over to the scavengers pretty soon, so I relaxed and began to enjoy getting there. "They've got all those naval warehouses down there, and the Mayor has had every one of them explored."

"Uh huh. One moment; I have to go downstairs and get another bottle."

The second his head disappeared down the stairs Melissa and I kissed. I could taste the rum on her tongue. I put my hand on her knee and she tugged her dress up so I was holding her bare thigh. More kissing, and my breath got short. I kept pushing the dress higher and higher, until I found she wasn't wearing anything under it. Blood knocked in my ears with the shock of the discovery. Her belly pulsed in and out and she rocked over my hand, pushing down on it. We kissed harder, her hand squeezed my cock through my pants, and my breath left me entirely, whoosh, whoosh!

Thump, thump, answered Add's boots on the ladder, and Melissa twisted aside and threw her dress down. Fine for her, but I had a hard-on bulging my pants, and Melissa gave it a last malicious squeeze to make it harder still, giggling at my expression of dismay. I drank my rum and scrunched around in the corner of the couch. By the time Add had gotten in the room and broken the seal on the new bottle I was presentable, although my heart was still pounding double time.

We drank some more. Melissa left her hand on my knee. Add got up and wandered the dimly lit room, peering out the windows and opening first one and then another, adjusting the circulation, he said. The rum was clobbering me.

"Doesn't lightning ever hit your house?" I asked.

"Sure," they both said, and laughed. Add went on: "Sometimes it'll hit and a whole wall of shingles will pop off. Later when I check them they look all singed."

"My hair stands right on end," said Melissa.

"Aren't you afraid of being electrocuted?" I asked, patiently rolling out the last word.

"No, no," Add said. "We're pretty well grounded here."

"What's that mean?"

"It means the lightning runs down the corner poles into the ground. I had Rafe out to look at the place, and he said we're in no danger. I like to remember that when the lightning hits and the whole house shakes, and blue sparks are bouncing around like hummingbirds."

"It's exciting," Melissa said. "I like it."

Add continued to play with the windows. When he was looking away Melissa took my hand and put it in her lap, trapping it between her legs. When he turned our way she released it and I yanked back upright. It was driving me wild. It got to where I didn't wait for her to take my hand, but plunged for her whenever I could. We drank some more. Finally the windows were adjusted to Add's satisfaction, and he stood over the side of the couch, looking down at me as if he knew what we had been up to.

"So what do you think that Mayor of San Diego is really after?" he said.

"I don't know," said I. I was in a daze—impatient to get back under Melissa's dress, but very aware of Add standing right over me.

"Does he want to be king of this whole coastline?"

"I don't *think* so. He wants the Japanese off the mainland, that's all."

"Ah. That's what you said before, in the meeting. I don't know if I believe it."

"Why not?"

"There's no sense to it. How many men does he have working for him, did you say?"

"I don't think I said. I never really knew, exactly."

"Do they have any radio gear?"

"Why, how did you guess? They've got a big old radio down there, but it doesn't work yet."

"No?"

"Not yet, but they said they were planning to get a man over from the Salton Sea to fix it."

"Who said this, now?"

"The folks in San Diego. The Mayor."

"Well what do you know."

With all these questions I judged that it was a perfect time for some questions of my own. "Add, where *did* you get all this glass from?"

"Why, at the swap meets, mostly." He was looking at Melissa, now—they exchanged a glance I didn't understand.

"From the scavengers?"

"Sure. They're the ones selling glass, aren't they?"

I decided to tack a little closer to the wind. "Do you ever trade directly with the scavengers, Add? I mean, outside the swap meets?"

"Why no. Why do you ask?" He was still grinning his crooked grin, but his eyes got watchful. The grin left.

"No reason," I said, feeling all of a sudden like he could see through my eyes and read what I was thinking. "I was wondering, that's all."

"Nope," he said decisively. "I never deal with the zopilotes, no matter what you hear. I trap crabs under Trestles, so I'm up there a lot, but that's the extent of it."

"They lie about us," Melissa said tragically.

"No matter," Add said, the grin back in place. "Everyone collects stories of one sort of another, I reckon."

"True," I said. And it was true; everyone who didn't live right on the valley floor, where their lives were under constant examination, had stories told about them. I could see how rumors would grow especially fast around Addison, him being such a private man. It really wasn't fair to him. I didn't know what to say. Obviously Steve was going to have to find some other way to get information for the San Diegans. I blinked and breathed deep and regular, trying to control the effects of the rum. Add had never lit more than the one lantern, and even though the single flame was reflected in five or six windows, the room danced with shadows. There were a couple more swallows of the amber liquor in my glass, but I resolved to pass on them. Addison moved away from the couch, and Melissa sat up. Add went to the kitchen corner and consulted a large sand clock.

"It's been fun, but it's getting late. Melissa, you and I ought to be abed. We've got lots of work to do in the morning."

"Okay, Daddy."

"You walk Henry down and say goodnight to him real quick. Henry, come back and give us a visit sometime soon." I got to my feet, unsteady but eager, and Add shook my hand, squeezing hard and grinning at me. "Careful walking home."

"Sure. Thanks for the rum, Add." I followed Melissa down the ladder to the ground floor, and then out the door into the night. We kissed. I leaned back against the sloping wall of their house to keep myself upright, one leg thrust between Melissa's as she pressed against me. It reminded me of the first time we fooled around at the swap meet, only this time I was drunker. Melissa rubbed up and down my thigh, and let me feel her some more as she kissed my neck and breathed *umm, umm*, very softly. Then:

"He's waiting. I'd better go upstairs."

"Oh."

"Good night, Henry."

A peck on the nose and she was gone. I shoved off from the wall and staggered across the little clearing into the woods. There were foundations out there from the old time, the remnants of houses it looked like. Everything was gone except the concrete slabs, cracking under the weeds. I stumbled onto one of these and sat down for a bit, looking back through the trees at the Shankses' tower. There was a silhouette in front of the lights in the living room. I tasted the finger that had been feeling Melissa. The blood rushed to my head. It seemed a terrible amount of trouble to stand again, so I sat awhile and recalled the feel of her. I could see her, too—the silhouette was her —moving about the kitchen part of the upper room. Cleaning, I guessed. I don't know how much time passed, but suddenly their kitchen lantern went dark, then reappeared—once, twice, three and then four times. That seemed a little odd.

Off to my right I heard a twig snap. I knew instantly it was people, walking over another foundation. I crawled silently between two large trees and listened. Around to the north of the house there were people, at least two of them, not doing a very good job of moving through the woods quietly. Valley people would never have made such noise. And there was no reason for any of them to be up there anyway. All this occurred to me rapidly, no matter that I was drunk. Without thinking about it I found myself flat on my stomach behind a tree, where I could see the Shankses' door. Sure enough, shadows on the other side of the little clearing resolved into moving shapes, then into people, three of them. They walked right up to the door, said something up at the second story.

It was Melissa who let them in. While they were still on

the first floor I slipped through the trees quiet as owlflight, and hauled butt over to the wall of their house. I blessed my speed (fastest in Onofre by far) and held my breath. Only then did I wonder if I really wanted to be there. That's drunkenness for you—sometimes it can speed action by cutting out the thought.

From the ground I could hear their voices, but I couldn't make out enough of what they were saying to make sense of it. I remembered seeing blocks of wood nailed to the side of the house next to the door, making a ladder to the roof. I shifted along the wall to them, and step by step I ascended the blocks, taking a minute for each block so they wouldn't creak. When my head was under one of the windows I stopped and listened.

"They've got a radio," Addison said. "He says it isn't working yet, but they have someone from the Salton Sea coming out to try and fix it."

"That's probably Gonzalez," said a nasal, high voice.

A deeper voice added: "Danforth is always bragging he's got equipment right on the edge of working, but it doesn't always happen. Did he describe the radio's condition?"

"No," Add said. "He doesn't know enough to judge it, anyway."

They had been pumping me! Here I had gone up there thinking to pump them for information, and they had been pumping me instead. My face burned. And what was worse, Melissa had probably arranged with Add to come on to me after I had gotten good and drunk, to distract my attention from the questions! Now that was ugly.

And then Melissa said scornfully, "He doesn't know any more than the rest of those farmers."

"He knows books," Add corrected her. "And he was digging around trying to find out something, I don't know what. Glass? Or Orange, more likely. He may have just been curious. Anyway, he's not as ignorant as most of them."

"Oh, he's all right," Melissa said. "Can't hold his liquor, though."

One of the scavengers was moving about the room, and I could make out the bulk of him as he passed above me. I pressed into the wall and tried to look like a shingle. If they caught me . . . well, I could beat any of them through the woods at night. Unless I fell. I was in no shape for running, and suddenly I was scared, like I should have been all along.

They continued to discuss the San Diegans, and Addison

and Melissa told them everything I had said. I was surprised
at how much I had told them; I didn't even remember some
of it. They had pumped me good, that was sure. And I hadn't
learned a thing from them. I felt like a fool, and gritted my
teeth with dislike for those two.

But now I was getting back at them. And despite what she
had done and what she was saying, part of me wanted to get
Melissa's dress up again.

"Our island friends were planning to bring over people and
goods soon," the nasal one said. "We need to know how much
Danforth knows, and what he could do about it if he did know
anything. Maybe we should move the landing."

"They don't know anything," Add said. "And Danforth is
nothing but talk. If they could touch Dana Point they wouldn't
be asking the Onofre folks for help."

"They may just want a good harbor up the coast here," the
man above me said. He was facing my way. "Las Pulgas has
got too many sandbars, and it's too far away."

"Maybe. But from the sound of it they're nothing to worry
about."

The nasal one seemed to agree: "Danforth doesn't abide his
best man, from what I hear—he can't be much of a leader."

They discussed Danforth and his men in some detail, and
on my wooden step I trembled. To know so much they must
have spies everywhere! We were ignorant simpletons, compared to such a network.

"We should be off," said the nasal guy. "I want to be in
Dana Point at three." He went on, but the moment he mentioned
leaving I started inching down the blocks, shifting my weight
ever so slowly, and praying that the man above me was looking
into the room. I was stuck against the house; no matter which
way I left, there was a good chance someone would see me.
The shortest gap was to the west, so I went to that side of the
building and waited. Had they started downstairs? I guessed
that they had, and stole off into the trees. Foxes couldn't have
crossed that ground as fast as I did.

Sure enough, the scavengers quickly appeared at the front
door, and I saw Melissa in the doorway waving goodbye, still
in her white dress. I was tempted to approach the house again
and spy on the two of them, but I didn't want to press my
luck. As long as they didn't know I had overheard their meeting
with the scavengers, I had turned the tables on them. That felt

good. I started off for the river, walking slowly and quietly. In the end I had gotten more information than they had, and they still thought I was a dimwit; that might give me an advantage later. I wanted fiercely to get back at them. If only the scavengers had said exactly *when* the Japanese landing was going to be. . . . But I knew it was to be soon, and at Dana Point, and that was something substantial to tell Steve. Would I have a story for him. He would be envious again, I judged with drunken clarity. But I didn't care. I would get the Shankses—show Steve what I could do—whip the Japanese —get Melissa's dress off—triumph every which way—

A tree creaked and I jumped out of my shoes, practically. I started paying attention to my progress through the forest. It took a long time to get home, and then a long time to get to sleep. Such a night! I recalled hanging on the wall of the Shankses' house. Why, I had done it again. That Melissa, though—she had hurt my feelings. But all in all I felt good. Escaping the Japanese ship, foxing scavengers and their spies . . . smart work all round. . . . After some more of this drunken fuddle I fell asleep. That night I dreamt there were two of me, chased by two of the Japanese captain, and in a house over the river that didn't exist two Kathryns rescued us.

Chapter Fifteen

"Well, Henry," Steve said when I told him about my night (juicing it up a little, and leaving out the part where Add and Melissa had pumped me for everything I knew), "we're going to have to know *when* they're going to land at Dana Point, or we don't have anything. Think you can find out?"

"Now how am I going to do that?" I demanded. "Add isn't going to tell me a thing. Why don't you find that out?"

He looked offended. "You're the one who knows Melissa and Add."

"Like I said, that's no help."

"Well—maybe we could spy on them again," he suggested dubiously.

"Maybe we could."

We went back to fishing in silence. Sun smashing down on the water and breaking bright white over every swell. Hot days like this were my special joy—the hillsides steamed, the water and sky were two shades of the same rich blue —but on this day I wasn't paying much attention to it. Steve

233

was speculating about how we might spy on Add, and planning what he would say to Lee and Jennings. He had worked out everything he was going to say to them to convince them to let us guide them into Orange. As we rowed back to the rivermouth I spoke for the first time since telling him my story: "You can put all that good planning to work—that's Jennings on the beach talking to your pa."

"It is?"

"Yep. Don't you recognize him?" Even with his face smaller than my little fingernail I knew him. At the sight of him all my San Diego trip came back to me at once, as something that had really happened to me. It made me shiver. There was no sight of Lee. Jennings was talking as usual. Now that I could see him in the flesh our whole plan seemed foolish. "Steve, I still don't think dealing with the San Diegans on our own is a good idea. What'll the rest of the valley say when they find out?"

"They won't find out. Come on, Henry, don't fade on me now. You're my best friend, aren't you?"

"Yeah. But that don't mean—"

"It means you've got to help me with this. If you don't help I can't do it."

"Well . . . shit."

"We've got to hear what they're saying there." He rowed like he was in a race to the flats. As we grounded over the sand I said,

"How will we get close enough to hear?"

We jumped out and lifted the boat forward on the next spent swell. "Walk the fish past them and listen while you're near. I'll follow you, and we'll piece together what we heard."

"That won't be easy."

"Shit, we know what Pa is saying. Just do it!"

I picked up a pair of rock bass by the gills and trundled slowly across the rimpled sand to the cleaning tables, walking right behind Jennings. He turned and said, "Why hello, Henry! Looks like you made it home safe enough."

"Yes sir, Mr. Jennings. Where's Mr. Lee?"

"Well, now. . . ." His eyes narrowed. "He's not with us this time. He sends his regards." The two men with Jennings (one had been on my train, I thought) smirked.

"I see." That was too bad, I thought.

"We went up to see your friend Tom, but he was in bed

sick. He told us to come and talk to Mr. Nicolin here."

"Which is what we're doing now," John said, "so clear out, Hank."

"Sick?" I said.

"Get going!" John said.

Jennings said, "Talk to you later, friend."

I carried the bass up to the cleaning tables and said hello to the girls. Walking back to the boat I passed Steve, then heard John say, "You got no call to be pressing on this, Mister. We don't want any part of it."

"All well and good," Jennings said, "but we need to use the tracks, and they run right across your valley."

"There are tracks back in the hills. Use those."

"Mayor doesn't want that."

And then I was out of earshot. It was tough hearing their voices with the gulls stooping us and screeching over the offal. I picked up a bonita and another bass and hurried back. Steve was just past them.

"Barnard wouldn't talk to me," Jennings said. "Is that because he wants us to work together?"

"Tom voted against helping you along with the majority of the people here, so that's that."

Over at the cleaning tables Mrs. Nicolin said, "Why is that man arguing with John?"

"He wants us to let them use the train tracks in the valley, and all that."

"But they're ruined, especially at the river."

"Yeah. Say, is the old man sick?"

"So I hear. You should go up and see."

"Is he bad?"

"I don't know. But when the old get sick . . ."

Steve nudged me from behind, and I turned to walk back.

"The Mayor ain't going to like this," Jennings was saying. "No one down our way is. Americans got to stick together in these times, don't you understand that? Henry! Did you know your trip to San Diego has gone to naught?"

"Um—"

"You know what's going on here?"

John waved a hand at me angrily. "You kids clear out," he ordered.

Steve heard that over the crying gulls, and he led me up the cliff path. From the top we looked back at the river flat;

Jennings was still talking. John stood there with his arms across his chest. Pretty soon he was going to grab Jennings and throw him in the river.

"That guy is a fool," Steve said.

I shook my head. "I don't think so. The old man is sick, did you know that?"

"Yeah." He didn't sound interested.

"Why didn't you tell me?"

He didn't reply.

"I'm going to go see how he's doing." He had been coughing a lot when he told his story. And even back at the meeting he had seemed listless and hacky. All I remembered about my mother's death was that she had coughed a lot.

"Not yet," Steve said. "When that guy gives up on Pa we can catch him alone and tell him our plan."

"Jennings," I said sharply. "His name is Jennings. You'd better know that when you talk to him."

Steve looked me up and down. "I knew it."

I walked down the path a ways, angry. Down by the tables John walked away from the San Diego men, brushing by one of them with his shoulder. He turned to say something, and then the San Diegans were left to look at each other. Jennings spoke and they started up the cliff trail. "Let's get out of sight," Steve said.

We hid in the trees south of Nicolins' yard. Soon Jennings and his men appeared over the cliff edge and started our way. "Okay, let's go," I said. Steve shook his head. "We'll follow them," he said.

"They might not like that."

"We have to talk to them where no one will see us."

"Okay, but don't surprise them."

When they were in the trees to the south we took off in pursuit, stopping every few trees to peer ahead, like bandits in a story.

"There they are," Steve said, flushed with excitement. Their dark coats flashed through the trees ahead of us, and I could hear snatches of Jennings' voice, carrying on as usual.

Steve nodded. "In these woods is as good a place as any."

"Uh huh."

"Well, let's stop them."

"Fine," I said. "I'm not holding you back."

Once again he gave me the eye. He stepped out from behind a tree. "Hey, stop! Stop up there!"

Suddenly the forest was silent, and the San Diegans were nowhere to be seen.

"Mr. Jennings!" I called. "It's me, Henry! We need to talk to you."

Jennings stepped out from behind a eucalyptus, putting a pistol back in a coat pocket. "Well, why didn't you say so?" he said irritably. "You shouldn't be surprising people in the woods."

"Sorry," I said, giving Steve a look. He was flushed red.

"What do you want?" Jennings said impatiently. His two men appeared behind him.

"We want to talk with you," Steve said.

"I heard that. So speak up; what do you want?"

After a pause Steve said, "We want to join the resistance. Not everyone in the valley is against helping you. In fact, it was a damn close vote. If some of us were to help you, the rest of the valley might come along, eventually."

One of Jennings' men snickered, but Jennings silenced him with a gesture. "That's a good thought, friend, but what we really need is access through your valley to the north, and I don't think you can give us that."

"No, we can't. But we can guide you when you're up in Orange, and that's more important. If that goes right, like I said, the rest of the valley will probably join in later."

I stared at Steve in dismay, but Jennings wasn't looking at me.

"We know scavengers who are on our side," Steve went on. "We can find out from them when the Japanese will be landing, and where."

"Who can tell you that?" Jennings asked skeptically.

"People we know," Steve replied. Seeing the doubtful look on Jennings' face he said, "There are scavengers up there who know about the scavengers dealing with the Japanese, and they don't like it. There's not much they can do about it, but they can tell us, and then we'll do something about it, right? We've been up there a lot, we know the lay of the land and everything."

Jennings said, "We could use information like that."

"Well, we can do it."

"Good. That's good." Slowly he said, "We might make arrangements for getting information from you now and then."

"We want to do more than that," Steve said flatly. "We can guide you up to whatever spot the Japanese are landing at, no matter where it is. There aren't any of you know the ruins like we do. We've been up there at night a whole bunch of times. If you're going up there on a raid, you'll need to have someone who knows the land, to get you there and back fast."

Jennings' face wasn't much at concealing his thoughts, and now he looked interested.

"We want to go up there with you and fight them," Steve said more vehemently. "We're like the Mayor—we want the Japanese too scared to come ashore ever again. You provide the men and guns, and four or five of us will guide you up there and fight with you. And we'll tell you when the landings are going to happen."

"That's quite a proposal." Jennings drawled, looking at me.

"We're young, but that doesn't matter," Steve insisted. "We can fight—we'd ambush them good."

"That's what we do," Jennings said harshly. "We ambush and kill them. We're talking about killing men."

"I know that." Steve looked offended. "Those Japanese are invaders. They're taking advantage of our weakness. Killing them is defending the country."

"True enough," Jennings agreed. "Still . . . that man down there wouldn't appreciate us dealing with you behind his back, would he. I don't know if we should do that."

"He'll never hear of it. Never know of it. There's just a few of us, and none of us will say a word. We go up into the ruins at night a lot—they'll think we're doing that again when we go with you. Besides, if things go well, they'll have to join us."

Jennings shifted his gaze to me. "Is that so, Henry?"

"Sure is, Mr. Jennings." I went right along with it. "We could guide you up there and no one would be the wiser."

"Maybe," Jennings said. "Maybe." He glanced back at his men, then stared at me. "Do you know right now when a landing party is coming in?"

"Soon," Steve said. "We know one is coming in soon. We already know where, and we'll find out exactly when in the next few days, I'd guess."

"All right. Tell you what. If you hear of a landing, you

come tell us at the weigh station where we stopped working the tracks. We'll have men there. I'll go back south and talk to the Mayor, and if he agrees to the idea, which maybe he will, then we'll bring men up and be ready to move. We got the tracks working again, did I tell you that, Henry? It was tough, but we did it. Anyway, you know where those buildings are, the weigh station."

"We all know that," Nicolin said.

"Fine, fine. Now listen: when you get word of a Jap landing, hustle to the station and tell us, and we'll see what we can do about it. We'll leave it at that for now."

"We have to go along on the raid," Steve insisted.

"Sure, didn't I say that? You'll be our guides. All this depends on the Mayor, you understand, but as I said, I think he'll want to do it. He wants to hit those Japs any way he can."

"So do we," Steve said, "I swear it."

"Oh, I believe you. Now, we'd better be off."

"When can we check with you and see what the Mayor said?"

"Oh—a week, say. But get down there sooner if you hear word."

Nicolin nodded, and Jennings pointed his men south.

"Good talking with you, friends. Good to know that someone in this valley is an American."

"That we are. We'll see you soon."

"Goodbye," I added.

We watched them slip through the trees in the forest. Then Steve struck me on the arm.

"We did it! They're going for it, Henry, they're going to do it."

"Looks like it," I said. "But what was that you said about how we'll know when the landing will come in a few days? You lied to them! There's no way we can be sure when we'll find that out, if we ever do at all!"

"Ah come on, Henry. You could see I had to tell them something. You pretend to object to all this, but you like it as much as I do. You're good at it! You're the fastest thinking, fastest running resistance man around, and the cleverest in figuring these kinds of things out. You'll be able to find out that landing date if you want to."

"I suppose I can," I said, pleased despite myself.

"Sure you can."

"Well . . . let's get back before anyone notices we're missing."

He laughed. "See? You are good at this, Henry, I swear you are."

"Uh huh."

And the thing is, I thought he was right. I was the one who had kept Jennings and his men from shooting us by mistake, back there. And every time I was in a spot, the right things seemed to happen to get me out of it. I began to feel that these things didn't just happen to me, but that I was doing them. I *made* them turn out right. And that meant I was in control of events; I could make sure that we joined the resistance, and fought the Japanese, without breaking the vote or getting the rest of the valley angry at us. I really thought I could do it.

Then I remembered the old man, and all my feeling of power vanished. We were still in the forest between the Nicolins' and Concrete Bay; if I headed inland I would soon run onto Tom's ridge.

"I'm going up to see how the old man is doing," I said.

"I've got to get back to the pit," Steve said. "But I'll—wait a minute!"

But I was already off, making my way through the trees inland.

Chapter Sixteen

The old man's yard always looked untended, with weeds growing over the collapsing fence and junk scattered everywhere. But now as I climbed the ridge path apprehension made me see it all again: the small weatherbeaten house with its big front window reflecting the sky; the yard drowning in weeds; the gnarled trees on the ridge tossing in the wind, and snatching at the steam clouds that were growing with every minute. It all looked abandoned. If the house's owner had been dead and buried ten years, it would all look as it did now.

Kathryn appeared in the window, and I tried to change my thoughts. Wind pushed the weeds up and down. Kathryn saw me and waved, and I lifted my head in hello. She opened the door as I walked into the yard, and met me in the doorway.

Casually I said, "So how's he doing? What's wrong with him?"

"He's asleep now. I don't think he slept much last night, he was coughing so bad."

"I remember he coughed some when he told us that story."

"It's worse now. He's all congested."

I studied Kathryn's face, saw the well-known pattern of freckles shifted by lines of concern. She reached out to hold my arm. I hugged her and she put her head to my shoulder. It scared me. If Kathryn was scared, I was terrified. I tried to reassure her with my hug, but I was trembling.

"Who's that out there?" Tom called from the bedroom. "I'm not sleeping, who's there?"

Then he coughed. It was a deep, wet, hacking sound, like he was choosing voluntarily to put a lot of force behind it.

"It's me, Tom," I said when he was done. I went to the door of his room. None of us had ever been welcome in there; it was his private place. I looked in. "I heard you were sick."

"I am." He was sitting up in bed, leaning against the wall behind it. He looked sick, there was no doubt about it. Hair and beard were tangled and damp, face sweaty and pale. He eyed me without moving his head. "Come on in."

I walked into the room for the first time. It was filled with books, like the storeroom down the hall. There was a table and chair, several books on each; a stack or two of records; and tacked to the wall under the one small window, a collection of curled photographs.

I said, "I guess you must have caught a cold on our trip back."

"Seems to me it should've been you who got it. You got the coldest."

"We all got cold." I remembered how he had walked on the seaward side of me to break the wind. The times he had held me up as we walked. I looked at the photographs, heard Kathryn move things around in the big room.

"What's she doing out there?" Tom asked. "Hey, girl! Quit that in there!" He stared to cough again.

When he was done my heart was pounding. "Maybe you shouldn't shout," I said.

"Yeah."

Lamely I added, "It's rotten to have a cold in the summer."

"Yeah. Sure is."

Kathryn stood in the doorway.

"Where's your sister?" Tom said. "She was just here."

"She had to go do some things," said Kathryn.

"Anybody home?" came a voice from the door.

"That must be her now," Kathryn said. But it had been Doc's voice.

"Uh oh," said Tom. "You didn't."

"I did," Kathryn said apologetically.

Doc barged into the room, black bag in hand, Kristen on his heels.

"What are you doing here?" Tom said. "I don't want you fussing with me, Ernest. You hear?" He shifted in his bed until he was against the side wall.

Doc approached him with a fierce grin.

"Leave me alone, I'm telling you—"

"Shut up and lie flat," Doc said. He put his bag on the bed, and pulled his stethoscope from it.

"Ernest, you don't need to do this. I've just got a cold."

"Shut up," Doc said angrily. "Do as I say, or I'll make you swallow this." He held up the stethoscope.

"You couldn't make me blink." But he lay flat, and let Doc take his pulse, and listen to his chest with the stethoscope. He kept complaining, but Doc stuck a thermometer in his mouth, which shut him up, or at least made him incomprehensible. Then Doc went back to listening.

After a bit he removed the thermometer from Tom's mouth and examined it. "Breathe deep," he ordered, listening again to Tom's chest.

Tom breathed once or twice, caught—held his breath till he turned pink—then coughed, long and hard.

"Tom," Doc said in the following silence (I had been holding my breath), "you're coming to my house for a visit to the hospital."

Tom shook his head.

"Don't even try to argue with me," Doc warned. "It's the hospital for you, boy."

"No way," Tom said, and cleared his throat. "I'm staying here."

"God damn it," Doc said. He was genuinely angry. "It's likely you have pneumonia. If you don't come with me I'm going to have to move over here. Now what's Mando going to think of that?"

"Mando would love it."

"But I wouldn't." And Tom caught the look on Doc's face. It was probably true that Doc could have moved to Tom's easier than Tom could move to Doc's. But Doc's place was the hospital. Doc didn't do much serious doctoring any more— I mean he did what he could, but that wasn't much, sometimes. Breaks, cuts, births—he was good at those. His father, a doctor gone crazy for doctoring, had made sure of that years ago when Doc was young, teaching him everything he knew with a fanatic insistence. But now Doc was responsible for his best friend, who was seriously ill—and maybe moving Tom to the hospital was a way to say to himself that he could do something about it. I could see Tom figuring this out as he looked at Doc's face—figuring it out more slowly than he usually would have, I thought. "Pneumonia, eh?" he said.

"That's right." Doc turned to us. "You all go outside for a bit."

Kathryn and Kristen and I went out and stood in the yard, amid all the rusty machine parts staining the earth. Kristen told us how she had located Doc. Kathryn and I stared out at the ocean, silently sharing our distress. Clouds were rolling in. It happened so often like that—a sunny day, blanketed by mid-afternoon by clouds. Wind whipped the weeds, and our hair.

Doc looked out the door. "We need some help in here," he said. We went inside. "Kathryn, get some of his clothes together, a few shirts he can wear in bed, you know. Henry, he wants to get some books together; go find out which ones he wants."

I went back in the bedroom and found Tom standing before the photographs tacked to the wall, holding one flat with a finger. "Oh, sorry," I said. "Which books do you want to take?"

He turned and walked slowly to the bed. "I'll show you." We went to the storeroom, and he looked around at the books stacked in the gloom. A pile near the door contained every book he wanted. He handed them to me from a crouch. *Great Expectations* was the only title I noticed. When my arms were full he stopped. He picked up one more.

"Here. I want you to take this one."

He held out the book that Wentworth had given us, the one with blank pages.

"What am I going to do with this?"

He tried to put it in my arms with the rest, but there wasn't room.

"Wait—I thought you were going to write your stories in that."

"I want you to do it."

"But I don't know the stories!"

"Yes you do."

"No I don't. Besides, I don't know how to write."

"The hell you don't! I taught you myself, by God."

"Yeah, but not for books. I don't know how to write books."

"It's easy. You just keep going till the pages are full." He forced the book under my arm.

"Tom," I protested, "no. You're supposed to do it."

"I can't. I've tried. You'll see the pages ripped out of the front. But I can't."

"I don't believe it. Why, the story you told the other night—"

"Not the same. Believe me." He looked desolate. We stood there looking at the blank book in my arms, both of us upset. "The stories I've got you wouldn't want written down."

"Oh, Tom."

Doc came in the room. "Henry, you aren't going to be able to carry those books. Give them to Kristen; she's got a bag."

"Why, what am I carrying?"

"You and I are carrying Tom here, young man, can't you figure that out? Does he look like someone ready to walk across the valley?"

I thought Tom would hit him for that, but he didn't. He just looked morose and tired and said, "I wasn't aware you owned a stretcher, Ernest."

"I don't. We'll use one of your chairs."

"Ah. Well, that sounds like hard work." He walked into the big room. "This one by the window is the lightest." He carried it out of the house himself, then sat in it.

"Put those books in Kristen's bag," said Doc.

"Ooof," Kristen said as I piled them in. I went to help Kathryn find Tom's shirts. Curiously I checked the photograph Tom had been looking at; it was a woman's face. Kathryn lifted an armful of clothes, and we went outside. The old man was staring at the sea. It was getting blustery, and halfway to the horizon a few whitecaps appeared and disappeared.

"Ready?" Doc asked.

Tom nodded, not looking at us. Doc and I got on either side of him and lifted the chair by its arms and bottom. Tom craned around to look back at his house as we stepped slowly down the ridge trail. Mouth turned down he said, "I am the last American."

"The hell you are," I said. "The hell you are." And he chuckled, faintly.

It was tricky getting down the ridge path, but on the valley floor he seemed heavier. "Change places with me," Kathryn said to Doc. We put the chair down; Tom sat there with his eyes closed and never said a word. So strange, to have the old man quiet! Though the wind was brisk, there was sweat beading on his forehead.

Kathryn and I lifted him. She was a lot stronger than Doc, so I had less to carry. Into the forest shade we went.

"Am I heavy?" Tom asked. He opened his eyes and looked up at Kathryn. Her thick freckled arms came together at the elbows, pinning her breasts together in front of his face. He mimicked a bite at them.

She laughed. "No more than a chairful of rocks," she said.

At the bridge we stopped for a rest, and watched the clouds roll over us, talking as if we were on a normal outing. But with Tom in the chair it wasn't natural. On the bank upstream a group of kids splashed in the water; they stopped to watch us as we got across the bridge, which was narrow enough to force me to lead, walking backwards. Tom stared mournfully at the naked brats as they pointed and shrieked. Kathryn saw the look on his face and she squinted at me unhappily. Fat gray clouds lowered over us, the wind tossed our hair, it was cold, and getting darker. . . . Miserably I tried to find a way to distract Tom.

"I still don't see what I'm going to do with that blank book," I said. "You better keep it, Tom, you might want to do some writing in it up at Doc's."

"Nope. It's yours."

"But—but what am I going to do with it?"

"Write in it. That's why I'm giving it to you. Write your own story in it."

"But I don't have a story."

"Sure you do. 'An American at Home.'"

"But that's nothing. Besides, I wouldn't know how."

"Just do it. Write the way you talk. Tell the truth."

"What truth?"

After a long pause, he said, "You'll figure that out. That's what the book is for."

He lost me there, but by that time we were working our way up the path to the Costas', and were almost to the little cleared terrace in the hillside that it sat on. I looked at Kathryn and she thanked me for distracting him with a quick smile. We hefted him up the last steps.

The Costas' house gleamed black against the trees and clouds. Mando came out and greeted us. "How are you, Tom?" he said brightly. Without answering Tom tried to stand up and walk through the door into their house. He couldn't do it, and Kathryn and I carried him in. Mando led us to the corner room that they called the hospital. Its two outer walls were oil drums; there were two beds, a stove, an overhead trap door to let sun and air in, and a smooth wood floor. We put Tom on the corner bed. He lay there with a faint frown turning his mouth. We went into the kitchen and let Doc look at him.

"He's real sick, huh?" said Mando.

"Your dad says it's pneumonia," Kathryn said.

"I'm glad he's here, then. Have a seat, Henry, you look bushed."

"I am." While I sat Mando got us cups of water. He was always a conscientious host, and when Mando and Kristen weren't looking, Kathryn and I smiled a little to see him. But not much; we were glum. Mando and Kristen talked on and on, and Mando got out some of his animal drawings to show her.

"Did you really see that bear, Armando?"

"Yes, I sure did—Del can tell you, he was with me."

Kathryn jerked her head at the door. "Let's go outside," she said to me.

We sat on the cut log bench in the Costas' garden. Kathryn heaved a sigh. For a long time we sat together without saying a word.

Mando and Kristen came out. "Pa says we should find Steve, and get him to come up and read from that book," Mando said. "He said Tom would like that."

"Sounds like a good idea," Kathryn said.

"I think he'll be at his house," I told them. "Or down the cliff right by the house, you know the place."

"Yeah. We'll try there." They walked on down the path, hand in hand. We watched them till they were out of sight, then sat silently again.

Abruptly Kathryn slapped at a fly. "He's too old for this."

"Well, he's gotten sick before." But I could tell this time was different.

She didn't answer. Her wild hair lifted and fell in the nippy onshore wind. Under the growing clouds the valley's forest was intensely green. All that life . . .

"I think of him as ageless," I said. "Old, but—you know —unchanging."

"I know."

"It scares me when he gets sick like this!"

"I know."

"At his age. Why, he's ancient."

"Over a hundred." Kathryn shook her head. "Incredible."

"I wonder why we get old at all. Sometimes it doesn't seem . . . natural."

I felt her shrug more than saw it. "That's life."

Which wasn't much of an answer, as far as I was concerned. The deeper the question the shallower the answer—until the deepest questions have no answers at all. Why are things the way they are, Kath? A sigh, arms touching, curled hairs floating across one's face, the wind, the clouds overhead. What more answer than that? I felt choked, as if oceans of clouds filled me to bursting. A strand of Kathryn's hair rolled up and down my nose, and I watched it fiercely, noted its every kink and curl, every streak of red in the brown, as a way to hold myself all in . . . as a way to grab the world to me with my senses, to hold it against me so it couldn't slip away. (So all our ways fail.) Kathryn said, "Steve is so tense these days I'm afraid he's going to break. Like a twenty-pound bowstring on a sixty-pound bow. Fighting with his pa. And all that shit about the resistance. If I don't agree with every word he says, he starts a fight with me. I'm getting so sick of it."

I didn't know what to say.

"Couldn't you talk to him about it, Henry? Couldn't you discourage him about this resistance thing somehow?"

I shook my head. "Since I got back, he won't let me argue with him."

"Yeah, I've seen that. But in some other way. Even if you're for the resistance yourself, you know there's no reason to go crazy over it."

I nodded.

"Something other than arguing with him. You're good with

words, Henry, you could find some way to dampen his enthusiasm for all that."

"I guess." What about my enthusiasm, I wanted to say; but looking at her I couldn't. Didn't I have doubts, anyway?

"Please, Henry." She put her hand on my arm again. "It's only making him unhappy, and me miserable. If I knew you were working on him to calm him down, I'd feel better."

"Oh Kath, I don't know." But her hand tightened around my upper arm, and her eyes were damp. This was Kathryn, the girl who had bossed me, now asking for my help friend to friend. With her hand touching me I felt connected with all this world that rushed over us, so chill and so beautiful. "I'll talk to him," I said. "I'll do my best."

"Oh, thank you. Thank you. No matter what you say, he listens to you more than anybody else."

That surprised me. "I'd think he'd listen to you most."

She pursed her lips, and her hand returned to her lap. "We aren't getting along so well, like I said. Because of all this."

"Ah." And I had agreed to help her there (I would always agree to help her if she asked, I realized) at the same time that I was conspiring with Steve in every spare moment to take the San Diegans into Orange County! What was I doing? When I thought about what I had just done it made me feel sick. All my connection with the green and white and the sea smell and the trees' voices disappeared, and I almost said to Kathryn I can't do it, I'm with Steve on this. But I didn't. I felt a knot tie inside me, over my stomach.

Steve appeared on the path below, leading Mando and Kristen and Gabby, carrying the book in one hand and waving with the other. Mando and Kristen had to jog to keep up with him.

"Halloo!" he cried cheerfully. "Ahoy up there!"

We stood and met them at the Costas' door.

"So Doc brought him here, eh?" Steve said.

"He thinks he has pneumonia," said Kathryn.

Steve winced and shook his head. Under his thick black hair his brow was wrinkled with worry. "Let's go keep him company, then."

Once inside I began to lose the knot, and when Steve and Tom went into their usual act I laughed with the others.

"What are you doing in the hospital, you old layabout? Have you bit any nurses yet?"

"Only to discourage them when they're washing my body,"

Tom said with a faint smile.

"Sure, sure. And is the food terrible? And the what d'you call thems, the bedpans is it?"

"Watch it, boy, or I'll turn a bedpan over your head. Bedpan indeed—"

And by the time they were done tussling and pounding each other, Steve had Tom up in his bed and leaning back against the oildrums. The rest of us crowded into the hospital and sat on the other bed, or the floor, and laughed like we were at one of Tom's bonfire parties. Steve could do that for us. Even Kathryn was laughing. Only Doc stayed serious through it all, his eye on Tom. Over here Tom was his responsibility, and already you could see the strain on him. I don't think Doc liked being our doctor. He'd rather have stuck to gardening, if he'd had his way. But the custom was that he did the doctoring in the valley, and though he had trained Kathryn to assist him, and swore she knew everything he did, only he was trusted with the care of our sick. He was the one with the knowledge from the old time, and it was his job. But even in the mildest cases I could see he didn't like it; and now, with his best friend, the only other old timer around, in his care, he looked truly distressed.

Mando was wild about *An American Around the World*, even worse than Steve, and now he clamored for it. Steve sat on the bed at Tom's feet, and Kathryn sat on the floor beside his legs, where he could tousle her hair as he read. Gabby and Doc and I sat on chairs brought in from the kitchen, and Mando and Kristen took the empty bed, holding hands again.

The first chapter Steve read was Chapter Sixteen, "A Vengeance Symbolic Is Better Than None." By this time Baum was in Moscow, and on the day of the big May parade, when all the tyrants of the Kremlin came out to review Russia's military might, Baum smuggled a packet of fireworks—the strongest explosives he could get his hands on—into a trash can in Red Square. At the best part of the parade the fireworks went off, spewing red, white and blue sparks, and sending the entire government of the Soviet Union under their chairs. This prank, a tiny echo of what Russia had done to America, gave Baum as much pleasure as the tornado had. But he also had to hightail it out of the capital, as the search for the culprit was intense. The things he had to do in the next chapter to make it to Istanbul would have tired a horse. It was one adventure after another. Doc rolled his eyes and actually began to chuckle in some places, like when Baum stole a hydrofoil boat in the Crimea, and piloted it over the Black Sea pursued by Soviet gunboats. Baum was in mortal danger, but Doc kept on giggling.

"Now why are you laughing?" Steve stopped to demand of Doc, annoyed that his reading of Baum's desperate last-chance flight into the Bosporus had been marred.

"Oh no reason, no reason," Doc was quick to say. "It's just his style. He's so cool when he tells about it all, you know."

But in the next chapter, "Sunken Venice," Doc laughed again. Steve scowled and stopped reading.

"Now wait a minute," Doc said, anticipating Steve's censure. "He's saying the water level is thirty feet higher there than it used to be. But anyone can see right out here that the water level is the same as ever. In fact it may be lower."

"It's the same," Tom said, smiling at the exchange.

"Okay, but if so, it should be the same in Venice."

"Maybe things are different there," Mando said indignantly.

Doc cracked up again. "All the oceans are connected," he told Mando. "It's all one ocean, with one sea level."

"You're saying this Glen Baum is a liar," Kathryn said with interest. She didn't look at all displeased by the idea, and I knew why. "The whole book is made up!"

"It is not!" Steve cried angrily, and Mando echoed him.

Doc waved a hand. "I'm not saying that. I don't know what all is true in there. Maybe a few stretchers, to liven things up, though."

"He says Venice sank," Steve said coldly, and read the passage again. "The islands sank, and they had to build shacks on the roofs to stay above the water. So the sea level didn't have to rise." He looked peevishly at Doc. "It sounds likely to me."

"Could be, could be," Doc said with a straight face. Steve's jaw was tight, his face flushed.

"Let's go on reading," I said. "I want to know what happens."

Steve read again, his voice harsh and rapid. Baum's adventures picked up their pace. He was in as much danger as ever, but somehow it wasn't the same. In the chapter called "Far Tortuga," when he parachuted from a falling plane into the Caribbean, with several others who then inflated a raft,

Doc left the hospital and went into the kitchen, his face averted to conceal a wide grin from Steve and Mando. The men on the inflatable raft, by the way, perished one by one, victims of thirst and giant turtle attacks, until only Baum was left to land on the jungle beach in Central America. It should have been pretty dramatic, and sad, but when Baum met up with a jungle headhunter Tom went "heee, heee, heee, heee," from his bed, and we could hear Doc busting up in the kitchen, and Kathryn started laughing too, and Steve slammed the book shut and nearly stomped on Kathryn as he stood up.

"I ain't reading for you folks any more," he cried. "You've got no respect for literature!"

Which made Tom laugh so hard he started to cough again. So Doc came in and kicked us all out, and the reading session was done.

But we came back the next night, and Steve agreed sullenly to read again. Soon enough *An American Around the World* was done, which was probably just as well, and we went on to *Great Expectations,* and took the parts to read in *Much Ado About Nothing,* and tried some other books as well. It was all good fun. But Tom kept coughing, and he got quieter, and thinner, and paler. The days passed in a slow sameness, and I didn't feel like joining in the joking on the boats, or memorizing my readings, or even reading them. Nothing seemed interesting or good to me, and Tom got sicker as day followed day, until on some evenings I couldn't bear to look at him, lying on his back hardly aware of us, and each day I woke up with that knot over my stomach, afraid that it might be the last day he could hold on to this life.

Chapter Seventeen

Mornings I got up at dawn before the boats went out, and went up to check on him. Most mornings he was asleep. The nights were hard, Doc said. He got sicker and sicker, right up to the edge of death—I had to admit it—and there he hovered, refusing to pass on. One morning he was half awake and his bloodshot eyes stared at me defiantly. Don't write me off yet, they said. He hadn't slept that night, Mando told me. Now he didn't feel up to talking. He just stared. I pressed his hand—his skin was damp, his hand limp and fleshless—and left, shaking my head at his tenacity. Living a hundred years wasn't enough for him. He wanted to live forever. That look in his eyes told me, and I smiled a little, hoping he could do it. But the visit scared me. I hustled down the hill to the boats as if I was running from the Reaper himself.

Another morning I noticed it was aging Doc to care for him. Doc was over seventy himself; in most towns he would have been the oldest one. Pretty soon he might be ours. One morning after a hard night I sat with Mando and Doc at the kitchen table. They'd been up through the small hours trying to ease Tom's coughing, which had lost power but was more constant. All Doc's wrinkles were red and deep, and there were rings under his eyes. Mando let his head rest on the table, mouth open like a fish's. I got up and stoked their fire, got some water on, made them some tea and hot cereal. "You're going to miss the boat," Doc said, but smiled his thanks with one· corner of his mouth. His hand trembled his tea mug. Mando roused at the smell of corn and scraped his face off the table. We laughed at him and ate. I trudged down the hill with the knot over my stomach.

That was Saturday. Sunday I went to church. There were people there who (like me) hardly ever went to church: Rafael, Gabby, Kathryn, and hiding at the back, Steve. Carmen knew why we were there, and at the end of her final prayer she said, "And Lord, please return our Tom to health." Her voice had such power and calmness, to hear it was like being touched, being held. Her voice knew everything would be right. The amens were loud, and we walked out of the church like one big family.

That was Sunday morning, though. The rest of the week the tension made folks irritable. Mando lost sleep, and took the short end of Doc's temper; he didn't much care what books I read from, or even whether we read at all. "Armando!" I said. "You of all people have *got* to want to read." "Just leave me be," he said blearily. Around the ovens the women talked in quiet voices. No boisterous tattling, no shrieks of laughter tearing the air. No old man jokes on the boats. I went out to help the Mendezes gather wood, and Gabby and I nearly got in a fight trying to decide how to carry a fallen eucalyptus tree to the two-man saw. Later that day I passed Mrs. Mariani and Mrs. Nicolin, arguing heatedly at the latrine door. No one would have believed me if I had told them about that. I hurried down the path unhappily.

One day at the rivermouth it got worse. They were pulling the boats onto the flat when I arrived—I was spending a week helping the Mendezes, and only came down to help clean up. I joined those moving fish from the boats to the cleaning tables. Gulls wheeled overhead, piercing the air with their shrill complaints. Steve was over with Marvin, pulling the nets out of the boats and washing them in the shallows, then rolling them up. Usually Marvin did this by himself; John saw Steve and called, "Steve, get over and help Henry!"

Steve didn't even look up. On his knees on the hard sand of the flat, he tugged at the stiff wire rope at the top of the net. Answer him! I thought. John walked over and looked down at him.

"Go over and help get the fish out," he ordered.

"I'm folding this net," Steve said without looking up.

"Stop it, and get over to the fish."

"And just leave the net here, eh?" Steve said sarcastically. "Just let me be."

John grabbed him just under the armpit and yanked him to his feet. With a stifled cry Steve twisted and jerked out of John's grasp, staggering back into the shallows. He pulled up and charged John, who walked straight at him and shoved him back into the shallows again. Steve stood and pulled back a fist, and was about to swing when Marvin jumped between them. "For God's sake!" Marvin cried, shouldering John back a step. "Stop this, will you?"

Steve didn't appear to hear him. He was rounding Marvin when I seized his right wrist in both hands and dragged him away, falling in the shallows to duck a left cross. If Rafael hadn't wrapped Steve in a bearhug he would have pounded me and gone after John again; his eyes were wild, they didn't recognize any of us. Rafael carried him down the beach a few steps and let him loose with a shove.

Every man and woman on the beach had stopped what they were doing. They watched now with faces grim, or expressionless, or secretly pleased, or openly amused. Slowly I stood up.

"You two are making it hard to work in peace around here," Rafael scolded. "Why don't you keep your family matters to yourself."

"Shut up," John snapped. He surveyed us and with a chopping motion of his hand said, "Get back to work."

"Come on," I said to Steve, pulling him up the flat and away from the boats. He shrugged free of me impatiently. We stumbled over the net where it had all started. "Come on, Steve, let's get out of here." He allowed me to pull him away. John didn't look at us. I decided against the cliff path, worrying that Steve might throw rocks down on his pa, and led him up the riverbank. I was shaken, and glad that Marvin had had the wit to jump between them. I was supposed to be the fast one, but Marvin was the one who had recovered from the shock of it first. If he hadn't been so quick . . . well, it didn't bear thinking about.

Steve was still breathing heavily, as if he had just bodysurfed every wave of a big set. Between his clenched teeth he was cursing, repeating the words in an incoherent string. We took the river path to the broken end of the freeway, and sat under a torrey pine that hung over the whitish boulders and the river below. Going for cover, like coyotes after a scrap with a badger.

For a while we just sat. I swept pine needles into stacks, and then scraped through the dirt to concrete. Steve's breathing slowed to normal.

"He's trying to make me fight him," he said in a voice straining for calmness. "I know he is."

I doubted it, but I said, "I don't know. If he is, you shouldn't rise to it."

"How am I supposed to do that?" he demanded.

"Well, I don't know. Just avoid him, and do what he says—"

"Oh sure," he cried, twisting to his feet. He leaned over and bawled at me, "Just keep on crawling around on my belly eating shit! That's a real help! Don't you try to tell me what to do with my life, Mister Henry Big Man. You're just like all the rest! And don't you get in my way again when I go after him, or I'll bust your face instead of his!" He stalked down the freeway, cut into the potato patch and disappeared.

I let out a deep breath, relieved that he hadn't hit me right then and there. That was my best feeling; other than that I was pretty low.

Kathryn had said that Steve listened to me more than to anybody else. Maybe that meant he didn't listen to anybody anymore. Or maybe Kathryn was wrong. Or maybe I had said the wrong thing—or said it in the wrong way. I didn't know.

It took me a long time to get up the spirit to stand and walk away from that place.

One day I took off up the river path, past the gardens and the ovens and the women washing clothes at the bridge bend, on up to where the hills closed together and the forest grew right down into the water on both banks. Here the path disappeared and everyone had to make their own way. I moved back into the trees and sat down, leaned back against the trunk of a big pine.

Wandering into the forest, to sit and be with it, was something I had done for a long time. I started when my mother died, and I imagined I could hear her voice in the trees outside our house. That was dumb, and soon I stopped. But now it was a habit again. With Tom sick there was no one I could talk to, no one who didn't want something from me. It made me lonely. So when I felt that way I went out into the woods and sat. Nothing could touch me there, and eventually the knot would leave my stomach.

This was a particularly good spot. Around me trees clustered, big torrey pines surrounded by littler daughter trees. The ground was padded with needles, the trunk bowed at just the right angle for a backrest, and the curly branches above blocked most of the sun, but not all of it. Patches of light swam over my patched blue jeans, and shadow needles fenced with the brown needles under me. A pinecone jabbed me. I scrunched against the flaky bark of my backrest. Rolling on it, I turned and picked some of the dried crumbly gum out of a deep crack. Pressed it between my fingers until the still-liquid center burst out of the crust. Pine sap. Now my fingers would be sticky and pick up all sorts of dirt, so that dark marks would appear on my hands and fingers. But the smell of it was so piney. That smell and the smells of sea salt, and dirt, and wood smoke, and fish, made up the odor of the valley. Wind raked through the needles and a few of them dropped on me, each fivesome of needles wrapped together by a little bark nub at their bottoms. They pulled apart with a click.

Ants crawled over me and I brushed them away. I closed my eyes and the wind touched my cheek, it breathed through all the needles on all the branches of all the trees, and said *oh, mmmmmmm*. Have you heard the sound of wind in pine trees— I mean really listened to it, as to the voice of a friend? There's nothing so soothing. It about put me to sleep; it put me in a trance more like sleep than anything else, though I still heard. Each buffet or slacking shifted the hum or whoosh or roar of it; sometimes it was like the sound of a big waterfall around the bend, other times like the waves on the beach—still again, like a thousand folk in the far distance, singing *oh* as deep and wild as they could. Occasional bird calls tweeted through the sound, but mostly it was all that could be heard. The wind, the wind, *oh*. It was enough to fill the ear forever. I didn't want to hear any other voice.

But voices I heard—human voices, coming through the trees by the river. Annoyed, I rolled on my side to see if I could see who was talking. They weren't visible. I considered calling out, but I didn't feel obliged to them; they were invading my spot, after all. I couldn't blame them too much, it was a small valley and there weren't that many places to go if you wanted to get away from folks. But it was my bad luck that they'd come to this one. I laid back against my tree and hoped they would go away. They didn't. Branches snapped off to my left, and then the voices took up again, close enough so that I could make out the words—just a few trees over, in fact. That was Steve talking, and then Kathryn answered him. I sat up frowning.

Steve said, "Everybody in this valley is telling me what to do."

"Everybody?"

"Yes!... you know what I mean. Jesus, you're getting to be just like everybody else."

"Everybody?"

Just that one word and I knew Kathryn was mad.

"Everybody," Steve repeated, more sad than angry. "Steve, get down there and catch fish. Steve, don't go into Orange County. Don't go north, don't go south, don't go east, don't row too far out to sea. Don't leave Onofre, and don't do anything."

"*I* was just saying you shouldn't deal with those San Diegans behind the backs of the people here. Who knows what those folks really want." After a pause she added, "Henry's trying to tell you the same thing."

"Henry, shit. He gets to go south, and when he comes back he's Henry Big Man, telling me what to do like everyone else."

"He is not telling you what to do. He's telling you what he thinks. Since when can't he do that?"

"Oh, I don't know.... It ain't Henry."

I scrunched down behind my tree uncomfortably. It was a bad sign, them talking of me; they'd sense me by the way my name sounded to them, and search around and see me, and I'd look like I was spying when I had only been trying to get some peace. I didn't want to hear all this, I didn't want to know about it. Well...that wasn't strictly true. Anyway I didn't move away.

"What is it, then?" Kathryn asked, resigned and a little fearful.

"It's...it's living this little life in this little valley. Under Pa's thumb, stuck forever. I can't abide it."

"I didn't know life here was that bad for you."

"Ah come on, Kath. It isn't you."

"No?"

"No! You're the best part of my life here, I keep telling you that. But don't you see, I can't be trapped here all my life, working for my dad. That wouldn't be a life at all. The whole world is out there! And who's keeping me from it? The Japanese are. And here we have folks who want to fight the Japanese, and we're not helping them. It makes me sick. So I've got to do it, I've got to help them, can't you see that? Maybe it'll take all my life to make us free again, maybe it'll take longer, but at least I'll be doing something more with my life than gathering the food for my face."

A scrub jay flashed blue as it landed in the branch above me, and informed Steve and Kathryn of my presence. They weren't listening.

"Is that all the life here is to you?" Kathryn asked.

"No, shit, aren't you listening?" Annoyance laced his voice.

"Yes. I'm listening. And I hear that life in this valley doesn't satisfy you. That includes me."

"I *told* you that isn't true."

"You can't *tell* something away, Steve Nicolin. You can't act one way for months and months and then say, no it isn't that way, and make the months and what you did in them go away. It doesn't work like that."

I'd never heard her voice sound like it did. Mad—I'd heard it mad more times than I'd care to count. Now that angry tone was all beaten down flat. I hated to hear her voice sound that way. I didn't want to hear it—any of it—and suddenly that overcame my curiosity, and my feeling that it was my place. I started crawling away through the trees, feeling like a fool. What if they saw me now, lifting over a fallen branch to avoid making a sound? I swore in my thoughts over and over. When I got out of the sound of their voices (still arguing) I stood and walked away, discouragement dogging every step. Steve and Kathryn fighting—what else could go wrong?

Beyond the neck at the end of the valley, the river widens and meanders a bit, knocking through meadows in big loops. It's easier to travel in this back canyon by canoe, and after walking a ways I sat down again and watched the river pour into a pool and then out again. Fish tucked under the overhanging bank. The wind still soughed in the trees, but I couldn't get back my peace no matter how hard I listened. The knot in my stomach was back. Sometimes the harder you try the less it will go away. After a while I decided to check the snares that the Simpsons had set up on the edge of the one oxbow meadow, to give me something to do.

One of the snares had a weasel caught in it. It had been going after a rabbit, dead in the same snare, and now its long wiry body was all tangled in the laces. It tugged at them one last time as I approached; squeaked, and baring its teeth in a fierce grin, glared at me murderously, hatefully—even after I broke its neck with a quick step. Or so it seemed. I freed the two little beasts and set the snare again, and set off home with them both in one hand, held by the tails. I couldn't shake that weasel's last look.

Back in the neck I walked along the river, remembering a time when the old man had tried to detach a wild beehive from a short eucalyptus tree up against the south hillside. He had gotten stung and dropped the shirt wrapping the hive, and the furious bees had chased us right into the river. "It's all your fault," he had sputtered as we swam to the other side.

Sun going down. Another day passed, nothing changed. I followed a bend to the narrows where the river breaks over a couple knee-high falls, and came upon Kathryn sitting alone on the bank, tossing twigs on the water and watching them swirl downstream.

"Kath!" I called.

She looked up. "Hank," she said. "What are you doing here?" She glanced downstream, perhaps looking for Steve.

"I was just hiking up canyon," I said. I held up the two dead animals. "Checking a couple of the Simpsons' snares for them. What about you?"

"Nothing. Just sitting."

I approached her. "You look kind of down."

She looked surprised. "Do I?"

I felt disgusted with myself for pretending I could read her that well. "A little."

"Well. I guess that's right." She tossed another stick in.

I sat down beside her. "You're sitting in a wet spot," I said indignantly.

"Yeah."

"No big deal, I guess."

She was looking down, or out at the river, but I saw that her eyes were red. "So what's wrong?" I asked. Once again I felt sick at my duplicity. Where had I learned this sort of thing, what book of Tom's had taught me?

A few sticks rode over the falls and out of sight before she answered. "Same old thing," she said. "Me and Steve, Steve and me." Suddenly she faced me. "Oh," she said, her voice wild, "you've got to get Steve to stop with that plan to help the San Diegans. He's doing it to cross John, and the way they're getting along, when John finds out about it there'll be hell to pay. He'll never forgive him. . . . I don't know what will happen."

"All right," I said, my hand on her shoulder. "I'll try. I'll do my best. Don't cry." It scared me to see her cry. Like an idiot I had thought it impossible. Desperately I said, "Look, Kathryn. You know there isn't much I can do, the way he is these days. He almost hit me for grabbing him when he went after his dad the other day."

"I know." She shifted onto her hands and knees, leaned out over the water and ducked her head in it. The wet spot on the wide seat of her pants stuck into the air. After a good long time she came up blowing and huffing, and shook her head like a dog, spraying water over me and the river.

"Hey!" I cried. While she was under I had wanted to say, look, I can't help you, I'm with Steve on this one . . . but looking at her face to face, I didn't. I couldn't. The truth was, I couldn't do anything: no matter what I chose to do, I would be betraying someone.

"Let's go to my house," she said. "I'm hungry, and Mom made a berry pie."

"Okay," said I, wiping my face off. "You don't have to ask me twice when it comes to berry pie."

"I never noticed," she said, and ducked the scoop of water I sent her way.

We stood. Walked down the riverbank until the trail appeared—first as a trampled-down line in the weeds and shrubs, then as scuffed dirt and displaced rocks, then as trenches through the loam that became little creeks after a rain. New paths appeared beside these as they became too wet or deep or rocky. It reminded me of something Tom had said before we went to San Diego, about how we were all wedges stuck in cracks. But it wasn't like that, I saw; we weren't that tightly bound. It was more like being on trails, on a network of trails like the one crossing the bog beside the river here.... "Choosing your way is easy when you're on established trails," I said, more to myself than to Kathryn.

She cocked her head. "Doing what people have done before, you mean."

"Yes, exactly. A lot of people have gone that way, and they establish the best route. But out in the woods..."

She nodded. "We're all in the woods now." A kingfisher flashed over a snag. "I don't know why." Shadows from the trees across the river stretched over the rippled water and striped our bank. In the still of a side pool a trout broke the surface, and ripples grew away in perfect circles from the spot —why couldn't the heart grow as fast? I wanted to know... I wanted to know what I was doing.

The more I feel the more I see. That evening I saw everything with a crispness that startled me; leaves all had knife edges, colors were as rich as a scavenger's swap meet outfit.... But I only felt fuzzy things, oceans of clouds in my chest, the knot in my stomach. Too mixed to sort out and name. The river at dusk; the long stride of this woman my friend; the prospect of berry pie, making my mouth water; against these, the idea of a free land. Nicolin's plots. The old man, across the shadowed stream in a bed. I couldn't find the words to name all that, and I walked beside Kathryn without saying a thing, all the way downriver to her family's home.

Inside it was warm (Rafael had put pipes underneath their place to convey heat from the bread ovens), lamps were lit, the pies were on the table steaming. The women chattered. I ate my piece of pie and forgot everything else. Purple berries, sweet summer taste. When I left, Kathryn said, "You'll help?"

"I'll try." In the dark she couldn't see my face. So she didn't know that on the way home, at the same time I was thinking of arguments to get Steve to abandon his plan, I was also trying to figure out a way to get the landing date out of Add. Maybe I could spy on him every night until I heard him say it....

*   *   *

I kept thinking about it, but no good trick to fool the date from Addison came to me. The next time I fished with Steve, it got to be a problem I couldn't sidestep.

"They're down at the station ruins," Steve said as we rowed out of earshot of the other boats. "I went down there and they were setting up what looked like a permanent camp in the ruins. Jennings was in charge."

"So they're here, eh? How many of them?"

"Fifteen or twenty. Jennings asked where you were. And he wanted to know when the Japanese were landing. When and where. I told him we knew where, and would find out when real soon."

"Why'd you tell him that?" I demanded. "I mean, first of all, the Japanese may not be landing soon at all."

"But you said you heard those scavengers say they would!"

"I know, but who's to say they were right?"

"Well, shit," he said, and tossed his lure into the channel. I stared at the steep back wall of Concrete Bay unhappily. "If you go at it that way, we can never really be sure of anything, can we. But if these scavengers told Add that much, it means Add is in on it, so he'll know when they're going to land. I told Jennings what we told him before, that we'd find that out for him."

"What *you* told him before," I corrected.

"You were in on it too," he said crossly. "Don't try and pretend you weren't."

I slung my lure out the opposite side from Steve's, and let the line run out. I said, "I was in on it, but that doesn't mean I'm sure it's a good idea. Look, Steve, if we get caught helping these folks after the vote went against it, what are people going to say? How are we going to justify it?"

"I don't care what people say." A fish took his lure, and he hauled the thing up viciously. "That's if they do find out. They can't keep us from doing what we want, especially when we're fighting for their lives, the cowards." He gaffed the bonita like it was one of the cowards he had in mind, pulled it into the boat and whacked it on the head. It flopped weakly and gave up the ghost. "What is this, are you backing out on me now? Now that we got the San Diegans up here waiting for us?"

"No. I'm not backing out. I just don't know if we're doing the right thing."

"We *are* doing the right thing, and you know it. Remember all those things you said at the meeting! You were the best one there—what you said was right, every bit of it. And you know it. Let's get back to the matter at hand, here. We've got to get that date out of Add, and you're the one who knows the Shankses. You've got to go up there and get to Melissa somehow, that's all there is to it."

"Umph." Now it was getting to be very inconvenient that I hadn't told Steve the whole truth about how much Melissa and Add had fooled me. . . . I felt a bite, but I pulled too hard and the fish didn't take. "I guess." I couldn't admit that I'd lied to make myself look good.

"You've *got* to."

"All right all right!" I exclaimed. "Let me be, will you? I don't notice you suggesting any smart schemes for getting him to tell us if he don't feel like it. Just lay off!"

So we fished in silence, and looked after our lines. Onshore bobbed the green hillsides, all tinted pollen color by the afternoon sun.

Steve changed the subject. "I hope we try whaling again this winter, I think we could make a go of it if we harpooned a small whale. From more than one boat, maybe."

"You can leave me out of that one, thanks," I said shortly.

He shook his head. "I don't know what's got into you, Hanker. Ever since you got back—"

"Nothing's gotten into me." Bitterly I added, "I could say the same about you."

"How come? Because I think we should try whaling again?"

"No, for God's sake." The only time we had tried to kill one of the gray whales in their migration down the coast, we had gone out in the fishing boats and harpooned one. It was an excellent throw by Rafael, using a harpoon of his own manufacture. Then we stood in the boats and watched all of the line attached to the diving whale fly out of the boat, until it was gone. Our mistake was tying the end of the line to an eye in the bow; that whale pulled the boat right down from under us. The bow was yanked under the surface and *slurp* it was gone. We ended up fishing men out of that cold water rather than whale. And the line had torn across Manuel's fore-arm, so that he almost bled to death. John had declared that whales were too big for our boats, and as I had been in the boat next to the one that went under, I was inclined to agree with him.

But that wasn't what I was thinking about. "You're pushing things," I said slowly, "till your pa isn't going to take it. I don't know what you think'll happen—"

"You don't know what I think at all," he interrupted me, in a way that made it clear he didn't want me to pursue the matter. His mouth was tight, and I knew he could explode. Our dogs get that look from time to time: nudge me once more, the look says, and I'll bite your foot off. A fish took my hook, so I could drop the matter easily enough, and I did. But obviously I was on to something. Maybe he thought John would kick him out of the valley, so he'd be free of it all. . . .

It was a big rock bass, and it took me a lot of time and effort to get it in the boat. "See, this fish is no longer than my arm, and I could barely get it in. Those whales are twice as long as this *boat*."

"They catch them up in San Clemente," Steve said. "They make a lot of silver off them at the meets, too. Why, one whale is how many jars of oil, did Tom say?"

"I don't know."

"You do too! What's this *I don't know*. I tell you. This whole valley is going to the dogs."

"No lie," I said grimly. Nicolin snorted, and we went back to fishing. After we got several more aboard he started again. "Maybe we could poison the harpoons. Or, you know, harpoon a whale twice, from two boats."

"We'd get all tangled. The boats would be pulled together and crushed."

"What about poison, then."

"It would be better to put three boats' worth of line on the end of one harpoon, so we could let the whale run as far down as it liked."

"Now see, there you're talking." He was pleased. "Or how about this, we could have the harpoon at the end of a line that extended right back to the beach—held up by little floats or something. And then when the harpoon struck, the playing of the thing would be from the beach. Eventually we could just haul it right into the rivermouth."

"The harpoon would have to be pretty well fixed."

"Well of course. That would be true no matter what you did."

"I guess. But it's also a hell of a lot of line you're talking about. Usually those things are a mile or so offshore, aren't they?"

"Yeah. . . ." After some pondering, he said, "I wonder how those folks in San Clemente *do* catch them monsters."

"You got me. They sure aren't telling."

"I wouldn't either, if I was them."

"What's this? I thought you were telling me all the towns have to stick together, we're all one country and all that."

He nodded. "That's true. You've said so yourself. But until everyone agrees to it, you got to protect your advantages."

That seemed to have some application to me, but I couldn't figure out exactly what it was. Anyway, I had made the mistake of bringing the subject back to the political situation, and as we rowed our full boat back to the rivermouth, Steve pressed me one more time.

"Remember, now, we've promised Jennings. And you *know* you want to go up there and fight those Japs. Remember what they did to you and Tom and the rest of you out there in that storm?"

"Yeah," I said. Well, Kathryn, I thought, I tried. But I knew better than that. Nicolin was right. I wanted those Japanese out of our ocean.

We negotiated the mouth break, and coasted in on the gentle waves that the high tide was shoving up the throat of the river. "So, get up there and see what you can do with Melissa. She's got a feeling for you, she'll do what you want."

"Umph."

"Maybe she'll ask Add for you."

"I doubt it."

"Still, you've got to start somewhere. And I'll see if I can't think of something myself. Maybe we could eavesdrop on them like you did last time."

I laughed. "It might come to that," I agreed. "I've thought of that myself."

"Okay, but do what else you can first, all right?"

"All right. I'll give her a try."

I spent a couple of days thinking about it, trying to figure something out—living with the knot over my stomach, so that it was hard to sleep. One morning before dawn I gave up trying and walked over the dew-soaked bridge to the Costas'. Doc was up, sitting at the kitchen table drinking tea and staring at the wall. I tapped at the window and he let me in. "He's asleep now," he said with relief. I nodded and sat down with him.

"He's getting weaker," he said, looking into his tea. "I don't know.... Too bad you guys had such miserable weather coming back from San Diego. You're young and can take it, but Tom...Tom acts like he's young when he shouldn't. Maybe this will teach him to be more careful, to take better care of himself. If he lives."

"You should remember the same thing yourself," I said. "You look awful tired."

He nodded.

"If the train tracks had been left alone we would have come back easy as you please," I went on. "Those bastards..."

Looking up at me Doc said, "He may die, you know."

"I know."

He drank some tea. The kitchen began to get lighter with the dawn. "Maybe I'll go to bed now."

"Do it. I'll stick around till Mando gets up, and keep an eye on things."

"Thanks, Henry." He shoved the chair back. Lifted himself up. Stood and collected himself. Stepped into his room.

So I hiked onto Basilone Ridge that afternoon, to see if I could find Melissa at their house. Through woods and over the cracked greeny concrete of the old foundations. When I walked into the clearing around their tower I saw Addison, at leisure on his roof, smoking a pipe and kicking his heels against the side of the house, thump-thump, thump-thump. When he saw me he stopped kicking, and didn't smile or nod. Uncomfortable under his stare, I approached. "Is Melissa home?" I called.

"No. She's in the valley."

"No I'm not," Melissa called, emerging into the clearing from the north side—the side away from the valley. "I'm home!"

Add took the pipe from his mouth. "So you are."

"What's up, Henry?" Melissa said to me with a smile. She was wearing baggy burlap pants, and a sleeveless blue shirt. "Want to go for a hike up the ridge?"

"That's just what I was going to ask you."

"Daddy, I'm going with Henry, I'll be back before dark."

"If I'm not here," Add said, "I'll be home for supper."

"Oh yeah." They exchanged a look. "I'll keep it hot for you."

Melissa took my hand. "Come on, Henry." With a tug we

were off into the forest above their house.

As she led the way uphill, dancing and dodging between the trees, she threw questions back my way. "What have you been doing, Henry? I haven't seen you very much. Have you been back to San Diego? Don't you want to go see all that again?"

Remembering what she had said to the scavengers that night, I could hardly keep from smiling. Not that I was amused. But it was so transparent what she was doing, pumping me for information once more. I lied with every answer I gave. "Yes, I've been down to San Diego again, on my own. It's a secret. I met a whole..." I was going to say a whole army of Americans, but I didn't want to show I knew what she was up to. "...a whole bunch of people."

"Is that right?" she exclaimed. "Why, when was that?" She was quite the spy. But at the same time, she was so lithe and springy slinking through the trees, and shafts of sunlight caught and broke blue in her black hair, and I wouldn't have minded having my hands all tangled up in that hair, spy or not.

Farther up the ridge the trees gave way to mesquite and a few stubborn junipers. We followed a little trickle ravine up to the ridge proper, and stood on it in the wind. The ridge edge was sandstone perfectly divided, like the back of a fish. We walked along that division, commenting on the views out to sea, and up San Mateo Valley. "Swing Canyon is just over that spur," I said, pointing a little ahead of us.

"Is it?" Melissa said. "You want to go there?"

"Yes."

"Let's." We kissed to mark the decision, and I felt a pang; why couldn't she be like one of the other girls, like the Marianis or the Simpsons?... We continued along the ridge. Melissa kept asking questions, and I kept on lying as I answered her. After Cuchillo, the peak of Basilone Ridge, several spurs headed down from the main ridge into the valley. The steep box canyon formed by the first two of these spurs was Swing Canyon; from our vantage we could look right down it, and see where its small stream made the final fall into one of Kathryn's fields. We slid on our butts down the steep walls at the top of the canyon, and then stepped carefully through thick low mesquite. All the while she questioned me. I was amazed at how obvious she was; but I suppose if I hadn't known what she was up to, I wouldn't have noticed. It was just like plain curiosity, after all, or almost like it. Reflecting on this, I decided I could be more bold in my own questions to her. I knew more than she did. A bit more bold in every way: helping her down a vertical break, I used her crotch as a handhold and lifted her down; she held one knee wide so it would work, and giggled as she twisted free on landing. With a kiss we headed down again.

"Have you ever heard about the Japanese that come over from Catalina to look at what's left in Orange County?" I asked.

"I've heard it happens," she said brightly. "But nothing more than that. Tell me about it."

"I sure would like to see one of those landings," I said. "You know, when the Japanese ship picked me out of the water, I talked with the captain for a while, and I saw he was wearing one of the high school rings that the scavengers sell!"

"Is that right," she said, astonished. You're overdoing it, I wanted to say.

"Yeah! The captain of the ship! I figure all those Japanese coast guard captains must be bribed to let through tourists on certain nights. I'd love to go up there and spy on one of those landings, just to see if I could recognize my captain again."

"But why?" Melissa asked. "Do you want to shoot him?"

"No, no. Of course not. I want to know if I'm right about him or not. You know, whether he helps the landings like I think he does." It didn't sound very convincing to me (and I shouldn't have said the word *spy*), but it was the best I could think of.

"I doubt you'll ever find out," Melissa said reasonably. "But good luck at it. I wish there was some way I could help, but I wouldn't like going up there."

"Well," I said, "maybe you could help anyway."

We were down to the sink at the very head of the box canyon, and I stopped the conversation to give her a long kiss. After that we walked to the swing tree, near the spring that starts the canyon's stream. The spring made a little pool before tumbling over a sandstone rib down the canyon, and beside the pool was a flat spot, protected by a ring of spruce trees. It was a favored spot for lovers. Melissa took my hand and led me right to it, so I guessed she was as familiar with it as I was. We sat in the gloom and kissed, then laid on the leaf and needle bed and kissed some more. We pressed against each other, rolled aimlessly over the crackling leaves. I nudged my fingers under the tie of her burlap pants, and slid them down her belly, into tightly curled hair . . . she held my hard-on through jeans, and squeezed hard, and we kissed, and kissed, and our breath got short and jerky. I was excited, but . . . I couldn't forget about everything else and just feel her. The other times I had lain with a girl—with Melissa before, or Rebel Simpson the previous year, or that Valerie from Trabuco, who had made several swap meet nights so interesting—I would get started and my brain would melt into my skin, so that I never thought a thing and when we were done it was like coming to. This time, at the same moment I was feeling her and kissing her neck and shoulders I was wondering how I could make my desire to see the Japanese landings sound convincing, even essential; how I could ask her again to ask Addison. It was strange.

"Maybe you *can* help," I said between kisses, as if it had just occurred to me. My hand was still in her pants, and I nudged her with a finger.

"How so?" she asked, squirming.

"Couldn't your dad talk to some of his contacts about it? I mean, I know he doesn't have many contacts up there, but you said he has one or two—"

"I did not," she said sharply, and pulled back from me. My hand slid out from her pants and it groped over the leaves for her; *no, no*, it said. . . . "I never told you anything of the sort! Daddy does his own work, like we told you before." She sat up. "Besides, why should you want to go up there? I don't get it. Is that why you were up talking to him today?"

"No, of course not. I wanted to see you," I said with conviction.

"So you could ask me to ask him," she said, not impressed.

I shuffled to her side and nuzzled her hair and neck. "See, the thing is," I said indistinctly, "if I don't see that Japanese captain again, I'm going to be afraid of him for the rest of my life. He's giving me nightmares and all. And I know Add could help me to find one of those landings."

"He could not," she said, irritated. I tried to put my hand back down her pants to distract her, but she seized it and pushed it away. "Don't," she said coldly. "See? You did get me up here to ask me to pester my dad. Listen—I don't want you bothering him about Orange County or the Japanese or any of that, you hear? Don't ask him nothing and don't get him mixed up in anything you do." She brushed leaves out of her hair, crawled away from me to the edge of the pool. "He's got enough trouble in your damn valley without you trying to give him more." She cupped some water and drank, brushed her hair back with angry slaps.

I stood up unsteadily, and walked over to the swing tree. She had made me feel awful guilty and calculating; and she looked beautiful, kneeling there by the dark pool; but still! All that holy innocent routine, after the way she had talked to the scavengers that night—after she and Add had welcomed them into their house, to tell them what they had learned by spying on our "damn valley" and its most foolish citizen Henry Aaron Fletcher...it made me grind my teeth.

The swing tree grows out of the rib that holds the pool in. Long ago someone had tied a thick piece of rope to one of the upper branches, and the rope was used to swing out over the steep canyon below. Angrily I grabbed the rope by the knots at its loose end, and walked back from the drop-off. Taking a good hold above the knot, I ran across the clearing at an angle away from the tree, and swung out into space. It had been a long time. Swinging around in the shadows felt good. I could see the canyon wall opposite, still catching some sun, and below me, treetops in shadow. I spun slowly, looking back to locate the tree's thick trunk. I missed it by a good margin on landing. One time Gabby had taken a swing while drunk, and had come right into the tree, back first, hitting a little broken-off nub of a branch. That had taken the color out of him.

"Don't you talk to us about that stuff anymore, are you listening to me, Henry?"

"I'm listening."

"I like you fine, but I won't abide any talk about Daddy dealing with those folks up there. We get enough grief about that as it is, and for no good reason at all. There's no cause for it." She sounded so sorrowful and put upon, I wanted to yell down at her, you get grief for it because you're a pair of scavengers, you bitch! I've seen you spy for them! You don't fool me with your act! But I clamped my jaws together and said "Yeah," and started another swing. "I hear you," I said bitterly to the air. She didn't reply. The rope creaked loudly. I tapped my feet together, spinning nice and slow. When I came in I went out again, and then again. For a moment I felt how wonderful it was to swing, and I wished I could swing out there forever, spinning slowly at the rope's end, free of the earth and with no worries but clearing the tree, with nothing to think about but the air rushing by me, and the shadowed trees spinning around me, and the dark green pool below to one side. Surely the knot in my stomach would leave me then. When I landed I almost smashed face first into the treetrunk. That was just the way of it: spend your time in wishing and a tree smacks your face for you.

Melissa was crouched by the pool, holding her hair back with a hand, leaning over to drink directly from the spring. "I'm leaving," I said harshly.

"I need help getting up the ridge." She didn't look at me.

I considered telling her she could go down the canyon and around the valley and not need any help, but I thought better of it.

We didn't have much to say on the way back. It was hard work climbing up the final walls of the box canyon, and we both got dirty. Melissa refused to let me help her except when she couldn't get up without it, perhaps remembering the handhold I had used on the way down. The more I thought about the way she had worked on me, the angrier I got. And to think I had still wanted her. Why, I was a fool—and the Shankses were no better than thieves. Scavengers. Spies. Zopilotes! Not only that, but there was no way I was going to be able to get the information I needed out of them.

We walked down the Basilone slope a few trees apart. "I don't need your help anymore," Melissa said coldly. "You can go back to your valley where you belong."

Without a word I turned and cut across the slope down toward the valley, and heard her laugh. Seething, I stopped behind a tree and waited a while; then I continued on toward the Shankses', and circled around so that I came on it from the north, moving from tree to tree with great caution. From the notch of a split pine I could see their weird house perfectly. Addison was by the door, in earnest conference with Melissa. She pointed south to the valley, laughing, and Add nodded. He had on his long, greasy brown coat (a good match for his hair), and when he was done questioning Melissa, he opened the door and sent her inside with a slap on the butt. Then he was off into the woods, passing just a few trees from me as he headed north. I waited, and then followed him. There was a bit of a trail through the trees—made by Add himself, no doubt, in his many trips north—and I hustled along it tippytoe, watching for twigs on the ground, and Addison ahead. When

I saw him again I dodged out of the trail and hid behind a spruce, breathing hard. I stuck my head around the tree and saw that he was still walking away from me; hopping around the trunk I highstepped through the trees, landing on the balls of my feet, on dirt or pine needles, and twisting my legs like I was dancing to avoid twigs or leaves that might snap under me. At the end of each crazy run I fetched up against a tree, and glanced around it to relocate Add. So far, so good; he didn't seem to have the slightest notion he was being followed. Time after time I checked to make sure his back was to me, and waited until he was obscured by the trees in between us, so I couldn't be sure which direction he was going in; then I leaped from cover and darted in whatever zigzag through the woods I thought would be the quietest. After several more batlike runs, I began to enjoy it. It wasn't that I was just losing my fear, either—I was positively enjoying it. After all the shit that Add and Melissa had pulled on me, it was a real pleasure to be tricking him—to be better at his business than he was.

There was pleasure in flitting through the woods like that, as well. It was like trailing an animal, only now it was possible in a way that chasing an animal wouldn't have been. Any animal in its senses would have been aware of me in an instant, and I never would have seen it again, nor known where it had gone to. A human, however, was very trackable. I could even choose which side of him I planned to come up on, and then cross over and trail him from the other side. Like it was a kind of hide and seek. Only now it was a game with some real stakes.

About halfway across San Mateo Valley I realized I was going to have a problem following him across the San Mateo River. The freeway was the only bridge, and it was as exposed as any bridge could be. I reckoned I would have to wait a long time after Add crossed it, and then hurry over, get back in the trees, and hope I could hustle ahead and relocate him.

I was still figuring all of this out when Add reached the bank of the San Mateo, considerably downriver from the freeway. I ducked behind yet another tree, a eucalyptus that was a bit too narrow for my purposes, and wondered what he was up to. He started looking all around, including back in my direction, and I crouched down and kept my head behind the trunk, so that I couldn't see him anymore. The scruffy bark of the eucalyptus oozed gum; breathing hard, I stared at it, afraid to poke my head out again. Had he heard me? At the thought my pulse went woodpecker, and suddenly trailing a man didn't seem pure fun after all. I lay flat, careful not to make a sound in all the eucalyptus crap behind me, and, holding my breath, I slowly stuck one eye's worth of face around the trunk.

No Add. I stuck both eyes around and still didn't see him. I scrambled to my feet again, and then I heard the sound of a motor, out on the river. Add came into sight again, still on the bank, looking seaward, waving a hand. I stayed put. Add never looked around again, and soon I caught sight, between the trees, of a little boat with three men in it. There weren't any oars; there was a motor, mounted on the aft. The man in the middle was Japanese. The one in the bow stood as they approached the bank, and he leaped to shore and helped Add secure the boat with a line around a tree.

While the other men clambered out of the boat, I crawled catlike from tree to tree, and finally slithered over a thick mat of eucalyptus leaves and pine needles, to a thick torrey pine only three or four trees from them. Under its low branches, and behind its trunk, I was sure they'd never see me.

The Japanese man—who looked somewhat like my captain, but was shorter—reached back into the boat and pulled out a white cloth bag, tied at the top. He handed it to Add. They asked Add some questions, and Add answered them. I could hear their voices, especially the Japanese man's; *but I couldn't make out what they were saying.* I drew in breath between my teeth, and cursed horribly in my mind. I really was very close to them—I couldn't risk going any closer, and that was that. But except for an occasional word they said, like "how" or "you," I could only get the tone of their voices. I was as close to them as I had been to Steve and Kathryn, when I overheard that conversation—but here the speakers were on a riverbank, and though the river didn't seem very noisy, it was just noisy enough. You can't eavesdrop on a riverbank successfully, I was learning; and so all my chasing and stalking was going to go to waste. I couldn't believe my bad luck. Here was Add talking with a Japanese, probably discussing exactly the stuff I wanted to know; and here was I, just where I wanted to be, no more than four boat lengths away. And it wasn't going to do me a bit of good. I wanted to sink my head into the pine needles and cry.

Occasionally one of the two scavengers (scavengers I assumed they were, though they dressed like country folk) would laugh and kid Addison in a louder voice, so that I heard whole sentences. "Easy to fool fools," one of them said. Add laughed at that. "This'll all come back to us in a month or two," the other said, pointing at Add's bag. "Back to our whores, anyway!" the first one crowed. The Japanese man watched each of them in turn as they spoke, and never smiled at their jests. He asked a few more questions of Add, and Add answered them or so I assumed; with his back to me I could hardly hear Add at all.

And then, right before my eyes, the three men got back in the boat. Add untied the line and threw it to them, pushed off, and watched as they drifted downstream. They were out of my sight immediately, but I heard the motor start again. And that was it. I hadn't learned a thing I didn't know before. I pressed my face into the pine needles and ground a few of them between my teeth.

Add watched them for only a moment or two, and then hiked right past me. I lay without moving for a bit, got up and headed after him. I actually pounded some of the trees I passed with my clenched fist. And Add was nowhere to be seen. I slowed down, so angry and frustrated that I didn't know if I wanted to spend the patience to hunt him down. What was the point? But the alternative—hiking back to Onofre alone—was somehow even worse. I started ranging forward in big diagonals, dancing between the trees again in my silent run.

I never even saw him until he had slammed into me with his shoulder and knocked me to the ground. He pulled a knife from his belt and came after me, nearly falling on me. I rolled and kicked the forearm above the knife, twisted and kicked his knee, scrambled to my feet, dodged and struck my clasped hands into his neck, as fast as I could move. He crashed into a tree, lay stunned against it; I quick snatched the bag from his left hand, leaping back to avoid a swing of the knife. I held the heavy little bag up like a club and retreated rapidly.

"Stay right there or I'll run and you'll never see this bag again," I rattled off. Thinking just ahead of my words, I said "I'm faster than you, and you won't catch me. Nobody catches me in the woods." And I laughed triumphantly at the look on his face, because it was true and he knew it. Nobody's quicker than I am, and beating Add and his knife around in the trees, faster than I could think, faster than I could plan my moves, made me *feel* it. Add knew it too. Finally, finally, I had Addison Shanks where I wanted him.

With his free hand he rubbed his neck, glaring at me with the same hateful expression I had seen in the eyes of that snared weasel. "What do you want?" he said.

"I don't want much. I don't want this here bag, though it feels like quite a bit of silver, and maybe stuff more important than that, eh?" I might not have guessed the contents right, but one thing was sure—he wanted the bag. He looked at it, shifted forward, and I took three steps back and to the right, along an opening in the trees. "I reckon Tom and John and Rafael and the others would be mighty interested to see this bag, and hear what I have to tell about it."

"What do you want?" he grated.

I stared back into his hating gaze, unafraid of him. "I don't like how you've been using me," I said. The knife in his hand jerked, and I thought, don't tell him how much you know. "I want to see one of those Japanese landings in Orange County. I know they're doing it, and I know that you're in on them. I want to know when and where the next one lands."

He looked puzzled, and let the knife drop a hand's breadth. Then he grinned, his eyes still hating me, and I flinched. "You're with the other kids, aren't you. Young Nicolin and Mendez and the rest."

"Just me."

"Been spying on me, have you? And John Nicolin doesn't know about it, I bet. No."

I raised the bag. "Tell me when and where, Add, or I'm back to the valley with this, and you'll never be able to set foot there again."

"The hell I won't."

"Want to try it?"

A snarl curled his lips. I stood my ground. I watched him think it over. Then he grinned again, in a way I didn't understand. At the time I thought he was like that weasel, giving one last fierce grin of rage as it was killed.

"They're landing at Dana Point, this Friday night. Midnight."

I threw the bag at him and ran.

At first I ran like a hunted deer, leaping big falls of wood and crashing through smaller ones in my new luxury of sound, scared that I might have thrown Add a gun, or that he would turn out to be a knife thrower, and put that thick blade in my back. But after crossing most of San Mateo Valley I knew I was safe, and I ran for joy. Triumphantly I danced between trees, leaped over bushes where I could have run around them, tore small branches out of my path. I ran up to the freeway, and sprinted down it at full speed. I don't think I've ever run faster in my life, or enjoyed it more. "Friday night!" I crowed at the sky, and flew down that road like a car, the knot in my stomach gone at last.

Chapter Eighteen

But the knot didn't stay away for long. I ran into the valley straight to the Nicolins', only to be told by Mrs. N. that Steve was out somewhere with Kathryn. I thanked her and left, uneasy already. Were they arguing again? Making up? Was Kathryn talking him out of all this? (That didn't seem likely.) I checked a few of our regular hangouts, none too anxious to find Kathryn, but compelled by a desire to see Steve immediately. No sign of them anywhere. No way of guessing where they were or what they were doing. Climbing back down Swing Canyon I realized I didn't understand the two of them anymore, if I ever had. Where do you go after a fight like the one I had overheard? The private lives of other couples—there's few things more private than that. Nobody but the two know what's going on between them, even if they talk about it with others. And if they don't then it's a complete mystery, hidden from the world.

So that was Wednesday evening. I went back to the Nicolins' twice that night, but no one showed up. And the longer I waited to tell Steve, the more uneasy I got about it. What would Kathryn say when she learned my part in this? She would think I had lied to her, betrayed her trust. On the other hand, if I didn't tell Steve about the landing, and let it pass—and if he ever found out what I had done—well, that didn't bear thinking about. I'd lose my best friend at that very moment.

After my second visit to the Nicolins' I went home and went to bed. It had been such a day I thought I would have trouble falling asleep, but a few minutes after I lay down I was out. A couple of hours later I woke up, though, and for the rest of the night I tossed and turned, listened to the wind, considered what I should do.

Just after dawn I woke up with the knot in my stomach, and trying to get back to sleep only made it worse. I faintly remembered a dream that was so awful I made no attempt to recall it more clearly—something about being chased —but a few moments later I wasn't even sure of that. Stepping outside for my morning pee I discovered a Santa Ana wind —the desert wind that pours over from the hills to the east and pushes all the clouds out to sea, and heats up the land, and makes everything dry for a time. Santa Anas strike three or four times a year, and change our weather completely. This one was picking up even as I watched, twisting the trees all backward to their natural onshore bent. Soon pine branches would be snapping off and gliding seaward.

The empty water bucket gave me a shock when I picked it up. Static electricity, Tom called it, but try as he would he couldn't make me understand it. Something about millions of tiny fires rushing around (of course you remember how well he explained fire to me) . . . and all the wires strung between towers like the Shankses' place had carried this electricity around, and it had powered all the automatic machines of the old time. All that power from little snaps like the one I had felt.

Walking to the river in the raw morning sun it seemed that everything was packed with color, as if static electricity might be something that filled things and made them brighter. The hair on my arms stood away from my skin, and I could feel the roots in my scalp as the wind pulled my hair this way and that. Static electricity . . . maybe it gathered in humans over the stomach. At the river I stepped in to my knees, ducked my head under, sloshed water down my throat and back up, hoping the electricity might catch to the water and leave with it. It didn't work.

Wide awake now. Cat's paws fanned across the river's surface, one after another, helping it down to sea. Already the air was warm and dry; it felt like it would be burning soon. The sky was a bright pale blue. I drank half a bucket of water, threw rocks at a fallen tree stuck against the other bank. What to do? Gulls wheeled and flapped overhead, complaining at how hard they had to work in this backwards wind. I walked back to my house and ate a loaf of bread with Pa.

"What you doing today?" he asked.

"Checking snares. That's what old Mendez told me, anyway."

"That should make a good break from the fishing."

"Yeah."

Pa looked at me and wrinkled his nose. "You sure aren't one for talking much these days."

I nodded, too distracted to pay much attention to him.

"You don't want to get so's people can't talk to you," he went on.

"I'm not. I'd better be off, though."

I went to the river again, thinking to get up to the snares eventually. Sat down on one of the tiny bluffs that overhang the bank. Downriver the women appeared one by one, the Mariani clan and the rest of them, out while the Santa Ana was blowing to bathe and wash clothes and sheets and blankets and towels and anything else they could haul to the water. The air was a bit hotter every minute, and dry so you could feel it in your nostrils. The women got out the soap and stripped down, moved into the shallows at the bend with washboards and baskets of clothes and linens, and went to work, chattering and laughing, diving out into the mainstream to paddle around a bit and get the soap off them. The morning sun gleamed on their wet bodies and slicked-down hair, and I could have stayed longer to watch them, such sleek white creatures they were; like a pod of dolphins, I thought, splashing water at each other, tits swinging together as clothes were scrubbed over washboards, mouths open to laugh and grin at the sky. But they had seen me sitting upriver, and pretty soon if I stayed they would be throwing rocks, and lifting their legs to embarrass me, and calling out jokes like, Hey, isn't something rubbing you the wrong way? or Do you need some help with that? or

Careful it'll wash away like this here bar of soap.... And besides I had other things on my mind anyway, so with a last glance I turned and walked upriver, forgot about the women and began to worry again. (But what would they think of all this?)

See, I could have not told him. I could have said, Steve, I didn't find anything out and I don't know how I could, and left it at that. And Friday night would have come and gone and we would never have known the difference. They wouldn't have, anyway. And everything would have gone on as before. Walking the river path it occurred to me I could do this, and as I hiked from snare to snare I considered it. In some ways it appealed to me.

But I remembered my fight with Add; how I'd knocked him against a tree when he held the knife and I didn't. And after clearing a rabbit out of a snare and resetting it, I remembered my escape from the Japanese, my swim to shore, my struggle up that ravine. It seemed like great adventure to me now. I remembered climbing up the side of the Shankses' house to hear the conversation with the scavengers, and my silent bat-runs after Addison through the woods. I had enjoyed that more than anything that had ever happened in Onofre. I'd never felt such power. It seemed to me more than ever that these things were not just happening to me, but that I was *doing* them, that I was choosing to do certain things and then I was going out and doing them. And now I had the chance to do something better than anything else had been so far, to fight for my lost country. This land I walked over was ours, it was all we had left. They had to stay off it or suffer for it. We weren't a freak show, a bigger version of those little ones that visited the swap meets sometimes, exhibiting pathetic radiation cripples, both animal and human.... We were a country, a living country, living communities on living land, and they had to leave us alone.

So when I returned to the valley through the neck, I dropped off three rabbits and a smelly skunk, and continued downriver to the Nicolins' house. Steve was out front, shouting furiously at his mother in the doorway. Something about John again, I gathered, something he had said or done to enrage Steve.... I winced and waited until Steve was done shouting. As he stalked away toward the cliffs I approached him.

"What's up?" he said as he saw me.

"I know the date!" I cried. His face lit up. I told him all about it. When I was done I felt a certain chill, and I thought, well, you've told him. I had never really decided to; the act itself was the decision.

"That's great," he kept saying, "that's great. Now we've got them! Why didn't you tell me?"

"I just did," I said, annoyed. "I just found out yesterday."

He slapped me on the back. "Let's go tell the San Diegans. We don't have much time—a day, whoo! They might need to get more men from south or something."

But now that I had told him, I was more uncertain than before that it was the right thing to do. It was stupid, but that's what happened. I shrugged and said, "You go on down and tell them, and I'll tell Gabby and Del and Mando if I see them."

"Well"—he cocked his head at me curiously—"sure. If that's what you want."

"I've done my share," I said defensively. "We shouldn't both go down there; it might draw attention to us."

"I guess you're right."

"Come by tonight and tell me what they said."

"I will."

When he came by that night the wind was blowing harder than ever. The big eucalyptus's branches creaked against each other, and its leaves clicked and spinnerdrifted down on us. The pines hummed their deepest chord, and tossed up and down across the bright stars.

"Guess who was at their camp?" Steve demanded, all charged up and even bouncing on his feet. "Guess!"

"I don't know. Lee?"

"No, the Mayor! The Mayor of San Diego."

"Is that right? What's he doing up here?"

"He's here to fight the Japs, of course. He was really happy when I told him we could lead them to a landing. He shook my hand and we drank some whisky and everything."

"I bet. Did you tell him where it was?"

"Course not! Do you take me for a fool? I said we weren't getting the final word till tomorrow, and that we'd tell them when we were up there ourselves with them. That way they'll have to take us, see? In fact—I told them that only you know where they're landing, and that you wouldn't tell anyone."

"Oh, fine. Now why should I do that?"

"Because you're a suspicious kind of guy, naturally, and

you don't want the Japanese to find out somehow that we know. That's what I told them."

That suggested something to me that I hadn't thought of before, believe it or not: the Japanese could find out we knew from Add. The landing might not take place after all. Another possibility occurred to me: Add could have lied to me about the date. But I didn't say anything about that. I didn't want to bring up any problems. All I said was, "They must think we're crazy."

"Not at all, why should they? The Mayor was real pleased with us."

"I bet he was. How many men were with him?"

"Fifteen, maybe twenty."

"Was Jennings one of them?"

"Sure. Listen, did you tell Del and Gabby and Mando?"

"What about Lee? Was Lee with them?"

"I didn't see him. What about our gang?"

I was worried about Lee. I didn't understand or like the way he had disappeared from the group. "I told Gabby and Del," I said after a while. "Del's going over to Talega Canyon with his pa Friday to trade for some calves, so he can't come."

"And Gabby?"

"He's coming."

"Good. Henry, this is it! We're part of the resistance!"

The hot push of the Santa Ana burned in my nose, and I felt the static electricity all through me. Stars danced in the leaves. "True," I said, "true." I was so excited I trembled.

Steve stared at me through the darkness. "You aren't scared, are you?"

"No! I am a bit tired, I think. I'd better get some sleep."

"Good idea. You're going to need it tomorrow." With a slap to the arm he was off into the trees. A powerful blast of wind carried a soaring branch over my head. I waved at it and went back inside, where Pa was sewing.

I didn't get much sleep that night. And the next day was the longest one I could remember. The Santa Ana blew strong all day; the land was drying out and heating up, and it got so hot that just to move was enough to break into a sweat. I checked snares in the back country all day—not an animal in any of them. After I forced down the usual fish and bread I got so fidgety that I just had to do something. I said to Pa, "I'm going up to see the old man, and then we're going to work on the treehouse, so I'll be home late."

"Okay."

Outside it was twilight. The river was a silvery sheen much lighter than the trees on the other bank. The western sky was the same silvery blue, and the whole arch of the sky seemed lighter than usual—the land was dark, but the sky still glowed. I crossed the bridge and went up to the Costas'. From their vantage I could see the whole valley forest bouncing in the gloom.

Mando met me outside the door. "Gabby told me about it and I'm going, you hear?"

"Sure," I said.

"If you try to go without me, I'll tell everyone about it."

"Whoah, now. No need for threats, Armando, you're going with us."

"Oh." He looked down. "I didn't know. I wasn't sure."

"Why?"

"I thought Steve might not want me to go."

"Well . . . why don't you go down and talk to him. I bet he's still at his house."

"I don't know if I should. Pa's asleep, and I'm supposed to keep an eye on Tom."

"I'll do that, that's what I came here for. You go tell Steve you're coming along. Tell him I'll be up here till we leave."

"Okay." Off he went, running down the path.

"Don't threaten him!" I shouted at his back, but the wind tore my words off toward Catalina, and he didn't hear me. I went inside. The Santa Ana was catching around the sides of the house, whistling in all the oil drums, so that the house said *Whoooo, whoooo, whooooo.* I looked in the hospital, where a lamp burned. Tom was flat on his back, head propped up on a pillow. He opened his eyes and looked at me.

"Henry," he said. "Good."

It was warm and stuffy in the room; Doc's sun heating was working too well during these hot days, and if the vents were to be opened completely the wind would have torn through and made a shambles. I walked to the bedside and sat in the chair left there.

Tom's beard and hair were tangled together, and all the gray and white curls looked waxy. They framed his face, which was smaller and whiter than I had ever seen it. I stared at it like I'd never seen it before. Time puts so many marks on a face:

wrinkles, blotches, sags and folds; the bend in his nose, the
scar breaking up one eyebrow, the caved-in cheek where those
teeth were missing. . . . He looked old and sick, and I thought,
He's going to die. Maybe I was really looking at him for once.
We assume that we know what our familiars look like, so that
when we see them we're not really looking, but just glancing
and remembering. Now I was looking newly, really observing
him. Old man. He pushed up onto his elbows. "Put the pillow
so I can sit up against it." His voice was only half as loud as
it usually was. I moved the pillow and held him up while he
pulled himself back to it. When we were done he was sitting
upright, his back against the pillow, his head against the con-
cave end of an oil drum. He pulled his shirt around so it was
straight on his chest.

The one lamp that was lit flickered as a draft plunged down
one of the partially opened roof vents. The yellow glow that
filled the room dimmed. I stood and leaned over to give the
flame a little more wick. The wind bent at an especially noisy
angle around the corner of the house.

"Santa Ana blowing, eh?" Tom said.

"Yeah. A strong one, too. And hot."

"I noticed."

"I bet. This place is like an oven. I'm sure glad I don't live
in the desert if it's like this all the time."

"Used to be. But the wind isn't hot because of the desert.
It gets compressed coming over the mountains, and that heats
it up. Compression heats things."

"Ah." I started to describe the effect of the Santa Ana on
the trees, that were so used to the onshore wind; but he knew
about Santa Anas. I fell silent. We sat there a while. There
was no rush to fill silences between us. All the hours we'd
spent sitting together, talking or not talking, it didn't matter.
Thinking about all those hours made me sad. I thought, You
can't die yet, I'm not done learning from you. Who's gonna
tell me what to read?

This time Tom made an effort to rouse things. "Have you
gotten started on filling that book I gave you?"

"Oh, Tom, I don't know how to do such a thing. I haven't
even opened it."

"I was serious about that," he said, giving me the eye. Even
in that wasted visage the eye had its old severity.

"I know you were. But what am I going to write? And I

don't even barely know how to spell."

"Spelling," he said scornfully. "Spelling doesn't matter. The six signatures of Shakespeare we have are spelled four different ways. You remember that when you worry about spelling. And grammar doesn't matter either. You just write it down like you would talk it. Understand?"

"But Tom—"

"Don't but me, boy. I didn't spend all that time teaching you to read and write for nothing."

"I know. But I don't have any stories to write, Tom. You're the one with the stories. Like that one when you met yourself, remember?"

He looked confused.

"The one where you picked yourself up hitchhiking," I prompted him.

"Oh yeah," he said slowly, looking off through the wall.

"Did that really happen to you, Tom?"

The wind. Only his eyes moved, sliding over to look at me. "Yes."

Again the wind, whistling its amazement, *whoooooo!* Tom was quiet for a long time; he started and blinked and I realized he had lost track of what we were saying.

"That was an awful long time ago for you to remember it all so clearly," I said. "What you said and all. There's no way I could do that. I can't even remember what I said last week. That's another reason I couldn't write that book."

"You write it," he commanded me. "Everything comes back when you write it down. Press the memory."

He fell silent, and we listened to the wind's howls. A branch thumped the wall. He clutched at the sheet covering his legs, clutched and twisted it. It had a frayed edge.

"You hurting?" I asked.

"No." Still he kneaded it, and looked at the wall across from me. He sighed a few times. "You think I'm pretty old, don't you boy." His voice was weak.

I stared at him. "You are pretty old."

"Yes. Lived a full life in the old time, was forty-five on the day—that makes me a hundred and eight years old now, is that right?"

"Sure, that's right. You know it best."

"And I look that old too, God knows." He took a deep breath, held it, let it go. I noticed that he hadn't coughed since

I had arrived, and thought that the dry wind might be a help to him. I was about to remark on that when he said,

"But what if I wasn't?"

"What?"

"What if I wasn't that old?"

"I don't understand."

He sighed, shifted around under the sheet. Closed his eyes for a time, so that I thought he might have fallen asleep. Opened them again.

"What I mean is . . . is that I've been stretching my age a bit."

"But—how can that be?"

He shifted his gaze and stared at me, his brown eyes shiny and pleading. "I was eighteen when the bombs went off, Henry. I tell you true for the very first time. Got to while I have the chance. I was going to go to that ruined school on the cliffs that we saw down south. I went for a trip in the Sierra the summer before and that's when it happened. When I was eighteen. So now I'm . . . now I'm . . ." He blinked several times in succession, shook his head.

"Eighty-one," I said in a voice dry as the wind.

"Eighty-one," he repeated dreamily. "Old enough, and that's the truth! But I only grew up in the old time. None of that other stuff. I wanted to tell you that before I go."

I stared at him, stared at him; got up and walked around the room, and ended up at the foot of the bed where I stared at him some more. I couldn't seem to get him in focus. He stopped meeting my eye and looked uncomfortably at his mottled hands.

"I just thought you should know what I've been doing," he said apologetically.

"Which is what?" I asked, stupefied.

"You don't know? No. Well . . . having someone around who lived in the old time, who knew it well, too—it's important."

"But if you weren't really there!"

"Make it up. Oh, I was there. I lived in the old time. Not for long, and without understanding it at the time, but I was there. I've not been lying outright. Just stretching."

I didn't believe it. "But why?" I cried.

For the longest time he was silent, and the wind howled my distress for me.

"I don't know how to put it," he said wearily. "To hold on to the part of our past that's of value, maybe? To keep our spirits up. Like that book does. Can't be sure if he did it or not. Could be a Glen Baum that did go around the world. Could be Wentworth wrote it right there in his workshop. Doesn't matter—it's happened now because of the book. An American around the world. We needed it even if it was a lie, understand?"

I shook my head, unable to speak. He sighed, looked away, bonged his head lightly on the oil drum. A million thoughts jammed in my mind, and yet I said something I hadn't thought, in a voice thick with disappointment. "So you didn't meet your double after all."

"No. Made it up. Made a lot of things up."

"But why, Tom? *Why?*" I started walking around the room again so he wouldn't see me cry.

He didn't answer me. I thought of all the times that Steve had called him a liar, and how often I had defended him. Ever since he had shown us the picture of the Earth taken from the moon, I had believed him, believed all his stories. I had decided he was telling the truth.

In a voice I could barely make out he said, "Sit down, boy. Sit down here." I sat in my chair. "Now listen. I came down and saw it, see? See? I was in the mountains, like I said. That part of the story was true. All the lies were true. In the mountains on a hike to myself. I didn't even know the bombs went off, can you believe it?" He shook his head like he couldn't believe it yet. And suddenly I realized he was telling me what he had never told anybody. "It was a fine day, I hiked over Pinchot Pass, but that night smoke blotted the stars. No stars. I didn't know but I knew. And I came down and saw it. Every person in Owens Valley was crazy, and the first one I met told me why, and that moment —oh, Hank, thank God you won't ever have to live that moment. I went crazy like the rest of them. I was just older than you and all of them were dead, everyone I knew. I was mad with grief and my heart broke and sometimes I think it never did get mended...."

He swallowed hard. "Now I see why I don't talk about it." He bonged the oil drum with his head, blinked to clear his eyes. In a fierce whisper he said, "But I got to, I got to, I got to," banging his head lightly, bong, bong, bong.

"Stop it, Tom." I put my hand behind his head, against the

resonant metal drum. His scalp was damp. "You don't have to."

"Got to," he whispered. I leaned forward to hear him. "At first I didn't believe it. But the greyhound wasn't running and I knew. It took me a work of walking and hitching rides with madmen to get home, but when I came down five it was still burning pillars of smoke everywhere, the whole city. I knew it was true then and I was afraid of the radiation so I didn't go on to see my home. Up into the mountains looting and scavenging for food. How long I don't know, lost my mind and only really remember flashes like flames through smoke. Killing. I came to in a cabin in the mountains and knew I would have to see it to believe they were all dead. My family, see? I didn't care about the radiation anymore, don't think I even remembered it. So I went back to Orange County, and there, oh, oh," he exclaimed; his hand was clutching at the sheet over and over, and I held it. It was feverish.

"I can't tell that," he whispered. "It was . . . evil. I ran and came here. Empty hills, I was sure the whole world was destroyed, world of insects and people dying on the beaches. When I hoped, I thought it might be just us and Russia, Europe and China. That the other countries would get help to us eventually, ha ha." He nearly choked, and held onto my hand hard. "But no one knew. No one knew anything beyond what they could see. I saw empty hills. That was all I knew. Marines had kept them clear. I saw I could live in these hills without going mad, if I could avoid getting killed by someone or starving. It could be done. See up to that point I didn't know if it could be done. But here was the valley and I knew it could be done. And I never set foot in Orange County again."

I squeezed his hand; I knew that he had been up there since.

As if to contradict me he said, "Never, not to this day." He tugged my hand and whispered rapidly, "It's evil, evil. You've seen them at the swap meets, scavengers, there's something wrong with them, wall-eyed or something burst inside —there's something wrong in their eyes, you can see it's driven them crazy to live in those ruins. Insanity's horse. And no surprise either. You got to stay out of that place, Henry. I know you've been up there at night. But listen to me, now, don't go up there, it's bad, *bad*." He was leaning off the pillow toward me, both hands on my side of the bed to prop himself up, his face intense and sweaty. "Promise me you won't go up there, boy."

"Ah, Tom—"

"You can't go up there," he said desperately. "Tell me you won't, not ever."

"Tom, I mean sometime I'm gonna have to—"

"No! What for? You get what you need out of there from scavengers, that's what they're for, *please*, Henry, promise me. There's evil up there so bad it can't be spoken of please *I'm asking you not to go up there*—"

"All right!" I said. "I won't go up there. I promise." I had to say it to calm him down, you see. But the knot tightened across my stomach until I had to hold my left arm over my ribs, and I knew I had done wrong. Done wrong again.

He collapsed back against the pillow, *bong*. "Good. Save you from that. But not me."

I felt so awful I tried to change the subject. "But I guess it didn't harm you, not in the long run. Here you are all these years later."

"Neutron bombs. Short term radiation. So I guess, but I don't know. Something like that, though. The earth will revenge us, but it's no solace. Revenge is no solace. Their suffering won't pay off ours, nothing will ever, we were *murdered*." He squeezed my hand so hard my knuckles hurt. He sucked in air. "The ones of us left were so hungry, so hungry, we fought each other and finished the murder off for them, ah, that was the worst of it. So crazy. In the year after more people died than had been killed by the bombs, I'm sure, and more and more until it looked like every last one of us would die. Civil defense, yeah. Stupid Americans so far from the earth by then that we couldn't figure out how to live off it, or those who could were swamped by those who couldn't, killed and the fighting was bitter. It got so's a friend you could trust was worth more than the world to you. Until there were so few left there was no need to fight anymore, no one to fight. All dead. The deaths, Henry. I saw Death walking down the road more times than you'd care to imagine. Old man in a black coat, axe over his shoulder. Got so I waved to him and walked on by. Then out of the sky the storms, weather turned bad and the storms came. There was a winter that lasted ten years, good limerick. But the suffering was too much to bear. I live to show what a person can bear and die not, good poem, remember it? Did I give you that one? It got so when you saw a living human face that wasn't insane you wanted to hug the person right then and there. Years of solitude like he never thought of. You need people, easier to get food the more of you there are, up to a point. So that when we settled here . . . it was a start. New. Weren't more than a dozen of us. Every day a struggle. Food . . . I used to wonder what for . . . we're slaves to it, boy, I learned that. Grew up and didn't learn a thing about it, not really. In that America was evil. The world was starving and we ate like pigs, people died of hunger and we ate their dead bodies and licked our chops. It's true what I say to Ernest and George, we were a monster and we were eating up the world and they had reasons to do it to us, but still, still we didn't deserve it. *We were a good country.*"

"Please, Tom. You're going to hurt your voice going on so, you can't!" He was sweating and his voice was so strained and torn up I really did think he would hurt it. I was scared, trembling. But now he was wound up; he took a few deep breaths, and went on again, squeezing my hand and ordering me with his eyes to let him talk, to let him speak at last:

"We were free then. Not perfectly so, you understand, but it was the best we could do, we were trying, it was the best so far. Nobody else had ever done it better, we . . . it was the best country in history," he whispered, like he had to convince me or die. "I tell you true now, no baiting George or babbling, with all the flaws and stupidities we were still the leader, the focus of the world, and they killed us for it. Malicious envy they murdered us for, killed the best country the earth ever had, it was genocide boy do you know that word? Genocide, the murder of a whole people. Oh it had happened before, we did it ourselves to the Indians. Maybe that's why this happened to us. I keep coming on reasons but they're not enough. Still it would be better to think that than to think we were killed out of hateful envy of the other countries, we didn't deserve that, no nation could deserve such desolation, we were wrong in a million ways and had flaws big as our strengths but *we didn't deserve this.*"

"Calm down, Tom, *please* calm down."

"They'll suffer for it," he whispered. "Tornadoes, yes, and earthquakes and floods and droughts and fires, and murder for no good reason. See I went back to see. I had to see. And it was all smoking and blasted flat. Home. And just a few blocks away it still stood, blasted flat all around it but not it, ground zero is that still spot. It really was the magic kingdom when I was a child." Now his whispering got so rapid and desperate I could barely hear him, and what he said made no sense, and I held his forearm with both hands as he went on. "Main Street was all full of trash, dead people here and there, ruins, the smell of death. Around the corner the steamboat used to come, one time when I was a little boy my folks took me and as the steamboat rounded the corner we could hear that horn cutting across the water like Gabriel's last call and the whole crowd knew it was him in an instant, Satchmo it was, Henry, Satchmo playing louder than the steamboat whistle, but now the lake was chock with corpses. I went to talk with Abraham Lincoln, leaned my head in his lap looked in his sad eyes and told him they killed his country like they killed him but he knew already and I cried on his shoulder. Went through the castle to the giant teacups, big blowsy woman and two men in the dead silence laughing drunk and trying to get the teacups to spin, she let a big green bottle go smash it went over the concrete and that instant I knew it was all true, and the man—the man he took his knife, oh—oh—"

"*Please*, Tom!"

"But I survived! I survived. Ran from evil I don't know where or how, came to in the valley like I said. I ran all the way and learned what I had to to survive. Didn't learn a damned thing in the old time. Schoolbook rubbish, nothing more. Idiot America. Roger's the model of reason next to it, I nearly died learning what I had to know, nearly died twenty times and more, Jesus I was lucky to live, luck boy it's real and so real it makes the differences between life and death a million times in your life. Just luck. Until it turns up ace of spades I saw that happen to friends right before my eyes and me not able to do a thing but wonder my ace hadn't turned up too, it was hard. Sometimes me or them, he fell in the torrent and maybe I could have—or the time they took her, no Troy for us . . . harsh, harsh, harsh. Tiger justice, we're Greek now boy, it's as hard for us as it was for them, and if we can make something beautiful out of it it'll be like what they made, that fine carved line pure and simple just to describe it the way it is. And Death fine curve sitting there always, skull under flesh in the sun, no wonder the tragedies, the harshness, verse rituals the vase, the curved line, they were just a way of talking about what's real then and now, real as hunger, a way to take nothing out of the pain, sometimes I can't bear to think of it. We were the last of those plays, great pride a great flaw, the two the same and they killed us for it, blasted us to desolation struggling in the dirt to scratch out thirty years and die like Greeks, oh, Henry, can you see why I did it, why I lied to you, it was to keep you knowing it, to keep you from the nothing, to make us Greek ghosts on the land and defying what fell to us and make that something pure and simple so we can say we're still people, Henry, *Henry*—"

"*Yes*, Tom. *Tom!* Calm down, *please.*" I was standing, holding him by the shoulders, leaning over him, shaking at his delirium. Twisting he started to speak again and I put my hand over his mouth, clamped it there. He struggled to breathe and I let my hand off him. "You're not making any sense," I told him. The lamp sputtered, our shadows wavered against the black circles of the wall, the wind shrieked around the corner. "You're working yourself up too much, talking wild. Listen to me now, lie down here. Please. Doc would be furious at us if he came in. You haven't got the strength for such carrying on."

"Do too," he whispered.

"Good, good. Simmer down some though, simmer down, simmer down."

He seemed to hear me, finally. He leaned back. I wiped the sweat from my forehead, and sat down again. I felt like I had been running for miles. "Jesus, Tom."

"Okay," he said. "I'll keep it down. But you got to know."

"I know you survived. Now we're past that and that's all I need to know. I don't want to know any more," I said, and I meant it.

He shook his head. "You got to." He relaxed back into the pillow. *Bong, bong, bong, bong, bong, bong.*

"Stop that, Tom."

He stopped. The wind picked up again, filling the silence. *Whoooo, whoooooo, whooooooooooo.*

"Aye, I'll be quiet," he said softly, the strain gone from his voice. "Wouldn't want Doc mad at me."

"No you wouldn't," I said seriously. I was still scared; my heart still pumped hard. "Besides, you've got to save what energy you've got."

He shook his head. "I'm tired." The wind howled like it wanted to pick us up and knock us down. The old man eyed me. "You won't go up there, will you? You promised."

"Ah, Tom," I said. "Some time I may have to, you know that."

He slumped down onto the pillow, stared at the ceiling. After a time he spoke, very calmly. "When you learn things important enough that you feel like teaching them, it always seems possible. Everything's so clear given what you've gone through—the images are there, even sometimes the words to convey them with. But it doesn't work. You can't teach what the world has taught you. All the tricks of rhetoric, the force of personality, the false authority of being teacher, or pretending to be immensely old . . . none of that's enough to bridge the gap. And nothing else would be either.

"So I've failed. What I did end up teaching you was no doubt exactly backwards to my purpose. But there's no help for it. I was trying to do the impossible, and so I got . . . confused."

He slid down the pillow until he was flat on his back. Snuggled under the sheet, so that it looked like he would fall asleep right then, for his eyes were closed and he was breathing deep, in the way of an exhausted man. But then one brown eye opened and stared at me, pierced me. "You'll be taught by something strong as this wind, boy, picking you up and blowing you into the sea."

Part Four

ORANGE COUNTY

Chapter Nineteen

Outside it was dark, and the wind howled. I stood at the log bench in the garden and watched wind tear at the potato tops, felt it tear at me. To the west Cuchillo poked into the last blue before night's black. It all looked different, as if I had walked out of the drum house into another time, a time when winds blasted the land like bombs. Wind tore my breath from me, shoved it back in. I tried to collect myself.

"Ready?" Steve said sharply, and I jumped. He and Mando and Gabby were behind me. Impossible in the wind to hear anybody come up on you.

"Very funny," I said.

"Let's go."

Mando said, "I have to make sure Pa's awake to look after Tom."

"Tom's up," I said. "He can call your pa if he wants him. If you wake him up, what will you tell him you're going to do?"

In the dark Mando's blurred, uneasy face.

"Let's go," Steve insisted. "If you want to come along, that is."

Without a word Mando took off down the trail, back into the valley. We followed him. In the woods the wind became no more than a gust here and there. Trees creaked, moaned, hummed. Over Basilone we hiked, steering clear of the Shankses' house. Through the overgrown foundations to the freeway, where we picked up the pace. Quickly enough we were in San Mateo Valley, and past the spot where I had confronted Add. Steve stopped, and we waited for him to decide what to do.

He said, "We're supposed to meet them where the freeway crosses the river."

"We'd best keep going, then," Gabby said. "It's ahead a bit."

"I know, but . . . seems to me we shouldn't walk right down there. That doesn't seem like the right way to do it."

"Let's get down there," I put in. "They might be waiting, and we've got a long way to go."

"Okay. . . ."

We walked close together so we could hear each other in the wind. A ball of tumbleweed bounced across the freeway and Mando shied. Steve and Gabby laughed. "Pretty dangerous, that brush," Gabby observed. Mando didn't answer, but pressed on ahead. We followed him to the San Mateo River. Nobody was there.

"They'll see us and let us know where they are," I guessed. "They need us, and they know we'll be on the freeway. They can hide."

"That's true," said Steve. "Maybe we should cross—"

A bright light flashed on us from below the freeway's shoulder, and a voice from the trees said "Don't move!"

We squinted into the glare. It reminded me of the Japanese surprising us in the fog at sea, and my heart hammered like it wanted to bound off by itself.

"It's us!" Steve called. Gabby snickered disgustedly. "From Onofre."

The light went out, leaving me blind. Under the sound of the wind, some rustling.

"Good." A shape loomed on the sea side of the freeway. "Get on down here."

We felt our way down the slope, bumping together in a

clump. There were a lot of men around us. When we got to the bottom of the slope we stood in bushes that came to our waists. A dozen or more men surrounded us. One of them bent over and opened the shade on a gas lantern; most of its light was caught in the lower branches of the brush, but standing in one dim beam in front of the lantern was Timothy Danforth, Mayor of San Diego. His trousers were muddy.

"Four of you, are there?" he said in his loud bray. His voice brought back every detail of my night at his house on the freeway island, and it was Nicolin who answered, "Yes, sir."

More men joined us, dark shapes coming up through the brush from the river. "That's all of you?" the Mayor said.

"Yes, sir," Steve said.

"That's all right. Jennings, get these men guns."

One of the men, looking like Jennings now that he had been named, crouched over a large canvas bag on the ground.

"Is Lee here?" I asked.

"Lee doesn't like this sort of thing," Danforth said. "He's no good at it, either. Why do you want to know?"

"He's someone I know."

"You know me, right? And Jennings here?"

"Sure. I was just wondering, that's all."

Jennings gave a pistol to each of us. Mine was big, and heavy. I crouched and looked at it in the lantern's light, holding it in both hands. Black metal business end, black plastic handle. It was the first time I had held a gun outside a swap meet. Jennings handed me a leather pouch filled with bullets, and kneeled beside me. "Here's the safety catch; you have to push it to here before it will shoot. Here's how you reload." He spun the cylinder to show me where the bullets fit in. The others were getting instructions around me. I straightened and blinked to help my night sight return, hefting the pistol in my hand. "You got a pocket it'll fit in?"

"I don't think so. Well—"

"All right, men!" If it weren't for the wind, the Mayor's voice would be heard all the way back in Onofre, it seemed. He limped over to me, and I had to look up at him. His hair danced over his shadowed face. "Tell us where they're landing, and we'll be off."

Steve said, "We can't tell you till we're up there."

"None of that!" said the Mayor. Steve looked at me. The Mayor went on: "We've got to know how far away they're landing, so we can decide whether or not to take the boats." So, I thought, they had boated up the coast to get past Onofre. "You men have got guns, and you're part of the raid. I understand your caution, but we're all on the same side here. I give you my word. So let's have it."

The circle of men stood around us silently.

"They're landing at Dana Point," I said.

There it was. If they wanted to leave us now, there was nothing we could do about it. We stood watching the Mayor. No one spoke, and I could feel Nicolin's accusing gaze, but I kept staring into the underlit face of the Mayor, who looked back at me without expression.

"Do you know what time they're landing?"

"Midnight, I heard."

"And who'd you hear from?"

"Scavengers who don't like the Japanese."

Another silence followed that. Danforth looked over at a man I recognized—Ben, his assistant.

"We'd better get going," Danforth said after this silent conference. "We'll go on foot."

Steve said, "It'll take a couple hours to walk to Dana Point."

Danforth nodded. "Is the freeway the best route?"

"Up to the middle of San Clemente it is. After that there's a coastal road that's faster, and less exposed to scavengers." Now that he was sure we were going, Steve's voice was filled with excitement.

"We don't have to worry about scavengers tonight," Danforth said. "They wouldn't attack a party this size."

We climbed back up the shoulder into the hot dry blast of the wind. Like me, Mando carried a gun in his hand; Steve and Gab had room in their coat pockets for theirs. When we were all on the roadway the San Diegans started north, and we followed. A few men disappeared ahead and behind us. They had all sorts of guns with them: rifles, pistols as long as my forearm, little fat guns on tripods.

Trees swayed on each side of the road, and branches tumbled through the air like injured night birds. The stars winked brightly in the cloudless black sky, and by their light I could see a great deal: shapes in the forest, the whitish slash of the freeway stretching ahead through the trees, the occasional scout jogging back down the road to us, to report to the Mayor. The four of us kept right behind Danforth, and listened silently as he discussed things and gave orders in a voice calculated to warn every scavenger in Orange County. Walking down the middle of the road, we topped the rise where brick walls tumbled into the freeway, climbed over them and were in San Clemente itself.

"I expect the wind will slow them coming in," Danforth remarked to Ben, unaware of the boundary we had crossed, the boundary I had promised Tom I would never cross. . . . "I wonder how much they had to pay those patrols to let them through? What do you think the going price is for a trip to the mainland, eh? Do you think they tell them it could cost their lives?" Nicolin kept right on the Mayor's heels, soaking in every word. I fell farther and farther back, but I could still hear him when the three men in the rearguard climbed out of the brick tangle and one said, "Either stay up there with them or get off the road with us." I picked up my pace and rejoined the Mayor's group.

Up and down, up and down, over the hills. Trees bounded in place under the wind's hard hand, and the wires still in the air swung like jumpropes. Eventually we came to the road Nicolin had mentioned, that would lead us through San Clemente to Capistrano Beach and Dana Point. Once off the freeway and down in the rubble-filled streets I was obsessed by thoughts of ambush. Branches flew out from between broken walls, planks slapped each other, tumbleweed ran at us or away from us, and time after time I clicked over the safety of my pistol, ready to dive for cover and shoot. The Mayor highstepped over the junk in the middle of the street easy as you please. "That's our point man," he shouted to us, aiming with his pistol at a silhouette dodging through the street ahead. "There's tails a block behind us, too." He gave us the whole strategy of our positions in the street, which seemed like accidents of the moment. The men all had their rifles at the ready, and they were spread out well. "No wreckrats are going to give us trouble tonight, I don't believe." He kicked a brick in the road and stumbled. "*Damn* this road!" It was the third time he had nearly fallen. In all the rubbish it was necessary to watch every step, but he was above that sort of thing. "Doesn't the freeway go right to Dana Point?" he asked Steve. "The maps showed that it did."

"It turns inland about a mile from the harbor," Steve said, his voice raised to carry over the clatter the wind was making.

He still sounded weak compared to the Mayor, who was talking in his everyday voice.

"That's good enough," Danforth declared. "I don't like the footing in this junk." He called to the forward scouts in a voice that made me wince. "Back to the freeway," he told them. "We need to hurry more than we need to hide." We turned up a street headed inland, and intersected the freeway after climbing over a fallen building. Once on the freeway we marched at good speed north, all the way through San Clemente to the big marsh that separates San Clemente from Dana Point.

From the south side of the marsh we could see Dana Point clearly. It was a curve of bluffs, not tall like the cliffs down in San Diego, but tall for our part of the coast, and the curve stuck out from the generally straight line of the land. Now it was a dark mass against the stars, not a light on it anywhere. Underneath the sheer part of the bluff was a tangle of marsh and island, trees and ruins, bounded by a rock jetty that protected a narrow strip of water. Once or twice when fishing to the north we had taken refuge there in storms. The jetty was invisible from where we stood, but Steve described it in as much detail as he could to the Mayor.

"So they'll probably land there," the Mayor concluded.

"Yes sir."

"What about this marsh here? It looks like a good-sized river. Is there a place where we can cross?"

"The beach road has held," Steve said. "It's a high bridge over the rivermouth, so it drains right and none of it's ever been washed out." He said this as proudly as if he were the bridge builder. "I've been across it."

"Excellent, excellent. Let's get over it, then."

The road leading from the freeway to the bridge was gone, however, and we were forced to descend a ravine, cross the creek at its bottom, and climb the other side. My pistol was getting to be quite an irritation in all this climbing, and I could see Mando felt the same. Danforth's exhortations kept us hurrying. Once on the beach road we hurried over the thick sand that covered it, to the mouth of the estuary. As Steve had said, the bridge was still there, in good shape. In a low voice Gabby asked me, "How does he know all this?" but all I could do was shrug and shake my head. Nicolin had made night treks on his own, I knew that—and now I knew that he had come all the way up here, on his own, and had never told me of it.

Out on the bridge we caught the full brunt of the wind for the first time since we had entered San Clemente. It peeled over the bridge with a force that made us stagger to walk forward, and it shoved the water of the river in choppy waves against the pilings. The waves burst into foam and rebounded into the channel, to be carried out to sea gurgling and sucking and hissing. We didn't tarry there, and were quickly over the bridge and under the bluffs of Dana Point, out of the wind's full power.

Tucked under the bluffs was the marshy flat that had once been the harbor. Only the channel directly behind the rock jetty was free of the sand and scrub that had drifted in and covered the rest of the little bay. We struggled through nettles and man-high brush to the beach facing the jetty, less than a stone's throw away from it. Swells broke over submerged sections of the line of rocks, giving it a white edging and making it visible in the starlight. Weak remnants of the swell washed up and back the pebbly beach. The jetty ended almost directly across from us; we stood at the entrance of what remained of the harbor.

"If they land here they'll have to get through this marsh here," Jennings said to the Mayor.

"You think they'll sail in there, then?" the Mayor said, pointing up the channel to where it ended against the curve of the bluff.

"Maybe, but when the swell is small like it is tonight, I don't see why they wouldn't avoid all this and sail over to the beach back there." Jennings pointed back the way we had come, at the wide beach stretching from the harbor south to the bridge.

"But what if we go there and they land here?" said Ben.

"Even if they do land somewhere in here," Jennings said, "they'll have to go by us over there if they're going to go up the valley to see the mission like we think they are."

"Like you think they are," Danforth said.

"Don't you agree?"

"Maybe."

Jennings said, "Well either way, if we're over there we'll have them. They'll come by us wherever they land—they won't be going up those cliffs." He waved at the north end of the channel. "If we stay here and they land on that beach, they'll be able to run inland. We want to trap them against water."

"That's true," Ben said.

Danforth nodded. "Let's get back there, then." Everyone heard him, of course, and we tramped back through the thick shrubs cursing and struggling. Back on the road that led to the bridge, the Mayor called us together.

"We've got to be well hidden, because the scavengers might come to greet this landing, and they'll be coming from behind us. So I want us all in buildings or thick trees, or some such shelter as that. We're assuming they're going to land at this beach here, but it's a good long stretch, so we may have to move after we sight them. If there's a group on the beach to greet them, we'll be able to adjust sooner, but we'll have to be very quiet about it." He led us from the road onto the beach. "Don't walk where fresh tracks will show! Now. Main force, over here behind this wall." Several men followed his pointing finger, and walked over to a low tumbled-down wall of broken brick. "Get tucked in there good." He walked south down the beach. "Another group in that clump of trees. That will make a good crossfire. And you Onofre men..." He came back north, passed the first wall, came to a pile of cement blocks. "In here. See, this was a latrine. Clear some of these out and hunker down in here. If they try slipping around into that harbor swamp, you'll be here to stop them."

Mando and I put down our guns, and we climbed into the blocks and weeds and tossed some blocks out to make more room for us.

"That's good," Danforth said. "We don't want to make too much of a disturbance, they may have landed around here before, in which case we don't want to change anything much. Get in that, let's see how well hidden you are." We climbed over the junk in the doorway and stood inside. Two of the walls didn't meet anymore, and we had a good view through the crack of the beach and the water. "Good. One of you stay where you can see down the beach."

"We can see through this break," Steve said, looking through the crack.

"Okay. That might be a good slot for shooting through, too. Stay out of sight, remember. They'll have night glasses, and they'll have a good look around before they land."

The rest of the San Diegans had disappeared in their various blinds. The Mayor looked around and saw they had dispersed; he checked the watch on his wrist and said, "Okay. It's still a couple hours before midnight, but the scavengers may come earlier to greet them, and they may land early anyway. When you see them come in, stay down. Don't even release the safeties of your guns until we fire on them, understand? That's very important. When we fire is your signal to fire too. Don't waste bullets. Lastly, if anything happens and we get separated in the fighting, we'll all meet on the bridge we crossed, and go back through San Clemente together. You know where I mean?"

"Sure," Steve said. "The big bridge."

"Good men. I'm going to join the main group. Keep quiet, and keep one man looking hard." He shook each of our hands in turn, leaning into the latrine to do it. Once again he crushed my hand. "One more thing—we'll hold our fire until they're all on the beach. Remember that. Okay? Okay, then"—clenching a fist and swinging it overhead—"now's our chance to get them!" Then he was off, limping across the soft sand to the broken wall down the beach.

No one in sight. Steve stood at the big crack facing the water and said, "I'll take the first lookout."

We each slid into the best seat we could make, and began to wait. Gabby settled down on a pile of disintegrating cement blocks. Mando and I got as comfortable as we could, sitting on each side of him. There was nothing to do but listen to the wind batter the ruins. Once I stood and looked over Steve's shoulder at the slice of the sea visible through the crack. Waves broke and sluiced up and down the beach; the offshore wind threw a little spray back, in white arcs barely lit by the star-pied sky. Whitecaps flecked the surface farther out to sea. Nothing else. I sat back down. Counted the bullets in my leather pouch. There were twelve of them. The gun was loaded, so theoretically I could kill eighteen Japanese. I wondered how many there would be. With my fingernails I could pluck the loaded bullets from their chambers and slip them back in, so I figured reloading wouldn't be a problem. Mando saw me and began fiddling with his gun, too.

"Do you think these things shoot straight?" he said.

"If you're close enough," said Gabby.

We waited some more. Leaning back against the cement wall I even dozed a bit, but I had one of those waking dreams, a quick vision of a green bottle tumbling my way, and I jerked awake again, my heart pumping. Still, nothing was happening, and I almost drifted off again, thinking in a disconnected dreamy way about the bricks of the latrine. Who had made such once-perfect bricks?

"I wish they'd get here," Mando said.

"Shh," Steve said. "Don't talk. It's getting close to time."

If they come at all, I thought. Overhead the stars flickered in the velvet black sky. I shifted to the other side of my butt. We waited. Off on the bluffs a pair of coyotes matched yowls. A lot of time passed, heartbeat by heartbeat, breath by breath. Nothing slower than time passing, sometimes.

Steve jerked and reached a hand back to snap in our faces. He leaned over, hissed "scavengers" in a whisper. We jumped to our feet and looked through the crack, peering around Steve. Dark. Then against the white gleam of the shorebreak I made out figures moving down the beach. They stopped for a while near the wall where the San Diegans were hidden, then moved north, until they were between us and the water. Their voices were almost loud enough to be understood. They clumped together and then moved south again, stopping before they had come even with the San Diegans. One of them leaned down and struck a lighter near the sand, and by its tiny flame several pants legs were illuminated. They were dressed in their finery: in the little circle of light were flashes of gold, ruby, sky-blue cloth. The man with the lighter lit five or six lanterns and left them on the sand with several dark bags and a couple of boxes. One of the lanterns had green glass. Another scavenger took that one and a clear one, went to the water and swung them overhead, crossing them once or twice. By the lanterns' light we could make out parts of the whole crew, silver flashing from their ears and hands, wrists and waists. Several more appeared, carrying dry brush and some bigger branches, and with difficulty they started a fire. Once it was going the kindling burst into flame, and the bigger pieces crackled and spit burning pitch into the sand. Now in the bouncing light they were all clearly visible: fifteen of them, I counted, dressed in yellow and red and purple and blue and green, and weighted down with rings and necklaces of silver and copper.

"I don't see any boat out there," Steve whispered. "You'd think if they were signaling we could make out the boat."

"Too dark," Mando whispered. "And the fire cuts what we can see."

"Shh," Steve hissed.

"Look," said Gabby in an urgent whisper. He pointed past Steve's shoulder, but already I saw what he meant: there was a dark bulk rising out of the water, just off the end of the jetty. Waves rolled over this dark shape, defining it.

"It's coming up from under the water!" Gabby said tightly. "It didn't sail in at all."

"Get down," Steve said, and we crouched at his sides. "That's a *submarine*."

The man on the beach waved one lantern overhead now, the green one. Their fire gusted in the wind and the bright light bounced off yellow coats, emerald pants.

"So that's how they get past the coast guard," Gabby said.

"They go under them," Steve agreed, awe in his voice.

"Do you think the San Diegans see it?" Mando said.

"Shh," Steve hissed again.

One of the submarine's lights came on, illuminating a narrow black deck. Figures came out of a hatch onto this deck, and in the water beside it they inflated big rafts. Others piled out of the submarine into the rafts. The scavengers' firelight reflected off the oars as the rafts were rowed to the beach. Two scavengers welcomed the raft by wading into the water up to their waists, and pulling it up the beach beyond the white wavefoam. Several men jumped out of the raft, and a couple more of them lifted packages and wooden boxes out of it. Scavengers handed them jars of amber liquid that glistened in the firelight, and as the Japanese visitors drank we could just hear the scavengers' greetings, raucous and jovial. The Japanese all looked very round, as if they were wearing two coats each. One of them looked just like my captain.

I pulled back from the crack. "We'll be too far from them when the ambush starts," I told Steve.

"No we won't. Look, here's another raft full of them."

I said, "We should get out of this latrine and get in the trees behind. Once they figure out where the firing is coming from, we'll be stuck here."

"They won't figure it out—how are they going to do that in the dark?"

"I don't know. We should be out of here."

One more raft was filled, rowed to shore, pulled up the beach. The thick Japanese men stepped out, looked around. The light on the submarine went out, but its dark bulk remained. Boxes were lifted out of the last raft, and some of the scavengers gathered around the boxes as they were pried open. One in a scarlet coat held up a rifle from a box for his fellows to see.

Crack! crack! crack! The San Diegans opened fire. Shot after shot rang out. From my crouch, looking past Steve's leg, I could see only the response of our victims on the beach: They fell to the sand, the lanterns were out in an instant, the fire knocked to sparks. From then on I couldn't see much, but already spits of flame showed they were firing back. I aimed to fire, and at the same moment there was a flat *whoosh-BOOM*, and we were in a cloud of oily gas, coughing and choking, gasping, crying—my eyes burned so badly I couldn't think of anything else—I feared the gas was eating them out of my head. As the wind swept the cloud out to sea there was another boom, and another, and the popping sound of our ambush was overwhelmed by tremendous long bursts of gunfire spraying off the beach. Through eyes burning with tears all I saw was the whitish flame spurting from the Japanese guns. I coughed and spit, feeling sick, raised my gun to shoot it for the first time (Steve was already shooting). I pulled the trigger and my gun went click, click, click.

A searchlight speared the darkness, originating on the submarine and lighting somewhere south of us, near the wall hiding the San Diegans. The whole area down there exploded. Gunfire ran in the street behind us, and another cloud of poison gas mushroomed over the beach. The Japanese and the scavengers trapped on the beach stood and marched toward us through the gas, wearing helmets and firing machine guns. Blocks of our latrine fell on us. "Let's get out of here!" Steve cried. We leaped over the latrine's back wall and ran for the trees backing the beach. Once on the trash-blocked street flanking the strand, we ran—hopped, rather—struggled over piles of soggy wood and old brick, tripped and fell, got up again. My nose was streaming snot from the poison gas; I threw away my pistol. In an eyeblink the whole area was bright as day, bright with a harsh blue glare, the shadows solid as rocks. In the sky over us a flare was sputtering light, revealing the tiny parachute holding it up. The whole unit quickly tumbled off to sea, lighting the harbor so that for an instant between trees I could see the submarine, and men on it firing a mounted gun at us.

"The bridge!" Steve was shouting. "The bridge!" I read his lips more than heard him. It was astounding how loud the gunfire was, I wanted to collapse and clamp my hands over my ears. We scrambled over rubbish, fallen trees, driftwood from storm tides; Mando caught his foot and we pulled him loose. Bullets whanged over us, tearing the air *zip, zip,* and I ran hunched down so far my back hurt. Another flare burst into life, higher and farther inland. It floated over us like a falling star, making our way plain but also showing us to everyone so we had to crawl, foot by foot. Rips of machine gun fire came from the sea side of us, and behind us were explosions at frequent intervals: with a blinding flash and a *crack* to break the ears a building down the street fell all over the rubble. The submarine. We got up from a tangle of planks and ran again, crouched over. Another flare lit the sky above. We fell and waited for the wind to take it to sea. A wrecked building up the hill exploded, then a trio of redwood trees were knocked down. The flare blew away and we stumbled through the shadows for a good way before another flare burst into life, and we lay flat in a copse of eucalyptus.

"Do you think—" Gabby gasped. "Did the San Diegans get away?" No one answered. Mando was still carrying his pistol. We were just a ways from the bridge, and I wanted to get over it before the submarine blasted it into the river. Dana Point still rang with gunfire, it sounded like a real battle was going on, but they could have been fighting shadows. I wasn't sure the San Diegans would have run like we had. We got up again and scurried over the trash in the streets. A waft of the poison gas. Another fire sparked, but this one plunged fizzing into the marsh. I fell and cut my hand and elbow and knee. We made it to the bridge.

No one was there. "We've got to wait for them!" Steve shouted.

"Get across," I said.

"They won't know we're here! They'll wait here—"

"They will not," Gabby said bitterly. "They're over it and long gone. They told us to wait here so we'd slow down the Japs."

Steve stared at Gab open-mouthed. Another flare burst right above us and I crouched by the rail. Looking between the concrete rail posts I saw several of the flares tailing out to sea, making a ragged string that fell closer to the water, until the ones farthest out lit patches of water. The latest one sailed offshore and over the submarine.

"Go before they put up another one," Gabby said furiously.

He stood and ran across the bridge without waiting for us to agree. We followed him, but another flare sparked the sky, lighting the bridge in ghastly detail. There was nothing to do but keep running, and run we did, because the submarine commenced shooting at us. The railing clanged and the air ripped like stiff cloth, like the first tearing sound of thunder. We got to the far side of the bridge and threw ourselves flat behind a stretch of canted asphalt. The submarine pummeled the bridge. From the hills inland a siren howled, low at first and then rising fast. Scavengers, sounding the alarm. But who were they fighting? Darkness, distant explosions, siren howls. The submarine stopped firing but my head rang so I couldn't hear. Little bangs ahead of us in San Clemente, felt more than heard. Steve put his face to my ear. "Go back through streets—" and something I didn't catch. The shooting to the south meant the San Diegans were already down there, I decided, and I cursed them for leaving us. We ran again, but the submarine must have seen us through its night glasses, because it fired again. Down we went. Crawled and hopped, ran doubled over through the ruins on the coastal road. The submarine stayed in the rivermouth, pounding away. We got off the coastal road, back against a low cliff, through trees and on another road. Into the wreck of San Clemente, the maze of trash. Mando was falling behind, limping. I thought it was his foot. "Hurry up!" Steve screamed.

Mando shook his head, limped to us. "Can't," he said. "They shot me."

We stopped and sat him down in the dirt. He was crying, he had his left hand up to his right shoulder. I lifted his hand away and felt the blood run over mine.

"Why didn't you tell us?" Steve cried.

"It just happened," Gabby said roughly, and pushed me away. He put his arm around Mando's. "Come on, we got to get him back as quick as we can."

By the distant light of the last flare I could make out Mando's face. He was staring at me as if he had something to tell me, but his mouth only jerked. "Help me *carry* him," Gabby rasped, his voice cracking. I could feel the blood soaking the back of his shirt. Steve picked up his pistol and we were off. We could only take several steps at a time before some beam or collapsed wall stopped us. "We've got to stop him bleeding," I finally dared to say. It was running inside my sleeve and down my arm. We put him down and I ripped my shirt into strips. It was hard getting the compress tight over the bullet hole. By accident I brushed the wound with my fingers: a little tear under the shoulderblade, on his right side. It wasn't bleeding fast. Mando still stared at my face with a look I couldn't read. He didn't speak. "We'll have you home in a jiffy," I said hoarsely. I stood up too fast and staggered, but Steve helped us get him up, and we were off again.

The center of San Clemente is one big ruin, no plan or pattern to it, no clear way through. Gabby and I carried Mando between us and struggled along, while Steve ranged forward pistol in hand to find the best way. Sirens cut through the wind's shrieking from time to time, and we had to hide more than once to avoid roving bands of scavengers. Gunshots echoed in the clogged streets. I had no idea who was firing at who. A wall fell in the wind. We hiked into dead ends more than once. Steve yelled instructions back to us but sometimes Gabby and I just picked the easiest way; this caused Steve to yell more, in a high desperate shout. Calls came from behind us and Gabby and I lowered Mando to the ground, stuck in the middle of the street. Three scavengers approached us, guns in hand. Steve ran up and fired, *crack crack crack crack!* All the scavengers went down. "Come on," Steve screamed. We picked Mando up and staggered on. Dead ends made us backtrack and after a long time trying to find a way we caught up to Steve sitting in the road, houses collapsed all around us, wind and gunfire beyond, no way forward—our way blocked by a giant mare's nest of bones.

"I don't know where we are," Steve cried; "I can't find a way." I prodded him to take my side carrying Mando, grabbed his gun and ran across the street. Through trees I saw the ocean, the only mark we really needed when it came down to it. "This way!" I called, and hopped over a beam, dragged it out of their path, ran down and got another fix on the sea, picked a road, did what I could to clear it. That went on and on, till it seemed like San Clemente had stretched out all the way down Pendleton. And scavengers on the prowl, setting off their sirens and guns, howling with glee at the hunt. They put us to ground more than once; I didn't dare shoot at them because I wasn't sure how many they were or how many bullets were left in Steve's gun, if any.

While we cowered in the dark of our cover I did what I could for Mando. His breath was choked. "How are you,

Mando?" No answer. Steve cursed and cursed. I nodded to
Gabby and we got Mando up again. I left Steve to carry him
and went out scouting. Scavengers gone, at least out of sight,
that was all I wanted. I set to finding a way again.

Somehow we got to the southern end of San Clemente,
down in the forest below the freeway. Scavengers were roaming
the freeway; we heard their shouts and occasionally I saw their
shapes. The only way across San Mateo River was the freeway.
We were trapped. Sirens mocked us, gunshots might have
marked a skirmish with the San Diegans, although I suspected
Gabby was right and they were long gone, on their boats and
under way. They wouldn't be back to help us. Gabby had
Mando resting on his lap. Mando's breath gurgled in his throat.
"We got to get him home," Gab said, looking at me.

I took the bullets from my pocket and tried to fit them into
Steve's gun.

"Where's your gun?" Steve said.

The bullets didn't fit. I cursed and threw the pouch at the
freeway. In the dirt we sat on was a rock I could just fit my
hand around. I hefted it and started for the freeway. I don't
know what I had in mind. "Bring him up close to the road and
be ready to move him across San Mateo fast," I told them.
"You *go* when I tell you to." But a series of explosions blasted
the freeway above us, and when they ended (burnt powder
smell blown by) it was quiet. Not a scavenger to be heard. The
silence was broken by the sound of a vehicle coming up the
freeway from the south. A little *whirrr*. I crawled up the shoulder of the road to take a look at it. I jumped out of the road
to wave at him. "Rafael! Rafael! Over here!" I screamed, the
words tearing out of me like no others ever had.

Rafael rolled up to me. "Christ, Hank, I almost shot you
dead there!" He was in the little golf cart that sat in his front
yard, the one he swore he could make work if he ever found
the batteries.

"Never mind that," I said. "Mando's hurt. He's been shot."
Gabby and Steve appeared, carrying Mando between them.

Rafael sucked air between his teeth. "Put him in back."

Scattered shots rang out from up the freeway, and one spanged
off the concrete near us. Rafael reached into his cart and pulled
out a metal tube, held by struts at an angle on a flat base. He
put it on the road and dropped a hand-sized bomb or grenade
(it looked like a firecracker) in it. *Thonk*, the tube said hollowly,

and a few seconds later there was an explosion just off the freeway, about where the shots had come from. While Gabby and Steve got Mando in the cart Rafael kept dropping grenades in, thonk, BOOM, thonk, BOOM, and pretty soon no one was firing at us. With a final burst of three he jumped in the cart and we were off.

"When we go uphill, get out and push," Rafael said. "This thing won't carry all of us. Nicolin, take this and keep an eye out to the rear." He handed Steve a rifle. "How about more bullets," Steve said. Rafael gestured at the floor beside him. "In the box there." We hit the steep hill at the very south end of San Clemente, and pushed the cart up it at a slow run. Sirens wailed off the hills; I could make out three different ones, wavering at different levels as the wind tore at their sound. We made the rise and rolled into the San Mateo Valley. I cradled Mando's head and told him we were close to home. There were faint shouts behind us, but now we were moving faster than men on foot could. We reached the rise to Basilone Ridge and Rafael said, "Push again." He was calm, but when he looked at me his eye was hard. When we reached the top of Basilone rise Steve cried wildly, "I'm going back to make them pay!" and he was off in the dark, back up the freeway to the north, rifle in hand. "Wait!" I shouted, but Rafael struck my arm.

"Let him go." For the first time he sounded angry. He drove the cart to his house and jumped out, ran inside and came back out with a stretcher. We got Mando on it. His eyes were still open, but he didn't hear me. Blood trickled from the corner of his mouth. Gabby was huffing beside the stretcher as Rafael and I carried him. We struck out through the forest, traversing the side of Cuchillo to get to the Costas' as fast as possible. I stumbled and groaned, and Gabby took over my end when he saw I couldn't see my way. We got to the Costas' place but I couldn't stop crying. Wind whistled over the oil drums; there was no way they could have heard us approach. Rafael propped the stretcher against his thigh, banged the door like he was out to break it. *Wham. Wham.*

"Get out here, Ernest," he said, still banging the door. "Get out here and doctor your boy."

Chapter Twenty

It must have been something Doc had imagined many times before, the moment when they came to the door and it was his own son hurt and in need of his care. When he pulled the door away from Rafael's banging he didn't say a word to us; he came out and picked Mando up off the stretcher and carried him through the kitchen into the hospital without a glance or a question for us.

We followed him. In the hospital he laid Mando on the second bed, a small one, and pulled it out from the wall. At the scraping Tom snorted, rolled over. One of his closed eyes opened a crack, and when he caught sight of us he sat up, ground his knuckles in his eyes, surveyed the scene wordlessly. Doc used scissors to cut off Mando's coat and shirt, gesturing for Gabby to pull off his pants. Gabby squinted as they peeled away the bloody cloth of the shirt. Mando coughed, gargled, breathed fast and shallow. Under the bright lamps Rafael carried in from the kitchen his body looked pale and mottled. Below his armpit was that little tear, surrounded by a bruise. Rafael nearly tripped over me walking in and out. I sat on my heels against the wall, knees in my armpits, arms wrapped around my legs, rocking back and forth, licking the snot off my lip, looking away from Tom. Doc looked at no one but Mando. "Get Kathryn here," he said. Gabby glanced at me, hurried out.

Tom said, "How is he?"

Doc felt Mando's ribs carefully, tapped his chest, took his pulse at wrist and neck. He muttered, more to himself than Tom, "Middle caliber nicked the lung. Pneumothorax . . . hemothorax. . . ." Like a spell. He cleaned the blood from Mando's ribs with a wet cloth. Mando choked and Doc adjusted his head, reached in his mouth and pulled his tongue around. A plastic thing from the supply shelf behind Doc served to clamp the tongue in place. Plastic vise on the side of Mando's face, stretching his mouth open . . . my spine rolled up and down the oil drum behind me. The wind picked up, *wheeeeee, wheeeeeee.*

"Where's Nicolin?" Tom asked me.

I kept my eyes on the floor. Rafael answered from the kitchen:

"He stayed north to fire some rounds at the scavengers."

Tom was shifting around against his back wall, and he coughed. "Quit moving," Doc said. A flying branch knocked the house sharply. Mando's breathing was rapid, harsh, shallow. Doc tilted his face to the side and wiped bright blood from his mouth. Doc's own mouth was a tight lipless line. Bright blood on cloth. Under me the floor, the grainy smooth boards of the floor. Knots raised above the worn surface, cracks, splinters all shiny and distinct in the lamplight, scrubbing sand in the corners against the walls. The bedpost closest to me was shimmied. The sheets were so old that each thread of the fabric stood out; needlework in the patches. I stared at that floor and never raised my eyes. My breath hurt so it might have been me shot. But it wasn't. It wasn't. Kathryn's legs walked into the room, bending down the floorboards a bit. Gabby's legs followed.

"I need help," Doc said.

"I'm ready," said Kathryn calmly.

"We need to get a tube between these ribs and drain the blood and air in the chest cavity. Get a clean jar from the kitchen and put a couple inches of water in it." She left, came back. Their feet faced each other under Mando's bed. "I'm afraid air's getting in and not getting out. Tension pneumothorax. Here, put down the tube and tape, and hold him steady. I'm going to make the incision here."

I put my hands over my ears. No sounds. No sight but silvery wood planks. Nothing real but wood. . . . But no. Muffled coughs from the old man. A quick glance up: Kathryn's back, in sweatshirt and string-tie pants; the old man, watching them with an unflinching gaze. Down on the floor went the jar, clear plastic tube stuck in the water at the bottom of it. Suddenly the water bubbled. Blood ran down the sides of the tube and stained the water. More bubbles. The old man's steady gaze: I wrapped my arms over my stomach and looked up. Kathryn's broad back blocked my view of Mando. Shudders rattled me. Broad shoulders, broad butt, thick thighs, slim ankles. Elbows busy as she pulled tape from a roll and applied it to Mando, where I couldn't see.

She looked at me over her shoulder. "Where's Steve?"

"Up north."

She grimaced, turned to the work at hand.

Tom coughed again, lightly but several times. Doc looked at him. "You lie back down," he said harshly.

"I'm okay, Ernest. Don't mind me."

Doc was already back at it. He leaned over Mando with a desperate look in his eye, as if the skills his father had taught him so long ago were not enough for this one. "We need oxygen." He tapped Mando's chest and the sound was flat. Mando's breathing was faster. "Got to stop the bleeding," Doc said. The wind gusted till I couldn't make out their voices over the house whistling. "Use the wound to put in another tube. . . ." Tom asked Gabby what had happened, and Gab explained in a sentence or two. Tom didn't comment on it. The wind dropped again and I could hear the snip of Doc's scissors. He wiped sweat from his forehead.

"Hold it. Okay, get the other end in the jar, and give me the tape quick."

"Tape."

Something in the way she said it made Doc wince, and look at Tom with a bitter smile. Tom smiled back but then he looked away, eyes filling with tears. I felt a hand on my shoulder and looked up to see Rafael.

"Come on out to the kitchen like Gabby is now, Henry. You can't do anything in here."

I shook my head.

"Come on, Henry."

I shrugged off his hand and buried my face in the crook of my arm. When Rafael was gone I looked up again. Tom was chewing on a curl of his hair, watching them intently. Kathryn put her head to Mando's chest. "His heart sounds distant."

Mando jerked on the bed. His feet were blue. "And his veins," Doc said, voice dry as the wind. "Tamponade, ohhh . . ." He drew back, his fist clenched up by his neck. "I can't help that. I haven't got the needles."

Mando stopped breathing. "No," Doc said, and with Kathryn's help he shifted Mando from his side to his back. "Hold the tubes," he said, and put his mouth and hands to Mando's mouth. He breathed in, holding Mando's nostrils shut, then straightened up and pressed hard on Mando's chest. Mando's body spasmed. "Henry, come hold his legs," Kathryn said sharply. I got up stiffly and held Mando by the shins, felt them twitch, struggle, tense up, slacken. Go slack. Doc breathed into him, breathed into him, pushed his chest till the pushes were nearly blows. Blood ran down the tubes. Doc stopped. We stared at him: eyes closed, mouth open. No breath. Kathryn held his wrist, feeling for a pulse. Gabby and Rafael were in the doorway. Finally Kathryn reached across Mando and put her hand on Doc's arm; we had all been standing there a long time. Doc put his elbows on the bed, lowered his ear onto Mando's chest. His head rolled till it was his forehead resting on Mando. "He's dead," he whispered. Mando's calves were still in my hands, the very muscles that had just been twitching. I let go, scared to be touching him. But it was Mando, it was Armando Costa. His face was white; it looked like the pinched face of a sick brother of Mando's, not like the face of the boy I knew. But it was him.

Kathryn got out a sheet from the cupboard against the wall and spread it over him, pushing Doc gently away so she could do it. Her sweatshirt was sweaty, bloodstained. She covered Mando's face. I recalled the expression his face had had when I was carrying him through San Clemente. Even that was preferable to this. Kathryn rounded the bed and pulled Doc to the door.

"Let's get him buried," Doc said intently. "Let's do it now, come on." Kathryn and Rafael tried to calm him but he was insistent. "I want it over with. Get the stretcher and let's get him down to the graveyard. I want it over with."

Tom coughed harshly. "Please, Ernest. Wait until morning at least, man. You've got to wait until daylight. Got to get Carmen, and dig the grave—"

"We can do that tonight!" Doc cried petulantly. "I want it over with."

"Sure we can. But it's late. By the time we're done it will be day. Then we can carry him over and bury him with people there. Wait for the day, please."

Doc rubbed his face in both hands. "All right. Let's go dig the grave."

Rafael held him back. "Gabby and I will do that," he said. "Why don't you stay here."

Doc shook his head. "I want to do it. I got to, Rafe."

Rafael looked to Tom, then said, "All right. Come on with us, then."

He and Gabby got Doc into his coat and shoes, and bumped through the doorway after him. I offered to go but they saw I was useless and told me to stay. From the front door I watched them walk down the path to the river. Predawn twilight, Gabby and Rafael on each side of Doc, holding him. Three little figures under the trees. When they were out of sight I turned around. Kathryn was at the kitchen table, crying. I went outside and sat in the garden.

The wind was dying down a bit with the coming of day. It only hit hard in gusts. The light grew; I could make out gray branches waving. Under the pale sky all distances seemed equal. Leaves fluttered and hung still, fluttered again, in waves that swelled across the treetops out to sea. The dome of the sky grew lighter and taller, lighter and taller. Grays took on color, colors seeped into the grays, and then the sun, leaf green and blinding, cracked the horizon. Wind gusted.

I sat in the dirt. My knee, elbow, and hands throbbed where I had cut them falling. It was impossible that Mando was dead, and that reassured me for long stretches of time. Then my hands felt his calves go slack. Or I heard Kathryn inside, clearing up—and I knew that impossible or not, it was real. But it wasn't a thought I could grasp for long.

The sun was more than a hand's breadth over the hills when Doc and Gabby came back up the path, Marvin and Nat Eggloff behind them. Rafael was down the river path, pounding on doors and waking folks up. Gabby fairly staggered up the last part of the path. His eyes were ringed red, and he was dirty, as were Doc and Nat. Doc looked up from the path at his house, stopped and waited. Marvin nodded to me and they went inside. I heard them talking with Kathryn. Then she started yelling at the old man. "Lie down! Don't be a fool! We got enough burials today!" Tom must have said his goodbyes to Mando inside. They came out with Mando on Rafael's stretcher, wrapped in the sheet. Unsteadily I stood. Everyone took a stretcher pole in hand, three on a side. We carried him down to the river, across the bridge. Sun brutal off the water. We took the river path through the trees. People given the news by Rafael caught up with us, family by family, looked shocked, or tearful, or withdrawn. Once looking back I saw John Nicolin leading all the rest of the Nicolins bar Marie and the babies, his face puffy with displeasure. My pa came to my side and put his arm around my shoulder. When he saw my face he squeezed my shoulders hard. For once he didn't look stupid to me. Oh he still had that vague look of someone who doesn't quite get it. But he knew. Suffering you don't have to be smart to understand. With the knowledge in his eyes was mild reproach, and I couldn't look at him.

Back in the neck of the valley we were in the shade. Carmen met us outside her home and led us to the graveyard. She was wearing her preaching robe and carrying the Bible. In the graveyard was a new hole in the ground, a mound of fresh earth on one side of it, Mando's mother Elizabeth's grave on the other. We laid the stretcher on her grave and all the people trailing us circled around. Most of the valley's people were there. Nat and Rafael lifted Mando's body and the sheet into a coffin twice Mando's size. Nat held the lid in place while Rafael nailed it down. Whap, whap, whap, whap. Sunbeams filtered through the branches. Doc watched the nails being driven home with a desolate look. Both his wife and Mando had been so much younger than him, their years didn't add up to half his.

When the coffin was nailed shut John stepped forward and helped them arrange the ropes under the coffin. He and Rafael and Nat and my pa picked up the ropes and lifted the coffin over the hole. They lowered it to John's curt, quiet instructions. When it was settled in the hole they pulled the ropes up. John gathered them and gave them to Nat, his jaw muscles so tight it looked like he had pebbles in his mouth.

Carmen stepped to the edge of the grave. She read some from the Bible. I watched a sunbeam twisting through the trees. She told us to pray, and in the prayer she said something about Mando, about how good he had been. I opened my eyes and Gabby was staring at me from across the grave, accusing, terrified. I squeezed my eyes shut again. "Into Thy hands we commend his spirit." She took a clod of dirt and held it over the grave; held a tiny silver cross over it with the other hand. She dropped them both in. Rafael and John shoveled the damp earth into the hole, it made the hollow sound. Mando was still down there and I almost cried out for them to stop it, to get him out. Then I thought, it could have been me in that grave, and an awful terror filled me. The bullet that struck Mando had been one of swarms of them; that one or any of the others could have hit me, could have killed me. It was the most frightening thought I had ever had in my life—the terror filled me entirely. Gabby kneeled beside Rafael and pushed dirt in with his two hands. Doc twisted away, and Kathryn and Mrs. Nicolin led him back toward the Eggloffs'. But all I did was stand and watch; I watched and watched; and it fills me with shame to write it, but I became glad. I was glad it wasn't me down there. I was so glad to be there alive and seeing it all, I thought thank God it wasn't me! Thank God it was Mando got killed, and *not me*. Thank God! Thank God!

Sometimes after a funeral quite a wake would develop at the Eggloffs', but not this morning. This morning everyone went home. Pa led me down the river path. I was so tired my feet didn't make it over bumps. Without Pa I would have fallen more than once. "What happened?" Pa asked, reproachful again. "Why'd you go up there?" There were people strung along the trail, shaking their heads, talking, looking back at us.

When we got home I tried to explain to Pa what had happened, but I couldn't do it. The look in his eye stopped me. I lay down on my bed and slept. I would say I slept like a dead man, but it isn't so. It's never so.

Sleep doesn't knit the raveled sleeve of care, no matter what Macbeth said (or hoped). He was wrong that time as he was so often. Sleep is just time out. You can do all the knitting you like in dreams, but when you call time in it unravels in an instant and you're back where you started. No sleep or dream was going to knit back the last day for me; it was unraveled for good. Past.

Nevertheless, I slept all through that day and evening, and when Pa's voice, or his sewing machine, or a dog's bark pulled me halfway out of slumber, I knew I didn't want to wake even though I didn't quite remember why, and I worked at returning to sleep until I slid back down the slope to dreams again. I slept through most of the evening, struggling harder and harder to hold onto it as the hours passed.

But you can't sleep forever. What broke my last hold on an uneasy half-sleep was the *w-whoo, w-whoo* of the canyon owl—Nicolin's signal, repeated insistently. Nicolin was out there, under the eucalyptus no doubt, calling me. I sat up, looked out the door; saw him, a shadow against the treetrunk. Pa was sewing. I got my shoes on. "I'm going out." Pa looked at me, hurt me once again with the puzzled reproach in his eyes, the slight hint of condemnation. I was still wearing the torn clothes I had had on the night before. They stank with fear. I was ravenous, and paused to break off half a loaf of bread on my way out. I approached Steve chewing a big lump. We stood together silently under the tree. He had a full bag over his shoulder.

When the bread was done I said, "Where you been?"

"I was in Clemente till late this afternoon. God what a day! I found the scavengers that had been chasing us, and sniped at them till they didn't know *who* was after them. Got some too— they thought a whole gang was after them. Then I went back up to Dana Point, but by that time they had all gotten away. So—"

"Mando's dead."

". . . I know."

"Who told you?"

"My sister. I snuck in to get some of my stuff, and she caught me just as I was leaving. She told me."

We stood there for a long time. Steve took in a deep breath and let it out. "So, I reckon I got to leave."

"What do you mean?"

". . . Come give me some help." My night vision was coming in and with the exhausted sound of his voice I could suddenly see his face, dirty, scratched, desperate. "Please."

"How?"

He took off toward the river.

We went to the Marianis', stood by the ovens. Steve made his owl call. We waited a long time. Steve tapped his fist against the side of the oven. Even I, with nothing at stake, felt nervous. That led me back to all that had happened the night before.

The door opened and Kathryn slipped out, in the same pants she had worn the night before, but a different sweatshirt. Steve's fingernails scraped the brick. She knew where he would be, and walked straight to us.

"So you came back." She stared at him, head cocked to one side.

Steve shook his head. "Just to say goodbye." He cleared his throat. "I—I killed some scavengers up there. They'll be out to get back at us. If you tell them at the swap meet that I did it and took off, that it was all my doing, maybe it will all stop there."

Kathryn stared at him.

"I can't stay after what's happened," Steve said.

"You could."

"I can't."

The way he said that, I knew he was leaving. Kathryn knew it too. She folded her arms over her chest and hugged herself as if she were cold. She looked over at me and I looked down. "Let us talk awhile, Henry."

I nodded and wandered to the river. The water clicked over snags like black glass. I wondered what he was saying to her, what she was saying to him. Would she try to change his mind when she knew he wouldn't?

I was glad I didn't know. It hurt to think of it. I saw Doc's face as he watched his son, the living part of his wife, lowered into the ground beside her. Helpless to stop myself I thought what if the old man dies tonight, right up there at Doc's place? What about Doc then? . . . What about Tom?

I sat and held my head but it didn't stop me thinking. Sometimes it would be such a blessing to turn all the thinking off. I stood and tossed rocks in the water. I sat down again when the rocks were gone, and wished I could throw away thoughts as easily, or the deeds of the past.

Steve appeared and stood looking over the river. I stood up.

"Let's get going," he said thickly. He walked down the river path toward the sea, cut into the forest. There was no talk between us, just the silent walking together, side by side, and briefly I recalled how it had felt for so long, for all our lives, when we had hiked together silently in the woods at night like brothers. Past.

He went down the cliff path without looking at it, going from foothold to foothold with careless mastery. There was a slice of moon, nearly on the water. I descended the obscure cliff more slowly. Once on the sand I followed him to the boats. We broke the sand's water crust, left big footprints in the loose sand below.

A couple of the fishing boats had sockets on the keel, where you could step a small mast and spread a sail. Nicolin went to one of those. Without a word we took bow and stern and skewed the boat from side to side in the sand. Normally four or five men push a boat into the water, but that's just for convenience; Steve and I got it moving pretty easily. When it was across the tide flat and in the shallows we stopped. Nicolin climbed in to step the mast, and I held the hull steady on the sand bottom.

I said, "You're going to sail to Catalina, like the guy who wrote that book."

"That's right."

"You know that book is a bunch of lies."

He never stopped unfurling the sail. "I don't care. If the book is a lie then I'll make it true."

"They aren't the kind of lies you can make true."

"How do you know?"

I did know, but I couldn't say. The mast was stepped and he started jamming the cotter pin through the socket. I didn't want to just come out and ask him to stay. "I thought you were going to spend your life fighting for America."

He stopped working. "Don't you think I'm not," he said bitterly. "You saw what happened when we tried to fight here. There's not a thing we can do. The place where something can be done is Catalina. I bet there's a lot of Americans already there who think the same, too."

I could see he would have an answer to everything. I shifted the boat's stern, got ready to push.

"I'm positive the resistance is strongest over there," he said. "Most effective. Don't you think so? I mean—Aren't you coming with me?"

"No."

"But you should. You'll regret it if you don't. This is a

little out of the way valley here. That's the *world* out there, Henry!" He waved a hand westward.

"No." I leaned over the stern. "Now come on, do you want help with this boat or not?"

He pursed his lips, shrugged. His shoulders drooped when the shrug was done, and I saw how tired he was. It would be a long sail. But I wasn't going to go, and I wasn't going to explain. He hadn't expected me to say yes anyway, had he?

He roused himself, got out of the boat to push. Quickly it floated clear of the sand. We stared at each other from across the boat, and he stuck out his hand. We shook. I couldn't think of anything to say. He leaped in and got the oars out while I held the stern. I shoved it into the current and he started rowing. With the crescent moon behind him I couldn't make out his features, and we didn't say a word. He rowed over a swell coming upriver. Soon he'd be out where what was left of the Santa Ana would clear the cliff, and catch his sail.

"Good luck!" I cried.

He rowed on.

The next swell hid the boat from me for a moment. I walked out of the river, feeling chill. From the beach I watched him clear the rivermouth. The sail, a faint patch against the black, flapped and filled. Soon he was beyond the break. From there he wouldn't hear me unless I shouted. "Do some good for us over there," I said, but I was talking to myself.

I climbed the cliff path, water dripping from my pants. By the time I got to the top I was warmer. I walked along the cliff. It was a cloudless night again, and the setting moon shone across the water, marking the distance to the horizon. It was a night to make you see how vast the world was: the ocean, the spangled sky, the cliff, the valley and the hills behind, they were all so huge I might as well have been an ant. Out there under a pale handkerchief patch was another ant, in an ant's boat.

On the horizon I could see it: dark mass of the sea below, dark sky above, and between them the black bulk of Catalina, bejeweled with white points of light both fixed and moving, and red lights to mark the highest peaks, and a few yellow and green lights here and there. It was like a bright constellation, the finest constellation, always on the verge of setting. For years I had considered it the prettiest sight I had ever seen. There was a cluster of light on the water at the south end that was invisible from the cliff—the foreigners' port—it could be seen from the height of Tom's house on a night like this, but I had no desire to go up there and see it. The dim patch of Nicolin's sail moved out of the narrow path of moonlight on the water, and disappeared. He was one of the shadows among the few moony glitters on the black sea, but strain my eyes as I might I couldn't tell which one he was. For all I could tell the ocean had swallowed him. But I knew it hadn't. The little boat was still out there somewhere, sailing west to Avalon.

I stayed on the cliff looking out to sea for a long time. Then I couldn't stand it, and took off into the forest. Leaves clacked and pine needles quivered as I trudged under the trees. The valley never seemed so big and empty as it did then. In a clearing I looked back; the lights of Catalina blinked and danced, but I turned and walked on. I didn't give a damn if I never saw Catalina again.

Chapter Twenty-one

The forest at night is a funny place. The trees get bigger, and they seem to come alive, as though during the day they were asleep or gone from their bodies, and only at night do they animate themselves and live, perhaps even pulling up their roots and walking the valley floors. If you're out there you can sometimes almost catch them at it, just beyond the corner of your eye. Of course on a moonless night it only takes a little wind to imagine such things. Branches dip to tousle the hair, and the falling-water sounds of the leaves are like soft voices calling in the distance. Two holes make eyes, a trail blaze is a smiling mouth, branches are arms, leaves hands. Easy. Still I think it may be true that they are a type of nocturnal animal. They are alive, after all. We tend to forget that. In the spring they sprout joyously, in the summer they bask in the sun, in the winter they suffer bare and cold. Just like us. Except they sleep during the day and come awake at night. So if you want to have much to do with them, night is the time to be out among them.

The different trees wake up in different ways, and they treat you differently. Eucalyptus trees are friendly and talkative. Their branches tend to grow across each other, and in a wind they creak constantly. And their hanging leaves twirl and clack together, making the falling-water sound, a rising and falling voice that caresses like a hug, or a brushing of the forehead. The eucalyptus has a great voice. But you wouldn't want to touch one, or give it a hug, unless you could see it and avoid the gum. The bark is smooth and cool, fragrant like the rest of the tree with that sharp dusty smell, but it doesn't grow as fast as the wood inside it, I guess, and there are a lot of breaks in it as a result, cracks that split it completely. These cracks leak gum like a dog slobbers, and in the dark you can't keep from getting your hands and arms in it, and coming away all sticky.

Pine trees are more forbidding speakers. In a breeze their quiet *whoooos* are fey, and the wild *ohhhhhhhs* they utter when the wind is up can raise the hair on the back of your neck. But pines feel good to the touch, and you can look at their black silhouettes against the sky forever. Torrey pines have the longest needles, and their little branches are all curly. They spiral off the main branches like pieces of the springs that Rafael keeps in his shop, and make lovely patterns against the others. And the rough, brittle bark feels wonderful against the skin, it's like a giant cat's tongue. Redwood bark is even better, all split and hairy; you can put your fingers in cracks around the sides and hold on for dear life. It's like hugging a bear, or holding on to your ma and crying into her hair. Good friends, pine trees, though you have to ignore their stern voice and touch them to find that out.

Of course there are real living things in the forest at night, mobile things I mean, animals like us. A whole bunch of them, in fact: coyotes and weasels and skunks and raccoons and deer, and cats and rabbits and possums and bears and who knows what all. But damned if you'd know it by just walking around. Even a lone human sitting in the forest for hours might not catch sight of a single creature—much less a human who is crashing around hugging trees and such. Someone like that isn't going to see a single animal, or even hear one except for frogs. Frogs don't scare easily, they've got the river to hop in and they don't care. You have to come close to stepping on them before they'll shut up, much less move. All the others, though, they hear you coming or smell you way off, and they get out of the way and you never know they've been there, except if you chance to hear a rustle off in the distance. Of course a big cat might decide to eat you, but you hope they'd be wary enough to stay out of the valley. Generally they avoid crowds, and in the fall they're not very hungry. So . . . if you walk about you don't see a creature anywhere, which is funny because you know they're around you, getting a drink, chomping on sprouts or dead prey, hunting for or hiding from each other.

But I forgot about the birds. Occasionally you'll see the quick black shape of an owl, flying without a sound. It's uncanny how complete their silence is. Or higher, geese or herons migrating, their heads poked ahead on those long necks, flying in V's that flow in and out of shape. Sometimes it looks like they're playing Change the Leader, each one taking a turn. (Crows on the other hand will play Follow the Leader, almost every fine evening at sunset.)

That night I saw a flock of geese, flying south. Two pairs of wide V's, passing over the valley in the hour before dawn, when the sky was blueing and I could see them quite clearly. Slow, steady wing strokes, and quite a conversation going on up there in that honk and squawk language. . . .

Of course they aren't part of the forest proper, but you can see them while in the forest. And I did see them that night. I slept earlier against a redwood, and then for a while curled between two gnarly roots. Mostly, though, I walked around. I had spent a lot of time in the forest, day and night, without paying the least attention to it. It was just home, nothing special. But this night I didn't want to think about anything. I was *determined* not to think about anything, so for long stretches I succeeded. I studied tree after tree, hung out with them and really got to know them well, touched them, climbed a couple . . . sat looking for the animals I knew were about, too, but as I said they don't like people watching them. I heard some scuffling a few times, but I didn't even see a squirrel.

Where the creek from Swing Canyon meets the river is a little meadow that always has a lot of animal tracks in it. I wandered that way when I woke up and saw the geese overhead, in hope of seeing some furry brothers taking a drink. Sure enough, after I lay in the ferns behind a fungus-riddled log for a while, watching a spider weave her morning web, a family of deer came down and drank. Buck, doe, fawn. The buck looked around and sniffed; he knew I was there, but he didn't care about it, which showed good judgment. The doe was fastidious in the mud banking the creek, but the fawn staggered around in it. It was about a three-month fawn, so it could have walked perfectly well, but it seemed to want to bother its ma. When they were done drinking they pushed off, across the meadow and out of sight.

I clambered up stiffly, went down to the creek and drank myself. My pants were still damp and my legs were cold, and I was stiff, and dirty, and cut up, and hungry, and dog tired, but mainly I felt all right. I walked down the west riverbank empty as an empty bowl. I wasn't going to start crying again, no matter whether I thought of Mando and Steve or not. I could think of them and not feel much of anything. It was done, and I was empty.

But then I rounded the bend above the bridge, and caught sight of a figure downriver on the same bank, at the foot of the cornfields. This was still early morning, when the whole world was nothing but shades of gray—a thousand shades of gray, but not a hint of color. Dew soaked every gray leaf and sprig and fern on the ground, a sign that the Santa Ana was ending. A mouse squeaked as I clumped by its home. I stopped, but not because of the mouse.

The figure downstream was a woman. (If a person is visible we know their sex, no matter how distant they are—I'm not sure how we tell sometimes, but it's so.) And the dark gray shade of this woman's hair would be brown in the sun, brown with a bit of red in it. Already in this world of grays I could see that touch of red. Kathryn it was, standing at the foot of her fields. From the knee down her pants were darker—wet, then, which meant she had been out walking for a while. Maybe she had been out all night too, I thought, yet another animal in the night forest that I had not seen. Her back was to me. I would have gone to her, but something held me. There are times when a back a hundred yards away is as expressive as ever our faces are. She started and began walking downstream, toward the bridge. At the end of the field she suddenly swung to her right and gave a fearsome kick to the last cornstalk. She wears big boots and the stalk shuddered and stayed tilted over. That didn't satisfy her. She got set and kicked it again and again, till it was flattened. The scene blurred before me and I stumbled away through the woods, all our catastrophes made real to me again.

So I was not as empty as I had thought. My capacity for feeling miserable was higher than I had imagined, a lot higher. I found I could feel miserable for *days*, that between feeling miserable and feeling empty as a dry gourd I could occupy every hour of every day. And that was what I did, day after day. It was a surprise to me, and not a pleasant one, but I couldn't help it. That was how I felt, and our feelings are not in our control.

I took to spending a lot of time on the beach. I couldn't abide being with people. One day I tried to rejoin the fishing, but that was no good; they were too hard. Another time I wandered by the ovens, but I left; poor Kristen had a look that pierced me. Even eating with Pa made me feel bad. And I couldn't visit the old man, he was too sick, it made me despair. Everyone's eyes questioned me, or condemned me, or watched me when they didn't think I was going to notice: they tried to console me, or to act like nothing was different, which was a lie. Everything was different. So I didn't want any part of them. The beach was a good place to get away. Our beach is so wide from cliff to water, and so long from the coarse sand at the rivermouth to the jumbled white boulders of Concrete Bay, that you can wander on it for days without crossing your path, hardly. Long furrows from old high tides, filled with brackish water; tangled driftwood, including old logs with their octopus roots sticking up; sandflea infested seaweed, like mounds of black compost; shells whole and broken; sand crabs and the telltale bubbles they leave in the wet sand; the little round white sandpipers with their backwards knees, charging up and down the shingle together to avoid the soup; all of these were worth investigating for hours and days. So I wandered up and down the beach and investigated them, and was miserable, or empty.

See, I could have not told them. Of course I *could* have refused to have anything to do with the whole plan right from the start. That is what I should have done. But even after I went along with it, I could have kept to myself what I had found out about the landing, and none of it would ever have happened. I had even considered it, and came close to doing just that. But I hadn't. I had made my decision, and everything that had happened—Mando's death, Steve's flight—all followed from that. So it was my fault. I was to blame for one friend's running away, another's death. And for who knows how many other deaths that had come that night, of people who were strangers to me, but who no doubt had families and friends grieving for them like we grieved for Mando. All of it came from my thinking, from my decision. How I felt it. How I wished I had thought it out better, and decided the other way! I would have given anything to change that decision. But there's nothing as unchangeable as the past. Striding up the river path to home I recalled what the old man had said there, about how we were wedged in a crack by history so our choices were squeezed down; but now I knew that compared to the way the past is wedged in there, the present is as free as the open air. In the present you have choices, but in the past you only did one thing; regret it with all your power, it won't change. I knew that, or I was learning it, but that didn't stop me from regretting the past, or wishing for a different one.

If I had been smarter, Mando wouldn't have died. Not only smarter—more honest. I had lied to and betrayed Kathryn, Tom, Pa—the whole valley, because of the vote. Everybody but Steve, and he was on Catalina. What a fool I had been! Here I thought I had been so clever, getting the time and place out of Add, leading the San Diegans up to the ambush.

But it was us who had been ambushed. As soon as I thought of it that way it was obvious. Those folks hadn't just been defending themselves on the spur of the moment—they were ready for us. And who else would have warned them but Addison Shanks? He knew we knew about the landing, and all he had had to do was tell the scavengers we knew, and they could prepare for us. Ambush us.

Well once I thought of it, it was as obvious as the sun in the sky, but it really hadn't occurred to me until then, walking up the river path and brooding over it. They had ambushed the ambushers.

And the San Diegans had set us farther north than them so that if anything went wrong, we would be the last over the bridge and would take up the attention of the enemy while the San Diegans escaped. Thrown in the road to trip them.

We had been twice betrayed. And I had been an incredible fool.

And my foolishness had cost Mando his life. I wished fiercely (now that the funeral was well past) that I had died and not him. But I knew that wishing was like throwing rocks at the moon (so I was safe).

Wandering the beach and thinking about it a couple days later, I got curious and went up Basilone to the Shankses'. I didn't have anything in mind to say to them, but I wanted to see them. If I saw their faces I would know if I was right or not about Add warning the scavengers, and then I could be shut of them for good.

Their house was burned down. Nobody was around. I stepped across the charred boards that were all that was left of the south wall, and kicked around in the piles of charcoal for a bit. Dust and ash puffed away from my boot. They were long gone. I stood in the middle of what had been their storage room, and looked at the black lumps on the ground. Nothing metal. It looked like they had emptied the place of valuables before they fired it. They must have had help moving north. After what I had caught Add doing, as soon as they heard of my survival they must have decided to move north and join the scavengers completely. And of course Addison wouldn't leave us such a house.

The north wall was still there, black planks eaten through and ready to fall; the rest of the wood was ash, or ends and lumps scattered about. The old metal poles of the electric tower were visible again, rising up soot-black to the metal platform that had once held the wires up. I felt as empty as always. It had been a good house. They weren't good people, but it had been a good house. And somehow, standing in the charred ruins of it, I couldn't bring up any feeling against Add and Melissa, although I could have easily moments before. It couldn't have been any fun to fire a good home like this and flee. And were they really that bad? Working with scavengers, so what. We all traded with them some way or other. Even helping the Japanese to land, was that surely so bad? Glen Baum had done it in that book of his (if he had done any of it), and no one called him traitor. Add and Melissa just wanted something different than I did. In ways they were better than I was. At least they kept their promises; they had their loyalties intact.

I dogged back into the valley, lower than ever. Stopped at Doc's: Tom sick, asleep and looking like death; Doc hollow-eyed at the kitchen table, alone, staring at the wall. I hustled down to the river, crossed the bridge, stopped at the bathhouse latrine to relieve myself. I walked out as John Nicolin walked in. He glared at me, brushed by me without a word.

So I went to the beach. And the next day I went back. I was getting to know the troops of little sandpipers: the one with one leg, the black one, the broken-beaked one. The tide moved in, drowning the flies' dining table. It moved back out, exposing the wet seaweed again. Gulls wheeled and shrieked. Once a pelican landed on the wet strand and stood there looking about aloofly. The shorebreak was big that day, however, and he was slow to get out from under a thick rushing lip. It thumped down on him as he hurried away and he tumbled, long wings and beak and neck and legs thrashing around in a tangled somersault. I laughed as he struggled up, all wet and bedraggled and huffy; but he walked funny as he ran to take off and glide down the beach, and when I was done laughing I cried.

The clouds came back. A gray wall sat on the horizon, and pieces of it broke loose and were carried onshore by the wind. The wind had backed at last. The Santa Ana had held the clouds out to sea for over a week, and now they were coming back to claim their territory. At first there were just a few of them, loose-knit and transparent except at their centers. Clouds beget clouds, though, and through the afternoon they came in darker and lower, until the whole wall picked up and advanced from the horizon, turning dark blue and covering the sky like a blanket. The air got cold, the gulls disappeared, the onshore wind picked up. The clouds grew top heavy, spat lightning onto the sea and then the land, sizzling waves and shattering trees on the ridges. I sat on a worn grey log and watched the first raindrops pock the sand. The iron surface of the ocean lost its sheen as the rain hit it. I pulled my coat around me and stubbornly sat there. The rain turned to hail. Hail fell until there was a layer of clear grains on top of the tawny ones: a beach of sand overlaid by a beach of glass.

I walked down the beach, climbed the cliff path. The hail turned back to rain. Hands in pockets I strode the river path, and let the rain strike me in the face. It ran down inside my coat, and I didn't care. I stayed out and walked through clearings and treeless patches on purpose, and it gave me pleasure because it was such a stupid thing to do.

I kept on up the valley until I stood at the edge of the little clearing occupied by the graveyard. Rain poured on it from low clouds just overhead, and in the dim gray light trees dripped and the ground splashed. I crossed the little section near the river where all the Japanese who had washed ashore had been buried. Their wooden crosses said *Unknown Chinese, Died 2045*, or whatever the date happened to be. Nat did a nice job carving letters and numbers.

Out in the clearing proper were our people. I squished from grave to grave, contemplating the names. Vincent Mariani, 1992-2038. A cancer got him. I remembered him playing hide and seek with Kathryn and Steve and me, when Kristen was a baby. Arnold Kalinski, 1970-2026. He had come to the valley with a disease, Tom said; Doc had been afraid we all would catch it, but we didn't. Jane Howard Fletcher, 2002-2030. My mother, right there. Pneumonia. I pulled out some weeds from around the base of the cross, moved on. John Manley Morris, 1975-2029; Eveline Morris, 1989-2033. Cancer for him; she died of an infected cut in the palm of her hand. John Nicolin, Junior, 2016-2022. Fell in the river. Matthew Hamish, 2034. Malformed. Mark Hamish, 2036. Luke Hamish, 2039. Both malformed. Francesca Hamish, 2044. Same. And Jo pregnant again. Geoffrey Jones, 1995-2040; Ann Jones, died 2040. They both died when their house burned. Endeavor Simpson, 2039. Malformed. Defiance Simpson, 2043. Malformed. Elizabeth Costa, 2000-2035. Some disease, Doc never figured out what. Armando Thomas Costa, 2033-2047.

There were more, but I stopped my progress and stood at the foot of Mando's grave, looking at the fresh carving on the cross. Even the Bible says something about men living their three score and ten, and that was ever so long ago. And here we were, cut short like frogs in a frost.

The dirt filling Mando's grave had settled, and it was sinking more in the rain. I went to the broken-up pit at the back of the clearing and took the shovel that Nat always leaves there, and started carrying dirt over to the grave, shovelful by shovelful. Mud stuck to the shovel, it spread out badly, it wouldn't tamp down right. Bad idea. I threw the shovel back at the pit and sat on the grass at the side of the grave, where I could hold the crossbar of the marker. Frogs in a frost. Rain thinned the mud, puddled on it. I looked around at our crop of crosses, all of them dripping in the gray afternoon light, and I thought, This isn't right. It isn't supposed to be like this. Mando was under me and yet he wasn't; he was plain gone, vanished, no more. He wouldn't come back. I took a handful of mud and squished it between my fingers. Mando had changed from a living person to no more than the mud in my hand. And the same thing was going to happen to every person I knew. And to me. Nothing we did was going to make any difference; nothing would last no matter what we said. I didn't see the point. It was too strange to live and work in the world till I broke, and then just go to mud. I sat there in the rain and squeezed the mud between my fingers. Squish squish. Squish, squish.

Chapter Twenty-two

But the old man lived.

The old man lived. I hardly believed it. I think everybody was surprised, even Tom. I know Doc was: "I couldn't believe it," he told me happily when I went up to see them on a cloudy morning. "I had to rub my eyes and pinch myself. I got up yesterday and there he was sitting at the kitchen table whining where's my breakfast, where's my breakfast. Of course his lungs had been clearing all week, but I wasn't sure that was going to be enough, to tell you the truth. But there he was bitching at me."

"In fact," Tom called from the bedroom, "where's the tea? Don't you respect a poor patient's requests anymore?"

"If you want it hot you'll shut up and *be* patient," Doc shouted back, grinning at me. "How about some bread with it?"

"Of course."

I went into the hospital and there he was sitting up in his bed, blinking like a bird. Shyly I said, "How are you?"

"Hungry."

"That's a good sign," Doc said from behind me. "Return of appetite, very good sign."

"Unless you got a cook like I do," said Tom.

Doc snorted. "Don't let him fool you, he's been bolting it in his usual style. Obviously he loves it. Pretty soon he'll want to stay here just for the food."

"When the eagle grins I will."

"Oooh, so ungrateful!" Doc exclaimed. "And here I had to shove the food right down his face for the longest time. It got so I felt like a mama bird, I should have digested it all first for him I guess—"

"Oh that would have helped," Tom crowed, "eating vomit, yuck! Take this away, I've lost my appetite for good." He slurped the tea, cursed its heat.

"Well, it was hard to get him to eat, I'll tell you. But now look at him go." Doc watched with satisfaction as Tom tossed down chunks of bread in his old starvation manner. When he was done he smiled his gap-toothed smile. His poor gums had taken a beating in his illness, but his eyes watched me with their old clear brown gaze. I felt my face stretched into a grin.

"Ah yes," Tom said. "There's nothing like a mutated freak immune system, I'll testify. I'm tough as a tiger. So tough! However, you'll excuse me if I take a little nap." He coughed once or twice, slid down under the covers and was out like one of his lighters snapping off.

So that was good. Tom stayed at Doc's for another couple of weeks, mostly to keep Doc company, I believe, as he was getting stronger by the day, and he surely wasn't fond of the hospital. And one day Rebel knocked on the door and asked me if I wanted to help move Tom and his stuff back to his house. I said sure, and we walked across the bridge talking and joking. The sun was playing hide and seek among tall clouds, and coming down the path from Doc's were Kathryn and Gabby, Kristen and Del and Doc, laughing as Tom cavorted at the head of the parade. "Join the crowd," Tom called to us. "The young and the old, a natural alliance for a party, you bet." Kathryn gave me Tom's books, heavy in a burlap sack, and I threatened to throw them off the bridge as we crossed. Tom swung at me with his walking stick. We made a fine promenade up the other slope of the valley. I had never allowed

myself to imagine this day; but there it was, right in my hands
where I could grab it.

Once up to his house the old man got positively boisterous.
With a dramatic flourish he kicked the door, but it stayed shut.
"Great latch, see that?" He puffed at the dust on the table and
chairs until the air was thick with it. There was a puddle on
the floor, marking a new leak in the roof. Tom pulled his
mouth down into a pouting frown. "This place has been poorly
tended, very poorly tended. You maintenance crews are fired."

"Ho ho," said Kathryn, "now you're going to have to hire
us back at wages to get any help cleaning up." We opened all
the windows and let the breeze draft through. Gabby and Del
yanked some weeds, and Tom and Doc and I walked up the
ridge trail to look at the beehives. Tom cursed at the sight, but
they weren't that bad off. We cleaned up for a bit and went
back down to the house on Doc's orders. Smoke billowed white
as the clouds from the stove chimney, the big front window
was scrubbed clean, and Gabby was balanced on the roof with
hammer and nails and shingles, hunting for that leak and shouting for instructions from below. When we went in Kathryn was
on a stool, thumping the underside of the roof with a broom.
"That's it," Tom said, "bust that leak right out of there." Kathryn took a swing at him with the broom, overbalanced and
leaped off the falling stool. Kristen dodged her with a yelp and
quit dusting, Rebel took the kettle off the stove, and we gathered in the living room for some of Tom's pungent tea. "Cheers,"
Tom said, holding his steaming mug high, and we raised ours
and said back cheers, cheers.

That evening when I came home Pa said that John Nicolin
had come by to ask why I wasn't fishing anymore. My share
of the fish was our main source of food, and Pa was upset. So
I started fishing again the next day, and after that I went fishing
day in and day out, when the weather allowed. On the boats
it was obvious the year was getting on. The sun cut across the
sky lower and lower, and a cold current came in and stayed.
Often in the afternoons dark clouds rolled off the sea over us.
Wet hands stung with cold, and hauling net made them raw
red; teeth chattered, skin prickled with goosebumps. Hoarse
shouts concerning the fishing were the only words exchanged,
as men conserved their energy. The lack of small talk was fine

by me. Blustery winds chafed us as we rowed back in the premature dusks. Under the blue clouds the cliffs turned brown, the hillsides were the green-black of the darkest pines, and the ocean was like iron. In all that gloom the yellow bonfires on the river flat blazed like beacons, and it was a pleasure to round the first bend in the river and see them. After getting the boats up against the cliff I huddled with the rest of the men around these fires until I was warm enough to go home. As the men warmed (hands practically in the flames), the usual talk spilled out, but I never joined in. Even though I was happy the old man was well and home, the truth was that it didn't do much to cheer me in the day to day. I felt bad a lot of the time, and empty always. When I was out fishing, struggling to make cold disobedient fingers hold onto the nets, I'd think of some crack or curse Steve would have made in the situation, and I longed to hear him say it. And when the fishing was done, there was no gang up on the cliff waiting for me to join them. To avoid climbing the cliff and feeling their absence I often walked around the point of the cliff to the sea beach, and wandered that familiar expanse. The next day I'd take a deep breath, push myself into my boots and go fishing again. But I was just going through the motions.

It wasn't that the men on the boats were unfriendly, either. On the contrary—Marvin kept giving me the best of the fish to take home, and Rafael talked to me more than he ever had, joshing about the fish, describing his latest projects (which were interesting, I had to admit), inviting me by to see them. . . . They were all like that, even John from time to time. But none of it meant anything to me. I was empty. My heart felt like my fingers did when the fishing was done, cold and disobedient, numb even next to the fire.

Somehow Tom figured this out. Maybe Rafael told him, maybe he saw it himself. One day after the fishing I clawed my way up the cliff path, feeling like I weighed as much as three of me, and there was Tom on the top.

I said, "You're getting around pretty well these days."

He ignored that and shook a knobby finger at me. "What's eating you, boy?"

I cringed. "Nothing, what do you mean?" I looked down at my bag of fish, but he grabbed my arm and pulled it.

"What's troubling you?"

"Ah, Tom." What could I say? He knew what it was. I said,

"You know what it is. I gave you my word I wouldn't go up there, and I did."

"Ah, the hell with that."

"But look what happened! You were right. If I hadn't gone up there, none of it would have happened."

"How do you figure? They just would have gone without you."

I shook my head. "No. I could have stopped it." I explained to him what had happened, what my part had been—every bit of it. He nodded as I got each sentence out.

When I was done, he said, "Well, that's too bad." I was shivering, and he started up the river path with me. "But it's easy to be wise afterwards. Hindsight et cetera. You had no way of knowing what would happen."

"But I did! You told me. Besides, I felt it coming."

"Well, but listen, boy—" I looked at him, and he stopped talking. He frowned, and nodded once to acknowledge that it was right for me to reject such easy denials of my responsibility. We walked for a bit and then he snapped his fingers. "Have you started writing that book yet?"

"Oh for God's sake, Tom."

He shoved me in the chest, hard, so that I staggered out of the path and had to catch my footing. "Hey!"

"This time you might try listening to me."

That stung. I was round-eyed as he went on. "I don't know how much longer I can take this sniveling of yours. Mando's dead and you're partly to blame, yes. Yes. But it's going to fester in you not doing you a bit of good until you write it down, like I told you to."

"Ah, Tom—"

And he charged me, shoved me again! It was the kind of thing he used to indulge in only with Steve, and at the same time I was getting ready to punch him one I was flattered. "Listen to me for once!" he cried, and all at once I realized he was upset.

"I do listen to you. You know that."

"Well then do as I say. You write down your story. Everything you remember. The writing it down will make you understand it. And when you're done you'll have Mando's story down too. It's the best you can do for him now, do you see?"

I nodded, my throat tight. I cleared it. "I'll try."

"Don't try, just do it." I hopped away so he couldn't shove

me again. "Ha! That's right—do it or face a beating. It's your assignment. You don't get any more schooling till you're done." He shook his fist at me, his arm a bundle of ligaments under skin, skinny as a rope. I almost had to laugh.

So I thought about it. I got the book down from the shelf, where it had been propping up a whetstone holder with only two legs. I looked through the blank pages. There were a lot of them. It was as clear as a stonefish is ugly that I would never be able to fill all those pages. For one thing, it would take too long.

But I kept thinking about it. The emptiness still afflicted me. And as the days got shorter the nights in our shack got longer, and I found those memories were always in my mind. And the old man had been awful vehement about it. . . .

Before I even lifted a pencil, however, Kathryn declared it was time to harvest the corn. When she decided it was time, all of us who worked for her worked dawn to dusk, every day. Right after sunup I was out there with the others slashing at stalks with a scythe, then carrying stalks to the wains, pulling them over the bridge to the barrows and warehouses behind the Marianis', stripping off the leaves, pulling off the husked ears.

The bad summer storms made it a poor harvest. Soon we were done and it was time for the potatoes. Kathryn and I worked together on those. We hadn't spent much time together since the night at Doc's, and at first I was uncomfortable, but she didn't seem to blame me for anything. We just worked, and talked potatoes. Working with Kathryn was exhausting. In the mornings it seemed all right, because she worked so hard that she did more than her share, but the trouble was she kept going at that pace all day, so I got hooked into doing more than a day's work every day no matter how much I let her go at it. And harvesting potatoes is dirty, backbreaking labor, any way you do it.

When the harvesting was done we celebrated with a little drinking at the bathhouse. No one got overjoyed, because it was a bad harvest, but at least it was in. Kathryn sat beside me in the chairs on the bathhouse lawn to watch the sunset, and Rebel and Kristen joined us. At the other end of the yard Del and Gabby tossed a football back and forth. The flames of a bonfire were scarcely visible against the salmon sky. Rebel was upset about the potato harvest, even crying a little, and Kathryn talked a lot to cheer her up. "Pests are something you have to live with. Next year we'll try some of that stuff I got from the scavengers. Don't worry, it takes a long time to learn farming. It ain't like those spuds are your children, you know." Kristen smiled at that, the first smile I had seen from her since Mando died.

"Nobody will go hungry," I said.

"But I'm sick of fish already," Rebel said. The girls laughed at her.

"You couldn't tell by the way you eat them," Kristen said.

Kathryn sipped her whiskey lazily. "What you been up to lately, Hank?"

"I've been writing in that book Tom gave me," I lied, to see how it sounded.

"Oh yeah? Are you writing about the valley?"

"Sure."

She raised her eyebrows. "About—"

"Yeah."

"Hmph." She stared into the fire. "Well, good. Maybe something good will come of this summer after all. But writing a whole book? It must be really hard."

"Oh it is," I assured her. "It's almost impossible, to tell you the truth. But I'm keeping at it."

All three of the girls looked impressed.

So I thought about it some more. I took the book off the shelf again, and kept it on the little stand beside my bed, next to the lamp and the cup and the book of Shakespeare's plays Tom had given me as a Christmas present. And I thought about it. When it had all begun, so long ago . . . those meetings with the gang, planning the summer. It wouldn't actually be grave-robbing, Steve had said, and I had snapped awake. . . .

So I started writing it.

It was slow work. Me trying to write is like Odd Roger trying to talk. Every night I quit for good. But the next night, or the one after, I would begin again. It's astonishing how much the memory will surrender when you squeeze it. Some nights when I finished writing I'd come to, surprised to be in our shack, sweat pouring down my ribs, my hand stiff, my fingers sore, my heart pounding with the emotions of time past. And away from the work, out on the boats heaving over the wild swells, I found myself thinking of what had happened, of ways to say it. I knew I was going to finish that book no matter what it took from me. I was hooked.

The evenings of the autumn took on a pattern. When the fish were on the tables I climbed the cliff. No gang to meet me. Steadfastly I ignored the ghost gathering and hiked home, usually through the early evening gloom. At home Pa greased the skillet and fried up some fish and onions, while I lit the lamp and set the table, and we made the usual small talk about what had happened during the day. When the fish was ready we sat down and Pa said grace, and we ate the fish and bread or potatoes. Afterwards we washed up and put things away and drank the rest of the dinner water, and brushed our teeth with a scavenged toothbrush. Then Pa sat at the sewing table, and I sat at the dinner table, and he stitched together clothes while I stitched together words, until we agreed it was time for bed.

I don't know how many nights went by like that. On rainy days it was the same, only all day long. Once a week or so I went up to Tom's. Since I promised I was writing he had relented and agreed to give me more lessons. He had me in *Othello*, and I was pretty sure I knew why. I thought I had things to regret, but Othello! He was the only man in Shakespeare more fool than I.

> ". . . O fool! fool! fool!
> When you shall these unlucky deeds relate,
> Speak of me as I am. Nothing extenuate,
> Nor set down aught in malice. Then must you speak
> Of one that lov'd not wisely, but too well;
> Of one not easily jealous, but, being wrought,
> Perplex'd in the extreme; of one whose hand
> (Like the base Indian) threw a pearl away
> Richer than all his tribe; of one whose subdu'd eyes,
> Albeit unused to the melting mood,
> Drop tears as fast as the Arabian's trees
> Their med'cinable gum. Set you down this . . ."

"So they had eucalyptus trees in Arabia," I remarked to Tom when I was done, and he laughed. And when upon leaving I demanded more pencils, he cackled wildly, and scrounged them up for me.

* * *

The days passed. The further I got in the story of the summer, the further away it was in time, and the less I understood it. Perplex'd in the extreme. One day it was raining and Pa and I both worked through the afternoon. We tried keeping the door open for light, but it was too cold even with the stove going, and rain kept blowing in when the wind shifted. We had to close it and light the lamps. Pa bent over the coat he was making. His hands moved as quickly as fingers snapping as he punched the holes, and yet the holes were perfectly spaced, in a line that could have been drawn by a straightedge. He slipped a thimble on his middle finger and stitched. Poke and pull, poke and pull . . . cross-stitches appeared in perfect X's, the thread tugged so that the tension on it was constant. . . . I had never paid such close attention to his sewing. His calloused fingers clicked along as nimbly as dancers. It was as if Pa's fingers were smarter than he was, I thought; and I felt bad for thinking it. Besides, it was wrong. Pa told his fingers what to do, no one else. They wouldn't do it alone. It was truer to say something like, Pa's sewing was the way in which he was smart. And in that way he was very smart indeed. I liked that way of saying it, and scribbled it down. Stitching thoughts. Meanwhile his deft fingers plied the needle, and it kept slipping through the pieces of cloth, pursing them together, pulling the thread taut, turning, piercing again. Pa sighed. "I don't think I see as well as I used to. I wish it were a sunny day. How I miss the summer."

I clicked my tongue. It was annoying to be sitting in a dark box in the middle of the day, using up good lamp oil. In fact it was worse than annoying. I felt my spirits plunge as I took stock of the bare insides of our shack. "Shit," I muttered with disgust.

"What's that?"

"I said, *shit*."

"Why?"

"Ah. . . ." How could I explain it to him, without making him feel bad too? He accepted our degraded conditions without a thought, always had. I shook my head. He peered at me curiously.

Suddenly I had an idea. I jerked in my chair. "What?" said Pa, watching me.

"I got an idea." I got my boots on, put on my coat.

"It's raining pretty hard," Pa said dubiously.

"I won't go far."

"Okay. Be careful?"

I turned from the open door, went back and punched him lightly on the arm. "Yeah. I'll be back soon, keep sewing."

I crossed the bridge and went up Basilone to the Shankses', and kicked around in the piles of burnt wood. Sure enough, buried in soggy ash inside the north wall was a rectangular piece of glass, as wide as my outstretched arms, and nearly that tall. One of their many windows. A corner of it was very wavy near the bottom, and a little pocked—it looked like it had melted some in the fire—but I didn't care. I crowed at the sky, licked down raindrops, and very carefully returned to the valley, window held before me, dripping. Like a car's windshield, eh? I stopped and knocked on the door of Rafael's shop. He was at home, black with grease and hammering like Vulcan. "Rafe, will you help me put this window in the side of our place?"

"Sure," he said, and looked out at the rain. "You want to do it now?"

"Well . . ."

"Let's wait for a good day. We'll have to be tramping in and out a lot."

Reluctantly I agreed.

"I always wondered why you didn't put a window in that place," he remarked.

"Never had glass to put in it!" I said happily, and was off. And two days later we had a window in our south wall, and the light streamed in over everything, turning every dust mote to silver. There was a lot of dust, too.

We even had good windowsills, thanks to Rafael. He peered at the wavy part of the bottom. "Yep, almost melted this one down, looks like." He nodded his approval and left, toting his tools over his shoulder, whistling. Pa and I hopped around the house, cleaning up and staring out, going outside to stare in.

"This is wonderful," Pa said with a blissful smile. "Henry, that was one great idea you had. I can always count on you for the good ideas."

We shook on it. I felt the strength in his right hand, and it sent a glow right through me. You got to have your father's approval. I kept pumping his hand up and down till he started to laugh.

It made me think of Steve. He never had that approval,

never would have had it. It must have been like walking around with a thorn in your shoe. I feel it in my mind's foot, Horatio. I began to think that I understood him more, at the same time I felt like I was losing him—the real, immediate Steve, I mean. I could only recall his face well in dreams, when it came back to me perfectly. And it was hard to get him down right in the book; the way he could make you laugh, make you sure you were really living. I sat down to work on it, under the light of our new window. "I'll have to sew us some good curtains," Pa said, eyeing the window thoughtfully, measuring it in his mind.

A while after that I joined the small group going to the last swap meet of the year. Winter swap meets weren't much like the summer ones; there were fewer people there, and less stuff being traded. This time it was drizzling steadily, and everyone there was anxious to get their trading done and go home. Debates over prices quickly turned into arguments, and sometimes fights. The sheriffs had their hands full. Time after time I heard one of them bellowing, "Just make your deal and move on! Come on, what's the fuss!"

I hurried from canopy to canopy, and in the shelter from the rain did my best to trade for some cloth or old clothing for Pa. All I had to offer were some abalone and a couple of baskets, and it was tough trading.

One of the scavenger camps had gotten a fire going by pouring gas over the wet wood, and a lot of folks congregated under the canopy. I joined them, and after a bit I finally found a scavenger woman willing to trade a pile of ragged clothing for what I had.

After we had counted it out piece for piece she said, "I hear you Onofreans really did it to that crew from down south."

"What's this?" I said, jerking slightly.

She laughed, revealing a mouthful of busted brown stumps, and drank from a jar. "Don't play simpleton with me, grubber."

"I'm not," I said. She offered me the jar but I shook my head. "What's this we're supposed to have done to the San Diegans?"

"Ha! Supposed to done. See how that washes with them when they come asking why you killed their mayor."

I felt the cold of that dim afternoon shiver into me, and I went from a crouch to sitting on my butt. I took the jar from her and drank some sour corn mash. "Come on, tell me what you've heard," I said.

"Well," she said, happy to gossip, "the back country folks say you all took that mayor and his men right up into a Jap ambush."

I nodded so she'd go on.

"Ah ha! Now he fesses up. So most of them were killed, including that mayor. And they're pretty hot about it. If they weren't fighting among themselves so hard to see who takes his place, they'd likely be on you pretty hard. But every man in San Diego wants to be mayor now, or so the back country folk say, and I believe them. Apparently things down there are wild these days."

I took another gulp of her terrible liquor. It went to my stomach like a big lead sinker. Around us drizzle misted down through the trees, and bigger drops fell from the edge of the canopy.

"Say, grubber, you okay?"

"Yeah, yeah." I bundled up the rags, thanked her and left, in a hurry to get back to Onofre and give Tom the news.

Another rainy afternoon I sat in Rafael's workshop, relaxing. I had told Tom what I had heard at the swap meet, and he had told John Nicolin and Rafael, and none of them had seemed overly concerned, which was a relief to me. Now the matter was out of my hands, and I was just passing the time. Kristen and Rebel sat crosslegged before Rafael's set of double windows, making baskets and gossiping. Rafael sat on a short stool and tinkered with a battery. Tools and machine parts littered the stained floor, and around us stood products of Rafael's invention and industry: pipes to carry a stove's heat to another room, a small kiln, an electric generator connected to a bicycle on blocks, and so on.

"The fluids go bad," Rafael said, answering a question of mine. "All the batteries that were full on the day are long gone. Corroded. But lucky for us, there were some sitting empty in warehouses. There's no use for them, so it's easy to trade for one. Some scavengers I know use batteries, and they'll bring the acids to the meet if I ask them. Only a few people want them, so I get a good deal."

"And that's how you got your cart out there running?"

"That's right. No use for it, though. Not usually."

We sat quiet for a while, remembering. "So you heard us that night?" I asked.

"Not at first. I was on Basilone and I saw the lights. Then I heard the shooting."

After a bit I shook my head to clear it, and changed the subject. "What about a radio, Rafe? Have you ever tried to repair one of those?"

"No."

"How come?"

"I don't know. They're too complicated, I guess. And the scavengers ask a lot for them, and they always look an awful wreck."

"So does most of the stuff you bring back."

"I guess."

I said, "You could read how they work in a manual, couldn't you?"

"I don't read much, Hank, you know that."

"But we could help you read. I'd read, and you could figure out what it meant."

"Maybe so. But we'd have to have a radio, and lots of parts, and I still wouldn't be sure at all that I could do anything with them."

"But you would be up for trying it?"

"Oh sure, sure." He laughed. "You run across a silver mine out there on that beach you been inspecting so close?"

I blushed. "Nah."

Rafael got up and rooted around in the big wall cupboard. I sat back lazily against the floor pillow behind me. Under the window Kristen and Rebel worked. The baskets they were weaving were made of old brown torrey pine needles, soaked in water so they were flexible again. Rebel took a needle and carefully bunched together the five individual slices of it, so that they made a neat cylinder. Then she curled the needle till it made a flat little wheel, and knotted several pieces of fishing line to it, splaying them out like spokes. Another pine needle was neatened up and tied around the outside of the first one. The first several needles were tied outside the ones before them, to make a flat bottom. Quickly it took two needles to make it around the circumference, then three. After that the nubs were set directly on top of each other, and the sides of the basket began to appear.

I picked up a finished basket and inspected it while Rebel

continued to whip the line around the needles. The basket was solid. Each needle looked like a miniature piece of rope, the five splits fit together so well. The four rows of nubs studding the sides of this particular basket rose in S shapes, showing just how much the basket bulged out and then back in. Such patience, arranging all the needles! Such skill, whipping all of them into place! I whapped the basket on the floor and it rebounded nicely, showing its flex and strength. Watching Rebel coax the line between two needles and through a complicated little loop of line waiting for it, it occurred to me that I had a task somewhat like hers. When I penciled in my book, I tied together words like she tied together pine needles, hoping to make a certain shape with them. Briefly I wished I could make a book as neat and solid and beautiful as the basket Rebel wove. But it was beyond hope, and I knew it.

Rebel looked up and saw me watching her, and she laughed, embarrassed. "This sure is boring," she said. Kristen nodded her agreement, a wet pine needle drooping from her teeth.

Another day the clouds would have given us a few hours for fishing, but the seas were running so high it was impossible to get the boats out. When I was done writing I walked to the cliffs, and there was the old man, sitting on a shelf under the cliff's lip, where he was protected from the wind.

"Hey!" I greeted him. "What you doing down here?"

"Looking at the waves, of course, like any other sensible person."

"So you think it takes sense to come down here and gawk at waves, eh?" I sat beside him.

"Sense or sensibility, yuk, yuk."

"I don't get it."

"Never mind. Look at that one!"

The swells were surging up from the south, breaking in giant walls that extended from one end of the beach to the other. The swells were visible far out to sea; I could pick one out halfway to the horizon and follow it all the way in. Near the end they built up taller and taller, until they were gray cliffs rushing in to meet our tan one. A man standing at the foamy foot of one of those giants would have looked like a doll. When the towering top of a wave pitched out and the whole thing rolled over behind it, spray exploded in the air higher than the wave had stood, with a crack and a boom that distinctly vibrated the cliff under us. The tortured water dashed over itself in a boiling race to the beach. There floods of white water swept up the sand, and sucked back to crash into the next advance. Only a strip of sand against the cliff was left dry; it would have been worth your life to walk the beach that day. Tom and I sat in a haze of white salt mist, and we had to talk over the explosive roar of the surf. "Look at that one!" Tom shouted again and again. "Look at that one! That one must be thirty-five feet tall, I swear."

Out beyond the swells the ocean stretched to the haze-fuzzed horizon. A low sheet of bumpy white and gray clouds covered the sky, barely clearing the hills behind us. Breaks in the clouds were marked by bright patches in the leaden surface of the water, and these patches made an uneven line to the horizon. They looked like the trail of a drunken scavenger with a hole in his pocket, scattering silver coins from here to the edge of the world. There was something about it all—the *presence* of that expanse of water, the size of it, the power of the waves —that made me stand back up and pace the cliff behind Tom's back, stop and stare as a particularly monstrous sea cliff collapsed, shake my head in wonder or dismay, pace and turn again, slapping my thighs and trying to think of a way to *say* it, to Tom or anybody. I failed. The world pours in and overflows the heart till speech is useless, and that's a fact. I wish I could speak better. I started to say things—spoke syllables and choked off the words—strode back and forth, getting more and more agitated as I tried to think exactly what it was I felt, and how I could then say that.

It was impossible, and if I had really held out for precision I reckon I would have stood there staring at those sea avalanches all day, mute and amazed. But my mind shifted to another mystery, I struck my hand to my thigh, and Tom glanced at me curiously. I blurted out, "Tom, why *did* you tell us all those lies about America?"

He cleared his throat. "Harumph-hmm. Who says I lied?"

I stood before him and stared.

"All right." He patted the sand beside him, but I refused to sit. "It was part of your history lessons. If your generation forgets the history of this country you'll have no direction. You'll have nothing to work back to. See, there was a lot about the old time we need to remember, that we have to get back."

"You made it seem like it was the golden age. Like we're just existing in the ruins."

"Well . . . in a lot of ways that's true. It's best to know it—"

I snapped my fingers at him. "But no! No! You also said the old time was awful. That we live better lives now than they ever did. That was what you *said,* when you argued with Doc and Leonard at the meets, and sometimes when you talked with us too. You told us that."

"Well," he admitted uneasily, "there's truth to that too. I was trying to tell you the way it was. I didn't lie—not much, I mean, and not about important things. Just once in a while to give you an idea what it was really like, what it felt like."

"But you told us two different things," I said. "Two contradictory things. Onofre was primitive and degraded, but we weren't to want for the old time to come back either, because it was evil. We didn't have anything left that was ours, that we could be proud of. You confused us!"

Abruptly he looked past me to the sea. "All right," he said. "Maybe I did. Maybe I made a mistake." His voice grew querulous: "I ain't some kind of great wise man, boy. I'm just another fool like you."

Awkwardly I turned and paced around a bit more. He didn't have any good reason for lying to us like he did. He had done it for fun. To make the stories sound better. To entertain himself.

I went over and plopped down beside him. We watched the sandbars plow a few more swells to mush. It looked like the ocean wanted to wash the whole valley away. Tom threw a few pebbles down at the beach. Gloomily he sighed.

"You know where I'd like to be when I die?" he said.

"No."

"I'd like to be on top of Mount Whitney."

"What?"

"Yeah. When I feel the end coming I'd like to hike inland and up three-ninety-five, and then up to the top of Mount Whitney. It's just a walk to the top, but it's the tallest mountain in the United States. The second tallest, excuse me. There's a little stone hut up there, and I could stay in that and watch the world till the end. Like the old Indians did."

"Ah," I said. "Sounds like a nice way to go." I didn't know

what else to say. I looked at him—really looked at him, I mean. It was funny, but now that I knew he was eighty and not a hundred and five, he looked older. Of course his illness had wasted him some. But I think it was mainly because living a hundred and five years was in the nature of a miracle, which could be extended indefinitely, while eighty was just old. He was an old man, a strange old man, that was all, and now I could see it. I was more impressed he had made it to eighty than I ever used to be that he had made it to one hundred and five. And that felt right.

So he was old, he would die soon. Or make his try for Whitney. One day I would go up the hill and the house would be empty. Maybe there would be a note on the table saying "Gone to Whitney," more likely not. But I would know. I would have to imagine his progress from there. Would he even make it forty miles to the north, to his birthplace Orange?

"You can't take off at this time of year," I said. "There'll be snow and ice and all. You'll have to wait."

"I'm not in any rush."

We laughed, and the moment passed. I began thinking about our own disastrous trip into Orange County. "I can't believe we did something that stupid," I said, my voice shaking with anger and distress.

"It was stupid," he agreed. "You kids had the excuse of youth and bad teaching, but the Mayor and his men, why they were damned fools."

"But we can't give up," I said, pounding the sandstone, "we can't just roll over and lie there like we're dead."

"That's true." He considered it. "And maybe securing the land from intrusion is the first step."

I shook my head. "It can't be done. Not with what they have and what we have."

"Well? I thought you said we don't want to play possum?"

"No, right." I pulled my feet up from the cliffside so I could squat and rock back and forth. "I'm saying we've got to figure out some other way to resist, some way that will work. We either do something that works, or wait until we can. None of this shit in between. What I was thinking of was that all the towns that come to the swap meet, if they worked together, might be able to sail over and *surprise* Catalina. Take it over for a time."

Tom whistled his weak, toothless whistle.

"For a while, I mean," I said. The idea had come to me recently, and I was excited by it. "With the radio equipment there we could tell the whole world we're here, and we don't like being quarantined."

"You think big."

"But it's not impossible. Not someday, anyway, when we know more about Catalina."

"It might not make any difference, you know. Broadcasting to the world, I mean. The world might be one big Finland now, and if it is all they're going to be able to do is say, we hear you brother. We're in the same boat. And then the Russians would sweep down on us."

"But it's worth a try," I insisted. "Like you say, we don't really know what's going on in the world. And we won't until we try something like this."

He shook his head, looked at me. "That would cost a lot of lives, you know. Lives like Mando's—people who could have lived their full span to make things better in our new towns."

"Their full spans," I said scornfully. But he had jolted me, nevertheless. He had reminded me how grand military plans like mine translated into chaos and pain and meaningless death. So in an instant I was all uncertain again, and my bold idea struck me as stupidity compounded by size. Tom must have read this on my face, because he chuckled, and put his arm around my shoulders.

"Don't fret about it, Henry. We're Americans, it ain't been clear what we're supposed to do for a long, long time."

One more white sea cliff smashed to spray and charged toward us. One more plan crumbled and swept away. "I guess not," I said morosely. "Not since Shakespeare's time, eh?"

"Harumph-*hmm!*" He cleared his throat two or three more times, let his arm fall, shuffled down the cliff away from me a bit. "Um, by the way," he said, looking anxiously at me, "while we're on the subject of history lessons, and, um, lies, I should make a correction. Well! Um . . . Shakespeare wasn't an American."

"Oh, no," I breathed. "You're kidding."

"No. Um—"

"But what about England?"

"Well, it wasn't the leader of the first thirteen states."

"But you showed me on a map!"

"That was Martha's Vineyard, I'm afraid."

I felt my mouth hanging open, and I snapped it shut. Tom was kicking his heels uncomfortably. He looked about as unhappy as I had ever seen him, and he wouldn't meet my eye. Gazing beyond me he gestured, with an expression of relief.

"Looks like John, doesn't it?"

I looked. Along the cliff edge above Concrete Bay I spotted a squat figure striding, hands in pockets. It was John Nicolin all right; he was recognizable from as far away as he could be seen, almost. He walked fast in our direction, looking out to sea. On the days when we were kept from going out, when he wasn't working on the boats he was on the cliffs, most of the time, and never more than when the weather was good and we were kept in by the swell. Then he seemed particularly affronted, and he paced the cliff grimly watching the waves, acting irritable with anyone unfortunate enough to have business with him. The swell was going to keep us off the water for two days at least, maybe four, but he stared at the steaming white walls as if searching for a seam or a riptide that might offer a way outside. As he approached us his pantlegs flapped and his salt-and-pepper locks blew back over his shoulder like a mane. When he looked our way and noticed us he hesitated, then kept coming at his usual pace. Tom raised a hand and waved, so he was obliged to acknowledge us.

When he stopped several feet away, hands still in pockets, we all nodded and mumbled hellos. He came a few steps closer. "Glad to see you're doing better," he said to Tom in an offhand way.

"Thanks. I'm feeling fine. Good to be up and around." Tom seemed as uncomfortable as John. "Magnificent day, ain't it?"

John shrugged. "I don't like the swell."

A long pause. John shuffled one foot, as if he might be about to walk on. "I haven't seen you in the last couple days," Tom said. "I went by your house to say hello, and Mrs. N. said you were gone."

"That's right," John said. He crouched beside us, elbow on knee. "I wanted to talk to you about that. Henry, you too. I went down to take a look at those railroad tracks the San Diegans have been using."

Tom's scraggly eyebrows climbed his forehead. "How come?"

"Well, from what Gabby Mendez says, it appears they used

our boys as a cover for their retreat after the ambush. And now it turns out that mayor got killed. I went and asked some of my Pendleton friends about it, and they say it's true. They say there's a real fight going on right now down there, between three or four groups who want the power that the mayor had. That in itself sounds bad, and if the wrong group ends up on top, we could be in trouble. So Rafe and I were thinking that the railroad tracks should be wrecked for good. I went down to look at that first river crossing, and it's pretty clear Rafe could destroy the pilings with the explosives he's got. And he says he can blast the track every hundred yards or so, easy."

"Wow," said Tom.

John nodded. "It's drastic, but I think it's the right move. If you ask me, those folks down there are *crazy*. Anyway, I wanted to know what you thought of the idea. I was going to just get Rafe and go do it, but..."

But it would have been too much like what Steve and I had done. Tom cleared his throat, said, "You don't want to call a meeting about it?"

"I guess. But first I want to know what some of you think."

"I think it's a good idea," Tom said. "If they think we were in on the ambush, and if that super-patriot crowd gets control...yeah, it's a good idea."

John nodded, looking satisfied. "And you, Henry?"

That took me aback. "I guess. We might want that track working for us someday. But it won't be soon," I added (John's eyes had narrowed), "and we've got to worry about keeping them at a distance first. So I'm for it."

"Good," said John. "We should probably try to talk with them at the swap meet, if we get a chance. And warn the others about them, too."

"Wait a bit, here," Tom said. "You still have to get a meeting together, and get the vote. If we start deciding things like the boys here did, we'll end up like the San Diegans."

"True," John said.

I felt myself blushing. John glanced at me and said, "I'm not blaming you."

I scratched the sandstone with a pebble. "You should. I'm as much to blame as anyone."

"No." He straightened up, chewed his lower lip. "That was Steve's plan; I can see his mark on it everywhere." His voice tensed, pitched higher. "That boy wanted everything his way right from the start. Right out of his ma. How he cried if we didn't jump to his wishes!" He shrugged it off, looked at me sullenly. "I suppose you think I'm to blame. That I drove him off."

I shook my head, though part of me had been thinking that. And it was true, in a way. But not entirely. I couldn't make it clear, even to myself.

John shifted his gaze to Tom, but Tom only shrugged. "I don't know, John, I really don't. People are what they are, eh? Who made Henry here want to read books so bad? None of us. And who made Kathryn want to grow corn and make bread from it? None of us. And who made Steve want to see the world out there? No one. They were born with it."

"Mm," John said, mouth tight. He wasn't convinced, even if it absolved him, even if he had been saying the same thing a second ago. John was always going to believe his own actions had effects. And with his own son, who'd spent a lifetime in his care . . . I could read his face thinking of that as clear as you can read the face of a babe. A wave of pain crossed his features, and he shook himself, and with a somber click of tongue against teeth reminded himself that we were here. He closed up. "Well, it's past," he said. "I'm not much of a one for philosophy, you know that."

So the matter was closed. I thought about how this conversation would have taken place at the ovens among the women: the chewing over every detail of event and motivation, the arguing it out, the yelling and crying and all; and I almost laughed. We men were a pretty tight-lipped crowd when it came to important things. John was walking in a circle like I had earlier, and quickly his nervous striding got to us, so that Tom and I stood to stretch out. Pretty soon the three of us were meandering in place like gulls, hands in pockets, observing the swells and pointing out to each other any particularly big ones.

Looking back at the valley, now filled with trees yellow among the evergreens, I stopped pacing and said, "What we need is a radio. Like the one we saw in San Diego. A working radio. Those things can hear other radios from hundreds of miles away, right?"

Tom said, "Some of them can, yes." He and John stopped walking to listen to me.

"If we had one of them we could listen to the Japanese ships. Even if we didn't understand them we'd know where

they were. And we could listen to Catalina, maybe, and maybe
other parts of the country, other towns."

"The big radios will receive and transmit halfway around
the world," Tom commented.

"Or a long way, anyway," I corrected him. He grinned. "It
would give us ears, don't you see, and after that we could
begin to figure out what's going on out there."

"I would love to have something like that," John admitted.
"I don't know how we'd get one, though," he added dubiously.

"I talked to Rafael about it," I said. "He told me that the
scavengers have radios and radio parts at the swap meets all
the time. He doesn't know anything about radios right now,
but he does think he can generate the power to run one."

"He does?" Tom said.

"Yeah. He's been working on batteries a lot. I told him
we'd get him a radio manual and help him read it, and give
him stuff to trade for radio parts at the swap meets this summer,
and he was all excited by the idea."

John and Tom looked at each other, sharing something I
couldn't read. John nodded. "We should do that. We can't
trade fish for this kind of stuff, of course, but we can find
something—shellfish, maybe, or those baskets."

Another huge set rolled in, washing all the way to the base
of the cliff, and our attention was forced back to the waves.
"Those must be thirty-five feet high at least," Tom repeated.

"You think so?" said John. "I thought this cliff was only
forty feet."

"Forty feet above the beach, but those wave troughs are
lower. And the crests are nearly as high as we are!" It was
true.

John mentioned that he wanted to get the boats out on days
like this.

"So you *were* thinking about that when you walked down
here," I said.

"Sure. See, follow the river current at high tide—"

"No way!" Tom cried.

"Look at the turbulance in the rivermouth," I pointed out.
"Even those broken waves must be ten or fifteen feet tall."

"You'd be capsized and drowned by the first wave that hit
you," Tom said.

"Hmm," said John reluctantly—with perhaps a gleam of
humor in his eye. "You may be right."

We meandered around our shelf again, talked about currents and the possibility of a mild winter. Out to sea shafts of light still speared the clouds to gild the lined ocean surface. Tom pointed out there. "What you *should* try doing is fishing the whales again. They're due through soon."

John and I groaned.

"No, really, you guys gave up on that one too fast. You either harpooned an extra tough one, or Rafael didn't put the harpoon in a place that would do the beast much harm."

John said, "Easy to say, but he's never going to be able to place the harpoon right where he wants to."

"No, that's not what I'm saying, it's just that most of the time a harpoon will do them more damage, and they won't be able to dive so deep."

"If that's true," I said, "and if we added more rope to the end of the line—"

"There's not room for it in our boats," John told me.

But I was remembering the time Steve and I had discussed it. "We could tie the bottom end to line that runs over to a tub in another boat, and have twice as much."

"That's true," John said, cocking his head.

"If we were to get into the whale business we could really make a killing at the swap meet," said Tom. "We'd have oil to spare, and animal feed, and tons of meat."

"If we could keep it from going bad," John said. But he liked the idea; what was it but fishing, after all? "Could you really get the line set so that it went from boat to boat?"

"Easy!" Tom said. He knelt and picked up a pebble to draw in the dirt. He started to scratch a plan, and John crouched at his side. I looked out at the horizon, and this is what I saw: three sunbeams standing like thick white pillars, slanting each its own way, measuring the distance between the grey clouds and the gray sea.

Chapter the Last

As the year fell away to its death the storms came more frequently, until every week or so one barreled in over the whitecaps and thrashed us, leaving the valley tattered and the sea a foamy pale brown from all the dirt sluiced into it. When we did get the boats out the fishing was miserably cold, and we didn't catch much. Most days I spent at the table under the window, where I read or wrote or watched black clouds bluster in. The clouds were the vanguard; after them a smack of the wind's hand, and maybe a low rumble of thunder, announced the arrival of the storm's main force. Raindrops slid down the windowpane in a thousand tributaries that met and divided again and again as they wandered down the glass. The roof ticked or tapped or drummed under the onslaught. Behind me Pa labored away on his new sewing machine, and its *rn, rn, rn rn rnnnn!* rebuked my idleness, sometimes so successfully that I buckled down and wrote a sentence or two. But it was hard going, and there were lots of hours when I was content to chew my pencils (writing epics on my teeth) and think about it, and watch it rain, lulled by wind, and roof patter, and the tea kettle's whistle, and Pa's *rn rn, snip snip*.

The first storm of December, it snowed. It was a real pleasure to sit in our warm house and look out the window at the flakes drifting silently through the trees. Pa looked over my shoulder. "It's going to be a hard winter." I didn't agree. We had enough food, even if it was fish, and more firewood was being dried in the bathhouse every day. After all the rain I was happy to see snow just for the way it looked, for the way it fell!—so slowly it didn't seem real, at first. Then to run outside, and hop white drifts, and slap snowballs together to throw at neighbors. . . . I loved the snow. The day after, the sun came out under a high pale blue sky (fishbone clouds smack against the highest part of it), and the snow melted before midday. But the next storm brought more snow, and colder air, and a thicker tail of high clouds, and it was four days before the harsh sun came out and the white dusting melted and ran into the river. That got to be the pattern: valley first white-green under black skies, then black-green under white skies. Week by week it got colder.

Week by week my story got harder to write. I got lost in it—I stopped believing it—I wrote chapters and had to take a walk over the soggy leaf carpets in the woods, distressed and angry at myself. Still, I wrote it. The solstice passed, and Christmas passed, and New Year's passed, and I went to all the parties and such, but it was like I was in fog, and afterwards I couldn't remember who I had talked to or what I had said. The book was the only thing for me—and yet it was so hard! Sometimes I wore out pencils faster biting than writing.

But the day came when the tale was on the page, pretty much. All the action done, Mando and Steve gone. I stopped then, and took one still day to read what I had said. It made me so mad I damn near burned the thing. Here all those things had *happened*, they had changed us for life, and yet the miserable string of words sitting on the table didn't hold the half of it—the way it had looked, the thoughts it had engendered, the way I *felt* about it all. It was like pissing to show what a storm is like. Why, there was no more of last summer in that book than there is of the tree in an old scrap of driftwood. And the work I had put in on it—well, it was discouraging.

I went out for a walk to try and recover. A few tall white clouds sailed above like galleons, but mostly it was a sunny

day, and dead still, though the air had a bite to it. Wet snow
lay on everything. Cakes of it were balanced on every branch,
dripping and sparking the various colors of the rainbow. On
the ground the snow crumbled to big clear grains under the
sun's glare, and the grains turned to drops of water that beaded
the white blanket. Suncones melted through to tufts of grass,
and snowbridges over the streams filling the paths collapsed,
leaving dirty chunks of ice in the mud, and snow hummocks
to each side, black with pine needles. I walked between these
hummocks and over the remaining bridges (the ones in shadow)
to the cliffs, thumping my boots in puddles and knocking snow-
cakes on branches into mush and spray.

Out on the point of the cliff overlooking the river I sat down.
No swell whatsoever; tiny waves lapped the strand as if the
whole ocean was shifting a hand's breadth up and down. There
wasn't any snow left on the beach, but it was wet and bedraggled, with blue-and-white puddles dotting it everywhere. The
scattered galleon clouds didn't hinder the sun much, but gave
its light a tint so that the long stretch of cliff was the color of
ironwood bark. No swell, still air, the ocean like a plate of
blue glass, the galleons hovering over it, holding their positions.

I noticed something I had never seen before. On the flat
blue sea were perfect reflections of the tall clouds, clearly
shaped so you could tell they were upside down. It looked like
they were floating underwater, in a dark blue sky. "Will you
look at that," I said aloud, and stood. Ever so slowly the clouds
drifted onshore over the valley, and their upside-down twins
disappeared under the beach. I stayed and watched that all day,
feeling like oceans of clouds were filling me. Later the afternoon onshore breeze ruffled the mirror clouds, and the sun got
too low and glared off the water. But I went home satisfied.

In the winter the scavengers hole up in some of the big,
shattered old houses—a dozen or more of them to a house,
like dens of foxes. At night they use the neighboring houses
for firewood, and light big bonfires in the front yards, and they
drink and dance to old music, and fight and howl and throw
jewelry at the stars and into the snow. A solitary man, gliding
over the drifts on long snowshoes, can move amongst these
bright noisy settlements without trouble. He can crouch out in
the trees like a wolf, and watch them cavort in their colored

down jackets for as long as he likes, undisturbed. Their summer haunts are open to his inspection. And there are books up there, yes, lots of books. The scavengers like the little fat one with the orange sun on the cover, but many more lie unattended in the ruins around them—whole libraries, sometimes. A man can load himself down till his snowshoes sink knee-deep, and then return, a scavenger of a different sort, to his own country, his own winter den.

At the end of January a particularly violent storm undermined the side of the Mendez's garden shed (they called it a barn), and as soon as the rain stopped all the immediate neighbors—the Marianis, the Simpsons, and Pa and I, with Rafael called in for advice—got out to give them a hand in shoring up that wall. The Mendez garden was as cold and muddy as the ocean floor, and there wasn't a patch of solid ground to set beams on, to prop up the wall while we worked under it. Eventually Rafael got us to tie the shed to the big oak on the other side of it. "I hope the framing was nailed together good," Rafael joked when we were back under the sagging wall. Kathryn and I worked one side, Gabby and Del dug out the other, and we practically drowned in mud. By the time we got beams set crosswise under the wall for foundations, all four families were ready for the bathhouse. Rafael had gone before us, so when we got there the fire was blazing and the water steamed. We stripped and hopped in the dirt bath and hooted with glee.

"My suggestion is you leave that rope there," Rafael said to old Mendez. "That way you'll never have to find out if those beams will hold it up or not." Mendez wasn't amused.

I rolled over into the clean bath and floated with him and Mrs. Mariani and the others. Kathryn and I sat on one of the wood islands and talked. She asked me if I was still writing. I told her I was nearly done, but that I'd stopped because it was so bad.

"You're no judge of that," she said. "Finish it."

"I suppose I will."

We talked about the storms, the snow, the condition of the fields (they were under tarps for the winter), the swells battering the beach, food. "I wonder how Doc is doing," I said.

"Tom goes up there a lot. They're getting to be like brothers."

"Good."

Kathryn shook her head. "Even so—Doc's busted, you

know." She looked at me. "He won't last long."

"Ah." I didn't know what to say. After a long pause looking at the swirling water, I said, "Do you ever think about Steve?"

"Sure." She eyed me. "Don't you?"

"Yeah. But I have to, with this book."

Under my reproachful gaze she shrugged, and her nipples bobbed on the bubbling surface. "You would book or not. If you're like me. But it's past, Henry. That's all it is—the past."

I told her about the day when the sea had been so glassy that it mirrored the clouds, and she sat back and laughed. "It sounds wonderful."

"I don't know when I've ever seen anything so pretty."

She reached over the wood island, and ran a finger down the crease between the muscles of the backside of my arm. I arched my eyebrows, and with a grin slipped off the seat to float around and tussle with her. She caught me by the hair. "*Hen*ry," she laughed, and held my head under, giving me more immediate matters to think about, like choking on water and drowning. I came up spluttering. She laughed again and gestured at the friends around us. "Well?" I said, and went under for a submerged approach, but she stood and sloshed away, leading me to the wall seats where the others were. After that we talked with Gabby and Kristen, and later old Mendez, who thanked us for our help with his barn.

But when Rafael declared the day's allotment of wood was burned, and we got out of the baths and dried off, and dressed, I looked around the room, and there was Kathryn looking at me from the door. I followed her out. The evening air chilled my head and hands instantly. There was Kathryn, on the path between two trees. I caught up with her and took her in a hug. We kissed. There are kisses that have a whole future in them; I learned that then. When we were done her mother and sisters were chattering out the bathhouse door. I let her go. She looked surprised, thoughtful, pleased. If it had been summer—but it was winter, there was snow everywhere. And summer was coming. She smiled at me, and with a touch walked off to join them, looking back once to meet my gaze. When she was out of sight I walked home through the dusk (white snow, black trees) with a whole new idea in mind.

Some afternoons I just sat before the window and looked at the book—left it closed, in the middle of the table, and stared at it. One of these times the snowflakes were drifting down through the trees as slowly as tufts of dandelion, and every branch and needle was tipped with new white. Into this vision tramped a figure on snowshoes, wearing furs. He had a pole in each hand to help his balance, and as he brushed between trees he sent little avalanches onto his head and down his back. The old man, out trapping, I thought. But he hiked right up to the window and waved.

I slipped on my shoes and went outside. It was cold. "Henry!" Tom called.

"What's up?" I said as I rounded our house.

"I was out checking my traps, and I ran into Neville Cranston, an old friend of mine. He summers in San Diego and winters in Hemet, and he was on his way over to Hemet, because he got a late start this year."

"That's too bad," I said politely.

"No, listen! He just left San Diego, didn't you hear me? And you know what he told me? He told me that the new mayor down there is Frederick Lee!"

"Say what?"

The new mayor of San Diego is *Lee*. Neville said that Lee was always in trouble with that Danforth, because he wouldn't go along with any of Danforth's war plans, you know."

"So that's why we stopped seeing him."

"Exactly. Well, apparently there were a lot of people down there who were behind Lee, but there wasn't anything they could do about it while Danforth and his men had all the guns. Neville said this whole fall has been a dog fight down there, but a couple months ago Lee's supporters forced an election, and Lee won."

"Well, what do you know." We stared at each other, and I found myself grinning. "That's good news, isn't it."

He nodded. "You bet it's good news."

"Too bad we blew up those train tracks."

"I don't know if I'd go *that* far, but it is good news, no doubt about it. Well"—he waved one of his poles overhead —"Lousy weather to be standing around chattering in. I'm off." and with a little whistle he snowshoed off through the trees, leaving a trail of deep tracks. And I knew I could finish.

The book lay on the table. One night (February the 23rd) the full moon was up. I went to bed without looking at the

book, but I couldn't sleep. I kept thinking of it, and talking to
the pages in my mind. I heard a voice inside me that said it
all perfectly, said it far better than I ever could: this voice
rattled off long imaginary passages, telling it all in the greatest
detail and with the utmost eloquence, bringing it back just as
lived. I heard the rhythms of it as sure as the rhythms of Pa's
snores, (though the sense of it was not as clear), and it put an
ache in me it was so beautiful. I thought, It's some poet's ghost
come to visit me, maybe, come to show me how to tell it.

Eventually it drove me to get up and finish the thing off.
Our house was cold, the fire in the stove was down to filmy
grey coals. I put on pants and socks, and a thick shirt and a
blanket over my shoulders. Moonlight poured in the window
like a silver bar, turning all the bare wood furnishings into
finely carved, almost living things. It was a light so strong I
could write by it. I sat at the table under the window and wrote
as fast as my hand would move, though what I wrote was
nothing like the voice I had heard when I was lying down. Not
a chance.

Most of the night passed. My left hand got sore and crampy
from writing, and I was restless. The moon was dipping into
the trees, obscuring my light. I decided to go for a walk. I put
on my boots and my heavy coat, and shoved the book and
some pencils in the coat's big pocket.

Outside it was colder yet. The dew on the grass sparkled
where moonlight fell on it. On the river path I stopped to look
back up the valley, which receded through the thick air in
patchy blacks and whites. There wasn't a trace of wind, and
it was so still and quiet that I could hear the snow melting
everywhere around me, dripping and plopping and filling my
ears with a liquid music, *plinka plonk, pip pip pip pip, gurgle
gorgle plop tik tik plop, plop plop plinka plop pip pip pip.* . . . A
forest water choir, yes, accompanying me as I slushed down
the path, hands in my big coat pockets. River black between
salt-and-pepper trees.

On the cliff path I had to step careful, because the steps
were half slush, half mud. Down on the beach the crack of
each little wave break was clear and distinct. The salt spray in
the air glowed, and because of it and the moon hardly a star
was visible; just a fuzzy black sky, white around the moon. I
walked out to the point beside the rivermouth, where a fine
sand hill had built up, cut away on both sides by river and

ocean. On the point where these two little sand cliffs met I sat down, being careful not to collapse the whole thing. I took out the book and opened it; and here I sit at this very moment, caught up at last, scribbling in it by the light of the fat old moon.

Now I know this is the part of the story where the author winds it all up in a fine flourish that tells what it all meant, but luckily there are only a couple of pages left in this here book, so there isn't room. I'm glad of it. It's a good thing I took the trouble to copy out those chapters of *An American Around the World*, so that it turned out this way. The old man told me that when I was done writing I would understand what happened, but he was wrong again, the old liar. Here I've taken the trouble to write it all down, and now I'm done and I don't have a dog's idea what it meant. Except that most everything I know is wrong, especially the stuff I learned from Tom. I'm going to have to go through everything I know and try to figure out where he lied and where he told the truth. I've been doing that already with the books I've found, and with books he doesn't know I borrowed from him, and I've found out a lot of things already. I've found out that the American Empire never included Europe, like he said it did—that they never did bury their dead in suits of gold armor—that we weren't the first and only nation to go into space—that we didn't make cars that flew and floated over water—and that there never were dragons around here (I don't think, although a bird guide might not be where they were mentioned, I don't know). All lies—those and a hundred more facts Tom told me. All lies.

I'll tell you what I do know: the tide is out, and the waves roll up the rivermouth. At first it looks like each wave is pushing the whole flow of the river inland, because all the visible movement is in that direction. Little trailers of the wave roll up the bank, break over the hard sand and add their bit to the flat's stippled crosshatching. For a time it looks like the wave will push upriver all the way around the first bend. But underneath its white jumble the river has been flowing out to sea all the while, and finally the wave stalls on top of this surge, breaks into a confused chop, and suddenly the entire disturbance is being borne out to sea—until it's swept under the next incoming wave, and the movement turns upriver again. Each wave is a different size, and meets a different resistance, and as a result there is an infinite variety of rippling, breaking, chopping, gliding. . . . The pattern is never once the same. Do you see what I mean? Do you understand me, Steve Nicolin? You rather be holding on to what can be made to last than out hunting the new. But good luck to you, brother. Do some good for us out there.

As for me: the moon lays a mirrorflake road to the horizon. The snow on the beach melted yesterday, but it might as well be a beach of snow the way it looks in this light, against the edge of the black sea. Above the cliffs stand the dark hillsides of the valley, cupped, tilted to pour into the ocean. Onofre. This damp last page is nearly full. And my hand is getting cold—it's getting so stiff I can't make the letters, these words are all big and scrawling, taking up the last of the space, thank God. Oh be done with it. There's an owl, flitting over the river. I'll stay right here and fill another book.